THE EAST INDIAMAN

THE EAST INDIAMAN

Richard Woodman

This first world edition published in Great Britain 2001 by
SEVERN HOUSE PUBLISHERS LTD of
9–15 High Street, Sutton, Surrey SM1 1DF.
This first world edition published in the USA 2001 by
SEVERN HOUSE PUBLISHERS INC of
595 Madison Avenue, New York, N.Y. 10022.

British Library Cataloguing in Publication Data

Woodman, Richard
  The East Indiaman
  1. United States – History – Revolution, 1775–1783
  2. Sea stories
  I. Title
  823.9'14 [F]

ISBN 0-7278-5749-5

Typeset by Palimpsest Book Production Ltd.,
Polmont, Stirlingshire, Scotland.
Printed and bound in Great Britain by
MPG Books Ltd., Bodmin, Cornwall.

PART ONE

THE HARROWING

The Taking of the *Sea Lyon*

'A God-damned Yankee!' Captain Clarkson exclaimed, shutting his glass with a snap and turning from the rail to rake his two officers and the knot of worried passengers with an ominous glare. 'I intend to fight,' he said, addressing the little assembly as it swayed to the roll and scend of the *Sea Lyon*. Under the captain's intimidating stare no one objected, though one man put his hand to his mouth as if stopping some utterance and looked at the approaching vessel.

'Mr Grove!' Clarkson turned to his chief mate. 'Call all hands; then do you look to clearing away the guns. Keep 'em inboard until I tell ye, but have 'em manned and loaded. I'll give the bugger a run for his money, and then swing and try and knock the sticks out of him. D'you understand?'

'Aye, sir, I do.'

'Mr Wise . . .' The second mate was still rubbing the sleep from his eyes and wondering how long the American privateer had been trailing them. The night had been moonless for the last hours of his watch, but the sudden appearance of the hostile sail at dawn suggested he had had the *Sea Lyon* in sight for some time. 'Mr Wise, when your watch turns out, do you see to the sails. Trim 'em to perfection, sir, perfection, d'you hear?'

'Aye, aye, sir.'

'As for the rest of you,' Clarkson went on as his two officers turned away and began shouting orders, 'you may take your choice of huddling below with the women, or assisting in the defence of the ship. You all have firearms and I'd welcome your help – and you all know what is at stake . . .'

3

Clarkson looked round the half-dozen well-dressed men, whose expressions of anxiety ranged from deep concern to outright funk. He was glad to have Jeffries and Allinson aboard, both were army officers returning home for furlough; and Corbett would be all right, Clarkson thought. He was a steady and sober enough fellow for a gentleman who had spent his mature years trading in the West Indies. Clarkson was less certain of Manton, whose nationality he suspected was French, though the man spoke perfect English and had lived for years in Antigua. But the man was sallow and had a rotten look about him; Clarkson's instincts had persuaded him to treat Mr Manton with a wary distance. As for Mr Gilbert, Clarkson thought him the greatest conundrum of them all, a thin, tall wisp of a man with the aspect of a lousy priest and the dress of an Italian paramour. The women loved him, though, Clarkson recalled with an inward sneer. How the hell would such a man stand under fire? Not well, Clarkson concluded, and the same could be said for the last of his six male passengers, Mr Wentworth. An affable enough man, and rich to the point of legend; a man whose hospitality Clarkson had enjoyed on many occasions, just as he had enjoyed the favours of Wentworth's wanton wife, who even now lolled below in her cot, but he doubted with the certainty of long prejudice that Wentworth would prove a coward when push came to shove of boarding pike. A gilt-horn cuckold was no man to rely upon in such a business as would shortly fall upon them.

Down below, along with Mistress Wentworth, the handsome octoroon Mistress Manton and a single woman named Miss Cunningham who seemed, insofar as the worthy captain could determine, to surreptitiously adorn the beds of both Jeffries and Allinson, lay a hoard of wealth. Wentworth he knew had a strongbox that had taken two large negroes to carry aboard, Manton also admitted to carrying home the greater part of his fortune in both money and bills of exchange, and the captain himself had a small quantity of specie, let alone the *Sea Lyon*'s valuable cargo of muscovado sugar. The thought sharpened his mind to the present predicament. Rich men could

4

buy themselves out of trouble and Wentworth's indecisive expression looked as if the very same thought was crossing his calculating mind. Clarkson knew that if Wentworth and Gilbert were to be prevented from infecting his crew with notions of surrender, they had best be given something useful to do. 'I should equally welcome loaders to hand up the small arms . . .'

'Molly Cunningham will do that, Captain,' offered Jeffries with a smile, 'and I'll happily point a gun for you, if you so wish.'

Clarkson nodded; this was more like it. 'Obliged to you, Major, then if Lieutenant Allison would direct the gentlemen volunteers on the poop here . . .'

'With pleasure, Captain Clarkson.' The younger Allison looked round, almost beaming at the prospect of a morning's duck-shooting.

'Mr Gilbert?'

'I'll load, if ye don't mind. I'm not much of a shot but I've a small sword that may prove handy.'

'Let us hope they don't get that close, Mr Gilbert, but I'm obliged to 'ee too.'

'I'll take a musket, Captain,' volunteered Corbett, and Clarkson acknowledged his offer.

'So will I, Captain, and my wife will help with the wounded or load, just as you please.'

'Thank you, Manton. Let us hope there'll be no wounded, so have her up here to load.' The male passengers dispersed to ready themselves for the coming action and Clarkson turned to the rubicund Wentworth and lowered his voice.

'You stand to lose most, Mr Wentworth; how say you? There's no dishonour in admitting you ain't much of a a shot.' The pale sheen of sweat gleamed on the fat merchant's unshaven face, despite the chill of the morning.

'Well, I'm not, Captain, as you sagaciously guessed, but I don't rate our chances very highly against yon privateers.'

'D'you suggest we strike?'

'After a shot or two, if you've a touchy sense of honour . . .'

'Oh, I've a very touchy sense of honour, Mr Wentworth, but I'd have thought yours might have been a little more robust.'

'Watch your mouth, Captain. You have been paid well to convey me safely to Liverpool and the imminent prospect of your failing to do just that now looms.'

'That is the misfortune of war.'

'You took little trouble to remain within convoy, Captain Clarkson, as you were both advised and bidden to do.'

'You think one naval sloop could protect forty laden West Indiamen, Mr Wentworth? You think the last two years have proved to me that the Royal Navy can do anything more than save the odd ship against men like these?' Clarkson gestured at the schooner on their windward quarter. 'Why I've been in the convoy of *two* fine frigates and listened to the blustering blather of their commanders about discipline and whatnot, but when a pair of Yankee gamecocks sally down from the north where are the naval johnnies, eh?' Clarkson paused only a second after this rhetorical question before he answered it. 'Why, Mr Wentworth, three miles ahead to the south-west a-showing us the way to Jamaica as if we'd never been there in our lives before. Bah!' Clarkson said with a dismissive wave of his hand. 'Don't talk to me of convoy!' He turned contemptuously away from Wentworth, raised his glass and studied his enemy again. There was no doubt about it. Beyond the leech of the foresail he could see the flutter of the ensign at her main peak. She was a Yankee privateer, all right! By the time a watery sun had broken through the thin layer of cloud and dried up the morning's dew from all but the deck lying in the shadow of the bulwarks, the Yankee was within two miles of them and had tried a ranging shot or two. Mr Wise had trimmed the sails to advantage. He had some ability in this, explaining, to anyone who cared to listen, that the trimming of sails was a matter of science, not merely of rote. Such an experimental approach certainly seemed justified, but it only postponed the inevitable. However, the respite that Wise's diligence had bought the company of the *Sea Lyon* had been put to good use and the ship was now in as defensive a posture as was possible. Then, just after three bells was struck in the forenoon watch, the cry went up that land was ahead.

'God grant that it is the South Bishop,' Clarkson muttered to his mate, who now stood alongside the master, his own glass levelled at the enemy schooner. Grove swivelled round and volunteered to go aloft. 'Do you oblige me, Stephen,' Clarkson responded without lowering his glass from his eye while the mate tucked his telescope away and walked forward to ascend the foremast rigging with a slow deliberation.

Clarkson swore softly to himself. He had given the damned Yankee a run for his money, but he knew that he could not hold out for much longer. It was possible, *just* possible, that a naval cruiser might be lying off the South Bishop or the Smalls, and the rickety lighthouse that rose above the latter should soon be visible. 'God grant that a frigate may rise above the horizon with the lighthouse,' Clarkson muttered, but the fervour of his prayer was swept aside in his bitter invocation against his fate. 'The damned Admiralty johnnies are always there to poach your crew on the plea of grave national necessity, but never there to offer protection when you want it!'

Clarkson stared once more at the approaching schooner. He could see the waist dark with men and then the flash of a forward gun was followed by a tearing noise as a ball passed close overhead. Clarkson closed his telescope for the final time and turned to Wise, who now stood alongside him. 'Watch her a moment, Mr Wise, I wish to grab my pistols.'

By the time Clarkson returned to the deck Grove had descended from the foretop and waited alongside the second mate.

''Tis the South Bishop, sir, and you can see the Smalls on the beam—'

'But not a cruiser in sight, I think,' Clarkson broke in, closing the frizzens on both his pistols.

'Unfortunately not.'

'Very well, then. Go to your posts. Major Jeffries is ready to point a gun or two, but aim high and see if we can knock the spars off that bugger.'

7

'Aye, aye, sir.'

Clarkson looked round his ship. The *Sea Lyon* was as prepared as she ever would be, even if the odd assemblage of warriors on the poop gave the impression of a frivolous yachting party. Jeffries and Allison had donned the scarlet coats of their regiment and while the major had gone forward with Stephen Grove to help with the *Sea Lyon*'s small broadside of 'cannonades', Allison was priming a short fusil with some care. Alongside him Molly Cunningham, swathed in a muslin morning dress that fluttered gaily about her buxom figure, rammed the charge into a musket and stacked it alongside the three or four already loaded and leaning against the mizzen fife rail. Her pleasant face bore a determined look and he watched as she exchanged a smile with Lieutenant Allison. Beyond her the octoroon beauty known to Clarkson as Lavinia Manton, but whom gossip said was a kept woman, was similarly employed. She lacked Molly's knowledge of firearms and Manton was showing her what to do. Corbett wore a hanger and had no less than three pistols stuck in his belt; he was a man with a rakish past, Clarkson recalled, with the reputation of a successful slaver and a ruthless streak that Clarkson might have reprehended in other circumstances, but just now was a boon. And there too was Gilbert, looking even more piratical as he clambered awkwardly on deck with an armful of muskets from the arms chest below, a hanger at his waist and a huge tricorne stuck precariously upon his poll. His powderless brown hair hung unclubbed halfway down his back and round his neck he wore a flaming scarlet neckerchief which was at odds with his purple-and-white-striped breeches, silk stockings and silver-buckled shoes. No, not piratical, Clarkson thought with a wry, almost amused, twitch to his mouth, more like an animated scarecrow!

'God, what company in which to put one's luck to the test!'

'Beg pardon, sir?'

'Eh?' Clarkson looked round at Wise. 'Oh, I was thinking aloud, Mr Wise, at the strange company we have aboard. Hardly the stuff of legend, don't you think?'

'Oh, I don't know, sir; I reckon Mistress Cunningham could show the Yankees a thing or two.'

'Where's Wentworth?'

'I don't think he'll be of much use,' Wise said with a wide grin, knowing his commander's liaison with the wealthy merchant's wife. 'But then no one thinks he's of much use, including the infamous Kitty!' Clarkson flushed. 'Thank you, Mr Wise, now . . .' But he got no further, for the flashes that sparkled briefly along the schooner's topsides translated themselves into a sickening rending sound before the concussion of the guns rolled over the interval of sea that ran between the two vessels, and several holes appeared in the mizzen topsail and driver.

Clarkson was beside the helm in a moment, shouting, 'Mr Grove! Major Jeffries! Watch for your moment now!' then turning to the helmsmen and ordering the rudder over to swing the *Sea Lyon* a couple of points to starboard. It was a risky manoeuvre, for it closed the lateral distance between the two ships and if they failed to shoot away any of the spars or sails of the enemy schooner there would not be much doubt as to the eventual outcome.

The *Sea Lyon* heeled as she brought the wind further onto her beam and Wise started forward to trim the braces but Clarkson stopped him. 'Leave her! I want the heel to throw our shot high . . .'

The captain's last words were drowned in the ragged thunder of *Sea Lyon*'s starboard broadside. Clarkson watched eagerly to see the result of their efforts, and for a moment he thought he had triumphed. Several holes appeared in the schooner's sails, and then a tottering of her foretopmast gave him cause for hope, but the master of the privateer was equal to Clarkson's challenge and himself bore away, so that the mainsail blanketed the damage forward and the schooner drove across the *Sea Lyon*'s stern with scarcely a falter in her speed. As she did so her starboard guns loosed off in turn, smashing into the stern of the British West Indiaman. Splinters flew up from the carved taffrail and the wind of passing shot soughed across

9

the poop so that the men and women there ducked and gasped. From below the tinkle of smashed crown-glass was accompanied by a shrill scream. A moment later a distraught Wentworth appeared on deck. No one took any notice of him, for at the same moment there was an ominous creaking from aloft. Looking up Clarkson saw the holes in the sails and then the sway of the mizzen topmast as the wounded spar, its supporting rigging shot away and under pressure from the wind-filled sails, leaned forward.

Even as Clarkson assessed the damage, Allison opened fire with his fusil and the whole poop-party loosed off at the enemy as she drove alongside to leeward. As Grove and Jeffries shifted the *Sea Lyon*'s crew across to the other side of the ship to man the larboard guns, the privateer fired another broadside. The shot hammered into the West Indiaman's rail, followed by screams and the curiously abandoned jerks of men flung back by the iron hail and the lancing splinters thrown up by the impact of shot.

'Do you strike, Captain?' a voice roared.

'No, sir, I do not!' Clarkson responded, and at that moment Grove discharged the larboard guns with a thunderous roar and Clarkson saw damage done amidships in the schooner where an explosion of lancing slivers of yellow wood looked like a shell burst amid the men crowded there.

He heard the screams of the Yankee wounded and the shouts of command re-establishing order. For five long minutes the two ships ran board-to-board, the British West Indiaman to windward, her broadside guns doing desultory damage among the Yankees, while the heeling schooner, half in the lee of the larger vessel, fired high on one roll and low on the next. To the play of the great guns was added the spiteful execution of the small arms, guns aimed deliberately at those exposed upon the upper decks of the opposing vessels. On the poop of the *Sea Lyon* Corbett was the first to be killed, shot through the throat by a musket ball so that he was bowled over with a gurgling moan and the bright surge of arterial blood. Then Lavinia Manton gave a restrained little scream and sat down with a shocked look on her golden face. There seemed nothing wrong with her, but she slumped sideways, her eyes staring, stark dead, shot through her spine as she turned to hand up a musket.

Clarkson exhorted his crew from the poop rail as Allinson, seeing Manton kneel beside the dead Lavinia, rallied the gentry and returned fire. Molly laboured beside him and he fired with the precision he would have expected of his infantry, a cool and devastating response to the Yankee's disciplined fire. But it was not enough, even with Gilbert now adding his own efforts to the defence of the British ship. There was a crash aloft and the maintopsail yard was shot away, plummeting down in a shower of ropes' ends and splinters. Then amidships, one of the inferior 'cannonades', cheap guns manufactured for merchantmen, blew its breech out with a terrible and devastating explosion, killing three of its crew and starting a fire.

As Grove and his seamen strove to douse the flames and Jeffries continued to serve the remaining guns, Clarkson took a musket ball in the shoulder and was flung round to collide with Gilbert.

'God damn it!' Clarkson clutched his shoulder. 'Get me a pledget, Mr Gilbert, if you please,' he gasped through clenched teeth.

'Strike, Captain! Strike your colours!' The Yankee voice stopped Clarkson from sliding into unconsciousness and he stood swaying.

'Never!' he bellowed as he slumped to the deck.

'Then take the consequences!' the American commander shouted back.

A moment later the schooner ran alongside and grappling irons snaked across to bind the two vessels together. Then a swarm of Yankee privateersmen swarmed over the rails of the two ships.

Gilbert drew his hanger and stood, a tatterdemalion sentinel over the fallen British commander; Allison drew his own sword and handed Molly a pistol while Wise grabbed the grieving

Manton and hauled him to his feet. Amidships Jeffries, Grove and the seamen were fighting for their lives, but for all their courage, the British were outnumbered and out-classed. Gilbert proved an able swordsman, but he was too tall and, denied the space of a *piste*, was quickly pressed and disarmed. Allison was shot through the thigh and only Molly saved him from being given the *coup de grâce*. An American officer fought his way aft and hacked through the ensign halliards so that the red bunting, with its stripes of blue and white, fell into the sea and, dragging astern in the *Sea Lyon*'s wake, was reduced to a mere rag.

When it was all over, Wentworth appeared on deck. He confronted the American lieutenant who was just then securing the prisoners and sending a man to take the *Sea Lyon*'s helm. He bore two loaded pistols which he held in front of him and, as someone called the Yankee officer's attention to the nervously approaching figure, he pulled both triggers. Flint snapped on steel and with a flash and puff of smoke the two firearms barked, but Wentworth's shaking fists sent the shots wide. A moment later the merchant fell dead from a dozen balls that the angry privateersmen discharged into his fat body.

Down below, Wentworth's unfaithful wife was already sprawled in ungainly death. Before the two vessels separated, the *Sea Lyon* with her prize crew aboard and already clearing away the wreckage of the action, Captain Clarkson and his surviving passengers were taken aboard the schooner. Here they were met by another American officer who, removing his hat, bowed and addressed them.

'Josiah King, commander of the schooner *Algonquin* of Newport, Rhode Island,' he said introducing himself. 'I am truly sorry to see you reduced to this extremity,' he continued, 'and must compliment you on your courage, but had you submitted to *force majeure* you would have saved much unnecessary effusion of blood.' Clarkson, held upright between Gilbert and Jeffries, a blood-sodden pledget bound to his shoulder, nodded as the major offered up Clarkson's sword.

'Well now,' said King with a smile, 'is that the gallant captain's sword, or your own, Major?'

'I was disarmed aboard the *Sea Lyon* by one of your licensed pirates, Captain,' Jeffries coolly replied. 'This is Captain Clarkson's sword.'

'Thank you, but you may return it to him. I have all the prize I wish from Captain Clarkson.' King turned to Clarkson, who was pallid from loss of blood. 'I shall have my surgeon attend you, Captain, but tell me, sir, I see you are from Liverpool, but who owns your vessel?'

'Captain William Kite, sir,' Clarkson replied through his teeth.

'Well, well, well,' said King with a wide grin.

Chapter One

The Honourable Company

M r Quentin Cunningham, Third Clerk to the Court of
Directors of the Honourable East India Company,
bit his lip with vexation. A man of less refinement than
Cunningham would have sworn, but the Third Clerk believed
firmly in personal inhibition as a mark of gentility; indeed
he attributed his position to this quality as much as to the
fine hand he wrote. Just at the moment, however, he was
finding it extremely difficult to concentrate on the practice of
handwriting and had not executed his last line of prose with
his customary ease. He looked across the copying room to
where his colleague, Anthony Burridge, the senior copy-clerk,
sat idle, his head raised, similarly arrested in his task by the
persistent interruption to their joint diligence.

Burridge, a man eleven years Cunningham's senior, felt
the Third Clerk's gaze upon him and, with a nervous twitch
that rippled across his shoulders and caused the older man to
wink one eye as his head jerked, bent again to his task with
a scratch of quill nib on paper. But Cunningham derived no
satisfaction from this manifestation of his power and remained
himself in suspended animation. The noise had an odd quality
of demanding attention; like the ticking of a clock its measured
regularity had become as much part of the neighbouring room
as the slightly creaking boards from which it was generated,
but, unlike a clock, it refused to fade from the consciousness
of the two clerks. It was strangely insidious, perhaps because
it was caused not by a mechanical device, but by a man of

such patience that its very regularity was its most alarming feature.

Cunningham found himself trying to work out at what point the man causing the intrusive footsteps turned about in his pacing and found that he could not do so. There seemed no hesitation in the regularity of each footfall after its predecessor and the Third Clerk found his mind's eye conjuring up the image of a man who walked endlessly forwards, yet remained in the same spot while the floor upon which he strode with slow precision moved under him. Cunningham also caught himself thinking that this was no military man, but a sea captain. Instead of the parade ground for which it seemed most suited, each step was measured in a slow time capable of absorbing the roll or pitch of a ship.

Cunningham drew out his half-hunter and consulted it. The man had been striding up and down – or on and on, Cunningham thought with a prickle of extreme irritation – for upwards of five and thirty minutes. Why on earth he had been left to vegetate for so long Cunningham could only guess. The Directors, upon whom the petitioner from Liverpool had come to wait, had their own reasons for most things and it was not Cunningham's prerogative to question such matters, but if the Third Clerk was annoyed, surely the petitioner would be irate: yet there was no hint of impatience in that measured tread. The worthy sea captain had asked the Court of the Honourable East India Company for a meeting months earlier, and Cunningham himself had signed the letter arranging this appointment. At eleven of the clock, he recalled, and the captain had arrived on the first stroke of the hour. Moreover Cunningham knew that the morning's conference of the Honourable Company's ship's husbands had broken up some quarter of an hour earlier. The superintending officers, who had been conferring upon the readiness of their respective ships to depart from the Thames outward bound for India and China, had handed him their conclusions as they had trooped out into Leadenhall Street. Even at that moment Cunningham was writing, or trying to write, to the Admiralty to finalize the allocation of four frigates to convoy the East India fleet. The two senior ship's husbands, who remained in the elegant court-room with its horseshoe-shaped table, would be enjoying a glass, no doubt, but, Cunningham assumed, their desire to allow the Liverpudlian mariner to cool his heels was having the very opposite effect upon the clerk's office beyond the waiting room!

It was no good, an exasperated Cunningham concluded: he would have to intervene. Laying his quill down he rose and, opening the doors between the clerk's office and the ante-chamber, he went through. Having committed himself, Cunningham realized he had acted on a foolish impulse, had forsaken his customary personal inhibition and had not the faintest idea what he should do next. Instead he was simultaneously aware of three things: that he had committed an impropriety; that Burridge, disturbed by the uncharacteristically precipitate movement of his superior, had ceased writing and was awaiting the outcome; and that he himself had in fact invaded the ante-chamber in order to find out how the captain reversed his direction of travel without the slightest faltering in his pace. In this at least fate granted the Third Clerk gratification, for the captain had his back to Cunningham as he closed the doors behind him, nor did he make any effort to turn prematurely. Perhaps he had not heard the doors open, but if not he evinced no surprise when, in a smooth swing of his body during which his pace altered not a whit, he confronted Cunningham. Cunningham realized in a flash of intuition that the captain was probably – no, certainly – an accomplished swordsman. Despite his middle years, he walked with a supple grace and a perfect balance so that, as he began a remorseless advance upon the Third Clerk, Cunningham, used to regarding any inhabitant who hailed from the north country as inferior, conceived a sudden wary respect for the petitioner. Cunningham recalled the man's name as giving no hint to any gentility. Captain Kite had seemed, at least by his letters, to be little more than a sea officer who came to his point without equivocation. It was true that upon his arrival Cunningham

16

had noted his dress was untypically sober. The effect this had upon Cunningham as Captain Kite now bore down upon him, fixing him with a stare above which one eyebrow lifted interrogatively, had the Third Clerk swallowing awkwardly. Captain Kite was dressed entirely in black, more like a priest than a sea officer, and, for an unnerving moment, Cunningham entertained the fantasy that the captain from Liverpool had mysteriously transmogrified into Beelzebub. Even more unsettling was the inexorable pace with which the man now approached Cunningham. The Third Clerk was on the very edge of retreat when he recalled the principle of personal inhibition and caught himself, aghast. Suddenly the Liverpudlian stopped in front of him and Cunningham could almost hear the sigh of satisfaction from Burridge behind him as the damnable pacing finally stopped.

'Well, sir? How long am I to be kept here?' Captain Kite asked.

'Er, not long, Captain Kite, not long. I do apprehend, sir, that it will not be more than a moment. I feel certain, Captain Kite . . .'

Then, as though the spell was now broken, a second door at the far end of the ante-chamber was opened. Looking beyond his interlocutor, Cunningham saw the portly figure of Captain Woolnough and behind him the lesser bulk of Captain Drysdale, the two ship's husbands who had remained to draft a minute to the Court of Directors over a congenial glass of wine. The drafted minute would in due process arrive on Cunningham's desk for formalization.

Aware of the movement behind him the black-clad Liverpudlian turned slowly and Cunningham watched in a motionless fascination as Captain Kite's back receded, crossing the wooden floor with exactly the same dreadful pace that had so disturbed the industry of the clerk's office.

'Captain Kite?'

'The same, gentlemen.' Kite stopped, bowed, and then held out his hand.

'I am Thomas Woolnough, Senior Ship's Husband and a

Director of the East India Company, Captain Kite,' the larger of
the two men declared, shaking Kite's hand, 'and this is Jeffrey
Drysdale, who occupies a similar position in our Court. Please
do you come in . . .'

And then the three men passed from Cunningham's sight
as the far doors closed. He sighed, as though relieved of an
intolerable burden, and returned to the clerk's office, where
Burridge looked up briefly.

'Thank heavens they've admitted him at last,' he breathed
as he resumed his seat.

'I thought they never would,' added Burridge, bent over his
desk again.

'Odd cove, I thought. Dressed more like a damned papist
than a sea captain.'

'He has an idiosyncratic reputation, I gather,' remarked
Burridge didactically.

'Oh?' responded Cunningham. Part of his self-denial rested
on his refusal to listen to gossip, but the curious disturbance
of his normally placid routine exposed him to a moment of
weakness.

Burridge, who did not eschew any form of intelligence and
derived a degree of satisfaction from possessing facts unknown
to his superior, explained. 'He was in a slaver and became
infatuated with one of the blackamoors to the extent of setting
her free in order to marry her.'

But Burridge's loquacity was a presumption, Cunningham
would not tolerate it and recalled the senior copy-clerk to his
sense of propriety. 'It is of no consequence to me that this
Captain Kite favours women of colour,' he responded primly.
'Indeed, if the half of what I hear is true, so do most of the
Company's servants in India . . .'

'I'm talking of a black slave from the Gambia,' Burridge
persisted, but Cunningham would have none of it.

'The devil you are, Burridge, and a deal too much of it, to
be sure. Kindly attend to your task.'

And with that Burridge twitched again, and a silence fell
once more upon the labours of the two men. It did not last,

however, for instead of the intrusive noise of pacing, a faint, slightly sickly odour now began to permeate the clerks' office and, like puppets manipulated by springs, the two men slowly looked round as they became simultaneously aware of this new intrusion.

An exceptionally large man stood panting and perspiring in the outer doorway. He held under one elbow a small seemingly odoriferous spaniel while his other hand rested upon a silver-headed cane.

Cunningham rose, unable to disguise the expression of real exasperation on his face at this further disturbance. 'Mr Hooker,' he began, 'I told you yesterday, your petition has been rejected. The Directors will not entertain your project. Do please accept this ruling as final and absolute . . .'

'Hold your tongue!' The large man lumbered forward and such was the stink he brought with him that Cunningham was compelled to retreat a step before recovering himself.

'Mr Hooker,' Cunningham protested with a deep breath, placing himself in front of the large man who seemed intent on invading the ante-chamber, 'I really must insist upon your leaving . . .'

'Damn your impudence, sir! Stand aside!'

The intimidating bulk rose above the slim figure of the Third Clerk, who seemed like a small sea-bird in danger of being swept aside by the bow of a great ship until Burridge suddenly rose from his desk and, with a surprising agility, threw himself in front of the intruder.

'Hold hard, Mr Hooker!' Burridge said sharply. 'The senior husbands are presently occupied with another petitioner.'

'So I gathered from your conversation,' Hooker said, revealing the fact that he had overheard the two clerks. 'And doubtless they will prefer this other petitioner above myself, eh?' Hooker frowned and looked at the two of them.

'I have no idea, sir,' Cunningham agreed, 'exactly what conclusion the Directors will come to since I have only the faintest notion of Captain Kite's business with the Honourable Company, but I do assure you they are as likely to reject him as you, Mr Hooker, for the matter of the fleet has gone too far forward to brook alterations in the financial arrangements . . .'

'Financial arrangements, d'ye say, eh?' Hooker's watery blue eyes focused upon the Third Clerk and Cunningham was almost overwhelmed by the smell of the dog, which also stared at him with a lachrymose and myopic glare. 'And what d'ye say this fellow's name is? Kite, is it?'

'Captain William Kite, Mr Hooker, from Liverpool.'

'And my own case . . .'

'Is irrevocably lost, I regret to say, sir,' said Cunningham smoothly, scenting victory and, after the morning's deep frustrations, glad of the triumph. He had the impression of a foot-bladder deflating. Hooker seemed suddenly impotent, the man's bluster vanished and he seemed almost frightened. He turned aside, apparently diminished in stature, and shuffled out as silently as he had arrived. Cunningham drew a perfumed handkerchief from his cuff and waved it under his nose.

'Obliged to you, Burridge,' he said, acknowledging his assistant's intervention and sufficiently relaxing after all the excitement to add, 'I think a man who walks the floor like a funeral drum and tups black wenches is preferable to one who appears like a ghost and nurses a poodle that stinks like a corpse.'

'Yes indeed,' Burridge chuckled nervously at Cunningham's sudden loose confidence. Then taking advantage of the Third Clerk's mood he asked, 'What does Captain Kite want with the senior husbands?'

'Much the same as Mr Hooker, I imagine,' Cunningham replied with a little technical evasion as evidence of his propriety. He seated himself again and picked up his quill, regarding the nibbed end with an expert eye: 'Money was at the root of both their petitions.'

'Ahhh,' sighed Burridge who had long ago relinquished any hope of acquiring much of the stuff. 'Money. So Captain Kite'll be no more successful then than was Mr Hooker.'

'I'll eat that damned dog if he is,' replied Cunningham with an uncharacteristic vulgarity that dismissed thoughts of missed fortunes from Burridge's mind and replaced them with a faint amusement that Mr Cunningham was not quite as genteel as he would like others to think.

'I hope you don't have to stoop to that, Mr Cunningham,' he added with a low irony.

Cunningham looked up, but Burridge was bent over his task once more, his nib scratching upon the paper as he drew out the spidery lines of his script. With a hand like that, Cunningham thought smugly, Burridge would never make anything more than a copying clerk.

The two men worked on for a few minutes and then the door to the ante-room opened and Drysdale showed Captain Kite out with a nod at Cunningham.

'Be so kind as to see Captain Kite out, Mr Cunningham, if you please.'

The Third Clerk stood and led the black-clad gentleman out into the entrance hall and watched as, without a word, Captain Kite was swallowed up in the noisy bustle of Leadenhall Street.

The black-clad figure stood undecided for an instant, then, turning in the direction of the Strand, he began to walk briskly, his face set, his gaze fierce. He had not advanced fifty yards before a young lad was plucking at his sleeve. Preoccupied, Captain Kite shook the youth off, but the boy was persistent.

'Please, sir, *please* . . .'

Kite stopped and regarded the lad. He wore a grubby pot-boy's apron and was clearly not a footpad.

'What d'you want?' he asked crossly.

'There's a gennelman in the Ship and Turtle as wants to see 'ee, sir. Says it's a matter of the gravest importance sir, an' if you come, sir, I'll get thruppence for my trouble, sir, so please, sir . . .' the youth pleaded.

'Thruppence, eh? That's a considerable sum for so negligible a task. But stay, what's the gentleman's name?'

The boy's expression grew crestfallen. 'Why, I dunno sir . . . but he's big, sir, big as a house, sir.'

'That big?' remarked Kite with a wry smile at the lad's resourcefulness.

'Well, p'r'aps not quite as big as that, but bloody big for a man, sir.'

Kite sighed. He had enough on his mind and he fished in his pocket. He produced some coins and dropped four pennies into the boy's outstretched hand. 'Tell the gentleman that I have no business with him, but I have no wish to rob you.'

The lad looked at the money and grinned. 'May I tell him where you're lodging, sir, in case he asks?'

Kite laughed at the boy's cunning. 'And how much will you sell that intelligence for, I wonder, eh? I'm for Vidler's Yard and the Liverpool mail, my lad, but it's no good coming after me. You may tell him that too.'

'Aye, sir,' said the grinning youth, touching his forehead and dodging off through the crowd of passers-by.

Kite watched for a moment and then turned to walk westwards. What a pitiful place the world was, he mused, with every jack out to trade to advantage off his fellow, and what a relative thing wealth was, to be sure. That pot-boy was happy with his fourpence while he, Captain William Kite, ship-owner of Liverpool, considered himself ruined with only five thousand pounds to his name!

Less fourpence, he added as a rueful afterthought; less fourpence.

Kite did not arrive at Vidler's Yard until much later, for he had had first to return to his lodgings and collect his effects. Now a porter followed him in anticipation of a small fee and Kite contemplated his much diminished fortune dwindling by another fourpence or so before he escaped from the stink and clamour of London. He had hoped to be in the city longer, but it was clear he could expect nothing from the Honourable East India Company. He had just sufficient funds to purchase an interest in one of their vessels, but it was clear the Bengal

Club had no interest in absorbing a north countryman who was teetering on hard times. The excuse advanced by Woolnough and Drysdale, that he was too late to invest in the year's expedition to the East, was no more than an unsubtle dismissal. He had owned ships too long himself not to know they were simply brushing his offer aside. No doubt they were fully capitalized and had no wish to diminish their profits. Well, perhaps they had a point, Kite thought, for he shuddered at the thought of helping these city gentry spread any losses. God knew he had taken more than sufficient himself!

'We have sound backing, Captain Kite,' Drysdale had said, 'and are content with our associates, whose influence and investment are considerable.'

'You Liverpool men are unfamiliar with our methods,' Woolnough had added and Kite had been stung to retort:

'Aye, because we have no opportunity to do so, nor do we have the protection of Their Lordships at the Admiralty in Whitehall.'

Drysdale and Woolnough had shrugged wearily. 'That is not our affair, Captain,' they had said, before wishing him well with a false courtesy that eased him towards the door.

'Damn them,' Kite had said but now, as he thought of returning to Liverpool and breaking the news to Sarah, his heart sank. It was not for himself that he grieved, but for her and the beautiful child she had borne him. He had come south full of high hopes and optimism, for a man must buoy himself up when he is near ruin. There was no tax on anticipation. But the world had been kicking him in the teeth for too long for him to sustain such hopes much longer. Ever since he had been hunted for a murder he had never committed, he had thought fate indifferent to him. He could have borne such indifference had it not been for the fact that others seemed to profit against all odds. He had lost Puella, his first wife, a beautiful black woman who had given him two sons, both of whom had died in infancy. Now he feared that he had blighted the life of his second wife, a Rhode Island loyalist whom he had married before this wretched rebellion of the American

colonists broke out. God, what a damnable mess the world
was in, with Burgoyne's army incarcerated in North America,
and the English Channel, North and Irish Seas full of conceited
Yankee privateersmen!

'Cap'n Kite! Cap'n Kite!'

The sound of his name being called out broke into his
thoughts as he swung into Vidler's Yard. A crowd of passengers gathered round the black and maroon mail coaches
assembled there. Ostlers were busy putting the six-strong horse
teams in their traces, and the smell of animals and dung was
pungent in the warm air of the August afternoon.

'Cap'n Kite! Cap'n Kite!'

'Who wants him?' Kite called out, looking round and
catching sight of a face that was now familiar to him. Since
Kite had last seen him, the pot-boy had shed his apron and
donned a scruffy coat and cap, but he danced up to Kite with
an expression of relief on his face.

'Cap'n Kite, sir, where *have* you been? I've been here an
age awaiting for you.'

Dragged from his melancholy thoughts by the sight of the
importunate young man, Kite regarded him with a not unkindly
smile. 'And what's it to you, cully? May a gentleman not go
where he pleases?' he asked.

'Aye, sir, and a street urchin too,' the lad cheekily responded.

'Well, then, why d'you hound me?' Kite asked. 'Surely not
for another thruppence?'

''Twas fourpence the last time, sir.'

'You have a true cockney cheek and I am out of sorts with
your citizenry,' Kite said. 'Now tell me what it is you want,
young shaver?'

'I have to ask you if you will please to wait upon a Mr
Hooker who has taken rooms only a short walk from here in
Gravitt's Yard.'

Kite shook his head. 'I have a seat booked in the Liverpool
mail. I am sorry to disappoint this Mr Hooker . . .'

'I am told to insist, sir.' The boy stood his ground with a
fierce expression.

'What is your name, boy?'

'Jack, sir, Jack Bow.'

'Well, Master Jack Bow, do you tell your paymaster that Captain Kite is his own man, at least for the time being . . .' Then a thought struck Kite; he had already concluded that he must return to sea himself, and give up all hope of restoring his fortunes by any means other than plying the trade he knew best, that of a ship-master. He feared that with the losses of ships from Liverpool he would be unable to find an employer willing to give him a vessel, despite his reputation as a privateer commander. That had been long overtaken by his ill-luck as a ship-owner. The capitalists of Liverpool did not like even an oblique connection with ill-luck, particularly in such ill-starred times with Yankee privateers skulking under every headland round the coast. But suppose this Hooker was a ship-owner? A London ship-owner who might be seeking him for the purpose of offering him a ship? Of course he would have to return to Liverpool and square matters with Sarah, but this Jack Bow had called him *Captain* Kite, so Hooker had clearly made some enquiries.

Kite pulled out his watch and looked from it to the boy, who had noted the hesitation in his quarry and waited expectantly.

'Where d'you say this Hooker is, Jack Bow?'

'Follow me, sir,' responded the boy eagerly, with a grin of unfeigned delight. Kite motioned the porter to follow and, with a sigh, set off in the lad's wake.

Chapter Two

The Nabob

K ite's surge of optimism proved momentary. Gravitt's Yard turned out to be a mean courtyard, reached through an archway of damp brick, flagged with uneven paving and surrounded by tall tenements from which numerous indeterminate smells emanated. From open windows came too the noises of a population long inured to a lack of privacy, a fact emphasized by a variety of apparel that hung to dry or air in an atmosphere that never, thanks to the precipitous nature of the architecture, felt the warmth of direct sunlight. With a plummeting heart Kite followed Jack Bow into a black opening which boasted a door of uncertain age, but which suggested by the rubbish swept up across its foot that it was never closed. They clattered up several flights of bare wooden stairs. On one landing a pair of grubby children squatted, their large eyes following Kite and Bow as they passed. Approaching the top floor where the gloom eased, relieved by a filthy skylight above the stairwell, they were confronted by two Indians in white coats and turbans, but Jack shoved past them, and running up the final flight stopped outside another door.

Jack knocked, then turned and grinned self-importantly at Kite.

'I thought you worked at the Ship and Turtle,' Kite remarked as he stared apprehensively around the dark and fetid landing, his heart pounding at the speed of their ascent.

'I did, sir, until this afternoon when Mr Hooker promised

26

me a berth in the first ship he has,' Bow answered and Kite raised an eyebrow. So, both he and this scruffy urchin were reduced to the same supplicant status. What a pass; thank God none of his Liverpool acquaintances could see him now!

'It would seem, Master Bow, that your new employer has departed and left us both in the lurch,' Kite remarked as the porter finally caught up with them, panting with the effort of lugging Kite's portmanteau up five flights of steep stairs.

'Sir, I hope—' But what the porter hoped was not known, for at that moment the door outside which they waited was suddenly alive with the thudding of drawn bolts and, a moment later Kite was confronted with the enormous figure of Mr Hooker and a nauseatingly sickly odour.

'Captain Kite, how good of you to come, and I do apologize for the importunity of my conduct in sending young Jack here in pursuit of you. Do come in, sir, do come in, and please do not be deceived by appearances. This humble apartment is but a posting stage, sir, an ephemeral moment on life's journey . . .'

Hooker backed into a narrow passage as he delivered himself of this assertion and, as Bow stood aside, Kite motioned the porter to deposit his bag and paid the man a generous shilling. Kite reluctantly entered the establishment, half falling over a small spaniel at his feet.

'Come, sir, do you follow me.' Hooker withdrew followed by the dog whose claws pattered on the bare boards. Kite hesitated a moment as Bow lifted his portmanteau over the threshold and then found himself shoved unceremoniously deeper into the passageway. A moment later the door was closed and Kite felt a sudden surge of alarm, as though he had been put in gaol.

He almost gagged at the smell of the air but Bow hissed, 'You'll get used to it, sir,' with a solicitude Kite found disconcerting. With an effort he mastered the nausea that rose threateningly in his throat, coughed and followed Hooker and his stinking dog.

Hooker led Kite into a room which opened onto the inner

courtyard. Being on the top floor, it was flooded with light from the westering sun that streamed in through the uncurtained windows, which were mercifully opened. It took Kite a moment to adjust to this, but when he had regarded his surroundings he was at least partially mollified.

Two brocaded upright chairs stood on a square of carpet Kite recognized as being of Indian manufacture. They were incongruously out of place in such a squalid setting, but hinted that perhaps Hooker's circumstances were indeed temporary and that these items of furniture and furnishing were all that he could bring with him. But as suddenly as this thought had occurred to Kite, Hooker turned and interposed his massive bulk between his guest and much of the window. As Hooker held out an indicating arm, the altered light threw a corner of the room into almost theatrical illumination.

As Kite's gaze was automatically attracted to it, partly by this relative shift in the value of the light in the room and partly by his host's gesture, he was even more astonished. For alongside a door which appeared to lead into another room stood a wide couch, upon which reclined a gaudily bedizened woman whom Kite saw from her bare feet upwards as he traversed his gaze to penetrate the darker corner of the chamber. Her bare feet were in full sunlight, the golden rings adorning her toes gleaming, as did the gilded thread woven into the hem of her flowing scarlet skirt. But then the figure receded into increasing shadow, so that the bangles upon her naked lower arms showed only highlights, while the lavish adornment about her neck, and the stone that showed in her nose, seemed no brighter than the whites of her dark eyes.

'My wife, Captain Kite . . .'

Kite covered his astonishment with a low and well-footed bow. 'Your servant, ma'am.'

Without a word the woman inclined her head in acknowledgement and with a faint rattling of gold and silver adornments drew her headscarf partially across her lower face in a gesture of modesty that, to Kite's heightened awareness, struck him as being at once and quite ridiculously coquettish.

'Do please sit down, sir, sit down.'

Hooker continued to sweep his gesturing hand round to indicate one of the chairs before flicking his skirts out from his bottom and lowering himself into the other. It groaned faintly under his weight, the spaniel leapt into his lap and Kite gingerly lowered himself into his chair.

'It is my intention to leave for Liverpool, Mr Hooker,' Kite said pointedly and restraining a hand that reached instinctively for his watch. 'I regret that I do not have much time . . .'

Hooker held up his hand and Kite noticed a ring in which was set a large emerald. At least Kite supposed it was an emerald, as Hooker's words, rather than his suspect jewellery, claimed Kite's attention. 'You will not, I think, wish to rush off too precipitately, Captain Kite, once you have heard all I have to say to you. I shall have Jack here run back and re-engage your lodgings for tonight . . .'

'No!' Kite almost shouted. 'No, forgive me, sir, but I am set upon the matter.' He took out his watch, consulted it and added, 'I may give you ten minutes, after which I insist that Jack carries my dunnage back to Vidler's Yard—'

'If you insist, Captain,' Hooker cut in, 'then let us waste no more time on the pleasantries.' He clapped his hands and a moment later a turbaned Indian servant wearing a plain, high-necked white coat, his feet as bare as his mistress's, stood before Kite with a glass of wine.

Astonished at the sudden manifestation, Kite took the glass and was compelled to listen to Hooker, who had abruptly thrown off his prolix, over-courteous manner and spoke with a rapid intensity, leaning forward every few moments to lend emphasis to a point, so that Kite realized with a shock that it was he and not his wretched spaniel that stank to high heaven.

'Quite fortuitously, I know a little of you, sir, having read of your recent loss in the newspapers. Perhaps I may have some consolation for you if you can overcome your prejudice and stay a little longer than the ten minutes you have allowed me to make my case, but let that pass. Pray heed me, sir, for what

I have to say may not be life and death to you, but it may prove so to me. Yet I cannot suppose that your own circumstances today are so very much different from my own . . .'

'If you would come to the point,' Kite interjected, a slight edge to his voice.

'Of course. I myself have been a petitioner at East India House in recent days, Captain Kite,' Hooker went on. 'I do not know your own business, but mine was to seek to invest a considerable sum in this year's fleets. I had thought that the present difficulties arising from the war with the American colonies would have made investors shy of such an undertaking and my approach most welcome. Unfortunately I was wrong and there are sufficient interests vested in the India and the China fleets to entertain prejudices against me as a man of no substance in this fair and inequitable city.' Hooker swept his arm about his mean lodgings. 'It is true that our current circumstances may lead you to suppose that I have no means, but this is a calculated deception. I tell *you* this, Captain Kite, because,' and here Hooker's heavily jowled and sweating face broke into an oddly engaging smile, 'I conceive you a man of honour and, in any case, if you are on the Liverpool mail this evening you can do me and my humble ménage little harm.

'There is, however, a quantity of cash in my possession amounting to the equivalent of forty-five thousand pounds . . . Ah, I see you have taken notice of your humble servant at last.' Hooker smiled again, sipped his wine and resumed. Kite nodded. He had found a faint current of fresh air wafting in through the open window and was feeling less faint. As if accompanying this change in his circumstances Mrs Hooker moved with a shimmer of gorgeous silks.

'Now, Captain Kite, I brought this small fortune out of India, intending to retire to this country of my forefathers, but alas I have an old enemy who, hearing of my arrival, has seen fit to poison the minds of those whom I thought to be my neighbours and I have decided to return to Calcutta. My wife, being a high-caste Brahmin, is not disappointed since she finds this city oppressive and the countryside, where we had hoped to reside, not to her liking. All this being the case,' Hooker went on as if his wife was a thousand miles away, 'I wished to invest my money at the same time as entrusting myself and my family, effects and household, to the East India Company in order to return to India. I suffered too much of anxiety on the voyage hither to London to wish to repeat the process in reverse. In addition I have no desire to hazard my entire capital and expose it to seizure by any American, French or Spanish privateers. Their activity has greatly increased of late, a fact of which I have no need to remind you. Instead I wished to invest it, thus removing the risk of its loss and the augmentation of the sum. Alas, however, the Directors, in the wisdom of their self-interest, have rejected my advance and I am compelled to seek out assistance from another source.

'Now, sir, you may consider my importuning you in this way and regaling you with my private woes as a story so incredible as to not warrant your consideration and only to earn your contempt. But the truth is that I conceive my stumbling over you as remarkably providential and it occurred in this wise.

'As I remarked, I read of the loss of your vessel, the *Sea Lyon*, I recall, and that she was the last of your ships, the others all having been taken in recent months. That, I think, was what impressed your name upon my mind and sharpened my desire to protect my own assets when I return to India.

'When I called upon the Directors this morning, in one last humiliating attempt to persuade them to change their minds, I overheard the copying clerks discussing you. Your name was mentioned and, if that was not sufficient a providential coincidence, it was remarked that you were formerly married to a woman of colour, a further circumstance, if such a thing were needed to convince me, that we were fated to encounter one another.'

Hooker paused, drew out his own, enormous watch and looked up at Kite. 'Captain Kite, the ten minutes you vouchsafed me has expired; the choice is yours. Do you wish to hear my proposal, or leave for Liverpool?'

Kite, taken aback at the entire train of events, still half repulsed by the stink of Hooker, yet fascinated by the fact that clearly Hooker had need of him, was trying to judge whether a man as wealthy as Hooker claimed to be would really hide in such appalling lodgings. It seemed to Kite that perhaps Hooker stood a greater risk of being robbed of his 'cash', a word Kite knew to be of Chinese origin and which suggested a sum in coin and highly vulnerable to theft, in the mean accommodation afforded by the tenements of Gravitt's Yard than if he had established himself in an hotel in the west end of London. Added to this confusion, Hooker had surprised him with his reference to poor Puella, yet the silent Mrs Hooker was an Indian, a 'woman of colour' herself, so was Hooker indicating that he and Kite therefore shared some confraternity in their sexual preferences? Should he tell Hooker that matters had altered since Puella's death and that Sarah, his present wife, was an American?

'Captain Kite . . . ?'

Kite was recalled to the present with a start. He drew in a deep breath and instantly regretted it, the sickly sweet smell of Hooker making him reel. He stood abruptly, full of the impulse to flee, to return to Liverpool, to Sarah and all the uncertainties of his own life. The room spun about him and he staggered across to the open window, drinking in great gulping drafts of what passed in London for fresh air. Somewhere across the roof-tops a clock began to strike six, and then another and another followed. He was already too late, the nightmare was not over and he must make up his mind. He needed a minute to collect himself and turned back into the room.

Kite's eyes adjusted to the gathering darkness. Mrs Hooker had risen to her feet and stood beside her husband, who remained seated. She was wrapped in folds of gold and scarlet silk, as tall as her husband. Yet she was far from ill-looking and her eyes were of an unfathomable darkness.

'Forgive me,' he apologized under their joint scrutiny, 'I am a little faint . . .'

'Captain Kite, pray sit down again. I fear I stink most damnably. It is an exudation of excess humours that too long a life in the tropical latitudes has induced. I had hoped that the English air would cure me of the affliction but it has not proved to be the case and, since I am not to stay here, I must perforce continue to endure it. I am told that time reduces its effect upon my acquaintances . . .'

As Mrs Hooker again withdrew to her couch, Kite reluctantly returned to his chair like a wine-sodden man with a headache. Since Hooker had mentioned his odoriferous state, Kite felt able to put a handkerchief to his face, from under which he said, 'Do please come to your proposal, Mr Hooker.'

'I will, sir, without more ado. I have need of you, Captain Kite. You have lost your ships, but I can purchase you another; you will have a crew upon whose services you can call, and I can pay for them. You are, I apprehend, a mariner capable of navigation and—'

'One moment, Mr Hooker. Do I understand that you wish to engage me in the capacity of a master?'

'That is correct, Captain. That is what you are, is it not?'

'It is, but I cannot entertain to convey a vessel to India against the monopoly of the East India Company, and if you purpose to become an interloper, as those are called who avoid the monopoly by registering vessels under the flags of foreign states, consider that the thing is now very difficult, with most of Europe ranged against us . . .'

Hooker airily waved aside Kite's objection. 'No, no, I have no intention of sailing under the Austrian flag and registering a vessel in Ostend or any other such place. No, Captain, I am more interested in acquiring a fast vessel, one that is both swift and well armed. Liverpool has a reputation for privateers and I would have one for a private yacht, appointing you master and commander of her. You would take me to India and I should pay you upon the safe delivery of myself, my household and my fortune. We would have to come to some arrangement over the vessel but, if all proves satisfactory it would be to your advantage. Come, what d'you say?'

Kite's mind was working fast. There was, perhaps, an opportunity for him, but there were also a host of doubts and questions. He strove to make sense of what Hooker was not telling him, as much as what he was. 'Tell me, Mr Hooker,' he said at last, 'if I take you at your word and assume you to be a nabob, albeit,' and Kite gestured round the room, 'a somewhat eccentric one, if these grim surroundings offer a clue to your character, what future is there for me in your proposal beyond the delivery of you and yours in India when the ship will be sold out from under me and I shall be left to rot upon the strand?'

'Before I reveal my purpose for you in India, sir, and I certainly have one if you wish to take advantage of it, may I ask you, in broad terms, what your business was with the Honourable Company?' Hooker's tone was ironic, but his question fair.

'I had some notion like your own, Mr Hooker. To reinvest what remained of my capital assets in an Indiaman on the basis that there was less risk than elsewhere. Like you I received short shrift, all the undertakings being oversubscribed. Moreover my offer was, I think, though they did not say so to my face, too poor to spark the slightest interest.'

'May I ask how much?'

'You may ask . . .'

'But you are reticent?'

Kite sighed. 'Not reticent, Mr Hooker, just reluctant to reveal that the sum is, alongside yours, insignificant.'

'Ahh. Ten thousand pounds?'

Kite laughed bleakly. 'Like much else in the world, insignificance is relative: five thousand.'

'Ahh, I see . . .'

'No, you do not see, but I can guess that you think my relative poverty puts me in your pocket.'

'Not at all, Captain Kite, not at all,' expostulated Hooker.

34

'Nor should I wish you to think that in any way I was trying to buy you . . .'

'Did you not buy Jack Bow?'

'Of course not!' Hooker retorted indignantly. 'I offered him an alternative position to that of pot-boy in an inn where the landlord beat him. I needed a messenger whose movements would be inconspicuous in this quarter, most notably to solicit your attendance here.'

'Very well, let that be as it may, but I have answered your question, now do you answer mine: what further advantage would there be for me once I had conveyed you to Calcutta?'

'I made all my cash in ship-owning myself, Captain Kite. You will have heard of those Country ships, which trade from both Bombay and the Hooghli River eastwards and southwards, along the coasts of Pegu, Sumatra, Java and as far east as the Moluccas.' Kite forbore from expressing his ignorance of the trade and let Hooker run on. 'Some go farther, as far as China, but my own interests lay closer to home. There, I have admitted that perhaps my heart does lie under warmer skies than these English clouds. If you convey me home, I shall have to buy or build new tonnage, and if you come into partnership with me and offer your own expertise as a ship's husband then you will thereby earn yourself a substantial share. It is a fair offer, Captain Kite.' Hooker clapped his hands and the Indian boy reappeared with fresh glasses of wine. Hooker lifted one off the tray in a massive paw and, half-draining it, asked, 'Come, what d'ye say, eh?'

Kite sipped his own glass and nodded. 'These are my own conditions. First, that I shall myself provide the vessel but that you bear the expense of fitting her out. It so happens that the *Sea Lyon* was not exactly my last vessel, though she was my last capable of loading a profitable cargo. I have a schooner named the *Spitfire*, formerly fitted as a privateer. She is fast and may be well armed. You shall bear all the running expenses, including the payment of the crew, and I shall charter her to you as a letter of marque. I shall bear the trouble and expense only of obtaining the necessary papers and we shall be joint owners in the enterprise. Since we shall carry no cargo, we may accommodate my own effects and my wife and child will come with us . . .'

'I need accommodation for twenty men,' interjected Hooker suddenly.

'Twenty men? What twenty men?' Kite asked.

'Some tame dacoits from Pegu.' Hooker pointed obscurely at the floorboards at his feet. 'They are currently living below and form my bodyguard. That is why I do not fear the loss of my treasure.'

'Dacoits are to be trusted, then?' Kite asked with a puzzled frown, recalling the pair of Indians on the lower landing. 'I had thought them a species of robbers.'

Hooker smiled. This time the expression was not pleasant and Kite felt a shadow of apprehension at the chill in Hooker's eyes. 'Oh, they are, but if one knows the trick of it, they may be made of use.'

Kite hesitated, wondering what Sarah would say when she heard she was to be shipped to India with a malodorous nabob, his Hindu wife and a score of reformed Oriental highwaymen! He needed to buy a little time and to call Hooker's bluff and test his probity. Nodding to Hooker he said, 'Very well. Now this is what I propose: that I return to Liverpool and put the refitting of my vessel in hand. For this I shall need two hundred guineas in gold. This shall be a pledge of *your* good faith. In ten days' time I shall expect you and your household.' Kite reached into his waistcoat pocket. 'Here is my card. I shall accommodate you and your immediate family – which amounts to what? Your wife, yourself and your personal servants?'

'The Hindu boy, a cook and my wife's maid.'

'And Jack Bow? Does he come too?'

'Yes, I think he will attach himself to my household. He tells me he has no known family and I think something may be made of him.' 'Very well, then. He will find some fellow spirits in my house, no doubts. As for the twenty dacoits, I shall quarter them in an ale house.'

Hooker shook his head. 'No, that will not do. They *must* remain in close contact with me, Captain Kite. Have you a stable and some hammocks? They are familiar with hammocks.'

'Are these fellows armed, Mr Hooker?'

Hooker nodded. 'Oh yes, they are.'

'Then may we compromise? A pair of them to be quartered in my house, the remainder in a warehouse where they may cook their curries or whatever they subsist upon. They may relieve themselves howsoever you wish. Do you agree?'

Hooker nodded again. 'I do, Captain, except that you wish to secure an earnest of my good faith with a purse of two hundred guineas. May I ask what you offer in return?'

Kite laughed. 'Once again, Mr Hooker, you may certainly ask but, having dragged me off the street and confined me to the extent of compelling me to remain another night in this pestilential city, I feel I have acted thus far in accordance with your wishes. Besides, I require the money to put work in hand. I cannot afford to speculate on so slender a chance as that this meeting will yield all you promise merely upon your word alone.'

'You do not trust me, Captain Kite,' Hooker said, heaving his vast bulk out of the chair and fishing a ring of keys out of a pocket let into his tight breeches.

'Would you in my position, sir?' Kite asked with chilly formality as he too rose to his feet. 'You are gambling on me, I admit, but for a man of your declared means, two hundred guineas seems a reasonable stake.'

With a grunt and a jingling of keys Hooker left the room. As he withdrew, his wife stirred from her couch and rose in a susurration of silk to glide across the fathom of bare boards and confront Kite. With a strange and supple gesture of her hands and a charming rolling motion of her head she thanked Kite. Her accent was wonderfully exotic so that, for the first time, Kite's thoughts focused upon their ultimate destination: India.

'My husband is very pleased that you are able to help us, Captain. And also am I too. I am certain that you will not regret this encounter and that your wife will become my friend.' Her English was almost flawless and Kite was touched by her artlessly graceful manner.

'I hope so too, madam,' he responded with some warmth, 'but you should know that I have been married twice. Your husband seems to set some store by the fact that I was married to a black woman. Sadly she died of the rice-water fever some years ago.'

'And now you are married to an English lady, no doubt,' Mrs Hooker said with a smile, the fading light catching the jewel in her nose as her head moved gently from side to side.

'My wife was born in America, madam. She too was widowed, though her bereavement was caused by the malice of man.'

'Her husband was killed?' A pained look crossed the woman's face, the interrogative leaving her head canted expectantly to one side.

Kite nodded. 'Yes; he was murdered by rebels, madam.'

'That must have been very terrible for her, Captain.'

'Yes, it was.'

At that moment Hooker came back into the room holding out a small leather purse. 'Here, sir, is what you demand. You need not count it.'

'I had no intention of doing so, Mr Hooker. I do not think you will make an appearance in Liverpool if you have cheated me.'

Expressionless, Hooker held out the purse. Kite took it and asked, 'May I borrow Jack Bow to carry my bags back to my lodgings?'

'Of course, Captain, of course.' Hooker clapped his hands and the turbaned boy appeared again. Hooker addressed him, Kite catching only the words 'Jack' and the repeated command, '*jildi, jildi.*'

'Then I shall take my leave.'

'And we shall meet in Liverpool in ten days' time.'

'That is agreed.'

'And the *Spitfire* will be fitting out for sea?'

'That too is agreed.'

Hooker held out his hand and Kite took it. The big man's clasp was firm, but not excessive, and Kite, recalling something Hooker had said earlier, asked, 'Before I leave, may I ask to what you referred when you said you might be able to offer me some consolation if I overstayed my self-imposed limit of ten minutes? I formed the impression that it was not directly concerned with the matter you wished to put to me.'

'Ah, no, Captain, no indeed,' Hooker wagged a self-admonitory finger and turned aside to where, on an adjacent table, a crumpled newspaper lay. He picked it up and began turning the pages and staring intently at them as he searched for something. 'I am glad you reminded me, for it was one more of those coincidences that cannot have been chance, but a fated contribution to our meeting . . . Ah, here it is . . .'

With a further rustle of the broadsheet Hooker folded a page back and held it out to Kite, his index finger making a paragraph which Kite read.

Falmouth, 20th August, 1780. Came in this day the American Privateer Schooner *Algonquin*, Prize to H.M. Frigate *Cyclops*, Captain Henry Hope. The Prize, taken off the Irish Coast, had been retaken by her Crew but this Turn in the Wheel of Fortune was Most Gallantly reversed by the Bold Actions of the Prize-Master, Midshipman Nathaniel Drinkwater, who thereafter conducted the Schooner into Carrick Roads and Delivered his Troublesome Prisoners to the Governor of Pendennis Castle.

The *Algonquin*, Commanded by a Captain King of Rhode Island, has Proved a Veritable Plague, eluding all attempts at her Capture, most recently Taking the *Sea Lyon*, of Liverpool, Thomas Clarkson, Master.

'Well, I'll be damned,' said Kite lowering the newspaper. 'That is a coincidence indeed, Mr Hooker. Not only did the *Algonquin* take my vessel the *Sea Lyon*, but she was herself captured by my sister's husband's ship, the frigate *Cyclops*!'

'There, sir!' exclaimed Hooker, his eyes afire in the last gasp of the daylight. 'Then the whole affair is ordained by Providence, as, my wife will tell you, are all things under heaven.'

Chapter Three

A Dubious Partnership

'Do I conclude that you do not trust this Hooker, William?'

Kite looked up at his wife. He would ring for candles in a moment, but the last of the daylight caught the side of Sarah's face and threw up the extraordinary beauty of her features. She was one of those unusually fortunate women to whom the passage of time was kind, for in her splendid maturity Sarah Kite was more handsome than he ever remembered her. But this thought turned like a knife in Kite's guts, reminding him that so precious a possession as Sarah was ought not to be subjected to the cruel vicissitudes of a fate that had already subjected her to the most harrowing of circumstances: Kite would never forget the charred remains of her first husband after the Yankee rebels had first tarred and feathered their political opponent and then set fire to him!* Now he too had failed to provide for her and was about to embark on a most singular risk.

'How can I, my dear?' he said, disturbed, and thrusting himself to his feet strode across the room and pulled the cord.

'But it seems to me you have taken adequate precautions for assurances as to his honour. You have two hundred guineas and at least you may refit *Spitfire* . . .'

'To what end, if this Hooker fails to materialize?' Kite snapped.

* See *The Privateersman.*

41

'But why should he not?' At this moment Maggie, the maid, appeared, bobbing in the doorway with a branch of lit candles. 'Thank you, Maggie, my dear,' Sarah said, continuing her remark to her husband, 'You have nothing to lose, William . . .'

'Heavens, Sarah, I have nothing *to* lose!' he exclaimed.

'Nonsense, William. Should Hooker not come, you may go back to sea and wreak some revenge upon these rebels!'

'What, recommission *Spitfire* as a privateer on my own account and chance my arm in the Atlantic? Come, my dear, I am too old for such adventures and am loath to leave you here in this place . . .'

'Too old? Why d'you say so? Because I proved more adept with my foil and bested you the other day?' She smiled and pulled a wry face at him. 'Anyway, you will be in no danger, I shall come with you, just as I shall come with you to India. This place,' said Sarah, suddenly serious and gesturing round the drawing room, 'is nothing. I shall hazard my life alongside yours, William, and, in addition to my foil, I can point a pistol better than you,' she concluded triumphantly.

Kite sighed and smiled. 'Would you truly splice your entire life to mine?'

''Tis what I promised before God.'

But Kite had little thought for God, though he looked kindly upon his wife. He was worried more about matters temporal than spiritual. He wanted to convince himself that Sarah was right and that he was fretting unnecessarily. Truth to tell, he had slept badly ever since returning to Liverpool from London. Disturbed by dreams in which phantasms reminiscent of Puella merged with fleshy images of Mrs Hooker, where pale mounds of inviting flesh divided to reveal dark pits of pleasure, he woke sweating in the half-light of dawn beset by guilt. Were these plaguing succubi manifestations of his own inner torment, or the warnings of fate? Though they might fade in the cold light of day, their power to unsettle him remained potent, simultaneously stirring the lusts of his ageing manhood and leaving him unmanned and trembling like a terrified child left alone in the night.

These carnal phantasmagoria soon withered, to be replaced by the horrors of his situation and the inexorable loom of financial ruin. Along with images of his corpulent Antiguan partner Wentworth, and his sexually rapacious wife Kitty, whose bodies were now rotting, Kite lay abed dawn after dawn miserable with apprehension. He had a child again now, a small and perfect daughter whose existence depended upon the success of her father's enterprises, and these were failing fast. Since the loss of *Sea Lyon*, his only commercial triumph had been the rather shameful extraction of two hundred guineas from Hooker's purse. Before travelling to London he had already put the refitting of *Spitfire* in hand, hoping to charter her to one of the several Liverpool consortia still game to send privateers to sea. He had had no plans to take her to sea himself, but now, it seemed, fate ordained otherwise.

Apart from the few thousand pounds he had been willing to invest in an East India voyage, he had little left. He had taken most of the risk of his own vessels himself and their loss yielded him no fat compensation from underwriters. There would be men on the Liverpool Exchange who would delight in his downfall – Jasper Watkinson, his former clerk, and Frith, with whom he had fallen out some years earlier, in particular. The news was already circulating that Captain Kite had lost his last commercial vessel to the Yankees.

As he lay and stared up at the ceiling, he thought of all those who depended upon him. Men had already died in his service, victims of the war at sea; their families hovered on the brink of destitution, though Sarah had done her best for them. Now there was the matter of his clerks and the stevedore who worked for him, his housekeeper, the maid and Bandy Ben, the odd-job man and messenger who could scarcely string a sentence together but who could manipulate numbers with an amazing speed. All these desperate souls looked to him for their living and it was beyond his powers to see how he could satisfy their hungry mouths for longer than a few more weeks.

Kite lay thus in the growing daylight, harrowed by anxiety, until an uneasy sleep took him for an hour into a blessed oblivion.

None of this was in any way obvious the following morning when the Kites' housekeeper, Mrs O'Riordan, brought news of the early arrival of the guests. Siobhan O'Riordan displayed a quite proper irritation, unintimidated by the huge size of the man standing upon the doorstep, his wig slightly awry and his wide skirts waving in the wind blowing up from the River Mersey.

'The master's not expecting you until tomorrow,' she protested, staring past the bulk of the man and catching the first whiff of Hooker's body odour as she saw the cavalcade of five coaches that lined the street. Mrs O'Riordan had not quite believed what Kite had told her to expect and the sight of an entourage as big as this ugly, smelly bear of a man's took her by surprise. 'Please step inside and I shall let the master know of your arrival.'

Leaving Hooker in the hall she passed through the kitchen, with a hissed aside to Maggie to 'clap yer eyeball to yon keyhole and watch the fella', then through into the long *salle d'armes* Kite had had built along one wall of the garden where he and his wife were accustomed to exercise with foils. Sarah was considered eccentric in this, though men forgave her most things when she smiled and the ladies of her acquaintance shrugged off such an odd accomplishment with a shudder and the observation that she was from America where a woman had to protect herself against the Iroquois or the Mohawks, or other red men whose designs on a white female were not to be imagined.

Mrs O'Riordan watched her employers for a moment, thinking that while Captain Kite was a fine figure of a man despite the ugly disfigurement of the mask, it was somehow demeaning that he should be in full retreat from his wife. To be sure Sarah Kite was a kind and considerate mistress, but Mrs O'Riordan, though entertaining no love for the English *en masse*, nevertheless liked to know where she stood. Moreover, Sarah Kite was too unpredictable to occupy the unequivocal status of an English gentlewoman in Siobhan O'Riordan's estimation. Why, look at the body! Just like a young man in those tight breeches! She had seen a few fast women wear breeches for riding and, thank Jesus, Mary and all the saints, Mistress Kite still favoured a skirted habit and the sideways saddle when she rode a horse herself. But seeing her shamelessly prancing up and down this strip of canvas – why, her round backside was too large for such a thing!

The fierce clash of blades was so swift that Mrs O'Riordan could not make out what was happening beyond noting the fact that the Captain was falling back fast before his wife's onslaught. In a moment or two he would come up against the far wall with a jarring crash but then she watched, quite forgetting the big man waiting for her in the hall, as Kite stood his ground and quickly parried his wife's lunge.

They were body to body now, and Mrs O'Riordan ached to put a bet on the outcome, but dared not think of such a thing for it was shameful to think of the Captain being beaten by a woman, even if that woman was his wife. No, by God! That made it all a thousand times worse!

Suddenly the clash of blades stopped. Both parties seemed locked together in a hiatus, foil pressed against foil, their bodies motionless apart from the expansion and contraction of their chests as they drew breath. Mrs O'Riordan recalled her purpose and seized her moment.

'Your guest is here, Cap'n!' she called and Kite's head, his face masked, turned towards her.

'What? Hooker?'

'That's what he calls himself, Cap'n.'

'Bring him through, Mrs O'Riordan, bring him through.' Then Kite addressed his wife. 'Well, you haven't hit me, Sarah, is it a draw, or shall we resume?'

Mrs O'Riordan hesitated, wanting to see what these two would do now.

'It most certainly is not a draw! Come, do your worst.'

With a shout, Kite thrust his wife bodily from him so that she fell back three steps before catching her balance. Before she could come *en garde*, Kite was attacking and she fell back with a quick succession of deft parries. Satisfied, Mrs O'Riordan retired herself, smacking Maggie's rump as the maid bent at the keyhole, remarking that 'the two fools are playing at soldiers when the whole household knows there's not'ing but ruination and penury for all of us'.

The bout was still in full swing when Mrs O'Riordan led Hooker through her own domain and into the *salle*.

'You'll have to wait till they've finished, sir,' she said; 'when one of them thinks they've killed the other they'll see you're here.'

But it was almost all over. As Sarah, again pressing Kite hard, forced him backwards and then made what she thought would be a triumphant thrust, Kite executed a circular parry, bound her blade and with a vicious flick of his wrist tore the foil from Sarah's grip so that it spun to one side and landed with a clatter two yards from Hooker's feet. With a ponderous groan he bent and picked it up. Holding it hilt first towards Sarah he bowed.

'Josiah Hooker at your service, ma'am.'

Sarah removed her mask and shook her hair. Her face was flushed and gleaming with sweat, yet she squared up to Hooker without demur. 'Mr Hooker,' she replied bobbing a curtsy and recovering her foil, 'you are most kind.' She flashed him a devastating smile and added, 'My husband hates to lose.'

Watching, Kite saw the look of admiration cross Hooker's face, following the first astonishment at her beauty.

As she drew her breath, Sarah inhaled Hooker's strangely repulsive odour and fell back a step. Hurriedly removing his own mask, Kite came forward and shook Hooker's hand.

'We are practising, Mr Hooker, for our lives may depend upon it.'

'Please, Captain, do call me Josiah.'

46

'Very well, and I am William and you have already met my wife Sarah. Come,' Kite gestured at the door, 'let us go through and welcome you properly. Where is your wife?'

'She remains in my carriage . . .'

'And you have your servants and the dacoits?'

'Indeed.'

'Then we had better get them quartered.'

'And your ship?'

'My *schooner*, Josiah,' Kite said pointedly. 'Tomorrow you shall see the *Spitfire*. You should not expect too much of her either.'

'I will go and welcome your wife, Mr Hooker.'

'Josiah, please, Sarah.'

'And what is *her* name, Josiah?'

'I call her by an English name, my dear,' Hooker said with presumptuous familiarity. 'Rose.'

'How charming,' said Sarah, flicking her husband a quick look and wrinkling her nose as she left the two men.

During the remainder of that day Kite's household was in turmoil as Mrs O'Riordan moved with a frantic resolution from one minor crisis to another in accommodating what she quickly denominated 'the flashy heathen'. The exotic Mrs 'Rose' Hooker had two attendant maids, said to be wives to the head dacoit, while Hooker had his turbaned 'boy'. As for the dacoit bodyguards, they were found an upper floor in Kite's counting house. This had formerly been used for the storage of small parcels of valuable cargo but, so far had Kite's business already collapsed, it was now empty. As for the heavy, iron-bound chest which Hooker had brought with him and which contained his putative fortune, this was lodged in the bedroom assigned to Hooker and his wife. Regarding the transfer of this heavy item, handled by two dacoits, Kite reflected that his own future might very well lie inside its padlocked and studded carapace.

By late afternoon, when Kite and Sarah, Hooker and the inimitable Rose sat down to dine, a sort of order had returned to the ship-owner's house. All seemed to augur well, despite the unexpectedly early arrival of the Hooker ménage. As Kite joined his wife in bed she said, 'You did not tell me he stank. How in God's name can we share the quarters of the *Spitfire* with such a man?'

Kite sighed and he shook his head as he eased himself down between the warmed sheets. 'I do not know; all I know is that beggars cannot be choosers.'

'Are matters that dire?'

Kite nodded, leaning over to blow out the bedside candles. 'Yes,' he announced to the sudden darkness, 'they are dire indeed.'

'Then we shall have to bear things as they are until they get better,' Sarah said, drawing close to him.

'Will they ever get better, Sarah?' he asked, his voice catching with emotion. 'All my life, it seems, I have been lifted up by fate just high enough to see a bright future, only to have such dazzling opportunities dashed from my grasp. Sometimes I wish I had never left the Lakes and had been hanged for a murder I did not commit.'*

'Don't be foolish, William,' Sarah said sharply. 'You would never have come to America and we should never have met. Besides, it is not for you to order Providence. The worth of a person, man or woman, is not how they rise in life, but how they withstand the onslaughts of fate. You pin too much hope on your enterprises.'

'But a man must, Sarah! Why else should he get out of bed each morning but in expectation of a small improvement in his life? Even the meanest of us works for his penny or indeed begs in hope.'

'That is what I mean, you silly fellow. It is hope backed by courage and endeavour that mark you. I adore you for this quality as much as for your other attributes, but fate is never kind, only indifferent. Be grateful for what you have, for it is not inconsiderable, and we have a new opportunity in this stinking Hooker and his Brahmin wife.'

* See *The Guineaman.*

Kite sighed. 'Perhaps,' he said, staring up into the darkness. 'But I worry about the child . . .'

'Shhh . . .' He felt her hand upon his face, stopping his mouth, then she moved against him and her lips found his. After they had kissed Sarah moved under him and whispered, 'Make us one, William, and we shall be inseparable.'

Next morning, a forenoon of low mist and Septembral chill, with the Mersey's ebb tide slapping pettishly along the quaysides, Kite and Hooker arrived to view the *Spitfire* lying in her riverside mud-berth. Under such a grey miasma she appeared small and unprepossessing, reduced to her lower masts with timber and debris littering her deck and her paintwork neglected. To all but an experienced eye she bore the superficial look of a vessel fit for the breakers, not a voyage to India.

To Kite, however, the signs of work in hand were encouraging. He knew the condition of the schooner's hull was sound, for he had coppered her in his days of affluence when he had taken her to sea to prey upon the enemy. Moreover the timber and lumber littering her deck were clear evidence not of neglect but of between-decks modification, alterations that would accommodate Hooker and his household in a modicum of comfort. From below came the noises of hammering and sawing, and the occasional appearance of a workman told of the activity taking place there.

Kite pointed these adjustments out to Hooker as the two men stood staring down upon the cluttered deck as the *Spitfire* lay with a slight list as she settled on the mud in the falling tide. A man emerged from the after companionway and, seeing the two gentlemen looking down upon the schooner, called out, 'Good morning.' A moment later he had scrambled ashore over a rickety gangway and stood beside them, wiping the palm of his right hand on the tail of his soiled brown broadcloth coat.

'Zachariah,' Kite said greeting the ugly man whose physical bulk rivalled that of Hooker, 'may I introduce Mr Hooker.' Kite turned to Hooker. 'Josiah, Zachariah Harper, a staunch servant of my shipping interest who will, I hope, consent to come with us as mate of the *Spitfire*. Do not be perturbed by his rebellious accent. A Yankee Zachariah may well be, but one well disposed to us . . .' Kite smiled as Hooker shook hands with the American-born Loyalist.

'I'd be honoured, Cap'n Kite.' Harper's ugly visage cracked into a grin of enormous enthusiasm.

'And you'd have no qualms about fighting your fellow countrymen?' Hooker asked rather pompously.

As Kite laughed, Harper shook his head. 'Not in the least, Mr Hooker, I'd welcome the chance. The damned Whigamore rebels took everything I once owned and I wish them naught but ill. As for any French or Spanish we might meet, well, they'll meet the same response from me, sir.'

'So how's she coming along, Zachariah?' Kite said, nodding at the schooner.

'Well enough. The carpenters'll be finished by the end of the week and we have already made up most of the rigging in the loft. I've a new main and foresail being cut and most of the stores are on order and due for delivery at the end of the month. I'd say that we should be ready to sail well before the middle of October.'

Kite considered matters for a moment, then nodded. 'Very well. From next week I shall attend the vessel daily myself to expedite matters and ease your burden. I should like to acquire a new stock of small arms and I'll have to arrange for powder and shot . . .'

After the three men had climbed aboard the schooner, the discussion turned to the minutiae of storing a vessel for a long passage in wartime. Taking notes in his pocket book, Kite consulted with both Harper and Hooker, planning and costing the many items to be considered in completing *Spitfire* for sea, so that it was late afternoon when Kite and Hooker returned to the terrace of houses from which the Mersey formed but a distant view.

Having shifted their clothes, the two men joined their wives. Kite detected a degree of chill between them, an assumption that Sarah confirmed with a slight raising of her eyebrow. It was scarcely to be supposed that the women would find anything in common and Kite knew that Sarah would have found the constraint of attending her guest very irksome. It was even less to be supposed that any true friendship would develop between them in the inevitable weeks which would pass before *Spitfire* was ready for sea. Once at sea perhaps the common experience of their lives would remedy this situation, but Kite was apprehensive as to the relationship between the two couples. The fact that he would be obliged to Hooker could hardly be countered by Hooker's dependence upon him for a safe passage. If they ran into trouble, it was a convention that Hooker would take his part in the defence of the schooner and, moreover, prime his dacoits for the same purpose, and they had already discussed this point. Hooker had been fulsome in his reassurances.

'Oh, you need have no apprehension upon that point, William,' he had soothed in a manner which Kite had found less than comforting. Growing acquaintance with Josiah Hooker suggested that he was all that he claimed to be, and yet a doubt lingered in Kite's mind and, in the lonely hours of the dawn, it was this that now filled his thoughts.

After the household had settled into its uneasy new regime, with the men out for most of the day and Mrs Hooker left to ruminate in her room, Sarah attended to her usual business and the winding up of her affairs in Liverpool. Kite determined to resolve his dilemma by opening up a frank discussion with his new, if dubious, partner, and one evening in mid-September, as the two men sat over their port and the women had withdrawn, he asked, 'Josiah, why did you decide not to settle in England? You will forgive my curiosity, but you clearly have the means.'

Hooker moved his vast body uneasily, so that the chair upon which he sat creaked in protest. 'Well, William, I suppose I know you well enough and our fates are so intertwined that little harm can come of my telling you. I suppose you have a right to know that you are not aiding and abetting a criminal, for you must have thought my hiding in the stews of Gravitt's Yard a strange matter. 'Tis a private affair, of course, and goes back a long time.' Hooker paused, as if wondering whether to confide in Kite. 'To be truthful,' he resumed, having apparently resolved this dilemma, 'it was a foolish thing to return at all. I am a not inconspicuous figure . . .' Hooker rumbled a self-deprecating laugh, drained his glass and refilled it. 'Many years ago, as a young man of modest means, I courted a young woman of great beauty. She rejected me and sent another suitor to tell me to keep my distance. The bugger was offensive in what he declared to me were the feelings of the person in question and I threw him down the stairs from my rooms. He limps to this day, but he afterwards married the lady upon whom I had set my deepest aspirations.' Hooker sighed. 'I was sorely affronted by the manner in which I had been treated, but the blade took it into his head that he was the wronged party. A week later he turned up at my rooms a second time. His leg was all splinted and he had half a dozen cronies with him, all half-drunk and all eager to revenge themselves. Naturally I defended myself and, it only being possible to ascend the staircase one at a time, I had no trouble in rendering them all down to an impotent heap at its foot in a matter of moments.

'That should have been the end of the affair, but two years later, as I prospered in business undertaking insurance risks, my offices were burned down. I later learned that this man's wife had had a still-born child and that he attributed this to me – a preposterous notion. I had not seen the young woman since she had rejected me, but I entertained no illusions about the malice her husband bore me for the disfigurement of his own beauty,' Hooker scoffed. 'So I betook myself and my money to India where, within ten years, I had acquired a fortune and a wife of my own. I began to consider what I should do, and determined to return to the place of my birth and buy an estate in the locality which was, I knew from correspondence with my former partner in risk, just then offered up for sale.

'Upon my arrival in the town our presence was made known and that very evening I received a call from my old enemy. He was by then a widower and informed me that I had blighted his life and the life of his wife, an odd reversal of perception, you'll allow, but this consumed him and he threatened me and told me to leave. I remained a few days but then one of my dacoits was found dead in a ditch. There was not a mark upon him and the night had been cold, so the coroner decided the fellow had been drunk – for an empty bottle was found near him. Two days after the inquest my enemy woke to find all his horses dead. Their stalls were soaked in their blood but no one had heard or seen anything. I knew my men had taken their revenge and, my wife now fearing the worst, I decided that I had little option but to return to India. Thus, my dear fellow, I went to ground in Gravitt's Yard where you found me.'

'I see,' Kite replied. 'Thank you for your confidence.'

Later, as they went to bed, he told Sarah of Hooker's account and she said, 'Do you suppose the young lady rejected his suit on account of his smelling so? I should have done, even had he come to me with all the fabled wealth of the Indies in his pocket! How do you suppose his poor wife copes?'

'She does not seem to notice,' Kite replied.

'Or it is the reason for her apparently permanent inertia?' Sarah added waspishly.

'Josiah tells me she is cold,' he said.

'Ah, well,' said Sarah, snuggling under the bedding, 'let us hope this odd partnership pays some dividend. I worry about little Emma; do you think that she will suffer in India?'

'I think we shall be at sea much of the time. I had thought to recommend that you take as many books as we can manage, even if we encase some of them for the outward voyage . . .'

And so their discussion turned to the uncertain future that now opened before them, and the day of their departure approached.

Chapter Four

Captain 'Topsy-Turvy'

K ite's optimistic hopes of an early departure were destined to be dashed. The sailing of the *Spitfire* was to be delayed for months. First Rose Hooker fell ill. Kite called in his old friend Joshua Bennett, a doctor whose skill Kite had long admired and who attended his exotic patient with a mixture of consolation, sympathy, patience and anodyne placebos. He sent his wife, the plain but capable Katherine, whose rogue of a father Kite had sailed with when he had first shipped outward aboard a Liverpool slaver, to visit daily and Mrs Bennett thereby eased a burden from Sarah's shoulders. After Captain Makepeace's death, his widow, and Katherine's mother, had remarried. Her new husband, the wealthy Frith, had long been an enemy of Kite's, though Katherine remained a firm friend of the Kite household, for Kite had saved her from a marriage with Frith, arranged by her devious mother who was already the man's mistress. Frith himself remained unforgiving, for Kite had once bested him and he now took delight in Kite's commercial ruin. Frith was instrumental in changing Kite's status to that of a pariah, of one no longer welcome on the floor of the Liverpool Exchange. Kite's only consolation as his creditors closed in upon him was that he could meet his debts, but this wore thin as time passed and he had to raise credit with Hooker.

Next, Hooker persistently postponed the date of sailing, uncertain as to whether his wife was sufficiently recovered to undertake the hazards of a voyage. To exacerbate this valetudinarian attitude, the weather now conspired with a series of hard westerly gales that mewed outward-bound shipping in the Mersey.

With Christmas, hard upon the heels of an improvement in the weather, came the unwelcome intelligence of further activity of American privateers in the Irish Sea and a further fit of nerves by Hooker and his wife so that, as the year turned, Kite became savage in his private opinion of his dubious partner.

'One would think,' he snarled vehemently at Sarah when undressing one night in mid-January 1781, 'that the damned lubber did not want to leave at all!'

Sarah, seeking to pacify her angry and frustrated husband who, she well knew, had perforce to maintain an air of equanimity in his daily intercourse with Hooker, replied that the delay was perhaps providential, and that a spring departure was preferable, allowing them to double the Cape of Good Hope and pick up the favourable monsoon in the Indian Ocean.

Kite reluctantly admitted the sense of this and Sarah, capitalizing upon her moral advantage, added that it was no concern of theirs, for such was their penury that Hooker was bearing the costs of the delay.

This was some consolation, but Kite was no less irked. He maintained a chilly formality with Hooker, bound by these humiliating ties, but this was not the end of the strain under which the delay compelled them all to exist. Kite's house was overcrowded; the dacoits were troublesome, feeding the more restive of their neighbours in the locality with rumoured causes for unwanted pregnancies, burglaries and other ills. Kite's eccentric reputation, earned by formerly having a blackamoor wife was now resurrected, and he once more became known as Captain 'Topsy-Turvy', a nickname attached to him as a flouter of convention. Moreover, his association with a vast and stinking partner whose wife was also a curious native from some foreign shore only added to the public hostility.

Kite was not the only man touched by the war. Losses and restrictions on Liverpool shipping had brought real hardship and privation to many in the port. Civil disorder and occasional full-blown riots were not uncommon. Once roused, the mob had to find its scapegoats. Again, as when he had first brought his beautiful black bride among them, the populace demonstrated their hatred of the eccentric by breaking Kite's windows.

Neither Kite nor Sarah viewed this indignity as the end of the world, but for Rose Hooker the ugly horror compelled her to retreat to her bed while her husband, now caught on the sharpening horns of a dilemma, suddenly considered their departure urgent. Tension between the tainted Hooker and his wife only added to the strain under which the household laboured. The daily change of the dacoit guard upon Hooker's treasure had long been a source of irritation to Mrs O'Riordan and it was only with difficulty that Kite persuaded her not to leave his service. But she was plagued too by an unexpected liaison between Maggie and Jack Bow who, having at first been a meek and grateful addition to Kite's ménage, had long since given in to his impudent nature. For three weeks Mrs O'Riordan had been consumed by anxiety that Maggie would fall pregnant, having discovered the maid and Jack in thoughtless intimacy. The beating which she gave the girl she afterwards claimed a specific against such an eventuality, having first convinced herself that the circumstances would most likely produce a conception. Accordingly she was mortified when, upon informing Dr Bennett, for whom she had the most profound respect, he dismissed the claim as 'a ridiculous conceit with no foundation in scientific fact and too much reliance upon the voiding effects of unwarranted violence'.

Mrs O'Riordan scarcely understood the doctor's dismissal, except that it was vitriolic in its contempt, but she afterwards greeted him with cold formality. As for the doctor's wife, whose devotion to Kite was well known to Siobhan O'Riordan, she was received with unveiled hostility so that, in due course, poor Katherine ceased to call upon her friends.

Thus did all the relationships slowly break down; only that between Sarah and Kite withstood the strain. But even this was threatened when, early in the new year, little Emma fell sick. Bennett admitted he was ignorant of the cause and had never seen the symptoms before; having chid Mrs O'Riordan for lack of science, all he could tell the anxious parents was that their daughter was 'consumed by a vapid decline that was not a consumption'.

Kite steeled his heart against the inevitable, but Sarah was inconsolable. Her conception had been late in her life and she knew that only Bennett's skill had saved her from puerperal fever. She knew another pregnancy would be dangerous, if not impossible, and she felt she had failed her husband, who had already lost two sons.

Kite, torn between the necessity of preparing the *Spitfire* for sea and supporting Sarah, bore this final onslaught of misfortune with an inscrutable fortitude. The change in his friend was remarked by Bennett, whose concern for the husband was as great as that for the wife.

'He has become cold as ice,' he told Katherine, shaking his head.

'But not with poor Sarah, surely?' Katherine asked. She had been half in love with Captain Kite when a girl, and had remained fond of him ever since.

Bennett shook his head again. 'No, but it is the very solicitude with which he treats her that in a curious and contrary way proves to me, who have known him for so long as you have, m'dear, that the man has buried his emotions deep in his soul.'

'But,' his wife queried uncertainly, 'why is that so bad? Surely if he wishes to hide his pain, for pain he must certainly feel if the child dies . . .'

'Oh, the child will most assuredly die, Kate. 'Tis only a matter of time.' Bennett shook his head and, removing his shoes, tossed them into a corner and sank back into his chair with an unhappy groan. 'But to answer your question, I apprehend that a man of William's humour will not contain his grief. 'Twill emerge most precipitately at some inauspicious moment. One can only hope that William is able to contain it.'

*   *   *

Emma died within a month of falling sick. Sarah spent the night locked in the child's room while Kite slept in a chair outside her door. When Sarah emerged and woke him in the dawn she said simply, 'It is time to go. We have no attachments here any more.'

Kite rose stiffly. Touching his wife gently on the cheek he nodded then passed into the room where he pressed his lips to the cold little forehead. Sarah retired to the bedroom to sleep until evening, and Kite went downstairs to arrange for the funeral. He then walked down to the river.

In his final harrowing, William Kite's only unconstrained association was with the *Spitfire*'s mate, Zachariah Harper. As an American Loyalist, Harper had lost everything. Harper's own descent into the abyss had profoundly affected his outlook on life and, in sympathy with his employer, he daily sought to raise Kite's spirits as the two men attended to every detail of the schooner. Since, to avoid unnecessary expense, they had delayed taking on a full crew until certain of their departure, Harper and his handful of employed seamen were joined by Kite whenever possible in the physical labour of preparation. Thus Kite, late a ship-owner and man of quality and means, had lost himself in the overhauling of rigging as much as the preparation of charts, submerging himself in the practicalities in a way that only added to his soubriquet of Captain 'Topsy-Turvy'. In this manner Kite found the means to sublimate his grief.

As for Sarah, after the interment and pretending a commission from her husband, she boldly travelled to London in the company of Bandy Ben and Maggie, taking up lodgings off the Strand found for her through an acquaintance. From here she laid out almost the last of Kite's disposable capital and a sum of her own, acquiring a quantity of haberdashery, fashionable knick-knacks, French pattern-books, cased pistols, two dozen hangers, a dozen fine-wrought fowling pieces and three sets of fine Spanish harness. While in town in a mood of brittle gaiety, she attended the theatre in the company of her sister-in-law Helen Hope, flirted harmlessly and broke several hearts. Having thus diverted herself and, like her husband, sublimated her unhappiness, she returned home with her booty and, she hoped, the means with which to start the revival of her husband's fortunes.

In the privacy of his own home Dr Bennett shook his grey head over Sarah's behaviour, expressing misgivings that little good could come of any of it. 'Such a curious expenditure of energy at such a time runs contrary to human nature,' he declared. For once his wife did not agree with him. Katherine understood exactly why Sarah had behaved in the way she had, and wished her free of her misery.

At the beginning of March Kite and his company finally boarded the *Spitfire* as she lay in the dock, gleaming with new paint and slushed spars.

The final departure of the schooner attracted a crowd which consisted of rather more than the casual dockside loafers who might otherwise have attended the departure of so small a vessel. The curious among Liverpool's growing numbers of wealthy were alerted to the event. Even in mourning Mistress Kite was sufficiently striking to attract a crowd of admirers among the men, and detractors among the women, but when her beauty was accompanied by the massive and malodorous bulk of her husband's strange new partner and the brilliant and swirlingly scarlet silk-clad figure of *his* voluptuously exotic wife, few could stay away.

The embarkation began with a little procession of turbaned dacoits in their white curtals, each with a Moghul sword strapped to his waist. They accompanied several carts bringing the last of the personal effects of the adventurers, among which was concealed the heavy chest containing Hooker's fortune. Then came those servants whom Kite had decided to take with him: Maggie and Hooker's protégé Jack Bow. Kite had also persuaded one of his counting-house clerks, a certain Michael McClusky, to join the party, and he too clambered aboard. Last came Hooker and the two ladies, attended by a wildly barking mongrel whose unwanted attentions amused the crowd and induced a few youths to draw attention to Hooker's unfortunate bodily dysfunction.

Captain 'Topsy-Turvy' was already aboard. Dressed like his wife in formal black, Kite ordered the warps carried out and the hands to the capstan. Then, to the tune of a fiddle and the cries of Zachariah Harper, the *Spitfire* cast off from the quay wall and was hauled out of the dock.

Closing the entrance, Kite braced the schooner's yards sharp up and let the square topsails fall. It was the moment of slack water as the breeze filled these high sails and, letting all her ropes go, *Spitfire* stood out into the Mersey. Here, in midstream, the first of the ebb caught her and, gently at first but with increasing strength, swept her down the river. The big quadrilateral main and foresails were hoisted and the red ensign was broken out at the main peak. The staysails and jibs were run up and the canvas filled, driving the schooner forward so that the curl of white water at her forefoot grew. At the truck of her mainmast a long blue pendant streamed out. Upon it in white letters was spelt the little vessel's name.

As she gathered way the crowd were already dispersing. Captain 'Topsy-Turvy' had gone, and with him his strange household and companions. Most wished him good riddance. A few, like Katherine and Joshua Bennett, wished him a quiet farewell and shed a tear or two. Mrs O'Riordan stared about the empty house, wondered whether she had been sensible to agree to stay on and keep the place aired, and what she would do with Bandy Ben. It was a place to live, of course, and Captain Kite had made arrangements with Dr Bennett to ensure she was provided for – quite how in his straitened circumstances Mrs O'Riordan could not understand. What Mrs O'Riordan knew, for as near a certainty as she could determine, was that India was a long way away and there was precious little chance of her ever seeing her employer again.

It was Kite's intention to get clear of the chops of the Channel as fast as possible. He feared interference not only from

American privateers, to whom rumour if not fact had now added a number of disaffected rogue Irish corsairs, but also from cruising British frigates whose commanders, if short of prime seamen, would not scruple to press men from a private vessel like the *Spitfire*. Given his luck to date, Kite's apprehension was unsurprising; in the event he was fortunate and reached the latitude of Cape Finisterre unmolested. Here, however, a strong south-westerly wind rapidly increased to gale force just as those of his passengers unaccustomed to the motion of the schooner had been on the verge of recovery from sea-sickness. Their relapse was spectacular; to queasiness, sweating and the urge to void one's stomach was now added a portion of terror. Rose Hooker shrieked while her husband groaned, poor little Maggie, now undoubtedly impregnated by the precocious Master Bow, suffered further indignity, while the dacoits succumbed to a man and lay like the dead in a heap between decks.

Below, amid the cabins and platforms the carpenters had erected and modified out of the former slaver-cum-privateer, the unhappy entourage made the best of it. Most anticipated an early death and few could even entertain the thought that the current state of affairs would not last until they reached India. For all but the seafarers it seemed that they had voluntarily cast themselves away on a foolhardy adventure that could only end in shipwreck and disaster. Anything less seemed impossible.

During the three days that the gale blew, Kite kept the deck with Zachariah, strangely elated by the trial to which his little vessel was put. The keen wind, dashing sheets of spray aboard, seemed to scour all the unpleasant associations of the land from his very soul, and Sarah too caught some of this sense of liberty and spiritual renewal. Forsaking her skirts, she adopted the form of dress in which she fenced, breeches, shirt and coat, male attire which caused some outrage among the dacoits, but which was greeted with wide grins by the *Spitfire*'s hands, most of whom had known and admired Mistress Kite for many years.

As the weather eased and *Spitfire* laid her course southwards for Madeira, spirits rose. The decks grew dry and the dacoits emerged to take exercise. A deckchair was produced for Hooker and his wife, the latter of whom began to bear up with more fortitude than she had hitherto displayed.

'It is not her fault that she is fearful of the immensity of the sea, William,' Sarah had reproved her husband when he made an offhand reference to his partner's wife. 'It is intimidating enough. Did you know Jackie Bow asked me if we'd reach India by the end of the week?' Sarah laughed at the recollection. 'He has no grasp of distance and it was quite beyond his conception that the earth was a sphere and that we had to travel round the greater part of its circumference in order to reach our destination.'

Kite had grunted; he had other preoccupations. Only that morning Zachariah had reported several casks of water to be stinking and others to be covered with the defecations of the dacoits who had voided both their stomachs and their bowels with equally enthusiastic disregard during the gale. Thus one of the advantages of the schooner having formerly been a slaver and able to carry a quantity of water was destroyed.

'I was intending to put into Madeira,' Kite admitted with a sigh, 'but not to undertake the cleaning of the hold.'

'Well, we may get the 'tween decks cleaned out easily enough,' Harper agreed, 'though those pesky heathens will have to sleep on deck tonight and they won't like that, I dare say.'

Kite nodded. 'See to it without delay, Zachariah, if you please. One stink is enough aboard here, to have the servants smell like their master is intolerable.'

Zachariah Harper laughed. He occupied a small cabin of his own and was the only member of the *Spitfire*'s afterguard who was relatively unaffected by Hooker's unfortunate body odour. 'I'll see to it right away, Cap'n.'

The dacoits neither liked nor understood their temporary eviction from their cramped quarters between decks. It seemed utterly perverse of the overbearing white men to souse their quarters just when they had become tolerably dry. They keened their resentment until, after an elaborate explanation in Hindi conducted by Hooker with much exaggerated gyrating of his head, and some supplementary remarks made by his wife, they hunkered down in the shelter of the boats lashed on the chocks amidships.

In the wake of Zachariah's departure to chivvy the dacoits out of their festering berths and the hands in with brooms and buckets, Kite ruminated on the problem of Hooker's stink. He had known the man long enough now to have observed his habits, and long enough to find the stench intolerable. Smells have a powerful nostalgic effect. If Hooker's odour reminded Kite too painfully of the foetid stink of slaves confined over-long in their leg-irons, the recollection came with a rush of remorse for Puella. Kite could never throw off the guilt of knowing that he might have saved Puella from her early death. That was only compounded by his present happiness with Sarah, whom he had first encountered in Rhode Island when she affronted Kite with the charge of being perverse in his attachment to a blackamoor.

Fortunately Sarah, realizing her great error, had quickly made amends and a friendship had been established, but none of these circumstances added to the feelings Kite entertained on Puella's behalf. Although he became inured to insults and innuendoes made about himself and his relationship with a manumitted slave, he had been powerless to guard his beautiful black wife from those aimed at her and he would always live with a sense of shame at the sheer injustice of such prejudice. This had detached him from all but the most intimate friendships in Liverpool and, he knew, those who revelled in his ruin would point out his unnaturalness as having incurred the just wrath of Providence.

Such underlying hostility made his closing down of his Liverpool enterprise easier. It contributed to his ability to stare the future squarely in the eye without looking over his shoulder at the uncomfortable past. Now Hooker's stink rammed his moral failure into his perception, hard upon the failure of his commerce. Moreover, it was interfering with the smooth running of their passage, doubling Kite's resentment.

'Confound it, I shall have to tackle the matter,' he murmured to himself, 'though God knows how.'

Early on the morning that they raised the summit of Madeira, Harper summoned Kite from his cot, pointing to windward when Kite stumbled on deck rubbing the sleep out of his eyes. The sharp peaks of two sets of widely spaced sails nicked the clean line of the horizon to windward.

'Damnation!' Kite swore. 'Go aloft, Zachariah, and see what you make of 'em.' Neither Kite not Harper were in much doubt, but neither man wanted to admit their suspicions prematurely. Then from the main crosstrees Harper shouted down his conviction that they were, 'God-damned Yankee pirates, Cap'n! Got New England written all over them!'

Kite swore. He had two choices and little time to decide which was the better. He could make for Madeira and, in addition to stumming and refilling his water casks, seek the protection of Portuguese neutrality. That ran two risks, the first being that he could be cut off before he arrived off Funchal, the second that the enemy privateers would lie off the islands until he emerged. His second choice was to abandon any attempt to make Funchal, but to make a run for it. The consequent drawback to this course of action was that he risked running out of water, for far more casks than had at first been suspected were now found to be tainted.

On balance he therefore thought that he should make for Funchal. He thought the Yankee skippers would lose patience before he did himself, and there was always the possibility, if not *probability*, that a British cruiser would turn up off Madeira to acquire some wine, if not a prize. The Yankees might hide in the Selvagems or the Desertas, lesser islands in the Madeiran archipelago, but Kite could inform the British naval commander of their presence. This, at the very least, would drive them off while he made his escape.

Looking up at Zachariah's ugly face with its expectant look, Kite shook his head. 'We'll try for Madeira, Zachariah—'

Harper blew his cheeks out and interrupted. 'They could cut us off, sir.'

Kite nodded. 'I know, but we must take the chance.'

Harper stared at Kite for long enough to let his commander know that he did not agree with Kite's decision. 'We have a fair wind, Zachariah, so let us set some more sail. Shake out the reef in the foresail and hoist the flying jib.' There was an edge to Kite's voice and Harper swung away to attend to his business.

Kite crossed the deck to stand a moment beside the helmsman and then, staring alternately at the swinging compass in its binnacle and the blue mountain rising above the horizon to leeward, he ordered an alteration of course.

It was soon clear that the two approaching vessels were indeed hostile and that while one was steering to intercept *Spitfire*, the other was outrunning her companion, in order to cut the British schooner off from her refuge.

Having set the extra sail and trimmed the braces, vangs and sheets to the best advantage, Harper came aft and stood beside Kite. From time to time Kite heard the mate suck the air in through his crooked teeth, an irritating reproach to Kite who grew ever more fretful. On deck the air of anxiety increased as time passed and the triangular relationship between the three vessels remained suspended. The bearings of each of the privateers from *Spitfire* changed little, though one slowly drew ahead as she closed Madeira ahead of her quarry. Only the distances shortened, a process as inexorable as the rising of the sun which cast a festive dazzle upon the blue waters of the Atlantic.

As Harper drew in his breath for the umpteenth time, Kite snapped, 'For God's sake stop that disgusting noise!'

Zachariah looked round, his face hurt, unaware that he had been making any noise at all. 'We can't do it, sir,' he offered.

'No, I can see that,' said Kite. 'Very well, then, call all hands and clear away the guns. I'm going to come round hard on the wind and see if we can dash past that fellow.' Kite indicated the enemy vessel whose course suggested a direct interception. She was brig-rigged and, if they got past her, would be less able to follow than the low rakish schooner that was heading to cut them off. 'We might knock a spar or two off her in passing.'

As the watch below was turned out, the watch on deck trimmed the sheets as Kite brought the schooner round to the east, into the sunlight dappling the water. In a quarter of an hour the distance between the two vessels was shrinking fast. To the south the second enemy privateer, the schooner like *Spitfire* herself, which had at first stood on to ensure that she could stop the British vessel reaching the safety of Funchal, now put about and began her own beat up to the assistance of her consort. It was, however, quite clear that she would not arrive in time. All now depended upon the result of the encounter between *Spitfire* and the brig.

All the men in Kite's crew were experienced; they had served in both privateers and slavers and could handle a gun and small arms as well as, and in many cases better than, the crew of a man-of-war. Most had previously served with Kite, or in one of his ships, and they cleared away and ran out the schooner's four-pounders with a degree of high spirits.

With the commotion transmitted below largely through the rumbling of the gun-trucks, first Sarah then McClusky and Hooker came on deck to be acquainted with their circumstances. Hooker volunteered the services of his dacoits, all of whom, he insisted, could fire muskets. Thus arrayed, and taking up their station behind the chocked boats by way of a breastwork and keeping them clear of the gun crews, these extempore and colourful marines topped with their red turbans might, at a distance, convey the impression that *Spitfire* was a man-of-war schooner.

Standing alongside the helmsman, Kite left the working of the guns to Harper. He told Sarah to take care of herself, well knowing she would refuse to go below. He had insisted that all other parties remain below, including Hooker himself, but the lumbering figure objected and demanded to be left on deck, in charge of his bodyguard. This seemed to Kite a reversal of roles, but Hooker was adamant, claiming that to go below would be to lose face and if he did so he might as well be dead as to call upon his dacoits to render any service in his defence afterwards. To this defiance, McClusky added his own: 'If your wife's to stay on deck, Captain Kite, how can Michael McClusky remain quartered below like a woman – beggin' yer pardon, Mr Hooker?'

In the urgency of the moment Kite acceded. Rose Hooker, her maids and Maggie remained below, the last named peering up the companionway so that, standing by the helm, Kite caught sight of her disconcerting face as she strove to see what was going on.

Jack Bow, of whom Kite had taken no account, had attached himself to Sarah, probably arguing with his brand of street-cunning that Mrs Kite as a woman would not be too much exposed to danger. With a grim acknowledgement of the lad's logic, Kite hoped Jack's faith was not misplaced. Besides, he had weightier matters to consider.

'Steady now,' he said to the helmsman as the two vessels closed rapidly. Although Kite was aware of Harper hopping from one gun to the other he kept his eyes on the enemy. He wondered whether Zachariah had drawn all the quoins in the hope of wounding the enemy brig's rigging, or told his gunners to aim for the hull. It was too late for him to intervene now and, in any case, hard on the wind as she was, *Spitfire*'s windward broadside would fly high until she came under the lee of the brig.

It always surprised Kite how the apparent speeds of vessels passing on opposite tacks seemed to accelerate at the last moment. The brig suddenly loomed large and, above the noise of the wind in the *Spitfire*'s rigging and the creak and groan of the schooner's fabric, there was suddenly a host of new noises: the moan of wind in the passing ship's rigging, the break of water under her bow, the shouts of last-minute command. Then a sudden lull as *Spitfire* passed into the brig's wind-shadow and her deck abruptly levelled. Kite saw a fast-traversing panorama of gun ports, muzzles, sails and faces. There were shouts aboard the enemy, then Hooker bellowed. The crackle of small arms fire broke out, smoke puffs and lances of fire from the rail of the enemy, and a louder response from the dacoits amidships. At almost the same instant the two vessels exchanged rolling broadsides, the terrible, ear-splitting thumping concussions of the successive guns thundering between the two hulls so that their echoes sounded like an encounter between line-of-battle ships in their reverberations.

Then it was all over, they were past and *Spitfire* was heeling to the wind and the sun was dazzling them from the surface of the sea ahead. For a long suspended moment it seemed as though nothing had changed, and then from aloft there came a stuttering that a moment later became the sound of tearing canvas. The foresail split from head to foot, two of the dacoits fell screaming to the deck with the splinters from the side of a boat sticking out of their faces and chests, and one man amidships had been killed stone dead from a musket ball with another three wounded. A hole had been battered in the larboard bulwarks and the carpenter was emerging from the companionway with a curious Maggie at his heels to report two balls in the hull.

There were several scrapes in the main boom, suggesting that most of the brig's shot had passed over their decks, and Sarah was nursing a nicked shoulder, but by and large they had got off lightly. The foresail, though badly torn and straining, had given way along a seam, the ball passing through it having obligingly parted it.

Staring after the brig Kite could see little damage there either. He did, however, catch her name and port of registry in gold letters across her stern: *Pegasus*, Boston. Above this flew the barred ensign of the rebel Americans.

He rounded on the helmsman and shouted for Harper. 'We'll run off to the south-east and, Mr Harper, do you ease that foresail . . .'

'We've another below, shall I rouse it out?'

'Aye, but secure the guns first and get those bloody Indians below decks!' The wailing from amidships was getting worse, but Hooker already had the matter in hand and Maggie, now on deck herself, was fussing over the wounded men.

'A creditable wench and no mistake,' he said to Sarah as she made light of her galling. 'Like my wife,' he added with a smile.

Sarah nodded astern. 'My husband has done pretty well too,' she said and he turned to see the foretopmast of the brig totter out of alignment with the main, and hang down at a drunken angle, retained for the time being only by its standing stays. The fore yards stuck out at a crazy angle and Kite shouted for Harper to take a look. The sight caused a cheer to run round the *Spitfire*'s upper deck.

'Don't fill yourself too full of self-conceit, William,' Sarah went on. 'Have you seen the other . . .'

Kite spun round before the warning was out of Sarah's mouth. The American schooner was in chase of them, away on their lee bow, with the steady bearing that betokened interception and, if held onto long enough, collision.

There would be no interval to change the foresail and, on their present course, no chance of making Funchal. He turned and, fishing out his glass, levelled it on the *Pegasus*. The foretopmast had crashed over the side and was trailing in the water, swinging the brig round and leaving her helpless for a while.

'Stand by the sheets and braces!' Kite roared and, turning *Spitfire* through the wind, he brought her round before the wind again, to run down in the wake of the Yankee brig.

Hardly had he steadied *Spitfire* on her new course than the pursuing schooner had followed suit. Ignoring her, Kite sent Harper and his men back to their guns. As they swept past the *Pegasus* along her starboard side, a second broadside was poured into the American brig. Although they sustained several shot in return, the Americans had not cleared their

69

starboard guns away and it was largely only musketry that *Spitfire* endured in passing.

Although their own shot achieved little more than had already been accomplished, Kite had the small satisfaction of having rendered one of his opponents temporarily *hors de combat*. The other, however, looked set to give him a good run for his money. In the next hours Kite's men set to plugging the shot holes in the hull, pumping out the well and making good the superficial damage to half a dozen ropes aloft. By running downwind the effect of the split foresail was not as marked as it would have been had they been clawing their way to windward, but the combination of loss of driving power and the additional weight of water within her hull was sufficient to render *Spitfire* the slower of the two vessels. The chase ran on throughout the forenoon, dropping the damaged brig over the horizon astern, while the peak of Madeira, the clouds curling about its lofty summit, drew out on the beam as a shift in the wind forced them to head away from safety.

As the hours passed, Kite watched as the American schooner drew closer and closer. Noon came and went, the afternoon drew on and Madeira faded from view. Kite began to hope that they might be able to hold off their pursuer until nightfall when some sudden alteration of course might throw the Americans off their scent. Then a new dilemma confronted him: should he start all the water casks and toss the guns over the side to lighten the schooner? His chances of escape would be proportionately increased if he did so, but he would be compelled to beat back to Madeira to top up with water and would almost certainly run into the arms of the Americans a second time. On the other hand, if he held on to his water, he might make the Cape Verde Islands before matters reached an extremity of want.

Making up his mind he called Harper aft again and ordered half their ordnance thrown overboard. 'It's our only chance,' he explained.

'Begging your pardon, sir, but have you seen over the side, sir?'

Kite shook his head and went forward to where, staring down into the rush of water past the hull, he caught the gleam of copper sheathing torn back and dragging in the sea.

'That shot must've torn it off, Cap'n,' Harper said and Kite grunted his agreement. 'I don't think jettisoning the guns will do more than prolong the agony, sir. Why not let him come up and we'll fight it out?'

'Because he'll be stuffed with men, Zachariah.'

'Not if he's sent most of 'em off in prizes,' countered the mate.

'We've no guarantee of that,' responded Kite quickly. 'No, I cannot risk the lives of all these women.'

Kite stared astern, havering. It was time to abandon all hope as futile. They must face the fact that *Spitfire* was about to be overtaken and they would all be taken prisoner. Kite sighed. 'I'm sorry, Zachariah, I'm not a lucky man and neither, it seems, are you for taking up with me—'

'Belay that gob-shite, Cap'n Kite!' Harper cut in sharply. 'See how she's running directly in our wake . . .' Harper nodded astern and Kite sought out his meaning. 'He's going to try and run us aboard! He's got no powder, d'you see? Or not enough to engage us! He can't afford a prolonged engagement; he's foregoing the chance of crippling us with his bow chasers and doesn't think we can get a stern chaser aft quick enough to damage him before he runs up alongside our quarter!'

Kite saw what Harper meant. 'Pray Heaven you're right, Zachariah, and look, he's assembling his sharp-shooters to pick off the likes of you and I!'

A cluster of men were forming about the knightheads of the pursuing schooner and Kite ordered all to seek what cover was available, taking the helm himself. He called to Sarah who, with Harper and the best shots Hooker identified among the dacoits, soon took cover behind the taffrail and, with others loading for them, began to send enough musket fire over the enemy's bow to disrupt this tactic for a while. In the few moments of grace this small triumph brought them, Kite suddenly realized he possessed a single opportunity.

If Harper was correct in his assumption that the Yankee commander really had run his stock of powder low, and it was quite probable that he had done so, then there was one manoeuvre he might try. If backed by gunfire of his own, it was just possible that they could yet escape! The only things it depended upon were the Yankee commander holding on to his own course and his marksmen missing Kite himself.

'Boatswain!' he called, and as the man came aft, ordered him to man the larboard after guns and then go forward and, concealing himself behind the fife rail, stand by with a knife to cut the forward peak halliard.

'Aye, aye, sir!' the man acknowledged and, going forward again, directed the men huddling in the waist to load and run out the after, larboard four-pounders. As he was thus occupied, Kite shouted aft to Harper.

'I'm going to try one last ruse, Zachariah. Do you and Sarah and the others keep them pinned down. I have to expose myself and I'd be obliged for your cover.'

'Aye, aye, sir!'

Kite caught Sarah's eye. She was pale with anxiety, but he flashed her a smile. She turned away, took a reloaded musket from a bearded dacoit and, levelling it upon the schooner looming over their stern, bent over the firelock.

Leaning against the heavy tiller Kite glanced astern. He was aware of a ball flying past him with a malicious buzz and wondered, in a distracted second, where it would end its wild trajectory. Then he looked up at the mainmasthead to where a tell-tale pendant streamed out to leeward. If he was to achieve anything he must watch his steering and judge matters to a perfection he felt himself incapable of. He swallowed and looked up again, then leaned on the tiller and steadied *Spitfire* on a slightly adjusted course. Turning, he stared astern. The American vessel's foresail was boomed out to larboard, her main to starboard. He hoped her commander's view of the *Spitfire* was sufficiently impeded.

The chasing schooner's bearing began to broaden on the larboard quarter and the distance between her masts opened

72

a little; but perceiving this slight alteration in his quarry's course, the American commander adjusted his own. The sight gave Kite hope: Harper was right!

Between glances at the compass, the masthead pendant and his pursuer, Kite watched as the American reduced the distance. While following close in Kite's wake, his enemy would have to voluntarily draw a little aside, in order to come up on the vulnerable quarter. Then, Kite guessed, he would devastate the *Spitfire*'s decks with langridge from his bow guns before running her aboard and releasing his boarders. In a moment this prolonged and agonizing chase would be over. Suddenly Kite saw the two masts open. This was the moment that the American commander had so carefully prepared for and, as if to confirm the hunch, Kite could see the men mustering on the enemy's foredeck.

He swung forward. 'Stand by the guns and fire when you will! Boatswain! Cut away!'

Kite turned swiftly back to watch the enemy, but he felt the jar as the peak halliard gave way and the heavy gaff drooped from the throat of the sail. The loss of effort slowed *Spitfire* and increased the relative motion of the overtaking enemy. As Kite had hoped, the American vessel apparently leapt forward through the water. Suddenly the Yankee's foremast was passing their quarter and, as the gun crews bent to their touch-holes, the British schooner lived up to her name and spat fire from her after guns. As if on the signal of their discharge, Kite threw his weight upon the tiller.

The *Spitfire* began to turn, then with a shout, the American came round too, following as he sought to make contact and get his men aboard. They crowded the rail, brandishing cutlasses, pistols and tomahawks and giving intimidating Indian whoops, all wearing wide grins as their fire kept the heads of Sarah, Harper and the dacoits below the rail. Kite felt a sudden pain in his shoulder, but at that instant he succeeded in passing the leech of *Spitfire*'s huge mainsail through the eye of the wind.

With a whoosh and a clatter of blocks as the wind caught the opposite side of its canvas, the heavy mainsail swept across the deck in a wild gybe; *Spitfire* heeled suddenly and, to Kite's jubilation, its iron-bound boom-end crashed across into the enemy's fore-rigging. As the would-be boarders were swept from the rail the starboard shrouds of the enemy's rigging parted like fiddle strings. There was confusion and shouting on the American schooner's deck and then, as her foremast went by the board, *Spitfire* drew away.

Free of his tormentors, Kite offered up a silent prayer and laid a course for the Cape Verde Islands. As they left the American schooner astern someone amidships piped up in an inimitable Liverpudlian accent: 'Three cheers for Cap'n Topsy-Turvy!'

Chapter Five

Thunder in the Bay

The *Spitfire* had not escaped unscathed from her encounter with the American privateers. In addition to the shot holes in the hull and the torn copper sheathing, the beaten-in bulwarks, damaged boat, rent foresail and wounded main boom, her maintopmast was found to have a ball embedded in it and the morning following the action announced the fact by carrying away. A second ball was found in the lower mast which fortunately stood the strain after it had been fished.

Thus shorn of her main upper spar and labouring under an over-full bilge, the British schooner sought a refuge in Porto Grande in the Cape Verde Islands, where Kite knew he could take water. There was, as far as Kite could see of the barren-looking mountains of the island of São Vicente, precious little verdant about them, but he was able to work *Spitfire* inshore, anchor and careen her sufficiently to get at the shot holes. Anticipating a prolonged stay in Indian waters he had also taken aboard a quantity of copper and from this prudently laid-in stock replaced the missing sheets which had been torn away during the ten-day passage from Madeira to São Vicente.

Unfortunately he was short of a spar suitable to replace *Spitfire*'s heavy lower mainmast. However, hearing of the arrival of a large British convoy under the escort of a naval squadron at the neighbouring island of São Tiago, he ordered *Spitfire* under weigh as soon as she was fit for sea and arrived there on 12 April, hoping to purchase a suitable spar from one of the convoy. He thought it unlikely that, having been in company with merchant transports for so long, any of the naval commanders would poach his own men. Besides, with the *Spitfire*'s mainmast in so shaky a condition, he had little choice.

Porto Praya Bay was crowded with anchored merchantmen and their escort, a small squadron of men-of-war. Besides frigates and sloops, Kite counted five ships-of-the-line, the chief of these being the 74-gun *Hero*, flying the broad pendant of a commodore. Passing through the anchored shipping, Kite brought *Spitfire* up to her own anchor close inshore and then, having hoisted out the repaired boat, made the rounds of the nearest merchantmen. He soon learned that the expedition was commanded by Commodore Johnstone and was bound for the Cape of Good Hope with the intention of taking that province from the Dutch. The merchantmen in convoy were therefore almost exclusively troop transports or military storeships and well provided.

Kite had little trouble finding a master willing to sell him a spar and in due course had this hoisted over-board and towed back alongside *Spitfire*. He then set the hands to work. The new spar was pulled ashore and drawn up onto the beach. Here, amid a curious little crowd of onlookers, it was cut to the appropriate size. Meanwhile on board the old mast was stripped of its rigging and all accessible ironwork and this latter was then taken ashore to be fastened to the replacement. By the evening of the 15th, having entirely stripped down the damaged mast and erected a short sheerlegs across the deck of the schooner, Kite's crew prepared to withdraw it the following morning. The transfer of the upper ironwork, once completed, would ready the new spar for substitution and these two tasks were expected to take the whole of the 16th, the hoisting in of the new mast and re-rigging being completed two or three days later. It was thus in considerably high spirits that all hands turned in that night. Kite lingered a while on deck, staring up at the distant constellations wheeling overhead. Beside him stood McClusky, less impressed by the firmament than his master, but pleased that Captain Kite had acknowledged his ability.

'You shall keep our anchor-watch while we employ the people so busily throughout the heat of the day, Michael,' Kite had said, 'and we shall turn you into a second mate before we reach Bombay, should you so desire.'

The quondam clerk, who alone among the *Spitfire*'s people had regretted the failure of the American privateersmen to board and allow him to prove his personal valour in hand-to-hand combat, expressed the fact that he should like nothing better.

'Is it true that the Indian seas are as warm and pacific as these hereabouts, Captain Kite?' he asked, for the novelty of standing on deck at midnight in his shirt-sleeves impressed McClusky.

'I am given to understand they are warmer, Michael, though, like the West Indies, they are occasionally subjected to wild and boisterous hurricanoes.'

McClusky did not think there was much to worry about in a wind described as wild and boisterous, and what he had gleaned during his years in Captain Kite's counting house about the West Indies suggested that much money and rum were the chief exports of such tropical places. He expressed his satisfaction and gratitude to Kite who, giving the matter little thought, wished McClusky a good night and left him to his lonely vigil.

Michael McClusky, whatever dreams of glory had been hatched out of his new situation in his imagination, remained at heart a counting-house clerk. He possessed no ingrained instinct as a seaman and was incapable of remaining absolutely alert throughout the night. Nevertheless he was not irresponsible and woke from a fitful slumber on the after grating, gritty eyed and possessed of a sudden anxiety. He could not at first say where this apprehension came from; it was not entirely his own guilt, for he was not that sensitive to such matters, but he felt a genuine unease worming in his guts. Rubbing his eyes

he stared about him: it was already light but the sun had yet
to rise. The deck looked as it had at midnight under the light
of the lantern. Then he knew why he had woken and what had
woken him, for the thunder came again, rolling across the bay
so that he jumped to his feet and stared wildly about him.

To seaward, beyond the veritable forest of masts and yards
that marked the anchored British shipping, the pale squares of
sails stood into Porto Praya Bay. Three ships approached, two
flanked by blooms of smoke, evidence of their hostile intent.
The fact that they were grossly outnumbered seemed not to
deter them, for they had caught Commodore Johnstone and his
men-of-war napping. From where he stood, McClusky could
see only the bold vanguard of the enemy, unaware that other
enemy vessels were offshore. Nevertheless, the noise of the
guns spurred him to action and he called all hands on deck.

There was little that anyone aboard the *Spitfire* could do;
they were mere spectators as the two large French ships-of-
the-line, followed by a smaller, came to their anchors amid
the British shipping. The most advanced opened a furious
cannonade on the British ships anchored on either beam,
while the second, penetrating deeper into the road, anchored
ahead of his commodore, but then seemed less anxious to get
into action. The lesser vessl's part was less spectacular as
she engaged an Indiaman from the convoy and then, having
grappled her, withdrew to seaward. Far in the distance two
other ships-of-the-line could now be seen, identified through
the tangle of the anchorage by the pale rectangles of their
wind-filled sails.

The engagement did not last long. Once the British seamen had manned their guns and returned the cannonade,
the French ships weighed, set sail and retired, taking with
them a solitary prize of the grappled Indiaman. The ships
offshore never got into action and the mood in the anchorage was one of jubilation that the 'impudent Frogs' had
been driven off. Owing to their preoccupation in drawing
the damaged mainmast and preparing its replacement, less
thought was given to the morning's thunder in the bay aboard

Spitfire than in any other British ship assembled off Porto Praya.

But in fact the apparently indecisive action in the Cape Verde Islands was to have a profound effect, for Commodore Johnstone had been discomfited. He remained at Porto Praya for a further fortnight and then, aware that the French would beat him to the tip of Africa, he threw up his intention of taking Cape Province from the Dutch and headed for home. The French Commodore, a certain Pierre André de Suffren, had scored a notable success over the Royal Navy of Great Britain. It was not to be the last.

The action off Porto Praya was soon forgotten aboard the *Spitfire*. If it kindled further dreams of glory in the heart of Michael McClusky that was because he was no seaman and had little or nothing to do with the stepping and rigging of the new mainmast. In fact, as the crew toiled, McClusky retired to his hammock, having stood the night watch alone. Here he lay for a while, contemplating the future and wondering whether he might reap some real profit from his master's adventure, until he fell asleep.

For Kite, Harper and the schooner's company, the intense labour of refitting the ship filled all their waking hours. With the new mast stepped, the standing rigging had to be set up and rattled down. Then the topmast had to be sent aloft and its rigging set up, before the score or so of blocks were moused and then the halliards and topping lifts rove through them. Next, the throat halliard was used to lift the heel of the heavy boom and secure it to the goose-neck, situated on the lower mast about a man's height above the deck. Once the boom was in position and its outer extremity topped up onto the gallows, the gaff saddle could be lodged about the mast, the mainsail relaced, hooped and tensioned along the boom prior to hoisting. At last, in the fresh breeze that blew constantly down from the heights of the island and kept the anchored vessels head to wind, the sail was set flapping.

Kite and Harper regarded it and pronounced themselves

satisfied, but that was not the end of their labours. When the hands had completed this complicated and laborious task it was again necessary to top up their water casks before sailing. While Kite and the schooner's company had been busy, Hooker, his wife and Sarah, taking Maggie to attend them, had, on the invitation of a Portuguese merchant, made an excursion into the island, dining with Senhor Soares and his family. Soares offered them a few days' welcome hospitality and here, on the eve of their departure, Kite joined them for dinner, enjoying for a few brief hours the riches of the shore.

After dinner, looking down over the bay from the cool elevation of the merchant's house, Kite stared at the anchor lights of the mass of shipping twinkling in the velvet darkness of the tropical night. From his vantage point at the window he was seeking out the glim in *Spitfire*'s forward rigging.

'Cannot you forget the ship, William?' Sarah called softly from the bed.

He turned and saw the pale shape of the netting over the bed and through the gauze, the stirring figure of his naked wife.

'Sarah . . .'

'Come, my darling . . .' She parted the netting and, slipping off his breeches, he slid beside her as she reached up for him and prompted a ready tumescence. It was the first time they had made love since the death of little Emma.

From São Tiago they carried the north-east trade winds south towards the Equator. In latitude 8° north the wind faltered and then died. They had entered the Doldrums and after a few days in the stultifying heat the lack of a breeze and any progress shortened tempers and brought to a head a simmering matter of contention.

One hot afternoon, as the watch slumped on deck having spent an hour trimming the sails in anticipation of a breeze which seemed to falter a mile short of them, McClusky turned in a fury upon Hooker and declared that he could no longer tolerate the man's stink.

Hooker, who had just followed McClusky on deck, stood

for a moment nonplussed, scarcely able to accept the vitupera-
tion. The hot weather and the consequent reduction in outer
garments had made the mountainous man's condition worse
and sorely tried the tolerance of his fellow voyagers.

'I come on deck,' McClusky railed, 'to avoid the stink
down below and then you follow me, damn you for a festering
bastard!'

Stunned, Hooker looked around. His insensitivity, allied to
a lack of awareness of the pervasive pungency of his bodily
smell in the confines of the schooner, meant that he had little
real appreciation of the nature of his offence in warm latitudes.
The man on the tiller gazed fixedly at the compass, even though
the schooner had no steerage way upon her and rolled with
a wearing and wearying slatting of gear and sails. From the
forward limit of his pacing an astonished Harper, who had
the watch, spun round to regard the two men standing aft by
the companionway, while the other seamen on deck, together
with the idlers lying about in various stages of indolence, stared
with interest at the principals in this promising altercation. The
dacoits, whose customary airing place was, by mutual consent,
right forward, stirred and three walked aft to their master's
defence.

Seeing himself the cynosure for all eyes, Hooker's ire broke
from the confines of surprise and reticence. He confronted the
impudent counting-house clerk before him, pulling himself
up to his full six and a half feet of outraged and trembling
corpulence

'Do you address me, sir,' he raged with a sudden anger, 'do
you, damn you?'

'I do, sir,' the provoked McClusky bellowed back, 'for you
have the stink of a corpse about you!'

'Why, damn your insolence!'

Hooker lumbered forward, a vast and sweating mountain of
a man, but McClusky, half his age and several stones lighter,
dodged away. Immediately a cheer went up from the now alert
and diverted crowd, followed by cries encouraging McClusky
to greater mischief.

But as McClusky retreated along the deck, he was suddenly seized from behind by two of the dacoits while the third, grabbing McClusky's hair, jerked his head back and put a knife at his throat. The former clerk froze in this hostile embrace.

As Hooker closed with his victim and the watchers froze, Zachariah Harper recalled himself to his duty and with a rapidity surprising in such a large man interposed his own bulk between the constrained McClusky and the triumphant Hooker.

'Now hold on there,' Harper remonstrated. 'First of all, Mr Hooker, there sure is a body of opinion on this vessel that you have about your person a distinct air akin to putrefaction . . .' Hooker was about to explode when Harper, almost his equal in height and a far fitter man, held up a powerful arm. 'Mr Hooker! Recall I command the deck, sir!'

'And I command your damned pay!'

'Be circumspect, damn it!'

'Stop!' The curt order cut through the hot air. Kite stood at the after companionway, his shirt stuck to his body. He had been dozing uneasily below when the altercation on deck had disturbed first Sarah and then her husband. Ordering his wife to remain where she was to restrain Rose Hooker from any intemperate outburst, he ran up the companionway ladder to intervene. Kite had caught the two large men on the point of trading blows for insults. Just beyond Harper, McClusky's face was white with terror as the dacoit's knife glittered at his throat.

Summing up the situation in an instant, Kite advanced on the dacoits and, without taking his eyes off them, said, 'Josiah, I'd be obliged if you'd call your dogs off this instant!'

Hooker mumbled a few words of Hindi and the three men let McClusky go. Released, the young man stumbled forward and fell abjectly on his knees. Kite ignored him as, gasping with shame and terror, McClusky clambered slowly to his feet. Kite rounded upon Hooker and Harper.

'Now, gentlemen,' he said in a low voice, 'let us have an end to this immediately. I am going to order the watch to man the fire buckets. Then I intend to strip myself of my clothes and order water thrown over me. I shall scour myself until I feel clean and both of you are going to do likewise.' Kite stared at each of the antagonists in turn and then regarded McClusky. 'You shall join us too, McClusky, but first go below and present my compliments to my wife and Mrs Hooker. Ask them to remain below but beg two bars of soap from my wife and bring them here. D'you understand me?'

'Yes, Cap'n,' said the humiliated clerk.

Kite caught the eye of a watching seaman. 'Ah, Stocks, do you and your mates stand by to fling the contents of the fire buckets over us. We are minded to bathe. You may have some sport in the matter, if you wish. Now, gentlemen,' Kite returned his attention to the two big men who stood at his either elbow, 'let us divest ourselves.'

He took off his shirt and, folding it, laid it over the gunwale of the chocked boat in the larboard waist. Around the three men the dacoits and the crew watched with interest. 'Zachariah,' Kite growled through clenched teeth, 'oblige me, if you please.'

With a marked reluctance Harper hesitated and then, as Kite stepped out of his breeches to a general snigger, he followed suit. More laughter accompanied this indecent exposure, but Stocks had already mustered his fellow seamen and, grinning widely, a quintet of them were assembling in a circle round the three gentlemen, giggling at the natural state of them. Kite's taut lean body appeared almost slight by comparison with the heavily muscled Harper. Both had the weatherbeaten head and forearms of seafarers, whereas Hooker's flesh, for all his years in the Indian sun, bore a pallid sheen which, it was immediately obvious, gave off a revoltingly sweet and obnoxious odour. Caught in the creases and folds of his lardy and corpulent mass, this subcutaneous secretion was revealed as the source of his unpleasantness. As for Hooker's face, it was scarlet with humiliation and embarrassment.

McClusky arrived with the soap, his face distorted with distaste at the manifestation of Hooker's problem. Ignoring the appalled young man, Kite retained one bar for himself and conspicuously handed the second to Hooker. 'There, Josiah,' he said in a low and insistent tone, half-gagging at his proximity to the obese monster, 'do you rub with the utmost vigour or, by God, I shall have you publicly scoured to put an end to this unpleasantness.'

'But this is an outrage, Kite, damn you . . .' Hooker hissed miserably, tears filling his eyes and the beginnings of sobs racking his wobbling frame.

'You *do* most assuredly *stink*, villainously, Josiah,' Kite muttered, his teeth clenched and his nose wrinkled, 'and I shall have an end to it or prove it unavoidable.' Kite turned to McClusky and raised his voice. 'Come, Michael, let us see what sort of a figure you cut. Hurry up now, there's a good fellow.'

The silly jest provoked a laugh among the assembled men as McClusky stepped out of his breeches. Kite looked at Stocks. 'You may soak us and then stay your hands while we soap ourselves. Afterwards, when I give the signal, you may throw as much water as you can draw from the sea and as fast as you can lift it.'

A gleeful mood of anticipation swept through the seamen. Then the first buckets were emptied over the four figures. Led by Kite they began to scrub themselves, Kite's bar of soap passing first to Harper and then to McClusky. Kite, keeping his eye on Hooker, kept chiding him. 'Come, sir, more ginger if you please, rub-a-dub-dub, sir, we are not three but four in the tub!'

Curiously the onlookers watched the folds of Hooker's skin exfoliate a grubby smegma. The obese figure seemed to possess recesses hitherto unknown to the human species, a corpulence long unexposed to the light of day or unexplored by soap and water. To Hooker's personal and malodorous exudations were added his neglect of even a primitive hygiene and it was as though he sloughed off an entire epidermal layer so that afterwards, recalling the strange events of that afternoon, the seamen pointed to a darker portion of *Spitfire's* deck, nicknaming it 'Hooker's grease-pan', or 'greasy shoal'. As Kite, Harper and McClusky completed their soaping, the sky grew suddenly dark and the first drops of rain began to fall. So absorbed in the incident and the subsequent ablutions had they all become, that no one had noticed the rapid approach of the cloud. The great cumulo-nimbus towered high into the sky but behind its vast shadow it drew not only rain but also a sudden, chilling drop in the temperature and a squall of wind. Within half a minute the hitherto becalmed *Spitfire* was driving along, her over-canvassed hull trying to bury its lee rail so that a roil of foaming water roared alongside, bursting over the rail and causing pools to form between the guns.

The sudden heel threw McClusky, Hooker and his unhandy dacoits off their feet and they tumbled to leeward, falling into the water swirling in the scuppers with cries of dismay that echoed the screams of the frightened women below. Harper, giving out his wildest Iroquois whoop, to which his nakedness added a bizarre aptness, leapt for the tiller, his face cracked into an immense grin. Kite grabbed the gunwale of the boat and kept his feet, stung by the icy chill of the rain which now turned into hailstones.

These beat a tattoo on the deck and felt like a flogging on the bare flesh. Hooker, McClusky and the dacoits now howled with real pain as Kite, gasping with the sharp agony, ducked under the bilge of the chocked boat, to the barely suppressed amusement of the soaked but gleeful crew.

Then it was all over; the bulk of the cloud had passed above them a mile away and the sun was abruptly warm upon their shoulders, setting the deck steaming, and as Hooker, McClusky and the Indians picked themselves up on the levelling deck they were confronted with the near hysterical laughter of the ship's company.

'You crowd of damned racoons!' Harper began, but then his natural sense of humour prevailed and he joined in the hilarity. Kite too found the welcome warmth of the sunshine restored his spirits in an instant. After some ten minutes of this mayhem, Kite bellowed for silence.

'Very well, my lads. Now let us pipe down. The watch on deck will take a wash like this every morning until we are ten degrees beyond the Tropic of Capricorn.'

And thus did Kite cure Hooker's skin condition and improve the cleanliness of his crew, burying in the jolly mood of levity the discomfiture of Josiah Hooker who, though he crawled below still humbled by what he had been forced to do, had the presence of mind to return on deck once he had dressed himself, and was thus held by the men to have behaved like a thorough sportsman. An Englishman could pronounce no greater compliment, and since he afterwards stank no more than anyone else on board, Josiah Hooker's dignity was thereby saved.

Chapter Six

To the Indian Sea

'Sarah?'

Kite addressed the shadowy figure approaching him from the companionway. The night air was like velvet on the skin and overhead the sky was ablaze with stars. There was sufficient light to throw shadows on the pale plane of the deck and Sarah's face took form as she drew close to him above the fluttering dressing gown she wore. Kite left the helmsman leaning sleepily against the tiller as *Spitfire*, her sails drawing in the light but steady breeze, ran northwards towards the Indian coast.

They were well north of the Equator, having doubled the Cape of Good Hope weeks earlier, standing well to the south of the Dutch territory. They had endured three weeks of strong wind and heavy, following seas before turning to the northwards, passing east of Madagascar and the off-lying French-held archipelago of La Réunion and the Île de France. Mercifully they ran for day after day without the sight of a sail.

They had had one scare before leaving the Atlantic; forty-odd hours of intense anxiety only a few days after the extraordinary dousing of Hooker. After clearing the Doldrums they had been frustrated by the wind. Ostensibly the south-east trade, the wind had stubbornly remained in the south, forcing them to make excessive westing and to pass well north of St Paul's Rocks before they could consider tacking. Thus they drew close to the north-east coast of Brazil which, like the Cape Verde Islands, was a neutral Portuguese colony. Unfortunately

87

Cabo São Roque was also the cruising station of a Spanish frigate which caught sight of them and gave energetic chase. Putting about, they stood to windward, hoping that their ability to sail closer to the wind would allow them to escape, but the Spaniard pressed them hard for almost two days. Then, by the greatest good fortune, they raised the tall 'Pico' of Fernando de Noronha and were able to lay a course towards it. The crooked finger of this ancient volcanic core, its surrounding slopes long since eroded, beckoned them on and in due course they ran in under the guns of Forte de Remedios and the neutral shelter of the Portuguese flag flying above it.

For three days the Spanish cruiser had stood on and off, just beyond cannon shot, in the hope that Kite would be driven out to fall under her guns, but the Portuguese governor had proved sympathetic and ordered a warning shot fired over the schooner, dissuading the Spanish commander from pressing his quarry. The governor had been content for the little British schooner, declared by her owner to be a private yacht with no mention of her letter of marque and reprisal, to remain at anchor. His Excellency's cooperation had been ensured by a generous gift from Hooker's chest, which had been received, or so that worthy man declared upon his honour, on behalf of the white church that stood on one side of the Placa dos Armas.

'We should not despise him,' Kite had remarked pointedly when Hooker had expressed his disbelief, 'for we have concealed enough about ourselves to risk charges of dissimulation.'

During this enforced wait, *Spitfire*'s crew landed and filled their water casks, a fortunate consequence of this impasse and one that determined Kite to press on directly for India without making a further stop if it were at all possible. In the end his patience was rewarded; the frigate withdrew to the north-west and, after a further precautionary wait of three days to ensure she had truly gone, Kite finally ordered *Spitfire*'s anchor weighed. Her sails were hoisted, her guns saluted the Forte de Remedios and, coasting along the northern shore of the island, the schooner doubled Ponta da Sapata. Here they found the wind blowing strongly from the south-east and, two hundred miles to windward of the Brazilian mainland, *Spitfire* had headed south and began to reel off the knots.

Gradually, as the southern latitude had increased and the wind had backed, they fetched more to the eastward, passing well off St Helena, and in due course they had driven far enough south to pick up the prevailing westerlies. Having then stormed through the great Southern Ocean for twenty-two days of running their easting down, Kite and Harper agreed on their longitude exceeding that of Rodriguez, easternmost of the French islands, whereupon they had hauled up to the northwards. It had been a passage to delight the true seaman, with strong but not overwhelming winds. The *Spitfire* had behaved gallantly, taking care of all but one of her company. The exception was Maggie who, in one particularly boisterous bout of squally weather, had been thrown across the cabin and fetched up heavily to leeward. The consequence of her untimely tumble was a miscarriage from which she was slow to recover, but which Sarah and Nisha concealed from Kite and Hooker, once they themselves had discovered the source of poor Maggie's indisposition.

Now Kite, along with all on board, was anxious to reach Bombay, for their water was again running very low, and the mood of expectation aboard the schooner had become almost palpable. Happiest, it seemed, were Hooker's dacoits, for whom this was a return to their native land, if not to their homes; for the seamen the anticipation of fleshpots and the excitement of meditated indulgence after a long passage brought broad smiles to their sun-burnt faces. Kite was uneasily aware that they had borne much temptation, for no man aboard *Spitfire* could be insensible to Sarah's allure, despite her masculine garb, or to Rose Hooker's voluptuously exotic form.

He felt lust prick now as Sarah came up to him in the star-light, and it struck him that his own anticipation, surmounting his anxiety over the dwindling water, was a compound of his love for Sarah and his hopes for rejuvenating his fortunes in

India. As Sarah took her place beside him at the rail it occurred to him that he should let slip the preoccupations and concerns of his duty so that, like the dacoits and the common seamen, he too might revel in the prospect of arrival on a foreign shore.

'Too beautiful a night for sleep,' he remarked. It was part question, part statement but he knew the moment the words had escaped him that she was burdened by uncongenial thoughts of her own, and instantly regretted his levity. The presence of Sarah on board, he had long since realized, brought a weight of responsibility which often offset the privilege of pleasure that came with her. 'You are troubled, my dear . . .'

'It is nothing.'

He gave a low laugh and remonstrated, 'Come, Sarah, you cannot fool me. You too often sleep the entire night through not to have some perturbation disturbing you now. What is it? Do confide it in me.'

Sarah sighed. 'It is too silly, William.'

'Ahh, it is intuition,' he mocked her gently.

'No,' she said sharply, hesitated, then added, 'Well, it is intuitive, but I should rather you considered it as insight . . .'

'Into what? The future?' He smiled in the night, staring at her as she stared out over the dark sea with its occasional white wave-cap and the bow wave curling away into the wake with a dim yet perceptible phosphorescent fire as *Spitfire* drove with apparent effortlessness through the fathomless ocean. He saw her shake her head and caught the familiar scent of her hair.

'I sense the past as it casts its shadow over the future.'

'Come, m'dear, you talk in riddles. I am not good at riddles at the best of times and decidedly not in the small hours of the night, no matter how beautiful that should be.'

'Oh,' she said, shaking her head, 'I am just worried about what is to happen to us in India.'

'Well, we have Hooker's backing . . .' he began patiently, intending to reiterate the intentions agreed between the two men, the one backing and the other carrying out their proposed joint enterprise.

'I'm not certain that we have, William,' she said looking

directly at him so that even in the gloom the intensity of her expression communicated itself to him.

'What do you mean?' He was suddenly intent, dismissing his mood of mild happiness as an indulgent foolishness. It was for the common seamen to build castles in Spain, men of business should concentrate their superior gifts upon more serious matters. He bent his attention to Sarah as she began to voice what he had called her perturbations.

'As you know, I have become close to Rose ever since that curious event in the rain storm.' Kite recalled that some days after the dunking which he had given Hooker, Sarah had told him that Rose had confided in her that she and Josiah had been intimate. The woman's glowing happiness was clear evidence that they had not enjoyed intercourse for a long time and, Sarah thought, Rose intended some oblique expression of her personal gratitude transmitted thus, woman to woman. Since this private exchange the enforced isolation of the two women among so many men had drawn them even closer. Kite's duty had inevitably contributed to throwing Sarah and Rose together in the isolation of the cabin, but Sarah had taken the opportunity of gaining information about India and of preparing herself for what she knew would be a bigger challenge to her adaptability than the simpler shift from New to old England.

Rose, she discovered, was a woman of considerable intelligence whose devotion to her husband derived in part from a past obligation and, it was hinted, some act of Josiah Hooker's that had, in some undisclosed way, saved Rose from an unspecified but dread and fateful event. Rose had admitted that this act, whatever it was, had turned her from her origins, leading her to abandon her given name and, while she still wore Indian clothes, it had filled her with a desire to assume the dress and manners of an English gentlewoman. Had she remained in England, as had been intended, she would have completed the transformation which, up until that time, had progressed little beyond her adoption of Josiah's name for her.

She had not, Sarah continued in her explanation, thought that

91

the time in Liverpool offered Rose any opportunity to continue, let alone complete, this process. Sarah was given to understand that Rose's disappointment in being forced to return to India was far greater than her husband's. However, and here Sarah laughed as Rose had done in the candid admission, she had at least succeeded in acquiring at least a share in an English lady's maid.

'A share, she said,' Sarah chuckled, 'as men own shares in ships. I hadn't the heart to explain that was not quite how we regarded Maggie's services.'

'I see,' Kite responded, pleased that Sarah's tale was not all gloom and perceiving perhaps that it arose from nothing more than the natural fears of the night. But then Sarah, as if recollecting herself, gave a deep sigh and stared again out over the sea.

'And what else has Rose confided in you?' Kite prompted.

'I'm not certain. There is a fear of returning to India, though I think this applied to Madras or Calcutta, rather than Bombay. No, fear may be too strong a word, but this apprehension is not what I find disturbs me, it is Josiah's changed mood. Surely you had noticed that?'

Kite considered Sarah's proposition with a faint air of exasperation. The concerns of running the *Spitfire*, of worrying about their stock of water and an outbreak of what looked like scurvy in two of the dacoits and one of the seamen, of the demands of navigation in these remote and unfamiliar seas and the constant, nagging fear of interception by an enemy cruiser to which now they were exposed, did not predispose him to the petty mood changes of Hooker. Unlike Sarah with her growing friendship with Rose, Kite did not like Hooker very much. His acquaintance had become a tiresome necessity and Kite maintained his distance with a barrier of courteous formality, broken only by the extraordinary events of that rain-sodden dunking, aware that he needed Hooker's backing and Oriental expertise if he was ever to restore his wife and himself to any position of standing in society.

But yes, since they had reached the bluer and warmer seas

of the mid-Indian Ocean he had noticed Hooker's change. The emergence of *Spitfire* from the damp and chilly latitudes was clear evidence that India was no more than a month away, perhaps less. No longer prostrated by sea-sickness, Hooker's thoughts turned to their destination and he expounded fulsomely on Indian affairs. In a bewildering series of monologues intended for the better understanding of Kite and his wife, Hooker expounded his views and interpretations of the position of the Honourable East India Company and its factories which, he explained, extended from Surat in the north-east of the Indian peninsula, to Benkulen on the coast of Sumatra. He had talked of opportunities lost in the past, of the Spice Islands of the Moluccas surrendered to the Dutch; he spoke too of the wider mercantile outposts at Bussorah in the Persian Gulf and of the difficulties of trading with the Mandarin-obstructed Hongs of Canton. He hinted at the possibilities of Japan and the secret and unsuccessful expeditions made by bold Country traders to reach the port of Nagasaki and break the monopolies of the Portuguese and Dutch. He regaled them with anecdotes of the presidencies at Madras, Calcutta and Bombay, told of the dangers of the French at Pondicherry; of the Portuguese at Goa and the turmoil of the entire country under the imperial domination of the Moghul Emperor Shah Alam upon the Peacock Throne at fabulous Delhi. There were European names too, familiar English names like Warren Hastings and Robert Clive, but cautionary names like that of the Frenchman Dupleix, and those of troublesome princes like Hyder Ali and Tipu Sultan of Mysore. He spoke of other high-ranking Indians, of nawabs, nizams and begums; of their tribes, like the Rohillas, Holkars and the Marathas, of the Gaikwars of Baroda and the Scindias of Gwalior; of territories called Oudh, Bengal, Hyderabad; of coasts called Malabar, Coromandel and the Carnatic, and of millions of rupees that passed by way of some mysterious agent (or was it agency? for Kite was never quite sure), known as the *Diwani*. Hooker's facts poured through their overwhelmed imaginations on a torrent of silver currency that suggested wealth beyond their grasping. From time to time Hooker's lectures homed in on more mundane facts, suggesting that difficulties exceeding even the labyrinthine complexities of Indian politics might lie in the paths of humble British merchants. He spoke of the difficulties of shipping saltpetre, essential for the manufacture of gunpowder, down the shoal-littered River Hooghli from Patna to Calcutta, and of the utility of teak, which was best extracted from the forests of the Mon Kingdom of Pegu, south-east of Bengal on the coast of the Burmese peninsula. Here, he cautioned, lay a vast swamp-land of mangroves, infested with pirates and known as the Arakan so that, all in all, it appeared to Kite that, between the Scylla of corrupt Moghul officials and their rebellious subjects and the Charybdis of lawless and unpredictable natives beyond the Moghul Pale, lay a narrow channel of opportunity for British merchant adventurers. But even this was studded with the rocks of Dutch hegemony and the ever-present and still potent challenge of the ambitious French.

'Now we are east of the Cape,' Hooker had declaimed, 'you can forget the monopoly of the Honourable East India Company.' Hooker had grinned and added, 'In fact, my dear friends, John Company's remit runs less and less to profit from trade, though her servants all indulge in private transactions. It is a fact that causes the Directors in London to grind their teeth, for their balances diminish as they acquire greater political and military responsibilities. They are, d'you see, driven to defend factories and forts with sepoy levies and their ships with their own marine while the chief beneficiaries are their servants and others, all of whom are directly or vicariously indulging in a private commerce.'

'But,' Hooker paused, his gleeful face assuming a sly, knowing look. 'But,' he repeated for great emphasis, 'as London and the whole of England grows ever more infatuated with tea, the greater opportunities for trade grow in proportion with China, not India. By an irony, however, that which we chiefly export, our guns and watches and woollen cloth, are not wanted in China and so we are driven of necessity to pay for our tea, not with goods but with silver. We must perforce *buy* the stuff . . .'

It was clear to Hooker that this necessity was utterly unacceptable. It constituted a serious drain upon the balance of trade and he expressed to Kite the gravity of this inequity. Or so Kite deduced at the time, though long afterwards he perceived in retrospect a greater and more significant meaning.

'The Chinese are obdurate,' Hooker added with an air of exasperation, pouring himself a third glass of wine and draining it at a single draught. 'They refuse almost all of our manufactures, indeed it would not be too strong to say they are contemptuous of them, and to this stupidity they add the burden of their damned *cumshaw.*'

Hooker had tossed yet another unfamiliar word at them, but Kite was too inured to Hooker's inexplicable additions to his vocabulary to remonstrate. He remained silent and left the more inquisitive Sarah to raise the query.

'And what is that, Josiah?'

'*Cumshaw? Cumshaw* is *baksheesh*, a *pour boire*, a *douceur* . . .'

'Bribes, then . . .'

'Exactly, dear lady,' Hooker was unrepentant at this deliberate obfuscation and merely smiled. 'And this only adds to our burden.'

'Then how are we to turn a profit?' Kite had realized the implications of Hooker's cautionary statement.

'Ah, you are awake, William,' Hooker remarked with an indulgent sarcasm.

'Well?' Kite prompted, ignoring Hooker's waspish retort and pulling himself upright in his chair as *Spitfire*'s stern lifted to a low swell and her hull groaned in attenuated protest.

Hooker's mood was one of resurgent triumph and he grinned broadly. 'That, my dear William, I would prefer not to divulge at this juncture, but rest assured that I have the greatest expectations of this enterprise.' And with this ambiguity Hooker refilled his glass and raised it in a toast to their mutual futures, thereafter skilfully diverting their debate to the primary task of acquiring a ship.

Since this dinner with its tones of optimism, which had taken place only five days earlier, Kite had indeed remarked a shift in Hooker's mood. It was, he presumed, to this that Sarah referred. Absorbed in his own business, he had given the matter little thought, but now that Sarah had drawn his attention to the fact, he sought a reasonable explanation.

'Yes, he has changed, I agree. But is this not reasonable given our approach to Bombay? He has much of a practical nature to occupy his mind. From the froth of his golden, or should I say silver, dreams he has to distil some means of advancing our cause.'

'You have not noticed, have you.' It was no question; Sarah had uttered a statement. Kite felt irritation rise in him and bit it off short.

'What have I not noticed in particular?' he asked in a tone of thinly suppressed irritation.

'He has begun to smell again.'

'Oh, for God's sake, Sarah! Must I needs bathe the man once more?' Exasperation burst from Kite.

'I do not believe Hooker smells from neglect of cleanliness. . .' Sarah persisted, lowering her voice.

'Well, I most assuredly do,' Kite said with a mixture of vehement conviction and amusement. 'Mercifully you did not witness the sloughing off of the man's past. Good heavens, it was a damned revolting revelation!'

'My dear,' Sarah affirmed with unshakeable conviction, 'he sweats from fear. He is in a constant state of agitation, of apprehension . . .'

'But what does he apprehend, for God's sake?'

'Some nemesis . . .'

'Nemesis? God Lord, Sarah, you talk like a damned witch!' Kite barked a short, unamused laugh.

'Oh, yes, and this obsession is now growing upon him, outweighing the optimistic anticipation with which he reasoned a few evenings since.'

Kite's brow furrowed. Sarah's persistence won her his attention at last. 'You have some privy knowledge of this from Rose?' he asked, turning to face his wife.

'No.' Sarah shook her lovely head. 'At least, not directly, though she has hinted that while she is looking forward to our arrival at Bombay, should the weather or any other circumstance—'

'Any other circumstance?'

'Well, an enemy, or something . . .'

'Go on.'

'Should anything disturb our passage and divert us elsewhere, neither Josiah nor Rose will regard our situation as fortunate as hitherto.'

'You mean that they are content with our arrival at Bombay, but that anywhere else, on the Coromandel coast, for instance, would not please them?'

'Yes. And I think that the purchase of your promised ship will be a hurried matter if Josiah can arrange it. He has said that he wishes you not to miss the favourable monsoon for the Bay of Bengal.'

Kite digested this information. He did not quite know what to make of it. He knew that the monsoon favourable to the Bay of Bengal made of the Malabar coast a long lee shore, but there was clearly some undercurrent evident to his wife. Sarah was no fool and would never have raised the matter had it not been troubling her. Intuition or insight, the fact that Sarah was raising an alarm ought to be warning enough. For Kite the future was clouded by his own private fears: he was no longer young and the Indian climate buried white men with almost as much brutality as that of the West Indies. If he ventured into Chinese seas or the vague yet threatening waters such as Hooker intimated existed along the coasts of the Arakan and elsewhere, what would he find? Chief among his own worries was what he was to do with Sarah. He could not leave her among strangers in Bombay, yet the risks of her accompanying him in the vaguely named Country trade filled him with a greater fear. Suppose he should fall sick and die, leaving her aboard ship, isolated among a crew whose appetites he knew only too well? The enervating climate of the tropics not only worked upon men, he recalled with an unavoidably disquieting fear, but loosened the morals and reticence of women. Had he not himself fought off the predatory advances of the infamous Kitty, whose lust had not been slaked by his partner and friend Wentworth, and which had embroiled other men? He did not care to consider Sarah consumed with such unbridled appetites, but the thoughts came to him unbidden, common to men of his age, aware both of their own failing powers and of the strong passions yet remaining in their women.

Kite shook his head to clear it. This was a train of thought engendered by the night; so too perhaps was Sarah's, but it would not do to put that theory to her now. Better he accepted her warning at face value.

'You are clearly worried, m'dear,' he said, placing a hand over hers as it clasped the rail. He was suddenly disturbed by the tension in her grip, evidence of inner turmoil and conviction. It suddenly occurred to him that Sarah was as frightened of the future as he was himself, for she suddenly turned her wrist and clung onto his hand in a fierce grip.

'Yes,' she said, 'I am.'

'Well, do you try and speak further to Rose. Watch for an opening, perhaps an allusion to congress applied discreetly. Hint that you are concerned that Josiah is worried and that you attribute his returning stink to his preoccupations. Pretend that you like her.'

'But I *do* like her,' Sarah protested. 'There is much more to her than you imagine. You see her only behind Josiah's intervening bulk, as an appendage to him, not as a person in her own right with a life and existence of her own . . .'

'Well, will you do what I suggest?' Kite said, not paying his wife any attention. Not since she had so charmingly thanked him for his help in that disgusting stew in London had he been immune from Rose's ample charms.

'I shall try.'

'And you should go back to bed. It will be an hour before I come below.'

'Very well.' She gave his hand another squeeze and then relinquished it and walked forward, her body perfectly balanced against the scend of the schooner. A second later she had disappeared down the companionway.

But Kite was not thinking of his wife, nor of Rose Hooker, he was remembering the strange circumstances of Hooker's incongruous London lodgings, of the allusions to 'an enemy', and to the rejections of investment by the Directors of the Honourable East India Company behind their great horseshoe table. What in the devil's name was the man truly up to?

PART TWO

THE SOWING

Chapter Seven

Bombay

The monsoon favourable to eastward voyaging prevailed north of the equator and the *Spitfire* soon picked up its strong south-westerly wind. All thoughts of Hooker were dismissed, for Kite was anxious about their position. Before their departure from Liverpool, Kite had sent out McClusky to obtain adequate charts of the Indian seas. But there was a paucity of these, it being argued that all hydrographic secrets were the property of the Honourable Company and that only those meditating the illegal, monopoly-breaking trade of the so-called 'interlopers' had need of such things. The arguments that the *Spitfire* was fitting out as either a yacht or a privateer carried little weight in such a seller's market. Charts of the Indian and China seas, McClusky had reported, were few and far between and commanded high prices. Despising himself for doing so, Kite had approached Hooker for money and the nabob had obliged but now, faced with the testing of their accuracy, Kite was confronted with their inadequacy.

What McClusky gleaned at an exorbitant price proved almost useless. The folio was old and, although it attributed its authority to the hydrographic efforts of several humble servants of the Honourable East India Company, Kite doubted the accuracy of the positions of any of the plotted atolls, relying only upon the observed positions of such well-established places such as Bombay Castle, Fort George at Madras, or the Company's factory at Surat on the River Tupti.

As they drove to the north-north-west, into the great bight of the Arabian Sea, the south-west monsoon frequently occluded the sky so that he was obliged to resort to latitude sailing, and first head well clear of the Malabar coast and the off-lying archipelagos of the Maldive and Laccadive Islands until, on the latitude of Bombay, he could turn east and run along the appropriate parallel. It added considerably to their time on the passage, reducing their stock of both water and food to a minimum. Rain showers enabled them to eke out the former a little, but it seemed an age before, one warm and breezy day, to Kite's relief they caught sight of other sails, not the squares of enemy cruisers, but the triangular peaks of two large baggalas, swooping along to the north and heading in the same direction as themselves. These Arab craft possessed a speed and grace equal to the schooner and kept them distant company until, in due course, they were joined by a kotia coming down from the north and then four swift, triple-masted pattamars.

Later that morning they sighted the lighthouse and by late afternoon the anchor was let go under the guns of Bombay Castle. Secure behind the ramparts nestled the large, rectangular gubernatorial villa, above which flew the barred colours of the East India Company. A forest of masts belonged to the dhows and mashwas both at anchor and drawn up on the various beaches fringing the shoreline. Above them rose the taller spars of Indiamen and Country vessels, filling the basin between the Bunder Pier and the docks to the south. Farther off they could see the green of vegetation and the waving fronds of tall coconut palms. In the outer bay, lying wind-rode at anchor like themselves, lay two large Indiamen and a snow-rigged despatch vessel belonging to the Bombay Marine.

Minutes before they dropped the anchor from the cathead they had been surrounded by small bum-boats selling fruit and vegetables, many unseen before by Kite and his crew. These craft were manned by small, active men in ragged skirts and shirts; some wore turbans, others wore sun hats woven from palm fronds, but all cried out their wares and solicited trade with energetic eagerness. Two or three of the boats, though sculled by men, bore groups of huddling women, painted trulls in bright squares of silk and cotton, their eyes outlined with kohl, their hair brightened with henna.

Contrary to Kite's expectations, Hooker was in voluble mood. As the boats closed in on the schooner, Hooker stood at the rail and, addressing them in an incomprehensible native tongue, waved them away. The bum-boats circled warily, as though seeking a weakness in *Spitfire*'s defences or the removal of Hooker. After anchoring he called out for a boat to be made available for him, giving every appearance of eagerness to go ashore. Kite passed orders for Harper to hoist out their larger cutter and remarked that he would go below and shift his coat, but Hooker objected.

'I think it best that you do not come ashore yet, my dear fellow. We must keep these vultures at bay and withal play up the fiction of this being a yacht,' he explained, 'and there may be a question of quarantine,' he added as an afterthought. 'I shall make the appropriate calls and see what progress I am able to make in the matter of a new vessel for us.'

Kite might have felt this a slight, but after the weeks of anxiety he was content to go below and rest. Hooker had been nothing more than a passenger for weeks and as Harper had reported the anchor brought up, Kite had felt the weight of responsibility slip from his shoulders. He could not care less about the bum-boats, he had met them in the West Indies and, the whores notwithstanding, felt that McClusky could keep them at bay. Hooker, however, had other ideas.

'Post a couple of seamen with loaded muskets,' he ordered imperiously. 'I'll leave half my dacoits. They all have knives and know how to use them should the need arise. Let one of those vermin aboard and they'll swamp you, you'll lose every moveable object you possess and I must mind my . . . well, you know to what I refer.'

Hooker issued these instructions as he waited for the body-guard of dacoits that had been assigned to accompany him ashore to clamber down into the waiting boat which, with Harper at the helm, bobbed alongside. They were all chattering excitedly with frequent obvious references to the shore, though they fell silent as Hooker barked some orders to them and four detached disconsolately, a quartet assigned to remain aboard. Then he turned back to Kite. 'By the way, William, I shall soon remove my wife and myself ashore; do you too require a lodging? It shall have to be at your expense, of course . . .'

There was something unkind about that 'of course', compounding the sudden domination of the deck and the trans-formation of *Spitfire* into Hooker's yacht. Hooker's changed tone revived the suspicions Kite had entertained days earlier when Sarah had first voiced her own worry about the man's mood. As if to sharpen his instincts, Kite smelt Hooker's body odour and, in an instant of catalysed perception, linked his unnecessary remark to Hooker's desire to go ashore alone. He was seized by the conviction that Hooker was up to something and he immediately prevaricated.

'Quarantine or not, Josiah, I shall need to clear the vessel inwards. I am, after all, the master.' In that 'after all', he sub-consciously sought to match the message implicit in Hooker's 'of course', but Hooker was too preoccupied.

'No matter, William, these things can be dealt with shortly. This is not the London River, this is India . . .' Hooker turned away and prepared to swing his ungainly bulk over the rail.

'Well, it may be India,' Kite began as Hooker lifted one huge thigh, 'but there is one thing I insist upon before you go.'

'Oh, and upon what do you *insist*?' Hooker looked into Kite's eyes, his tone surprised. He was sweating copiously as he held himself halfway over the rail and Kite had a sudden, reactive impulse to thrust him over the side so that he fell into the waters of the anchorage. Restraining this irrational desire left his voice curiously vehement, a fact to which he afterwards attributed Hooker's admission. Had Hooker been standing upon the deck, or seated below with a wine glass in his hand, Kite knew he would never have released the intelligence with such ease. But, poised as he was betwixt wind and water, balancing unfamiliarly in an attitude which, however familiar it might have been for a seaman, was perilous for a man of Hooker's disposition and bulk, Hooker gave up his secret without hesitation.

'By what method are we to cheat the Chinese of their silver?' Kite snapped.

'Opium,' Hooker said as his weight forced him to seek the next step down *Spitfire*'s tumblehome before his arms gave out. Almost immediately he regretted his candour, for he slipped, recovered with a gasp and, his head now almost comically level with the rail, his chin set between his white-knuckled hands, he hissed, 'You must tell not a soul, William. It is my turn to insist . . .'

Then he was gone and Kite moved quickly to the rail to see Hooker in Harper's massive arms, being eased onto the stern-sheet bench. Harper's averted face bore an expression of distaste and Kite could scarcely suppress his smile as Hooker looked up.

'Damn you, Kite,' the discomfited Hooker called out, 'I *insist* . . . Do I have your word?'

'Aye, of course, and Josiah,' Kite added, 'my wife and I shall remain on board for the time being.'

'You are unkind, sir,' Sarah said as he walked aft after watching the boat pull away for the shore, pitching in the short, steep waves thrown up by the wind as it scoured in from the open sea. 'I heard what you said about staying on board and I would dearly love to get ashore.'

Kite held up his hand and walked aft to the taffrail, beckoning Sarah after him. She still wore breeches and a shirt, the ruffles of which lifted in the cool breeze. Dark clouds were building over the sea and already the westering sun was obscured. Against the cloud the line of the horizon was jade green, broken here and there by the lateen sails of native pattamars and mashwas which were running in for the shelter of the harbour.

'What is it, William?'

Kite frowned. Then he said, in a low voice, so that no sound of their conversation filtered down to Rose below, 'It is odd, Sarah, but I *am* now convinced that Hooker is up to something, that he has some secret matter in hand from which he denies me any part. We are so much in his hands that I am thrown into all confusion and . . .' Kite fell silent.

'And?' Sarah prompted.

Kite shook his head, as if throwing off a bad dream. 'I had the oddest impulse to throw him overboard,' he said, nodding down at the water under them.

'Dear God,' Sarah exclaimed, drawing back from the rail. A large shark, with its attending remora, turned languidly in the shadow of *Spitfire*'s stern, predatory and sinister, seemingly unperturbed by the wind-ruffled surface of the harbour.

'I felt a . . . a premonition,' he whispered, and Sarah put out her hand and touched his.

'My husband has gone ashore to secure us lodgings.'

They both turned as Rose approached them under a parasol. She came aft in a swirl of green and gold silk, her tall, well-proportioned figure upright and confident as she walked on the unfamiliarly level deck. Rose Hooker had never really accustomed herself to the slightest movement of the schooner at sea. Now, with the breeze pressing the brilliant silk closer about her, she presented a graceful picture of happiness, her smile wide in the shadow of her parasol, her oiled hair gleaming as she turned and waved a bangled brown arm towards the pale ramparts of the castle and Fort George beyond.

'It is so good to be home,' she said simply as she turned back to them.

'I suppose Josiah will have no trouble in finding you somewhere to live?' Sarah asked. 'Are houses to be had easily, or will he seek out some friend?'

'Oh, don't worry, Sarah, Josiah has much influence here; all will be well now.'

Rose stared again at the distant fort and Kite, watching this exchange, thought he caught a wistfulness in her face, then dismissed the thought: he had become too damned suspicious. What if Rose Hooker *was* wistful? She had been away a long time and, even if her expectations of England had been blighted, the prospect of getting ashore from the confines of the schooner must have raised even a short-term anticipation in her. Then Rose swung back to them.

'Yes, all will be well now, for all of us.' She smiled, then added, 'He will be back by nightfall with good news.'

Yet somehow Kite was not reassured. There was something fey about Rose's lack of conviction and he felt a sudden chill in the air.

Hooker was not back by nightfall. Nor were Harper and the boat. The day was eclipsed by the sudden chill and sweeping hiss of rain which came a few minutes before sunset. The fresh monsoon breeze of the day turned into a near gale so that *Spitfire* snubbed at her cable and Kite's only consolation as he huddled on deck cursing the ill-luck that kept him from a full night's sleep yet again was that they were able to fill several casks with water as the rain poured down from the furled sails in torrential spouts.

It was all over before midnight as the cloud eased, the stars appeared again and the wind moderated. Kite heard the hail of Harper's voice and a few minutes later the mate, sodden to the skin, his ugly face cracking in a grin of pleasure at getting back on board, stood in the cabin with a glass of toddy Sarah had prepared for him. The boat lay astern on its painter and Harper looked exhausted.

'Well, Zachariah, where is Mr Hooker?'

Harper looked round. Mistress Kite was in her dressing gown, the Indian woman was wrapped in yet another of her extravagant silk confections and Captain Kite, his hair plastered on his skull, had at least kept his trunk dry. Harper noted his stockinged feet rose from puddles on the square of carpet the cabin-deck was graced with. He set down his glass and withdrew a note from his breast.

'I fear the ink has run,' he said, handing it to Kite.

Kite read it through quickly and then handed it to Rose. 'He says he is detained and will be back in the morning. He is apparently spending the night with a certain Wadia.'

'A native shipwright, I think,' Harper offered in his American drawl.

'A ship-builder whose reputation is celebrated throughout the land,' Rose added. 'Did he send a topass with this?' she asked Harper, holding up the soggy note.

'A topass?'

'A boy. A runner . . .'

'A messenger,' Kite added for Harper's benefit.

'Yeah, he sure didn't come himself. It was raining.'

'Very well. You had better get some sleep, Zachariah. Now the wind has dropped I'll turn out McClusky; he can stand the anchor watch.'

When Harper, refreshed from his sleep and in dry clothes, returned to the landing place next morning he was met not by Hooker but by the same Indian messenger who had brought him Hooker's note the previous evening. An hour after leaving *Spitfire* he was back alongside with the Indian, who had insisted upon being taken out to the schooner with a large bundle wrapped in a cotton sheet.

'He demanded a passage out to the vessel, Cap'n Kite,' Harper explained as he brought the man aft to where Kite and Sarah were enjoying a cup of coffee on deck.

Kite regarded the Indian. Apart from Rose and the dacoits, who had kept themselves to themselves throughout the voyage, this was the first native Indian he had met. The man was impressive: tall and turbaned with an attractively hawklike face and fierce moustaches. His long coat was of dark blue and he wore leggings bound at the ankle, while his feet were bare. In his belt was a dagger. Meeting Kite's eye he inclined his head in a civil though not a servile manner and made a gesture with his hands that indicated some degree of obligation to Kite's station.

'You are the Captain Kite?' he asked in an English that was almost perfect.

'I am. You have news of Mr Hooker?'

'I am called Muckbul Ali Rahman. Hooker Sahib has

assigned me as topass to you, Captain Kite, that is to say I am to be your interpreter, guide and, I hope, your friend.' The man smiled and shot a glance at Sarah. Rahman's dark, almost liqueous eyes bore a look of astonishment as though, Kite thought, it had just dawned upon him that beside himself stood an English woman. He footed her a bow and muttered, 'Memsahib.'

Sarah smiled and dipped in a half-curtsy.

'Hooker Sahib wishes me to inform you that he is currently waiting upon the House of Wadia and is sanguine that a ship may be chartered before the sun sets this evening—'

'Forgive me, sir,' Kite broke in uncertainly, 'but I have a need for water and fresh food; moreover I must clear the vessel inwards—'

But it was Rahman's turn to interrupt. He held his hand up, palm outwards, waving it in a negative. 'It is all arranged, Captain Kite, an officer from the Custom House will attend you if you send a boat to the landing place at noon, there is a gun from the fort at that time, and Hooker Sahib will rejoin you then. If you give me a list of your requirement for stores I shall see to the matter, and as for water, sahib, you can land your casks at the dockyard when it is convenient and you will be shown where to draw potable water.'

Kite digested this intelligence. Rahman had arrived like the god he had once seen appear in a machine lowered out of the paper clouds suspended over the stage of a theatre in Liverpool. Was this some form of Oriental magic, like the beds of nails and climbing ropes of which he had heard Hooker speak? All his worries would, Rahman seemed to promise, melt away like the puddles of dew and rain drying from their decks in the hot sunshine that now consumed those real clouds that had hitherto lowered over Bombay harbour.

'Very well . . .'

'You should call me Topass, Captain, if you cannot manage my name.'

'I am obliged to you, Topass,' Kite said smiling at the dark-skinned man, surprised that quite inexplicably he found himself liking Rahman. Despite the Indian's arrival at the behest of Hooker, Kite thought he would trust the man before he would trust his master.

'And yet,' he muttered to himself, 'I hitherto trusted Hooker, or else I should not be here with Sarah.'

The unease of premonition returned to dog him through that busy morning as they fought off the sporadic attempts of the bum-boats to work alongside while they strove to hoist the water casks out of the hold. Nor did the sensation diminish when Hooker returned. For an hour he closeted himself with his wife and Sarah drew him away on deck when he sought to eavesdrop through the temporary bulkhead by which means they had given each couple privacy.

In due course, however, Hooker sent word for Kite and he had descended from the deck, his head aching from overexertion in the heat.

'You should not drive yourself,' Hooker said expansively, smoking a long cheroot. He was sodden with sweat and gave off the old aroma of neglect as he leaned back in a creaking chair with a glass of wine.

'All is well then, Josiah?' Kite enquired, helping himself to a glass and, mopping his own face, eased himself onto the transom shelf.

'Very well indeed, my dear fellow. I have had a stroke of luck. I called upon the chief factor. I ascertained, after we had discovered a mutual acquaintance in Calcutta whom we both held in high esteem, that a large Country ship has just been made available for charter. Her owner, a Scotchman named Buchanan, has just expired. The man had no issue and no partners. She is loaded with cotton piece goods and her commander has, with some partners of his own, Parsees I gather, raised sufficient capital to buy half her bottom and her freight. She is fully manned and cleared for China. But without Buchanan's letters of credit Captain Grindley is unable to proceed and he is thus urgently seeking further backing. I was able to provide the missing capital—'

Kite broke into Hooker's enthusiasm: 'Captain Grindley? She has a commander, this vessel of yours?'

'Yes, yes . . .'

'Then what is to become of me? Was it not agreed that I should command your ship?'

Hooker blew smoke at the white-painted deckhead and smiled dismissively. 'Yes, yes, of course, William, but don't you see what a golden opportunity this was? Why, it fell into my lap, it was fate, was I to pass up such a chance? It was an opportunity to move matters forward, d'you not see, without delay. Besides, you have your schooner.' Hooker waved his wine glass about in an airy gesture that slopped the residual contents. 'She will make you a fortune . . .'

Kite felt the cold certainty of betrayal clutch his guts; it was the fulfilment of Sarah's premonition and the reason for Rose's lack of confidence. He leaned forward. 'You are reneging, sir,' he said coldly.

'Not at all, not at all. There will be other opportunities . . .' Hooker blustered and then, sensing Kite's change of mood, added, 'I shall of course pay you for my passage outwards.'

Kite was affronted, but a life in commerce had trained him not to react passionately.

'Surely you have not invested *all* your capital in this venture with this Captain Grindley?'

Hooker shook his head. 'No, no, of course not. I called upon the Parsee builder Wadia, he is laying down two ships and has offered me a share or two in either . . .'

'A share or *two*?' Kite stared at his so-called partner in disbelief. He set his jaw and awaited more of Hooker's bluster but Hooker was consumed by the euphoria of self-esteem. Hooker was very pleased with himself and Kite could go hang!

'It is another great opportunity and, mark my words, Kite, there will be others, upon my soul there will be, of that I am certain but, for the time being, we shall settle matters between us by my paying for my passage and your costs to date, as we agreed. This will give you a small sum of personal capital to add to your own fortune.'

His *fortune*? Kite was conscious of having been completely deceived, outmanoeuvred and utterly humiliated. By God, this would make them laugh in Liverpool! Inwardly he was seething with a cold fury but, for the time being he had perforce to affect acceptance of this. With an effort he pretended indifference and shrugged. 'Very well, you shall pay me as you say, but since I must rely upon my own wits, you must satisfy my curiosity: does this Captain Grindley of yours take silver or opium to China?'

Hooker looked at Kite sharply. Kite caught the guile in his eyes and watched as they softened. 'Ah, that eh? Opium or *cash*, as the Chinese call it . . .'

'Well?'

'I believe Captain Grindley has a consignment of opium on board, yes.' Hooker paused, and then as though thinking of some fact with which to placate Kite, he added, 'There is a certain risk inherent in the voyage to which I did not wish you to be exposed.'

'Risk? You mean the Chinese are unwilling to permit uncontrolled imports of opium into China without it paying duty?'

Hooker shrugged. 'As I say, there are some risks and I wished to protect you from any chance of your losing . . .' Hooker's voice trailed off and then he said in the cheerful tone of one forcing a change in the subject of the conversation, 'You have met the industrious Ali Rahman?'

'Yes,' replied Kite, 'I have.' He bit off his inclination to add that he trusted the Indian topass more than the hideously obese and by now thoroughly repugnant Englishman sitting before him.

The mood at supper that night was strained, even though the cook had butchered a fresh fowl for their table and neither man had acquainted his respective wife with the disagreement that lay between them. Ship-owning and ship-broking had inured Kite to making too free a demonstration of his personal feelings, while Hooker's own plans precluded any free and frank discussion of their prospects. Instead Hooker gave the ladies an account of his hours ashore, of whom he had met on what sounded like an uncomfortable whirl of social and commercial visits. He dropped names to little effect as far as either Sarah or Kite were concerned, though clearly Rose was impressed and her face bore excited little smiles and, from time to time, she gave an anticipatory squeak that Kite found faintly salacious.

In due course, however, they retired to their beds, the Hookers for the last time aboard ship. Aware of her husband's preoccupation, Sarah asked what the matter was.

Putting his finger to his lips Kite had whispered that it was best that he deferred an explanation until the morning. Personally he wanted time to think, and long after Sarah's breathing told him that she was asleep he lay awake, staring at the pale deckhead and wondering at the strangeness of fate that had brought them to this pass. He felt drained of all resolution, utterly defeated and devoid of resource. What was he to do now that Hooker intended to abandon him, for he had no further faith in the man's vague, half-promises? The one thing he was determined upon was to cut loose from Hooker and he rued the day he had succumbed to little Jack Bow's pleas in Leadenhall Street.

Kite was dreaming of his father and a cold Cumbrian morning in his youth when the screaming woke him. Sarah shot bolt upright beside him as he threw himself out of their cot. The piercing noise came from Rose, and Kite burst into their half of the cabin, almost tearing the flimsy door from its hinges.

The first light of dawn threw a pallid light into the space, revealing Rose, half naked, kneeling upon the deck, her hands tearing at her face so that the nails ploughed the flesh and dark streams of blood poured down her cheeks.

Before her lay her husband, his body a mass of fleshy folds that seemed almost fluid as it subsided under its own weight. At first in the half light Kite could not distinguish what was wrong with Hooker, so seamed was the body with its own corpulence. Then he saw that Hooker had had his throat cut and lay in an expanding pool of his own blood, the strong smell of which mingled with the fetid stink of the man.

Suddenly Hooker's feet twitched and Kite heard the faint bubbling respiration as he fought for his last breath through his severed windpipe. A second later it was all over. There was an expiring fart and the white corpse seemed to settle further, as though, half liquid itself, it sought the level equilibrium of its spreading lifeblood.

Chapter Eight

Hostages to Fortune

K ite's appearance had cut short Rose's screaming. Sarah, having followed her husband into the cabin, moved round the body and taking Rose by the shoulders drew her away. Kite's heart was thundering; he had been dragged from the depths of an exhausted sleep and for a moment could think of nothing but the dead body before him. Then Harper arrived, his presence announced by a sharp intake of breath. Next there were shouts from forward which rose rapidly in a crescendo of alarm. Kite raced up the companionway with Harper behind.

The planking of the deck was grey beneath the starlight and forward there was a swirl of shadows from which McClusky emerged.

'Cap'n Kite! The dacoits have gone, sir. Cleared out and gone . . .'

'No, they've been taken, sir,' another voice called. 'Look, there's blood all over the rail . . . and it runs across the deck here.'

As if reminded of something, Kite turned to Harper. 'Can you make out any blood on the after companionway, Zachariah?' he asked, staring at the pale shapes of his hands, as though he might have been contaminated by some of it during his rapid ascent. Then, leaving Harper to have a close look, Kite went to the rail and stared out over the harbour. He thought he saw the faint gleam of a phosphorescent wake, as if from a rowed boat, but it was gone behind the dull

117

half-manifestation of a Country trader and it might well have been nothing more than a fish jumping.

'William . . .' Sarah's voice, cool and measured, broke into the tempest of his thoughts. He turned and saw his wife, head and shoulders above the coaming of the companionway over which Harper still bent.

'Yes. What is it?' He saw her beckon and crossed the deck. 'Well?'

'The chest, Hooker's chest, it's gone . . .'

'That's what they came for, Cap'n,' offered Harper, 'that an' to despatch Hooker. Look, there's some blood smeared here . . . and here . . .' Harper straightened up. 'Damn me, Cap'n, begging your pardon, ma'am, but he made some enemies in a short time.'

'Or already had them, Mr Harper,' Sarah said, adding, 'You'll keep mum about the chest, won't you?'

'Of course, ma'am.'

'I think I had better raise the alarm,' Kite said at last, straightening up from staring at the dark bloodstains.

'I'll do that, sir. You stay here; I'll take a boat to that snow of the Bombay Marine,' Harper volunteered.

'Very well,' Kite said, 'and find out any scuttlebutt that you can, Zachariah, there's a good fellow, and what the devil the procedure is for a death like this.'

'I'll go back to Rose,' Sarah offered and Kite was aware of the keening whimper of the widow rising up from the hot and smelly interior of the schooner. As Harper went forward calling out for the boat to be manned and Sarah went below, Kite swore and stared about them again. Then, walking quickly to the taffrail, he looked for the boat lying astern on her painter. All he found there was the end of a cut rope. He turned forward.

'Belay that, Mr Harper. The boat's gone, you shall have to swing out the other.'

There was a pause during which Kite guessed that Harper swore fluidly under his breath and then came the acknowledgement of the order. 'Swing out t'other boat, sir, aye, aye.'

Leaving Harper and the men to their task, Kite turned to go below. He was just about to duck his head under the companionway when he saw McClusky walking aft.

'Cap'n Kite, sir, can I have a word?'

'What is it?' Kite asked shortly.

'Mr Harper says that Mr Hooker's been murdered, sir.'

'Yes . . . What about it?'

'Then does that mean any other dacoits are dead? Or did they have something to do with the killing of Mr Hooker?'

After the long, long voyage it was easy to forget that McClusky was no seaman but a clerk with the shrewdness natural to a town-bred and ambitious Irishman. Kite's tired brain was past grasping McClusky's allusion. He asked McClusky to explain himself.

'Well, sir, the dacoits who went ashore with Hooker didn't come back with him last night. Harper told me he thought it odd and asked if the fellows that Hooker had left behind were still on board. I told him they were and gave the matter no thought until, well, until this all happened. Now the mate tells me you're sending him over to the naval ship and I thought he should mention it.'

Kite forbore from correcting McClusky's assessment of the Bombay Marine's cruiser, it was not important. 'To tell the truth, Mr McClusky, I never gave the dacoits a second thought last night. We'd had such a drubbing what with wind and rain . . .' Kite paused a moment and then said, 'Look, you're a bright fellow. Do you go with Mr Harper and see what the commander of the cruiser says. Give him all the details including the intelligence about the dacoits.'

'Very well.' And when the boat was finally swung outboard and lowered into the water Kite watched her pulling towards the dimly perceived shape of the snow. Then he finally went below.

In their own half of the divided cabin Sarah was comforting Rose, sitting on the cross bench under the stern window, her arm about the Indian woman as she sobbed out her grief. Sarah pursed her lips for silence as Kite stumbled into the space and poured himself half a glass of wine. Taking a sip he put it down on the table, took a candle from the sconce and went through into the Hookers' half cabin. The stern window was open, a cool breeze wafted in bearing the exotic scents of the shore. Lighting a lantern he held it over the body, at the same time pressing a handkerchief to his own nose.

Hooker lay on his back, his legs straight. He wore a checked cotton *sarong* which had been pulled loose so that the whole of his vast torso was exposed. A feather of hairs ran upwards from his pubis and disappeared into the surprisingly neat coil of his navel. This delicate whorl of pallid flesh sat atop the repulsive mound of his belly which, subsiding abruptly under his ribcage, was replaced by white breasts. Confined by an artful corsetière, these might have flattered a woman; spread now in a lateral divergence, they failed to convey any impression of the physical strength that had once filled the disgusting corpse. It occurred to Kite in a perceptive if irrelevant moment that had Hooker not spent most of his life over-indulging in the tropics, he might have been a finer specimen than the muscular Harper.

'Well, well,' muttered Kite to himself. At all events Hooker had been overcome like a shorn Sampson, for he seemed to have put up little of a struggle. Judging by the lack of noise, Kite concluded he had known little of his end, for he had been sleeping on the deck where a blood-soaked blanket was spread out over a shallow palliasse. He had been dragged clear of this, it was true, but possibly only to ease access to the locker beyond, where, Kite knew, Hooker had stowed the chest containing his liquid assets.

Moving the lantern upwards over Hooker's corpse Kite illuminated the wound. The haemorrhage had ceased and the blood was already dark and clotted, blurring the edges of the knife's incision. Hooker's expression was barely one of astonishment. His eyes stared, but not from horror or fear, and though his mouth too was open, the effect was merely one of mild surprise. He looked much as he might have looked had Kite himself called him unexpectedly in the middle of the night.

Was that because he had not known what was happening to him? Or because the person upon whom he last set eyes was familiar to him? A dacoit, for instance?

Kite straightened up. Perhaps that was how some men died; awake but in ignorance of the fact that they were being murdered. There was something almost amusing about it, thought Kite as he stared down at the body, in the same way that Hooker's extreme corpulence was distantly amusing to an observer. But on close acquaintance amusement turned to repugnance and then revulsion. Kite's nose wrinkled and, in a fit of sudden coughing, he rejoined Sarah and Rose. Easing himself onto a chair he recovered his breath and contemplated the scene before him. Rose continued sobbing, though she was quieter now and Kite cleared his throat and said, 'Rose, I must talk to you. Would you like a glass of wine?'

Sarah shook her head. 'No, William, it is against her religion, I have already asked.'

'Will she answer me a few questions?'

Sarah turned to Rose. 'Rose, William wishes to ask . . .'

'Yes, I heard.' Rose stirred and drew apart from Sarah. Her face was ravaged by her self-mutilation, and streaked with kohl; in the lantern-light she looked hideous in her grief. Pressed with the urgency of affairs, Kite barely noticed. He was thinking of the brief talk which Hooker had had with his wife when he had returned from the shore.

'Rose, I have sent Harper across to the Company's cruiser to report what has happened, but there are some things that I must ask you. Did you see anything when . . . I mean to say, were you aware of anyone?'

Rose shuddered, then shook her head.

'You saw nothing, no one at all? Then what woke you?'

Rose tried to speak, but nothing more than a croak came from her. Instantly Kite advanced with his wine glass. Rose waved it away, but he pressed it on her.

'Come, my dear, a little wine will not hurt you.'

After hesitating a moment, Rose tentatively gave way and sipped the wine. A moment later she had drained the glass and Kite, kneeling before her and staring up into her eyes, asked again, 'Rose, my dear, what woke you?'

'They moved him,' she said as the wine uncoiled its warmth in her belly.

'Who moved him, Rose?' Kite asked softly staring up into her eyes.

She looked away evasively. She seemed frightened, but Kite did not wish to press her. He was almost certain he knew who had murdered Hooker; he also had some questions he wished McClusky to answer but which he had forgotten to ask before sending the clerk off with Harper. As suspicion clouded his mind, Kite thought of something else, something which inserted itself like a knife blade into his own consciousness: if anyone knew that Hooker had cheated him of a promised command, it was just possible that they might attribute the fact sufficient a motive as to make Kite himself a suspect. He was grateful that he had deferred mentioning the matter to Sarah, but how much did Rose know, and was this the reason for her present circumspection? He tried another tack.

'Rose, I know Josiah had agreed to put money into a venture, that he had had an excellent offer yesterday which he could not pass up. Do you know if he had actually paid any money?' Kite thought it unlikely, for Hooker could not have had the time to complete the transaction.

Relieved not to be pressed on the matter of the murder and with the wine doing its insidious work, Rose seized the change of subject almost eagerly and shook her head. 'No,' she said, her voice almost inaudible, 'he was to attend to the matter tomorrow . . . today . . .'

'And where is your money now? Is the chest stolen?'

Rose nodded. 'They dragged it out and passed it through the window.'

Kite recalled the open stern window, the sash lifted to admit the cool night air. 'The dacoits took the chest and passed it through the stern window into a boat.' He couched the sentence as a statement and Rose murmured yes, without realizing what she had done. Kite, pleased with the accuracy of his guess, knew now why the boat painter had been cut. He barely heard her mutter something about Josiah being sorry and 'paying it back', attaching no importance to this half-apology for her husband's deception of himself. As for the blood on the deck, it was clear that it was Hooker's, borne by the dacoit who had slit Hooker's throat. When they looked in daylight he guessed they would find the trail ran from the cabin, up the companionway and forward, where a native boat by which the dacoits who had been taken and left ashore by Hooker had returned to the schooner. Two boats made good sense too, the *Spitfire*'s, prepared to get away with the treasure, manned and most certainly hauled up under the stern by the two dacoits left aboard to keep the bum-boats at bay, and the native boat to create a diversion as the rest of the dacoits got away.

'I apprehend that Josiah was betrayed by his own men,' Kite said to Sarah, 'but what I doubt whether I will fathom is the reason why, unless it was simply their desire to seize his fortune.'

'That would seem a powerful enough motive to men of little means,' Sarah replied. 'They must have been aware of his wealth—'

'But he tried to keep it from them as much as possible,' Rose broke in and Kite wondered if this too was part of the extraordinary subterfuge of the London tenement.

'So that is what happened, Rose, is it?'

Rose stirred herself, suddenly sitting upright and plucking at the white silk wrap as though the gesture signalled a return to self-composure. Abruptly she held out the wine glass. 'Please, William, a little more wine.'

Kite took the proffered glass and, crossing to the decanter, refilled it and handed it back to Rose. Having taken a deep draught she shuddered and then looked from Kite to Sarah before shaking her head.

'What am I to do? I have nobody, no one, now Josiah is . . .' and she began to cry again, mumbling in her native tongue so that Sarah had to put her arm about her again and Kite contained his true feelings with difficulty, muttering a low, 'Damnation!'

Sarah looked up sharply. 'We must leave matters until the morning,' she admonished him. He contemplated sleep, but rest was to elude them, for there was a clatter on the companionway ladder and a second later Harper's ugly visage peered round the cabin door.

'Begging your pardon, Cap'n Kite, ma'am, but may I have a word?'

Kite sighed, looked at his wife and gestured to the deck above. Sarah nodded and Kite rose stiffly to his feet. 'Very well, Zachariah, I'll follow you up on deck.'

'Maggie's here wondering whether she can do anything,' Harper added, indicating the maid behind him, and Kite wondered what she had heard.

'Send her in,' Sarah said and Kite stood aside for the young woman as she entered the cabin; then he followed Harper on deck. McClusky stood expectantly at the head of the companionway and Kite said, 'Wait there, I want a word with you before you turn in.'

Kite heard McClusky sigh; he must have guessed what Kite wanted to ask him.

'Well?' Kite asked when Harper had withdrawn to the taffrail and both men stood staring out over the dark waters of the harbour.

'I was not well received,' Harper said in his engaging drawl. 'That snow is the *Artemis*, commanded by a Lieutenant Anthony Cavanagh, and the hour was somewhat late for him but I passed on what had happened and McClusky had his pennyworth.' Harper paused, then added, 'I got the impression that Cavanagh knew something of Hooker, if only by reputation. Anyway his reply was that he advised that you, Cap'n, did not tarry in harbour but put to sea and dumped the body before putrescence set in. He said once the flies get to it after sunrise . . . Well, I don't need to labour the point, sir.'

'So there was no suggestion that due process of law should in any sense take its course?' Kite asked astonished.

'Quite the contrary, sir.'

Kite was about to mention the missing chest of treasure, but then decided against it. Although he would have trusted Harper with his life, he did not think that extending his confidences or his inner thoughts at that moment would be fruitful. Instead he swung round and, seeing the figure standing beside the after companionway, called out, 'Mr McClusky?'

'Sir?' McClusky came aft.

'You had the deck, McClusky. Tell me what happened.'

There was a silence, then McClusky said, 'Well, sir, I heard the scream—'

'I mean what happened before the scream,' Kite broke in.

'Well, nothing, sir.'

'Nothing? Think carefully, man. You are telling me you neither saw nor heard a thing?'

'Not that I can recall, sir.'

'You were asleep!' Kite snapped.

'No, sir, I was *not* asleep!' McClusky protested.

'Mr McClusky, it is quite possible to be asleep and yet not to know it. I suggest to you that you were asleep, or perhaps, conceding you the partial benefit of the doubt, merely dozing, and that the scream woke you to full consciousness.' There was another silence. 'Well, sir? Am I correct?'

McClusky sighed again and mumbled, 'Yes, sir, it is possible.'

'Very well, now try and recall what, of those comatose moments, you remember.'

'Well . . . nothing, Captain Kite . . .' McClusky's tone was unhappy.

'Nothing at all? Let me prompt you. Did you see any strangers on deck? You have been keeping the anchor watch alone, with the—'

'Exception of the dacoits who had relieved each other,' McClusky volunteered with sudden excited recollection.

'Did you see the handover?'

'No . . . Yes . . . No . . . I don't recall, sir. I remember there was one we called Hassan. He was very tired having been up all day on guard and he kept nodding off . . . Then I *do* remember Mahmud, the tall thin one, coming towards me . . . Yes he seemed to . . . No, I was surprised and then he seemed startled, perhaps I *had* dozed off. He reported all was well, and I don't remember much else until the scream . . .'

'You were not struck from behind. You don't have a bump on the head, or anything?'

McClusky ran his hand over his head as if he might discover something. 'No, sir . . .'

'Mahmud had come aft to see if he was asleep and found him drowsy, Cap'n,' Harper said, 'and then he just backed away until Mac was asleep properly.'

Kite nodded. 'Yes, that's what I think.'

''Cause those damned dacoits did it, sir, I'm sure of it and that's why they didn't come back with Hooker; they'd deserted him and were annoyed that he'd left two of them aboard. I heard one of them saying something about having to come back and get their pay and their compatriots.'

'How did you understand them, Zachariah?'

'I know a little of their lingo, Cap'n. Not much, but I know they said it was all finished, that Hooker was a, well we'd say bastard, I dare say, Cap'n, and Hassan and Mahmud's names were mentioned. It makes sense,' Harper concluded in his logical way; the matter was beyond peradventure as far as Zachariah Harper was concerned.

Kite nodded his head. 'Very well. We can do no more tonight. I shall keep the deck, I've some thinking to do. Do you two turn in for a couple of hours and then I want Hooker sewn into a hammock.'

'I'll see to that, Cap'n, though I guess one will be insufficient,' Harper said, his grin, unseen in the darkness, articulated in the tone of his grim words.

'Very well. And I'll want your boat again early in the forenoon. I've some calls of my own to pay.'

As the two men went forward Kite fell to a restless pacing of the deck where, some minutes later, Sarah joined him.

'Will you not come below, William? Rose has fallen asleep. It was the wine, I expect; she is not used to it.'

'I must stand the anchor watch, Sarah. Do you sleep, my dear. We are come to a pretty pass and I must consider what is to be done.'

'What *can* be done?' Sarah asked. 'With Josiah and his money gone we are obliged to offer our protection to Rose . . .'

'God, I had not thought of that!'

'She has no one, as she said.'

'Well, we have precious little, Sarah. I did not even secure Hooker's damned passage money, and beyond what I have in bills of exchange, and that is little enough . . . Oh, God damn! We would have been better off in Liverpool playing fast and loose with our creditors . . .' Kite spoke through clenched teeth.

'Come, come, William, we have no creditors.' Sarah soothed.

'No, but how low we have been brought . . . Had I not trusted Hooker . . .' Kite brushed his hand through his hair and then his self-control broke down. He struck his fist violently on the rail. 'God rot that festering bastard! He has made a fool of me!'

Sarah remained silent as the anger ebbed out of Kite and he turned to his wife. 'What are we to do, Sarah, here in Bombay?' he asked in a low, almost tremulous voice.

'I don't know, my love,' she said, leaning forward and brushing his lips with her own, 'but it will seem less terrible in the morning.'

'God grant that you are not mistaken,' he muttered, holding her.

'God granted me a resourceful husband.'

'Then God grant he does not let you down,' Kite responded with bleak bitterness, 'for make no mistake but that we are hostages to an hostile fortune.'

Chapter Nine

A Matter of Suicide

The dawn was red and splendid; the scarlet ball of the sun
rose behind the line of distant hills and the nearer, harder
edges of domes, buildings and palm trees. The dark waters of
the harbour became limpid, then the colour of jade, and the
rampart of the castle white and pink, like some fantastical
confection. The noise of four bells, struck first on the *Artemis*,
was echoed by the other large Country ships while from the
dhows and pattamars rose the thin coils of smoke from the
cooking fires in their clay beds. Movements stirred the air.
Along the bund ox-carts began to move, carriers bore their
burdens and the bright splash of a dress told where a woman
took her produce to market. On board the ships men could be
seen at their daily chores and already fishing mashwas were
on their way to sea, their brown-skinned crews laughing as
they passed Kite pacing his lonely vigil on *Spitfire*'s deck.

In the daylight he found what he was looking for: the trail
of blood that went forward and over the rail where the dacoits
left ashore had returned for 'their pay' and the extermination
of Hooker. While he knew Rose had not told him everything,
it was curious that they had not despatched her too. And,
come to think of it, odd that they had left Kite himself
alone, or, worse still, had not set fire to the schooner. Then
it occurred to him that perhaps they had intended all these
things, only to take alarm when Rose had screamed. It was
unlikely, he concluded, that he would ever comprehend the
motives of men with whom he had nothing in common and

to whom he had paid scant attention. Perhaps his ignorance was reprehensible, if so it was a sin of omission and with all the preoccupations of command he felt acquitted of guilt. Moreover, since Hooker had hoodwinked him, he felt scant obligation to pursue justice, even supposing he knew how to go about the matter. As for recovering Hooker's fortune, he had not the slightest inkling of where to start. He would, he decided, call himself upon Lieutenant Cavanagh, and then pay the Honourable East India Company's factor a visit, but beyond that, what *could* he do?

He thought he possessed sufficient bills of exchange to refit and resupply *Spitfire* and thereafter he had better return to the Atlantic and, under the terms of his letter of marque and reprisal, he would descend upon the American coast and take a few prizes. That at least was better than rotting like Hooker, and the thought stirred him to action. There was the ship's company to be called and a deal of work to be done before William Kite could lie down and rest.

He waited upon Lieutenant Anthony Cavanagh while the commander of the *Artemis* was breaking his fast.

'Ah, Captain, pray take a seat and join me in a cup of coffee. We enjoy the finest Mocha, don't y'know,' said Cavanagh smiling and indicating one of two empty seats at his table. Two Indian servants moved silently about the cabin, ministering to Cavanagh's trivial wants with a solicitude that Kite found unnerving but which Cavanagh barely regarded, such was the extent of his indiscretion before them.

'Your mate came aboard rather late last night,' Cavanagh said, smiling and dabbing his mouth as one of his servants removed the plate of half-consumed fish kedgeree.

'Yes, Lieutenant, I regret the necessity to inform you, but I am not versed in the Indian trade and had hoped that you might advise me,' Kite looked pointedly at the Indian servants, 'of what, under the circumstances, I should do.'

Cavanagh looked amused. 'Why nothing, Captain Kite, as I told your mate. The man Hooker . . .' He paused, seeing the alarm registered on Kite's face and his eyes glancing at the Indians. 'Oh, please don't worry about my boys, they know all about whatever happens long before I do. I dare say they can tell you things about your Hooker Sahib that would surprise you, eh, Vikram?' And here Cavanagh rolled his head and addressed a few words in Hindustani to the servant who was just then setting a cup and saucer before Kite, at which point the second appeared with a silver coffee pot. 'But I will ask them to go, if it pleases you, though they will listen on the far side of the door.' And Cavanagh gave some instructions at which, having served Kite with his coffee, the two so-called 'boys' disappeared.

'I do not know the degree to which you are acquainted with Josiah Hooker, Captain, but we thought he had gone home. He is well known in Madras and even better known in Calcutta, where he fought a duel and shot a rather pleasant young fellow named O'Neil, a captain of sepoys who expressed some silly opinion about the woman Hooker passes off as his wife. Normally, of course, we would hear little of such matters here in Bombay, but word reached us that Hooker, having had the effrontery to suggest he might invest in an India voyage, had met rejection from the Company's Directors in London. It is unheard of for a nabob to return once he has made his fortune, so I have no idea what deterred him from settling in England unless he had made as many enemies there as it appears he had in Calcutta. It was the hottest news that came out aboard the *Walmer Castle* and word was passed along the coast. O'Neil survived the ball he took in his shoulder and is thirsting for revenge.'

'I see,' Kite replied, digesting this news. There had been ample time for the story to be transmitted from Leadenhall Street since he and Hooker had had their ill-fated encounter there all those months ago. Cavanagh seemed amused by the way events turned out and, sensing this, Kite remarked with a complementary levity, 'Then it is as well I am rid of him.'

'Absolutely, my dear fellow.' Cavanagh paused, then pointedly asked, 'So what brings you out here?'

'Oh,' Kite said as lightly as he could manage, 'I was the

owner of several ships, all of which were taken by American privateers. All I had left was the *Spitfire*, a former slaver and a privateer herself. Hooker engaged me to carry him out here and, well . . .'

'Here you are, eh?' Cavanagh broke in with a pleasant smile. 'I hope he paid you before he had his throat slit.'

'Tell me,' Kite asked as though abstracted and avoiding Cavanagh's implied question, 'what was the cause of the duel with O'Neil? Something about Hooker's wife, did you say?'

'Oh, the usual nonsense about miscegenation. I dare say O'Neil himself was drunk or he is an epicure and likes to play the buggeranto. There is a prejudice among some of the military officers against marrying native women. They like to annoy the established traders, almost all of whom have native wives. The silly infection came out here with the first of the King's officers sent with their troops to bolster the Company's sepoy regiments. The causes of such squabbles are of less consequence than the manner in which they touch a gentleman's honour. Now, had O'Neil been a sea-officer like myself, or indeed you, my dear Captain, he would not have had the time to trouble himself over with whom or with what Hooker slept . . . Tell me, they say he was a big man, is that true?'

'Indeed it is, Mr Cavanagh. He is, or was, an immense fellow.'

'God help you if he starts to putrefy. He will stink within hours! Do you take him to sea and bury him without more ado.'

Kite resisted the temptation to complain Hooker stank when alive and contented himself with an expression of gratitude.

'Well, thank you for your advice and for your excellent Mocha,' Kite said rising. He was glad of the coffee, for it drove some of the fatigue from him. 'But I feel I should report the circumstance of his death to some authority ashore.'

'I can report it, if you wish . . .' Cavanagh offered with an air of palpable reluctance.

'I am obliged to you, but I shall feel at ease when I have

acquainted the Company factor with whom Hooker spoke yesterday of his death.'

'Very well.' Cavanagh stood and held out his hand. Then with a smile he added, 'The head of the Company's factory here in Bombay is titled the president, Captain Kite.'

'I'm obliged to you, sir,' responded Kite taking his departure. In the boat he ordered her headed for the castle.

The pink and white confection appeared less lovely at close quarters. The white stone and stucco work had a shoddy finish, as though built in a hurry and seamed with cracks. Two sepoy sentinels, one each side of the crenellated entrance, stood guard but made no attempt to bar Kite's entrance. He wore the blue broadcloth coat and black tricorne hat traditionally adopted by merchant masters. Though highly unsuitable to the climate it identified him as British and therefore free to enter the Company's fortified headquarters at Bombay. Inside two men in similar garb stood in the shade of the walls. Kite interrupted their conversation and they indicated the entrance door that led to the president's office. He was passed by a file of sepoys under a corporal as he made his way towards it.

Outside a punkah-wallah sat patiently at his rope and it was only ten minutes later, when Kite was shown into the factor's room, that the regular swaying of the fan of the air-wafting punkah explained the fellow's labour. The president's room was light and airy, cooled by the punkah and situated on the upper ramparts of the castle where the sea breeze came in over a terrace that commanded a splendid view of the harbour. The white-coated servant who ushered him in announced Kite's name and the white-haired president looked up and introduced himself.

'Joseph Cranbrooke at your service, Captain Kite.' The two men shook hands and Cranbrooke introduced a younger man, clearly one of the Company's clerks, or writers as he afterwards learned they were called in the East. The younger man gathered up some papers from the president's desk and withdrew.

'It is good of you to see me, sir,' Kite began as the door

closed and he was alone with Cranbrooke. 'And I am sorry to intrude upon your time and patience, but I understand that my principal, Mr Hooker, waited upon you yesterday.'

'He did, Captain Kite, and I have to confess that his visit was a surprise. I do not know how long you have been associated with Mr Hooker, but you may not be aware that he has earned something of a somewhat disreputable reputation in India.'

'I have only today been acquainted of the fact, sir. Lieutenant Cavanagh of the *Artemis* was kind enough to appraise me. Hooker and I entered into an agreement that I should bring him back out to India only a few months ago. I am entirely ignorant of his history.'

'Well, I understand it matters little now, Captain, since Lieutenant Cavanagh sent word this morning that he, Hooker that is, has met with a fatal accident.'

'That is a somewhat euphemistic assessment, if you will forgive the presumption. In fact he was murdered . . .'

'Who by, Captain Kite?'

'By the dacoit bodyguard he employed.'

'Who looted him of his fortune, I assume, and have now vanished.'

'I have no idea whether they have vanished, sir, but they are certainly not to be found on board my vessel. I rather thought that you would take the view that the murder of one British merchant might prejudice the lives of others in Bombay.'

The president, a pleasant featured man with a sallow, rather unhealthy complexion, smiled thinly. 'Why so, Captain? We are not conquerors, merely traders, and we enrich the countryside by our presence. How would the native princes export the produce of their fields, their cotton and so forth, without the Company? Look what we have created here in Bombay, with its regulated harbour, its dry docks and its shipyards! Why, there are native people here that would starve were they left to their own subsistence and there are native people here whose wealth and state proves the benevolence of the Company's remit. Hooker's dacoits will vanish into thin air, for he was a man who made enemies both amongst the natives and among his own kind. You must have heard the story about O'Neil, but the captain of sepoys is not the only man to nurse a grudge against Hooker. 'Twas as well you came here to Bombay and did not sail direct to the Hooghli. I was myself in Calcutta until a year ago and can tell you that there are at least three trading houses in that busy city who found dealing with Hooker a less than profitable business.' The factor broke off and smiled again. 'So you see, Captain, no one is going to weep for Josiah Hooker.'

'Cavanagh told me to put to sea and bury him,' Kite said flatly. His sleepless night was catching up with him and he felt incapable of thought. If he had come ashore seeking a resolution to his own personal crisis he could not expect this kindly but disinterested gentleman to help him.

'That was sound advice, Captain,' Cranbrooke continued, 'and if you wish to register his demise with the authorities, I can advise you that a deposition over your signature attesting to the fact that Hooker expired by his own hand would find a ready lodgement with the governor. Since there is no estate . . .'

'There *is* a widow, sir,' Kite put in, troubled, despite his exhaustion by the notion of perjuring himself.

'Ah yes. So she is with you too, is she? A Hindu woman, I recall. She too caused some problems. What was she called? Rosemary or something *anglicé?*'

'I know her only as Rose, sir, and yes, she is aboard my schooner.'

'Well, sir, she is your problem. I should land her before you leave.'

'She would be destitute, sir,' Kite protested, disturbed by the president's callousness, 'unless you would subscribe to her subsistence.'

Cranbrooke appeared to ignore Kite's humanitarian plea. 'She should be dead,' he remarked obliquely, 'but if chivalry is your forte, Captain Kite, then you must decide the matter for yourself. I would, however, be obliged if you would take the late Mr Hooker to sea and bury him there and thus avoid us the tedious necessity of our having to deal with a suicide here in Bombay.'

135

Cranbrooke held out his hand in dismissal. Kite took it, feeling the weight of fatigue about to overwhelm him. He realized that the heat, despite the waving punkah, combined with the weight of his broadcloth coat and his sleepless night, rendered him almost comatose. He was vaguely aware that he had called at the castle to ask something, but he could no longer recall it and he no longer cared very much. He had much to think about and he needed to rest.

'Forgive me, sir,' he mumbled, 'I did not sleep last night . . .'

Cranbrooke smiled. 'Call upon me again, Captain Kite, when you have attended to the suicide. We must discuss your presence here in Bombay.'

He watched Kite leave the room. 'You are no longer a young man, Captain Kite,' the president murmured, 'and I wonder what will become of you, for you are untutored in our ways.'

It was late morning when the boat pulled him back out to the schooner. Harper helped him over the rail and gave him some good news. 'We got our boat back, Cap'n, the one the dacoits stole. It was found drifting off the dockyard and a sea-cunny from the *Artemis* brought it back to us.'

'A *what*?' mumbled Kite irritably.

'A sea-cunny, a quartermaster,' Harper explained.

'Then say a festering quartermaster, damn it!'

'But he was Indian, Cap'n, and I thought . . .'

'Did you think to sew Hooker up in a hammock?'

'All done, sir, and none too soon. He's still below but we've scrubbed the cabin out and . . . Are you all right, Cap'n Kite?'

Kite had reached the after companionway and leaned upon it, almost fearful of attempting a descent into the schooner's dark interior.

'Zachariah, can you get the vessel under weigh and take her out to sea? I must get some sleep.'

'William? Is that you back at last? I have been so worried,

my dear.' Sarah ran up the ladder and Kite recalled little more as she and Harper helped him below. He was vaguely aware of the swells lifting the *Spitfire*'s hull as Harper took her out to sea and her white wake cut through the brilliant blue of the Arabian Sea, mingling with the white wave caps of the moderated monsoon wind.

Kite woke after eight hours, stirring as Sarah gently shook him. 'My dear,' she was saying as he rose through a fog of semi-consciousness, 'Zachariah thinks we have gone far enough to sea and the wind is freshening. He thinks we must dispose of Josiah's body soon.'

Kite grunted, the events of the previous hours returning to him in distasteful recollection. 'Yes, yes, of course. Give me a moment . . . Is that Maggie? Maggie, do you tell Mr Harper to heave to and muster the hands. I shall be up directly.'

'Very well, sir.' Maggie bobbed a curtsy and the sight of her doing so as *Spitfire* drove her bow into a wave brought a smile to Kite's face. Perhaps things were not so bad; all he had to do was to adapt as Maggie had. He reached for his breeches and turned to Sarah. 'Does Rose know what we are about to do?'

Sarah nodded. 'She is very distraught, William, especially now that we are going to bury Josiah. There is something troubling her deeply, more deeply than mere grief or even fear for the future, for I have assured her that we shall not abandon her.'

Kite was surprised at this assurance, but it was no time for a quarrel with his wife, particularly as he knew he himself could never abandon the unfortunate woman; but the thought drove another from his mind, a slight feeling of unease that dogged him without him being able to nail it down. He dismissed the anxiety in his eagerness to get the present distasteful task over and done with.

The Order of Service for burial at sea according to the Anglican rite is a brief and seamanlike affair. To their credit the hands turned up in their best rig, some sporting the ribboned straw hats and bell-bottomed trousers of the true nautical dandy. Kite assumed that their good behaviour was not without motives of self-interest, which he guessed were associated with the desire for shore leave when they returned to Bombay. Looking at them over the prayer book, Kite thought that this unabashed currying of favour might be translated to his own advantage if he were shrewd enough to engineer matters properly. But he was pleased with the turnout. Even Jack Bow, whom he had hardly taken any notice of for weeks, was wearing clean clothes, though they were shabby and the lad had outgrown them. The sight reproached him: he ought to see the youth better clad. Maggie too was in her best and stood behind Sarah, who had donned a dark dress and looked inexpressibly lovely with her hair blowing about her face. But Rose was missing, the only exotic on deck being the turbaned Rahman, who seemed keen to pay his own respect at the strange ceremonial.

Kite read the final words and waited for Harper's burial party to heave Hooker's body over the side. The bulk of the corpse lay beneath the fluttering red ensign and then slid off the boards and fell into the sea with a loud splash. Kite stood for a moment, then closed the prayer book with a snap.

'Very well, Mr Harper, let draw the foresheets, then put up the helm and run her off before the wind.'

'Aye, aye, sir.'

As the crowd broke up on the moving deck Sarah approached him with a sad smile on her face. 'I think you should have been a priest, my dear, you read that beautifully.'

'I did? Well, perhaps I would have made a better success of the priesthood than I have of this venture.'

Standing close Sarah put her finger up to his lips. 'Shhh, my darling, you are a man of resource, you will find a way.'

'I am thinking of returning to the American coast,' he said unenthusiastically, 'it is the only place I can think of that will perhaps yield a prize. There are no enemy ships hereabouts to plunder.'

'So we turn privateer again?'

Kite shrugged. 'I see no other possibility.' But even as he spoke the words he dissembled. There was the germ of an idea at the back of his mind but he had no idea whether it stood the slightest chance of getting off the ground, let alone succeeding. At the moment it consisted of no more than a jumbled succession of vague notions and he needed advice, charts, and a, what was it Harper had called the native mariner? A sea-cunny?

'Damned funny word,' he murmured unconsciously.

'What is?'

'Eh?'

'You said, "damned funny word",' Sarah said curiously.

'Did I?' Kite shook his head. 'I am still rather dopey from lack of sleep, Sarah. I am not certain what I am saying.'

'Well, you bade Josiah farewell very eloquently.'

'And what of Josiah's widow?'

'Ah, *there* is a mystery. We can look after her, can we not?'

'I suppose we shall have to.'

'She has a little money of her own, but not a great deal.'

'Much like ourselves, then,' Kite said grimly catching hold of Sarah as she staggered on the canting deck. Harper had brought the schooner round and she was running before a quartering breeze, scending wildly in the tumbling following sea as she headed back for Bombay.

'I'll go below,' Sarah said and Kite watched her move swiftly across the deck, smile at Harper and the helmsman, and then disappear down the companionway. He followed her and stopped beside the mate.

'I'll take the deck, Zachariah,' he said, staring into the compass bowl set in the binnacle.

'It's all right, Cap'n, I'm fine, you could do with some more sleep I dare say.'

'I dare say I could, Zachariah, but I've a deal of thinking to do and I'll walk the deck to do it. Do you get some rest yourself, thank you.'

'Very well, sir, if you insist.' Harper shook his ugly head

as though in obedient disagreement with his commander, and the gesture brought a smile to Kite's face. Silently he thanked Providence for sending him Zachariah Harper. He only wished he could repay the American's loyalty with some material success. Kite caught Harper's eye and motioned the mate to withdraw a little towards the lee rail, out of earshot of the helmsman.

'By the by, Zachariah,' he said in a lower tone, 'we are to assume that Hooker cut his own throat.'

'We are, Cap'n?' Harper raised his eyebrows in surprise.

Kite nodded. 'Yes, we are, let it be known to McClusky, Maggie and the hands that that is what happened. All our other suspicions are unproven and are therefore groundless.'

'Groundless, d'you say, Cap'n Kite? Well, that's mighty odd.'

'Odd or not, Zachariah, it's important that we close the matter as a suicide.'

'But how do we explain the theft of Hooker's fortune, sir?'

Kite sighed and rubbed his chin. His palm rasped on the stubble and it occurred to him that, eloquent or not, he had conducted Hooker's funeral with an unseemly beard gracing his own chops. 'Well, Zachariah, we don't.'

'But it's common knowledge . . .'

'Yes, I had thought otherwise, but clearly we must establish the fiction that nothing was taken.'

'And how in Hades can we do that?' Harper asked in astonishment.

Kite looked at Harper's incredulous face with a smile. 'That's what I need to think about.'

'Well, good luck to ye, Cap'n, I'm sure glad that it's you that have to do it and not yours truly. Damned if I'd know where to start.'

'Damned if I do, Zachariah, but we're a long way from home and even there we've precious few friends.'

'Desperate measures, then, sir.' Harper's ugly face grew solemn.

'Aye, but are you with me, Zachariah?'

'Well, Cap'n, I've precious little choice and you've already brought me to the ends of the earth.'

Their eyes met and they both smiled. Then Harper turned away and, watching him follow Sarah down the companion-way, Kite reflected on the curious differences that exist in the friendships between men and women.

Chapter Ten

The Imperfect Wife

K ite was far from feeling as confident as he thought Harper considered him to be. There had been that familiar, knowing look in the mate's eyes, the look that signalled that he guessed his commander was cooking something up. Although Kite had been nursing an idea of his own even before Hooker's death, he had not the faintest idea of how to promote it without Hooker's intimate commercial knowledge. Now the scheme seemed remote, but irritatingly enough, now that he had to give his full attention to it, he was distracted by something else. Moreover, upon this distraction was piled another, for it occurred to him that the intrusion was but a means by which his tired brain refused to give its full attention to the primary problem. And yet was this mental diversion truly a distraction? Or should he consider this manifestation as a subconscious prompting to deal with first things first? Despite his long-held reservations about Hooker, had not the revelations about him materially altered Kite's situation? And perhaps that quick, half-forgotten aside of President Cranbrooke about Rose preyed upon his mind for entirely sensible reasons. She was, after all, the imperfect Hooker's legacy to him and he had to resolve her status, explore the reality of her own situation insofar as it might still affect him, before he could right his own.

Suddenly resolute, he passed word for McClusky and when the quondam clerk reported aft Kite ordered, 'Do you turn yourself into a sea-officer proper, Mr McClusky, and watch the con for me while I go below for a few moments. East-sou'-east is the course.'

'East-south-east, sir. Aye, aye, sir.' McClusky swallowed and stared at the compass as the card swung gently then Kite looked up and caught the helmsman's eye.

'And you can keep an eye on Mr McClusky, Pollard,' he said with a smile. The remark disarmed Pollard's resentment at McClusky's rapid promotion and he too smiled.

'Aye, aye, sir.'

Down below, in the tiny lobby from which the cabin doors opened, he hesitated. Harper's tiny box led off forward, the pantry lay to one side and the after door led directly into his own portion of the after cabin. Access to the partitioned half in which the Hookers had been accommodated was through his own and he did not wish to alert Sarah to what he was about to do in case she dissuaded him out of compassion for the bereaved Rose.

Slowly he turned the door handle and eased it open. Sarah was reading and he stepped inside, his finger to his lips as, startled, she looked up.

'Oh, my word, what . . . ?' Then she fell silent as Kite tiptoed across the cabin, changing his mind as he did so.

Bending to Sarah's ear he whispered, 'My dear, you may not agree with what I am about to do, but it is essential that we establish more details about Hooker. Unfortunately I learned a great deal from the chief factor that was not to Hooker's credit and I am now anxious about Rose. You may come with me or remain here, but I am determined to confront the woman.' With his hands on the arms of her chair Kite drew back and waited for Sarah's response.

For a moment she considered what he had said and then she nodded. Lowering her book she said, 'I'll come with you.' Kite straightened up under the deck beams as Sarah, still in the unfamiliar dress, rose with a rustle of silk, then he led her to the interconnecting door.

Rose Hooker lay on the palliasse, staring at the intruders, yet she made no other move and Kite was reminded of the inert form he had first seen long months ago in that filthy London tenement.

'Rose, my dear, we have buried Josiah according to the sea ritual of his Established Church and now I regret to say there are some matters which we must discuss, chief among which is your future.'

'Do not be too brutal, William,' Sarah whispered in his ear, but Kite knew of no other way other than to come directly to the point.

'Now unfortunately I have learned a good deal about your husband, Rose, and I know of the duel with O'Neil and other matters touching affairs at Calcutta.' Kite paused as Rose drew herself up into a squatting position equivalent to a European sitting upright in a chair, evidence that she was receiving this information in a formal sense. Seeing the wary hostility kindling in her eyes, Kite smiled kindly.

'Now, Rose, please rest assured that you yourself are among friends and that we shall not abandon you and you may stay with us if that is your wish . . .' Kite paused and Sarah smiled and reached forward and touched the Indian woman's bare forearm.

'What is it you have heard about me?' she asked in a low voice.

'That you should not be alive,' Kite said quickly, seeking to disarm the woman, but he was quite unprepared for the wail of naked anguish that sprang like a demonic spirit from the widow's throat, nor for his own wife's cry of protest at the unfeeling brutality of his remark. Rose was on her feet and had, with an abrupt gesture, drawn a knife from the folds of her sari. Her left hand wrenched at the silk about her until it tore to expose her left breast. She pressed the point of the knife so hard against the soft flesh that it drew blood.

'Stop!' shrieked Sarah but Rose backed away, her lustrous dark eyes shining with a silent exhortation for them to do nothing.

'Who told you that I should be dead?' she gasped. 'Who told you that?'

'The chief factor – the Company's president,' Kite said, his heart beating with the emotion of the moment.

'What are you going to do?' Rose asked, her breasts heaving with emotion. 'You promise me friendship like he did and then you cast me off . . .'

'No, Rose! No one here is casting you off. All that I wish to know is why did Mr Cranbrooke say—'

'Cranbrooke? Ah, so, I recall him at Calcutta.'

'He knew all about Josiah . . .'

'He knows *nothing* about Josiah,' Rose said vehemently.

'He spoke of Josiah's reputation among the merchants,' Kite pressed patiently, 'and I need to know more about you for fear that what I do not know compromises me in my attempt to . . . to . . .' Kite was lost for words, but Rose was not listening to any self-motivated explanation.

'You see,' she cried, 'you need to know more about me and when you know it, you will not protect me.'

'Rose,' Sarah broke in, her voice quiet and reasonable, 'put down that knife, please, my dear.' Sarah paused and was rewarded by Rose slowly lowering her hand. Beside her Kite expelled his breath as Sarah resumed her coaxing. 'All William wishes to know is whether or not to pursue a voyage of gain upon the Malabar coast or to abandon everything here and return to England. We are all lost if he makes the wrong decision, for there is great risk in returning without any profit and, in having acceded to your husband's wishes, you, as his widow, are under some obligation to us.'

Rose's eyes closed for a moment and then, when she looked at them again they were bright with tears. 'Mr Cranbrooke is right: I should be dead. It is a matter of shame that I am not, but Josiah bore me off before I could be burned with my husband.' She paused, but neither Kite nor Sarah understood the allusion nor thought to ask for any explanation. Sensing this, Rose went on, 'It is expected of a Hindu wife to accompany her dead husband into the afterlife. I was to be a *sati*, a true and perfect wife, bound to my husband in death as I had been in life, but Josiah had conceived a passion for me. It is true, I was not

145

in love with my husband for he was older than myself and it was an arrangement of my parents. Nevertheless, I should not have listened to Josiah and his honeyed words . . .'

'He took you from your funeral pyre?' Sarah's tone was incredulous.

Rose nodded. 'And in doing so burned himself so that I was bound to him too.' Rose hung her head again and her body was wracked by sobs. 'I lost caste and gained . . . a new husband . . .'

Kite was appalled, for it was clear that if Rose had not wished to marry the man contracted as husband by her parents, she had little liking for the gross and obese Englishman either. For her part, Sarah was contemplating the barbarity of the Hindu rite of suttee with equal disgust.

'Poor Rose . . .'

'No! Please, that was *his* name for me,' she protested and Kite sensed Josiah's romantic but predictable imagery. 'It is not my own name!' the distraught Rose continued. 'While I was bound to him I endured it: but no longer!' Again she raised the knife, but Kite took two strides towards her, grabbed her wrist and twisted it. The knife dropped to the deck and he stamped his foot upon it. She fell into his arms and he supported her as she fainted. Her voluptuous body was supple and he caught the scent of her as, in obedience to Sarah, he laid her down upon the palliasse in a susurration of silk and the faint jangling of her many bracelets. Rising, he looked down at Rose with a sharply unexpected pang of exquisite and adulterous desire as Sarah knelt and slapped Rose's cheeks to bring her round. Guiltily he knelt beside his wife and, as Rose's eyes fluttered open, asked in his kindest tone, 'What *is* your name, my dear?'

'Yes, tell us,' said Sarah almost as moved as Kite himself at the strange, pervasive intimacy of this moment.

For a moment Rose looked from one to another of them and then she held up her hands, and with a complementary spontaneous impulse both Sarah and Kite each clasped one. 'If you are my true friends, you may call me Nisha.'

'Nisha.' They both breathed the word and agreed it suited

her far, far better than Rose. Slowly Kite relinquished Nisha's hand and got to his feet. 'If you are so far fallen from grace, Nisha, could I tempt you with the smallest glass of wine, that we might put this ugly moment behind us all?'

Slowly Nisha nodded. 'But only a small one . . .'

'Of course.' As Kite withdrew into the adjacent cabin Sarah helped Nisha into a sitting position. As she did so the Indian woman reached up, put her arm round Sarah's neck and drew her face down to her own. 'I was not a perfect wife, Sarah, but I shall be a perfect friend,' and with that she kissed Sarah upon her lips so that as Kite returned with the tray of glasses his wife was flushed with embarrassment and pleasure as she still held onto Nisha's hand.

They drank the wine and under its mellowing they all acknowledged a change in their relationship. Nisha slowly discarded the guilt she had felt instead of grief at Hooker's murder and which had mixed inextricably with apprehension over her future. Under the unaccustomed influence of the wine she melted in the warmth of her benefactors' friendship.

'It is a great blasphemy to say so,' she said, 'but we three must be together much like the *Trimurti*, the Hindu Trinity. There is you, Sarah, who is like Vishnu the Preserver, and you, William, you are like Shiva the Destroyer from whom all regeneration must come and to whom we look for our new life . . .'

'And you, Nisha, to whom do you liken yourself?' Sarah asked, fascinated by this exhibition of a strange religion.

Nisha shook her head, as though regretting what she suddenly now considered a monstrous, wine-induced blasphemy. 'No, it is too much of a presumption for I have lost caste and must not mention such things.'

'Then you may tell us what is the third deity in your Trinity, surely?' said Kite, smiling and warming to the shift of mood within the woman and acknowledging the seed of attraction planted in himself.

'Well,' said Nisha, lowering her eyes, 'in addition to Vishnu and Shiva, there is Brahma, the Creator . . .'

'Ahhh, I see . . .' grinned Kite, 'and you could help us, could you not, Nisha?' he asked, adopting her real name with as much ease as had Sarah.

'Of course. I can tell you whether the Topass wishes to cheat you with his interpreting,' she said with a laugh.

'Ah, that is true,' said Sarah.

'And I may also be of assistance when you decide what to do, William,' Nisha added, meeting Kite's smile with a new happiness in her expression that seemed to add a strange beauty to her features so that the transformation from Rose to Nisha was given an especial significance.

Inconsequentially insinuating its way into his mind came a disturbing thought as he wondered whether his own first wife had ever resented the Latin name he had given her. For a moment the thought troubled him. He sighed; he was too old to linger over the regrets his life sometimes seemed to consist of. He finished his wine and stood up, smiling.

'I must resume my watch. There is much to be considered and I shall speak of it later. Let us dine together when we anchor on our return to Bombay, and mark our new partnership.'

And with that Kite left the two women alone together.

On deck he was confronted by McClusky, who still stood betwixt the helmsman and the binnacle. 'Well, Mr McClusky, is all well?'

'Yes, Captain Kite, except for this fellow here,' McClusky nodded. Turning forward Kite saw the pallid face of Muckbul Ali Rahman, the Topass, who rolled his head miserably and made shy gestures of supplication.

'Captain Sahib, are we returning to Bombay? I have a wife . . .'

'Ah, I apologize, I had forgotten you are not a seaman.'

'But that is not true, sir!' Rahman protested. 'It is only that I have not been to sea on so small a ship as this one and I am wondering that you must be a man of greatness to come so far as from England in this schooner.'

Kite ignored the compliment. 'Then what sort of ships have you been to sea on, Topass Rahman? Surely the native boats . . .'

'No native boat, Sahib! No, no! I have been Number One sea-cunny to Captain Bury in the *Shah Jehangir*, a great ship, Kite Sahib. A man is not so sick on a big ship.' Rahman pulled a face but Kite was frowning, hardly daring to believe that he might have just stumbled on some good luck.

'You were quartermaster in an Indiaman?'

Rahman shook his head. 'Oh, no, Sahib, not an East Indiaman, but a Country-wallah. A ship of nine hundred tons, Sahib, as big as an Indiaman, but owned by Banajee and Buchanan Company of Bombay.'

The name Buchanan rang a bell in Kite's mind. 'And what can you tell me of this company, Topass?'

'He is very much changed, Sahib, Buchanan Sahib is dead and Bomanjee Pestonjee Banajee is grown old. He has no sons and is sad. Now he has only three ships.'

'And Captain Grindley commands one of them, does he not?' said Kite, recollecting the news of Buchanan's death, the reason for the needed capital and Buchanan's alleged lack of partners. Hooker had been lying over this last point, Kite realized, though it did not surprise him now.

'Captain Grindley is not the best master on the Malabar coast, Captain Kite, and Pestonjee Banajee is too much old man now.'

'Did you know that Mr Hooker was intending to go into business with this Mr Banajee?'

'Oh yes. Hooker Sahib told me so himself.'

'And what else did Mr Hooker tell you?'

Rahman shrugged. 'Only that I was to assist you with your schooner, Sahib.'

'And nothing more?'

'No, Sahib, not before he was dead.'

'And you are a good sea-cunny, are you, Topass?'

'The best, Sahib.'

'And now that Mr Hooker is dead, what shall you do?'

Rahman looked shocked and he clapped his hand to his breast. 'Sahib, I am bound to you until you have no requirement for my services as a topass.'

'What about your services as a sea-cunny?'

'Is that what the Sahib wishes?'

'Perhaps. And suppose the Sahib also wished his topass to speak Chinese?'

Rahman cocked his head on one side and then smiled. 'It can be done, Sahib.'

'Very well. We shall talk of this some more.'

Rahman bowed. 'As the Sahib wishes,' he said, withdrawing forward and a few minutes later hunkering down under the shadow of the starboard boat on its chocks amidships.

And at last, relieving McClusky, Kite fell to pacing the weather rail, his brain racing.

Chapter Eleven

The Interloper

'Captain Kite, may I introduce Captain Grindley of the *Carnatic*, Country ship,' President Cranbrooke said as Kite was shown into his office and two men rose to meet him.

Kite shook hands with a short, yet powerful man with a disagreeably petulant face caused by too protuberant a lower lip which jutted out and hung over a small, pointed chin. This lower lip, Kite observed with some distaste, was kept perpetually moist, even in the heat, by a frequent and nervous application of Grindley's tongue. The compulsive habit made Kite think of a lizard.

'Your servant, Captain Grindley,' he said, adding, 'if I intrude, gentlemen, please do not hesitate to tell me. I am content to wait.' Kite had no wish to be rushed in his interview with Cranbrooke and most certainly did not wish to discuss his proposition with a third party present.

'Please take a seat.' Reluctantly Kite took up the offer and the other two men subsided in the chairs they had vacated as he had entered. 'You are not intruding at all, Kite,' Cranbrooke ran on. 'As a matter of fact your late partner was the subject of our discussion.'

'He was not my partner, sir,' Kite dissembled gently, 'rather my employer, since I undertook the commission of bringing him hither in my own vessel.'

'Then he paid you?' Grindley said, speaking for the first time. Kite noticed his voice seemed cracked, as though he suffered some defect in the throat. Curiously, it added to the impression of Grindley being reptilian.

'He was to have paid me.'

'He was to have paid me too,' grumbled Grindley.

'He was to have invested in your voyage, surely, Captain Grindley. That is not quite the same.'

'Well, that may be so,' broke in Cranbrooke, 'but it seems our Mr Hooker has, not uncharacteristically, disappointed both of your expectations. Captain Grindley, having suffered the death of his principal, Mr Buchanan, must now risk his voyage under-capitalized, while you, Captain Kite, if you will excuse my presumption, would seem to be cast on an unfamiliar shore with a similar lack of funds.'

Kite nodded. 'That is so, sir,' he said warily, wondering where the conversation was leading, for there was little doubt Cranbrooke was a man speaking with a purpose. Instead, Kite sought to turn the conversation away from himself and, recollecting the Topass Rahman's allusion to a Mr Buchanan, saw one means by which he might do this and, at the same time, provoke Grindley into leaving.

'But as I understand it, and this may be a presumption on my part, Captain Grindley's vessel is co-owned by a certain Pestonjee Banajee.'

'How the devil d'you know that?' croaked Grindley.

'I am learning the ways of the East, sir,' Kite said with what he hoped was a disarming smile, 'from a topass whom Hooker engaged to assist me in the management of my schooner whilst we are in Bombay.'

'Muckbul Ali Rahman,' Cranbrooke said with a meaningful look at Grindley.

'Do you have anything against this man, sir?' Kite asked sharply. 'If so, I should be obliged if you would let me know.'

'No, not at all. It argues Hooker's shrewdness. Ali Rahman is one of the best interpreters in Bombay and is a man of proven intelligence and integrity. I believe he was formerly a first-rate sea-cunny, was he not, Grindley?'

Grindley nodded. 'Yes, he was acknowledged to be so among the Country commanders, certainly. He left sea-going employment some three or so years ago after contracting a marriage and has eked out a precarious existence as a topass ever since.'

'Well, let us come to the matter in hand, gentlemen,' Cranbrooke said, turning to Kite, who realized his allusion to the Indian part-owner of the *Carnatic* had been neatly side-stepped. 'As it happens, Captain Kite, and in view of your circumstances, Captain Grindley has made a suggestion that might appeal to you and kill two birds with a single sling-shot.'

'He has?' Kite showed his surprise.

'Your schooner, Captain,' Grindley broke in, 'looks a fine, fast craft. What was she built as? A privateer-cum-slaver? Ah, I thought so. Well, she would find a ready market and realize you some capital . . . No, please hear what I have to say before you comment. Now, having solved the problem of your immediate fiscal needs, I am, in addition to being under-capitalized, in need of one officer. It is not difficult to find a suitable man, but if you were to accept the post as chief officer and were to invest in our voyage, I would ensure that you undertake few of the duties of the rank since I shall continue to rely upon the officer presently in that post for our day-to-day routine. The benefits which will accrue to us both would be considerable if our voyage is a success, and I see no reason why it should not be if we sail without delay. There are rumours of reinforcements to the French squadron at the Île de France, but there is little risk if we take the current favourable monsoon across the Bay of Bengal, so what do you say, Captain Kite?'

After his initial protest at the notion of selling *Spitfire* and investing the surplus profit in the *Carnatic*'s voyage, Kite had held his peace, curious to hear what Grindley, and by implication Cranbrooke, had to propose. Now he was able to nonplus them both.

'It seems hardly fair to the officer presently incumbent,' he remarked casually. 'Besides, what provision have you made in this plan for my wife, Captain Grindley?'

'Your *wife*, sir? You have your wife on board?'

'Aye, and my wife's companion.'

'Good Lord,' Cranbrooke murmured.

'You have *two* women aboard that schooner of yours?' Grindley was astonished.

Kite inclined his head, an amused smile playing round the corner of his mouth as he rose to his feet. 'Thank you for your kind offer, gentlemen, but I was not intending to sell the *Spitfire*. You are right to remark upon her speed, however, and I was therefore mindful of loading a cargo of my own. Indeed, sir,' and Kite turned towards the president, 'I was hoping to solicit your advice in the matter.'

'Please remain a moment, Captain,' Cranbrooke insisted and Kite sat down again. 'And what were you intending to load, Captain Kite?' Grindley asked in a tone of low apprehension.

'Well, opium, of course.'

'Of course,' breathed Grindley, his face setting in a mask of suppressed fury.

'I see,' said Cranbrooke. 'Well, of course, there is little we can do to prevent you, Captain.'

'Prevent me? Why should you wish to prevent me?' Kite asked, genuinely surprised.

'A surplus of such a delicate commodity depresses the market, Captain,' Grindley said as though teaching a child.

'Surplus? I thought the market inexhaustible. Ah, but I should arrive before yourself, is that it?'

'It is entirely possible, if you do not wreck yourself in the China Seas.'

'But surely the capacity of my schooner poses no threat to a ship the size of the *Carnatic*. She must measure all of nine hundred tons . . .'

'She exceeds one thousand, but that is not the point, the point is we should consider you an interloper.'

'And what precisely is an interloper?' Kite asked, affecting total ignorance.

Grindley sighed. 'You see, Captain Kite, you know nothing of our ways on this coast.'

'An interloper, Captain Kite,' Cranbrooke explained, breaking in on Grindley's patronizing, 'is a trader who breaks the monopoly. As you know, the Honourable Company has the chartered right to trade between Great Britain and India. Here, in India, it licenses what we refer to as "the Country trade", carried out in locally built ships like Captain Grindley's *Carnatic* which are free to carry goods between India, Pegu, Sumatra, the Malay ports and China, but must perforce trans-ship any goods bound for Europe into the Company's Indiamen. There are those who, under the device of a flag other than their own, circumvent these regulations and, reprehensibly enough, many of these adventurers are Englishmen and Scotchmen . . .'

'They chiefly use the ensign of the Austrian Netherlands,' Grindley added didactically, his tongue flickering over his lower lip, 'and register their vessels in Ostend, which is no great distance from London.'

'Of that at least I am aware,' Kite snapped sarcastically.

'The point at issue, Captain Kite,' Cranbrooke continued smoothly, 'is that you would become an interloper and your ship and cargo subject to due process of law, should you fall foul of it. It was our intention to assist you out of your problem.'

It was on the tip of Kite's tongue to counter with the remark that, far from assisting him, he would have supplied them with a fast vessel capable of shifting a small but valuable cargo of opium, a fact which he guessed had the potential to enrich them far more than the price of the *Spitfire* herself.

Kite stood up. He could not decide which was the more repugnant to him, the prospect of sailing as Grindley's subordinate, or selling the loyal little *Spitfire*. However, he knew which would deprive him of any chance of regaining his fortune. 'Gentlemen, there seems little point in continuing this discussion. My schooner is not on the market. It appears

that Captain Grindley and I are about to become competitors.'
Kite bowed. 'Your servant, gentlemen.'

Out in the sun Kite felt the sweat crawl down his skin
under his heavy clothes. He felt strangely exhilarated after this
unexpected encounter. The sense of being flung back upon his
own resources was at once a challenge and a profound concern,
but the expression upon the face of the odious Grindley
somehow elevated his mood. Now he almost laughed aloud
at the notion of serving under the man and yet Grindley's
reaction to the news that he, Kite, was contemplating loading a
cargo of opium was encouraging. The fact that it had unsettled
Grindley at least underlined the basic merit of the idea insofar
as recouping his own lost fortune was concerned. If he could
carry Rahman off to sea again and find himself some decent
charts of the Malacca Strait and South China Sea, he thought
that he might not return to England empty-handed.

In this buoyant mood Kite walked down to the landing place
and the waiting boat. His only real problem, a problem that he
had hoped Cranbrooke might out of charity have advised him
about, was how to discover a supplier of a cargo of opium.
However, it was understandable that Cranbrooke was not
in favour of interlopers. But Hooker in one of their many
conversations had indicated that no matter what restrictions
the East India Company placed upon trade, even their own
officials, such as the chief factor at Bombay, would willingly
indulge in any private commerce by which they gained. There
was, Hooker had assured him, ample scope under the principle
of the nod and the wink.

On board he broached the subject of a supplier of a shipment
of opium with Nisha, who advised him that while Cranbrooke
might well have helped, he should consult Rahman. So, that
afternoon, when the sun burned down on the green waters
of Bombay harbour, Kite summoned the topass aft to where
he lounged under the shade of the awning Harper had had
stretched over the main boom.

'Mr Rahman,' Kite began, uncertain how to address the
handsome Indian and yet wishing to assure the man that he

was offering him an alliance, 'I wish to load a consignment for China and I need a supercargo as well as a pilot for the China Sea, but more than this I need an agent through whom I might buy a cargo . . .'

'You are talking about opium, Sahib?'

'I am talking about opium, Mr Rahman.'

Rahman seemed to consider the matter for a moment and then asked, 'Kite Sahib, may I ask you a question?'

'Of course.'

'Did you know Hooker Sahib was intending to invest in Captain Grindley's ship, the *Carnatic*?'

Kite nodded. 'Yes, he told me that just before his death. I was introduced to Captain Grindley at the castle this morning. Now, might I ask you a question? Tell me, do you know why Grindley needs a backer when, although this Mr Buchanan is dead, I understand that his ship is also owned by a certain Pestonjee Banajee?'

'Ah, a famous Parsee, sir, and Captain Grindley is also an owner of the *Carnatic*. But Pestonjee Banajee holds only a small interest in the *Carnatic*, and anyway, he is an old man.' Rahman paused, cocked his head to one side in thought, then added, 'But he would be the man to find you a cargo of fine Malwa opium. If you will profit by my advice, Kite Sahib, you will call upon Pestonjee Banajee and, if you will permit me to come with you . . .'

'Of course.'

Rahman inclined his head in a gracious gesture of acceptance. 'Then I shall arrange the matter, Kite Sahib. Might I have the use of your longboat this afternoon after the sun is well past the zenith?'

Certainly, but Mr Rahman, are you prepared to accompany us to China? I would not have you think that I cannot pay you . . .'

'Give me five per centum of your gross profits, Kite Sahib. With that I shall be content.'

Kite met the Indian's eyes and held his gaze as he extended out his own hand. 'You must forgive my unfamiliarity with the customs of this coast, Mr Rahman. In my country we shake hands to seal an arrangement.'

'I have seen this often, Kite Sahib,' and Rahman took Kite's hand in a firm grasp.

'And you will not mind leaving your wife for a few months?'

Rahman smiled and rolled his head from side to side. 'Not for five per centum. Besides, my wife has a mother and has borne me many children, I shall not mind too much.'

And as they shook hands both men laughed together.

'May I have a word, Cap'n?'

'Zachariah,' Kite said looking up. He had been sitting on the deck, his back to the companionway, and must have dozed off in the heat. He brushed the flies off his face and crooked his right forearm over his brow as Harper's bulk loomed over him, dark against the brilliant blue of the sky. 'Of course. What is it?'

'It's the hands, Cap'n, they want paying.'

'You sound concerned; what is their mood?'

Harper shrugged. 'They could do with a run ashore.'

'Of course, and I shall pay them an advance this evening, but when I do so I shall remind them that we are about to depart upon a voyage that may yield us a handsome dividend. For the nonce, they may do what they please amid the stews of Bombay. I presume there are stews in Bombay, Zachariah?'

'So I'm given to understand, Cap'n, and the little nautch girls hereabouts are known for the extremity of their copulations.'

'Good heavens, Mr Harper,' Sarah broke in as she ascended the companionway behind Kite, 'in what way?'

'Well, ma'am, I don't rightly know how to . . .' Harper flushed at the unexpected interruption.

'Oh, don't be coy, Mr Harper, do enlarge.' Sarah was at her most charming and disarmingly improper.

Kite grinned at Harper's discomfiture. 'I believe they are excessively athletic, Sarah,' he said, turning back to Harper to add, 'Do you tell the hands that I'll pay them at sunset and the larboard watch can go ashore until dawn.'

'Thank you, Cap'n, I'll pass the word,' Harper said, turning to go forward.

'And what will you do yourself, Mr Harper, to tame the beast within *you*?'

'Sarah!' Kite protested as the colour mounted up Harper's bull-neck.

'Why, er, nothing, ma'am,' Harper said awkwardly.

'While my husband was hob-nobbing with the chief factor, or president, or whatever the worthy calls himself, I had cookie buy a pullet or two and we should be delighted if you would join us for supper tonight. Nisha needs a partner and I should not like my husband to too readily enjoy the company of two women. Come, will you say yes?'

Harper's ugly visage cracked in a wide grin. 'Why yes, of course, ma'am.'

'The matter is settled, then,' said Sarah and, as Harper resumed his progress forward with a jauntier stride, she winked at Kite. 'There is a match there, William,' Sarah whispered, 'for I am certain she is sweet on him.'

'Good heavens, Sarah, the fact that she could not tolerate her husband does not mean she is like a bitch on heat.'

'Ah, but she is,' Sarah hissed wickedly, 'and she is free of all constraint.' And with this assertion, Sarah ducked below, leaving Kite to a feeling of guilty disappointment.

Rahman reappeared before three hours had passed and requested that Kite accompany him immediately. Handing over the allocation of pay to McClusky, who had been assisting his master in the accounting, Kite donned his coat and hat and followed Rahman back into the boat. The oarsmen were obviously tired and Kite greeted them with the news that they would be paid on their return and that the larboard watch would be going ashore that night.

'But we're all in t'other watch, sir,' one man protested.

'Well, then,' Kite responded swiftly, 'your anticipation will make your liberty tomorrow night all the sweeter.'

And the laughter in the boat pleased Kite as the oarsmen bent to their task.

Pestonjee Banajee lived in considerable state, his fine house being fronted with a wide patio of black and pink marble on either side of which were laid out formal gardens on the English pattern of parterres. Two bearers waited on the old man, who sat, cross-legged and barefooted, upon a large cushion to receive his guests.

'You are welcome, Captain Kite,' said Banajee, waving Kite to a solitary French-made fauteil. His English was excellent, though his accent was thick, his words being spoken through a mouth devoid of teeth. His wizened face was shrewd, but not unkind, the dark eyes swimming, their whites brown with age. 'Your *dubash*,' and here Banajee indicated Rahman, 'is a good man and you may trust him. He tells me that you wish to load a consignment of opium for China.'

'That is so, sir,' Kite replied.

'I had expected a younger man, Captain Kite,' the old Parsee said with a faint smile increasing the wrinkles on his face.

'I had not expected to be a ship-master again, sir, but fortune plays tricks upon us.'

'You *owned* ships?'

'In Liverpool, yes, but the war with the Americans and the French has caused some of us to suffer grievously.'

'And are you seeking a freight or a cargo?' Beside him Rahman gave a low cough.

'It depends upon the price of the cargo.'

'You are a gambler, Captain?'

'No, sir, but I have only one chance. I must make the best of it; besides, I have Mr Rahman here to consider.'

Banajee transferred his attention momentarily to the standing topass. 'Oh? And what consideration is that?'

'He is to receive a percentage on the voyage.'

Banajee's face cracked into a wide grin. 'You are to be

160

congratulated, Muckbul Ali Rahman, to drive so hard a bargain. I hope, Captain, you gave him no more than two per centum . . .'

'I gave him five, sir,' said Kite, unembarrassed. 'I have need of his services as a pilot as well as interpreter.'

'Five per centum is a *partnership*, Captain Kite. I do not think you have the rapacity of most of your countrymen.'

Kite inclined his head. 'As you observed, sir, I am not a young man.'

Banajee seemed amused by this riposte. 'But age must confer wisdom if it is to have value,' he retorted, and turned again to Rahman to address a few words in Hindustani to the topass. Kite divined they were questions, for Rahman's responses were more complex. After a few moments of several such exchanges, they culminated in a longer statement from the Parsee, to which Rahman grunted his assent. Seemingly satisfied, Banajee returned to Kite.

'I have spoken with your *dubash*, Captain, on the subject of your cargo. I shall send you a sufficiency of best Malwa opium, bound and ready for shipment in chests. If you wish to purchase these, I shall offer them to you at seven hundred and fifty rupees a chest, that is to say that a ton of opium will require an outlay of eleven thousand, two hundred and fifty rupees. If you wish, I can advance you a loan on respondentia and also offer you an additional freight of tin and, should you have surplus space, a quantity of Gujerati cotton piece goods.'

Kite declined the loan, conferred briefly with Rahman on the rate of exchange and, after a moment's reflection, ordered five tons of opium. 'If I have the capacity, sir, I should be happy to load tin and cotton goods.'

Banajee nodded approvingly. 'You will do very well, Captain, especially if you arrive in the Pearl River before Captain Grindley.'

'But do you not have shares in the *Carnatic* yourself, sir?' Kite asked, puzzled.

Banajee gestured around him. 'What need have I of a few shares in one ship, Captain? They are of little importance to me now . . .' He smiled, implying more lay behind this disclaimer. 'The opium will be with you the day after tomorrow, Captain.'

It was clear the interview was at an end and Kite rose and bowed. 'I am indebted to you, sir.'

Banajee waved his right hand dismissively. 'Not at all, Captain, you are to pay, and it is you who will undertake the voyage.'

'But I am indebted to you for your kindness.'

'Thank you.' Kite was about to depart but Banajee held up his hand. 'By the way, I understand that Mr Hooker died by his own hand.'

'So it is assumed, sir,' Kite replied, looking directly into Banajee's eyes and wondering whether the old Parsee knew better or had had a hand in the affair.

'But one never knows the truth about so much, Captain.'

'Not all of it, certainly.'

'It is a pity you did not come out to India when we were both younger men.'

'I was in the West Indies and North America, sir.'

'Ah, America . . . It is far distant. I build ships and I own ships, but never have I wanted to sail in a ship, Captain.'

'You are very wise, sir.'

'Yes, I think you are right.' Banajee chuckled, adding, 'It is a better way of becoming rich.'

'It is generally more certain, sir, but is not always so when war intervenes.'

'As in your own case, no. But you have been unfortunate. It is time that Ahura Mazda smiled upon you. Good day, Captain Kite.'

'You made a great impression, Kite Sahib,' Rahman enthused as they made their way back towards the boat lying alongside the steps fronting the Parsee magnate's opulent dwelling.

'He is an extraordinary man. But tell me, who or what is Ahura Mazda, and what is a *dubash*?'

'Ahura Mazda is the supreme being, the Lord Wisdom of the Parsees, Kite Sahib, the followers of the path of Zarathustra.

Ahura Mazda is the creator of all that is good and is in perpetual conflict with Ahriman, the Lord of Evil. It is a creed peculiar to the Parsees, Kite Sahib, they are from far away and came here to Bombay many, many years ago.'

'And you are not a Parsee?'

Rahman shook his head. 'Oh, no! I am a Hindu.'

'And what is a *dubash*?'

'A man who possesses two tongues, Kite Sahib, like a topass but of greater skill.'

'Then you too are approved of, Mr Rahman, and you have done a good day's work.'

'We have done a good day's work together, Kite Sahib.'

'And we shall do many more, I hope.'

'I am hoping so too.'

'Then you shall go back to your wife tonight, and rejoin the ship when the cargo comes alongside the day after tomorrow.'

'And when I shall be wanting to go to sea again,' Rahman said with a smile, and both men were again laughing as they reached the boat.

Chapter Twelve

A Folio of Charts

K ite arrived back aboard *Spitfire* tired but modestly pleased with himself. In the after cabin Sarah was dressing and expressed her concern at his prolonged absence.

'I have given orders for supper,' she said reproachfully, 'but I had no idea where you had gone.'

Sluicing himself with water from the basin on its stand in the forward starboard corner of the cabin, Kite looked up at the reflection of his wife in the mirror on the bulkhead in front of him as the water ran down his face in a cool and revivifying stream. 'I apologize, my darling, but by the greatest good fortune, or perhaps under the benevolence of Ahura Mazda, I have secured a cargo which, if matters go well for us, will repay the outlay many times over.'

'You are to purchase a cargo of opium? And how much is the outlay?'

'Some fifty-six thousand, two hundred and fifty rupees for the opium, and I have agreed to ship also a quantity of tin and cotton piece goods, but these will be freighted and therefore only the opium has to be paid for.'

'A capital sum which you cannot offset with the freight rate for the tin and cotton goods?'

Kite shook his head. 'I am not sure, since, with the alterations to the vessel necessary to accommodate Hooker's entourage, I have no idea how much capacity we shall have. However, 'tis possible.'

'Then you speak of fifty-six thousand rupees as though it
were but pennies.'

'It amounts to little more than five thousand pounds at
the rate Rahman can secure for us, a little under a florin
per rupee.'

Sarah went white. 'But that is our *entire* capital, William,
every penny that we possess!'

'What else shall we do with it, my dear?' Kite replied,
unruffled. 'If we run a mere *five* tons of opium into China
we should double our investment at the very least. Rahman
takes a more optimistic view . . .' He paused and, having
dried his face, took Sarah in his arms. 'My darling, I tremble
at the thought of what this opportunity might offer. There are
rumours of a French squadron arriving in the Bay of Bengal,
such an event may increase the price in China.'

'You excite me, William,' Sarah breathed, kissing him, but
there was a cough and the steward wished to enter and complete
the laying of the table that he had suspended while his mistress
dressed. Kite, detaching himself from Sarah, waved him in and
turned to complete his own toilet.

The supper passed off well and by ten o'clock the company
was in mellow mood and went on deck to take the air while the
cabin table was cleared and the beds prepared. Harper had been
attentive to Nisha and she had glowed in his regard, so that Kite
sensed Sarah's assessment might have been correct. Certainly
Zachariah's appetites were aroused and on deck Sarah drew
Kite aside.

'We should leave them,' she whispered, 'give them the
opportunity of going below before us, if they so wish.'

'You would have them paired, then, would you?' Kite asked,
amused by his wife's intrigue.

'What harm is there in it?' she asked.

Kite shrugged. 'None, unless I am to bear the additional
burden of a bastard upon that of a widow.'

'William! You are outrageous. If I am not mistaken,

Nisha . . .' Sarah paused and then said, 'Do you not think how much nicer it is to call her that than "Rose"?'

'Indeed, but as you were saying,' Kite prompted, uneasy at references to Nisha's imposed name which brought Puella into his mind.

'If I am not mistaken,' Sarah continued, 'Nisha will know ways of avoiding impregnation.'

'Is this some Oriental skill?'

'Well, William,' said Sarah obliquely, suddenly darker in her mood, 'we have no children of our own.'

'No,' he agreed flatly.

Sarah looked forward. With half the schooner's company ashore, only a fraction of the watch remained on deck and they were hunkered down forward, out of sight. Then she looked aft. As she had hoped, Harper and Nisha were embracing. She turned to her husband, put her arms about him and thrust herself against him. 'Come, sir,' she whispered into his ear, 'the night is warm and lovely and I would have you take these heavy clothes from me.'

Kite felt the languor of the night air and the heavy, concupiscent pressure of Sarah's body against his own rising tumescence. 'They are going below, my darling. Let us follow them . . .'

As they entered their half of the bisected cabin the grunts of urgent coition were clearly audible through the flimsy bulkhead. Detaching herself with a giggle, Sarah tore at her stays and Kite undressed, blowing the lantern out and watching as his wife spread herself in the soft starlight that came in through the stern windows. A moment later he felt the moist comfort of Sarah surround his questing prick and then, as she arched her back and he bent to kiss the moving globes of her breasts, he drove home in a frenzy of passion from which they both fell back content.

In the darkness, as their hearts stilled, they became aware of a complementary quiet beyond the partition. Then, as they lay side by side and hand in hand, they heard a revival of passion. Sarah, propping herself on one elbow, her hair falling down over Kite's chest, looked down at him.

166

'You have left me alone too much lately, William. I understand your preoccupations, but it is not good that we should
be so distant.'

Kite sighed. 'It is difficult, Sarah. The schooner requires
my constant attention and I have only Harper to support me.
Perhaps, if I had another officer, it might be different, but I do
not see what I can do about that now. Perhaps you will have
to be patient a little longer. I am sorry,' he added as Sarah lay
back and stared at the pale rectangle of the deckhead above.
He could understand her annoyance, but it was unlike her to
be peevish. 'I am truly sorry,' he repeated, 'truly.'

Sarah sighed. 'I understand,' she said. There was a long
silence, then she added in a whisper as, next door, the sounds of
culminating and frantic passion rose, 'You see my dear, Nisha
and I have taken pleasure of one another.' But there was no
response from the man beside her. Kite was already asleep.

The opium arrived as promised and coincided with the return
of the starboard watch from their debauchery. 'Good God
Almighty,' Harper groaned, 'we shall have need of a physician
before a sennight is past.' Harper looked with unfeigned
disgust at the exhausted human wreckage that clambered
wearily over the rail from the cluster of bum-boats that
gathered around *Spitfire*'s sides. He was a man in love,
spiritually elevated and contemptuous of the grubby effects
of the lust of his shipmates. Moreover, his new intimacy with
Nisha had admitted him to his commander's counsels. It had
been impossible to disguise the fact that he had slept with the
Indian widow the morning following the supper, and Kite had
taken him to one side later that forenoon.

'Zachariah,' Kite said as the two men stood aft, their shirts
fluttering in the cool monsoon, and leaning back upon the
taffrail as they stared forward. The schooner's people had
been stood down from all but essential duties, the starboard
watch to sleep off their excesses, the larboard to prepare for
their own next foray ashore. As a consequence the upper deck
was a scene of men squatting down and washing, sewing

and generally making good their shore-going clothes. No one took any notice of the commander and mate as they chatted amicably aft.

'Zachariah, I would not have you misunderstand me and I have no objection to your liaison with the widow Hooker, but I must consider the situation. At the present time she inhabits a disproportionate amount of the after accommodation. It would not be good for discipline if your involvement was seen to be sanctioned by me and while I doubt you can keep it a secret from the people, I must not be seen to condone it or your privilege will be seen as overweening. Unkind though it may seem, do you take my point, Zachariah? Now is not the time for conspicuous self-indulgence.'

Harper nodded. 'I understand, Cap'n.'

'Moreover, there are only the two of us, notwithstanding McClusky's growing competence, and we are to undertake a perilous enough passage without charts or real knowledge beyond what Rahman can provide us with. I would not have you unduly distracted.'

'I understand all that, Cap'n, but the lady may have certain expectations.'

Kite grinned. 'I know you are able to satisfy the lady, Zachariah, you make enough noise about it!'

'I do? Good God, I never thought of it . . .' Harper blushed.

'I intend to knock down the bulkhead and to curtain off a corner for Nisha, who will otherwise join Sarah and myself. It will thwart your passion but may make it clearer to her that things must change, a change for which I will be to blame, not you. You may take your pleasure as you will, Sarah is sensitive enough to the matter not to embarrass you.'

'I'm obliged to you both,' Harper said wryly.

'And what the crew know they will assume is at my expense. It will keep the lid on the affair, but you may lose some respect if you are having what they desire but are denied.'

Harper laughed. 'Most of them will be pissing through colanders by the end of the month, mark my words.'

'Whores have their own means of protection, Zachariah,

they want the pox no more than their customers.'

'I hope you're right, Cap'n, but I'd not lay money on it, if I were you.'

'Well, we shall see. Now as to this opium . . .' And they fell to discussing the stowage of the chests of opium which was just then coming alongside in a round-sterned mashwa, on whose deck stood Muckbul Ali Rahman, a bundle beside him.

'Rahman's come to join us,' Kite remarked.

'Couldn't *he* keep a watch?' Harper asked suddenly.

Kite looked at the mate. 'That is a very practical notion, Zachariah,' he replied enthusiastically. 'He and McClusky could both stand a watch alongside us for a week or two, until we have confidence in them.'

'Aye, and if you have McClusky,' Harper added, 'you could stand down altogether, so that you were simply on call during his duty period. I'll have Rahman and soon tell you if he can handle the vessel.'

Kite took but a moment to make his decision. 'A capital idea, Zachariah, be so good as to put arrangements in train!'

Harper went forward as Rahman scrambled over the rail to dump his bundled chattels on deck before he came aft.

'I am reporting on board, Kite Sahib.'

'Very well, Mr Rahman, you are most welcome. Mr Harper, the mate, will acquaint you of your accommodation but first there is one other matter that troubles me.'

'What is that?'

'I have no charts of the Bay of Bengal, the Strait of Malacca or the China Sea.'

'Ah, it is *possible* that I could obtain for Kite Sahib good copies of Dalrymple's folios but, Kite Sahib,' Rahman said, rolling his head with an expression of great regret, 'these are expensive.'

'They are stolen?'

'Oh, not stolen, Sahib, they are *copied*.'

'But how accurately copied?'

'Very good copies, and also they are coming with tables of courses and distances, the establishment of the several ports and fixed positions of important places with up-to-date modifications by other Company officers like Commander Joseph Huddart.' Rahman paused. 'Kite Sahib will not be disappointed.'

'How much?'

Late that forenoon a smartly pulled gig approached in which a young writer from the castle leapt aboard, asking for the *Spitfire*'s commander. While he was waiting for Kite to come on deck he stared curiously about him and Kite, emerging from the companionway under its awning, formed the distinct impression that the young man was doing a little more than satisfy his curiosity.

'We mount twelve long guns, sir, if you are interested.' The writer turned with a start and flushed deeply, proving Kite's suspicion was not misplaced. 'Including a pair of six-pounder chase guns forward,' he added with a smile, 'though some are struck into the hold.'

'I . . . I was simply curious, sir, not being a sea officer myself.'

'Of course,' Kite said reasonably. 'And what, pray, can I do for you?'

'Oh, yes.' The young man was certainly rattled, Kite thought, amused at the other's discomfiture. 'I have this for you, Captain Kite. I was instructed to await your reply.'

Kite tore open the note. It was from President Cranbrooke. The chief factor requested the pleasure of Captain and Mrs Kite at the castle that evening.

'Hmm,' remarked Kite to Sarah after he had sent the writer off with an acceptance, 'I should very much like to have snubbed Cranbrooke on the pretext that we must sail immediately.'

'Oh, William . . . it will be most diverting and,' Sarah added as though inspired, 'it will give Zachariah and Nisha a little privacy.'

'Before that damned bulkhead comes down. Oh, you may have your own way. You have had little enough diversion in recent months, so I have accepted, though I suspect Cranbrooke only wishes to ogle you, my dear.'

'Then we should give him something to ogle,' Sarah said with a gleam in her eye.

Kite grunted. 'I expect Captain Grindley may well be there too,' he added, thinking of the espionage carried out on the deck above. He had watched the young man reboard his boat and, though it might be true that he was no sea officer, he had been very familiar with boats. 'Indeed it occurs to me that there may be some more sinister purpose designed to detain us further from sailing, possibly to compromise us, so you must beware of what you eat and drink.'

'You are being dramatic, surely?' Sarah said, intrigued.

'Nevertheless, do as I ask. Only eat and drink what is eaten or drunk by others. I am going to pass word that we shall weigh before dawn and slip out to sea when they think we are still sleeping off our excesses.'

And with that Kite returned to the deck and spoke to Harper. When he had kindled a lustful gleam in the mate's eye he said, 'I wonder if we have done right in leaving half our armament in the hold, Zachariah?'

Harper scratched his head. 'Well, Cap'n, six guns and their carriages come to over four tons and if we're running that'll enable us to carry canvas. If we're attacking or being attacked by something our own size, I reckon we've enough weight of metal to prevail over such as these native craft appear to be. Besides, it'll be rate of fire that counts, and we can serve the smaller number of guns better, in my opinion.'

Kite nodded. 'Very well. Let's hope you are right.' They were briefly silent, looking along the deck of the *Spitfire*, their eyes seeking out any last-minute tasks to be undertaken before their departure. 'Well, have the hands mustered to weigh at midnight, Zachariah, if Rahman is back by then with the charts he has promised to purchase for me.'

'Aye, aye, but what if he isn't?'

'Then we'll have to wait for him.'

*   *   *

The boat dropped them off at the landing place and Kite handed
Sarah out with a feeling of considerable pride and satisfaction.
She looked stunning in a blue-and-white-striped silk gown and
with her long hair loosely piled atop her head. She wore a
broad-brimmed hat with a long curling ostrich feather that
had somehow survived the vicissitudes of their voyage. So
infrequently had she worn such feminine attire that, with her
grace and beauty, the effect was overwhelming and, as they
were announced, Mrs Kite turned several heads among the
dozen or so people invited to dine.

Cranbrooke appeared to live in bachelor state, but several
of the Company's senior writers had their wives with them,
among whom were two Indian women, glorious in their
brilliant dresses, shot with gold and bejewelled and bangled
in exotic state. Two officers of the Company's sepoy regiments
gloried in their scarlet and white, resplendent popinjays whose
skin was almost as rubicund as their coats. As Kite had
predicted, Grindley was in attendance. He was unaccompanied,
dressed in the full panoply of a commander in the Honourable
East India Company's service and immediately attentive to
Mistress Kite. Used to having passengers in his ship, Grindley
was able to deploy a certain urbane charm though, as Sarah
was detached from him, Kite was aware that even as he took
her arm, Sarah was repelled by his darting tongue and wet
lip. Kite was glad he had warned Sarah to be careful, as she
was swiftly surrounded by several of the young, unattached
writers.

Cranbrooke monopolized Kite, introducing him to a second
Company commander, a Captain Robert Harling.

'Captain Kite is sailing for China, Harling, with a cargo of
opium.'

'Are you indeed,' Harling said, raising his eyebrows. 'Have
you ventured there before?'

Kite shook his head. 'No, I have not.'

'But you are embarking a pilot.'

'He has engaged Ali Rahman, d'you know him?' Cranbrooke
said.

Harling shook his head. 'Well, good fortune, Captain Kite. You must not expect any assistance from the Company if you run foul of the Mandarins.'

'I have learned to expect help from no one, Captain Harling,' Kite said, meeting the disapproval in the sea officer's eyes. 'One is so frequently let down.'

'But you are going to rely upon a pilot. There is an element of trust there, surely.'

'I may not be familiar with the China Seas, gentlemen, and you may wish to dissuade me, but needs must when the devil drives the chaise.'

'Well, well,' Cranbrooke said, but their conversation was terminated as a last guest was announced and Cavanagh arrived. On his arm was a tall Indian woman. 'Ah,' remarked Cranbrooke, 'here's Cavanagh, we shall go in.'

The gathering was dull, both in its content and its accompanying conversation. The Company's servants knew each other too well and shared too many experiences to make the latter anything but a tedious rodomontade of local gossip to which Kite and Sarah were not party. As for the supper dishes, these were all so excessively spiced that Kite found himself tempted to drink too much and at one point caught Sarah's eye, sensing she too was finding the occasion an ordeal.

When the women withdrew, the men's conversation degenerated to salacious stories and Kite was aware that most were drunk. Only Cranbrooke, Harling and Kite himself seemed in control of themselves. Grindley appeared the worse for drink and at one point it was clear that he was making some indecent comment about Sarah, for the two young writers with whom he was lolling with his cheroot and his glass of arrack shot glances in Kite's direction. One was the young man who had taken a look round *Spitfire*'s deck that afternoon, and again he flushed with embarrassment as he felt Kite's gaze upon him.

'I hope you told Captain Grindley what he wished to know about my schooner, sir,' Kite said across the table so that a silence fell and Grindley, hearing his name, turned towards the man he was insulting.

But drink had made the young writer less intimidated than he had been that afternoon and he replied boldly, 'I have no idea to what you refer.'

'Perhaps I am mistaken,' Kite said, smiling with charming dissimulation, 'but it seemed to me that you evinced a more than natural curiosity in my vessel. You have not seen such a schooner before, no doubt. She is North American built and tolerably fast.'

'Is that so, Captain Kite?' Grindley said. 'Well, she will have to be fast. You are a damned interloper, sir—'

'Come, come, gentlemen,' Cranbrooke broke in, 'Captain Kite is a guest among us. He has not broken any laws—'

'No, but he is no gentleman,' Grindley interrupted, his croaking voice insinuatingly unpleasant.

'Grindley, mind your tongue.' Harling rumbled the caution to his fellow commander, and Cranbrooke muttered, 'I'm sorry about this, Kite.'

'It is of no consequence, but thank you.' Kite acknowledged the president's apology then raised his voice. 'But I agree with Captain Grindley.' He smiled again, aware that he had their attention. 'I am certainly not a gentleman, gentlemen, if to be a gentleman requires one to drink too much and make lewd remarks about a guest's wife.'

Confused by the proliferations of social status in Kite's assertion, Grindley nevertheless realized he was being guyed. He went a deep purple while a smirk played on the faces of the young men with whom he had shared his confidences. 'What are you implying, Kite?'

'Whatever you are, Captain Grindley,' Kite riposted smoothly.

Even more confused, Grindley blurted out, 'When are you sailing, Kite?'

'When I am ready.'

'Ah!' Grindley exclaimed triumphantly. 'You mean when your topass has stolen you some charts!'

'I think I shall be *buying* them, Captain Grindley, which is rather different, don't you think.'

'Your *boy* will be stealing them just the same,' Grindley protested with pejorative emphasis on the juvenile noun, but no one seemed inclined to come to his aid before Cranbrooke caught Cavanagh's eye.

'Cavanagh has a fine voice. You'll oblige us, Cavanagh? Good. Shall we join the ladies and listen to him?'

As they walked out onto the veranda where the ladies lounged on chaises longues, Harling caught Kite's arm. 'I apologize on behalf of Grindley, Captain.'

'That is kind of you, but there is no need. He is offensive and, should he wish to pick a quarrel, I shall counter any challenge by claiming the primary insult. I am certain he has insulted my wife and I am extremely adept with a hanger.'

'I am sure it will not come to that.'

'But you will tell him, none the less.'

'If it becomes necessary, yes.'

'Thank you.'

Kite knew that Sarah would affirm the East India Company officer had been less than gallant. It was a condition common to men who claimed gentility, Kite had observed, but he doubted Grindley would press the point to a challenge. Anyway, Kite mused as he settled himself against the veranda rail and listened to Cavanagh's fine baritone dissipate into the velvet darkness, Grindley would not find him available to fight a duel in the dawn's mist. If Rahman had filched, stolen, borrowed or simply bought the folio of charts, Kite and *Spitfire* would be away.

After Cavanagh, one of the English wives with a mellow contralto rose and sang some pleasing airs with which Kite was not familiar, and she was followed by a declamation by one of the writers, who recited a tedious ode by a poet unknown to Kite. The chief virtue of the performance seemed to be to demonstrate the mental retention of the young man, but he redeemed himself with his encore, Oliver Goldsmith's 'Woman', which he addressed to the ladies present with generous gestures encompassing them all.

'When lovely woman stoops to folly,' he declaimed tragically, 'And finds too late that men betray,' the last word uttered with an insinuating sneer as he leaned forward, 'What charm can soothe her melancholy?' he asked, straightening up, pressing clasped hands to his bosom. 'What art can wash her tears away?'

The men were all grinning and the women wore amused, quizzical smiles, waiting for the poet's revelation.

'The only art her guilt to cover,' the writer went on, provoking moues of protest that no guilt attached to any of them or their sex in general; 'To hide her shame from ev'ry eye,' and now the mock indignation was almost voiced as the ladies looked from one to another and the men grinned ever more widely. 'To give repentance to her lover, and wring *his* bosom . . .' There was heavy emphasis on the personal pronoun which claimed the attention of them all as they awaited the bon mot: 'is – to *die.*' The last word was breathed with its single, awesome syllable attenuated in a note that was almost melodramatic. It faded into loud cheers and applause from the men and a little simpering approval and laughter from the ladies.

'Bravo, Douglas, such force of rhetoric would have done Cicero proud,' Cranbrooke said and for a while the conversation became general until the senior writer, acting upon some previous instruction, stood and made his excuses.

The company took the hint and Kite rose, handing up Sarah who smiled graciously at her admirers.

'We shall see you again before you leave us, I hope,' someone said.

'I am a mere passenger, I fear, you must ask my husband; he commands the ship.'

'You are not leaving immediately, are you, Captain Kite?'

Aware that several of the men, and especially Grindley, who stood swaying alongside Harling, showed an interest in his reply, Kite affected indifference. 'Oh, when we are ready,' he repeated before turning to thank their host. A moment later they had escaped into the soft, dark night.

'Well, thank heavens that's over,' Kite said as they walked

swiftly down to the landing place. 'Were you much troubled by that old goat Grindley?'

Sarah chuckled. 'Not much, but he is an obnoxious fellow for all his airs. He offered me a passage to China aboard the *Carnatic*. Said if my husband could not come he would give me a better *ride* in his Indiaman than ever I'd have at the hands of a schooner *skipper*. There was no mistaking his meanings, either.'

'I suspected as much. Well, we have done with him now, just so long as Rahman has obtained the requisite charts.'

They were pulled out to the schooner by oarsmen who had clearly enjoyed the evening in their own way and Kite affected not to notice the stink of arrack about them. Sarah was swung up and over the side of the *Spitfire* by a chair Harper had rigged earlier and Kite soon followed her up the tumblehome.

'Is Rahman back, Zachariah?' he asked.

'I am here, Kite Sahib, and I have obtained a first-class folio of the charts you are wanting.'

'Very well done. Then we shall weigh anchor in an hour.'

PART THREE

THE REAPING

Chapter Thirteen

A Long Chase

'Well, what d'you make of her?' Kite asked, his voice terse.

There was a pause as Harper, undeterred by his commander's impatience, took his time in studying the strange sail. Kite had held off asking the mate his opinion until he had called for the change of watch and was almost fuming with anxiety as the distant ship crowded on sail in obvious pursuit of the schooner.

'Damn it, Zachariah . . .' Kite began but then Harper closed the glass with a decisive snap and handed it back to Kite with his assessment.

'French frigate.'

Kite nodded. 'Aye, that's what I think.' The two men stood side by side, staring astern and effortlessly bracing themselves against both the heel of the deck and the movement of the *Spitfire*'s racing hull. Yet their bodies were tensed with expectation, as if waiting for their brains to galvanize them into action, and all along the deck the men changing watches also looked astern where the chasing ship was now hull up, her canvas taut with the strength of the monsoon, and the bone in her teeth just breaking the sharp line of the horizon.

It was a beautiful morning, the Indian Ocean sparkled a deep, sapphire blue beneath a sky of a lighter hue, dappled with small fluffy, fair-weather clouds. From the surface of the sea rose the curious shapes of a myriad flying fish which, with outstretched wings, somehow dodged the tumbling wave-crests

181

as they escaped the pursuing barracuda. From time to time dolphins flashed through the sea, leaping in the schooner's wake oblivious to the situation of the vessel whose hull sent manifold complex patterns of varying pressure out into the surrounding water. The wind was fresh, but not so strong as to prevent either vessel carrying full sail and both had the wind on their starboard quarters, broad-reaching so that every stitch of canvas drew.

Even the routine ringing of the bell, the four double-strikes that marked the end of the morning watch, failed to break the spell on the schooner's deck, for no one watching the approaching frigate could be in any doubt of the outcome of the long hours of daylight that lay ahead of them. The prospect of capture acted on each man in singularity, breaking up that synthesis of purpose that distinguished the men who manned the *Spitfire* as a crew, to turn them each into apprehensive individuals. This sense of forlorn and solitary exposure acted more powerfully upon Kite and now Harper, for both had women to think of, and this fuelled their private fears. It was a consequence of defying the ancient prejudice against allowing women aboard ship, and for those seamen who nursed such thoughts, the apparent paralysis of their officers was a direct consequence of their foolish conduct. For in addition to the likely prospect of capture by an enemy frigate and subsequent incarceration on the Île de France, several of the schooner's company were irrationally hostile to the handful of women who inhabited the *Spitfire*. Were they not sisters to the polluted nautch girls of Bombay whose promiscuity, eagerly embraced a week or so earlier, was now producing dire and painful consequences? And as if to emphasise that perverse perception, one of these lousy creatures now rose up from the after companionway, her dark hair blowing provocatively in the wind, provoking nudges and nods from those watching seamen infected by disease and a lack of charity.

'How do you know she is French?' Just as her appearance broke the hiatus among the watching hands forward, Sarah's voice ended the apparent paralysis of Kite and Harper. Sarah had learned the news from Jack Bow, who had come aft to attend the cabin as was his daily round after breakfast and had heard the dreadful word uttered by Harper.

'What?' Kite turned, his face irritable.

'How do you know she is French?' Sarah repeated her question, adding, 'May I take a look?' She extended her hand for Kite's glass.

'For God's sake, Sarah,' Kite expostulated, but handed over the telescope. Taking it, Sarah climbed over the sea-step and crossed the deck, to level the instrument and brace it against the thick rope tackle of the maintopmast backstay. As she focused the lenses every man on the schooner's deck watched the slim figure in her breeches and shirt, her unruly hair only half tamed by the black ribbon, her hip jutting, her shirt pressed against her back and her long legs terminating in short, hessian boots. Even the clapped seamen felt the twitches of lust momentarily overcome their indisposition.

'Could she not be British?' Sarah asked without lowering the telescope and seeking to moderate their collective fear by readjusting her query.

'No,' snapped Kite, 'not with those topsails . . .'

'What about those topsails?' Sarah persisted.

'The cut and colour of them, Mrs Kite,' Harper explained as Kite remained mute. 'Most of the British men-o'-war in these waters have worn sails . . .'

'That is one of the French ships which we last saw in the Cape Verdes,' Kite broke in.

'You think so?' Harper said, surprised at this assertion.

'I'm as sure of it as you are that she's French, and it makes sense if you think about it,' Kite reasoned. 'They were reinforcements and, after taking wood and water at the Cape, have come on into the Indian Ocean.'

'That would set the cat among the pigeons in these seas,' Harper added reflectively.

'She is over-hauling us, is she not?' Sarah asked, lowering the glass and turning to face them, one hand gripping the backstay.

Kite sighed and nodded.

Sarah looked aloft at the drawing sails. 'Can we do nothing about it?'

'What does the tension in that backstay tell you?' Kite asked.

'She's straining?' Sarah asked, taking her hand from the backstay and looking at her husband under her brow.

'She's straining all right,' Kite confirmed. 'We could jettison the guns on deck, we could start the water casks and pump their contents over the side out of the bilge, we could chop up the boats on the chocks and throw the debris overboard and ditch every piece of loose gear. We could even break open the opium bales and hurl our cargo into the wake but on what do we live and with what do we trade if we succeed in escaping?'

'But if capture is inevitable, is it not better to have tried to get away and then to leave so little a prize that the enemy profits little by it?' Sarah responded. 'Moreover he will weaken his own strength by having to secure the *Spitfire* with a prize crew and has us to feed.'

Kite shook his head. 'A ruthless and competent naval commander, and I have little doubt but that we are being pursued by a man of such mettle, would burn an unwanted and useless prize. As for feeding us, *you* might be well provided for, Sarah,' Kite said with a meaningful look, 'but apart from Nisha and Maggie, the rest of us could be conveniently neglected.'

Kite derived a cold satisfaction from the pallor that stole over Sarah's beautiful face. 'I see you understand me,' he added harshly.

'Then we must fight,' she said sharply.

Kite turned and looked at Harper, raising one eyebrow. 'Well, Zachariah?'

Harper nodded. 'We may sail under the British flag, Cap'n, and have Liverpool as our port of registry, but Mrs Kite and me are native-born Americans. We'll fight.'

Kite looked sharply at Harper, and then laughed. 'Damn me, Zachariah, I believe you're admonishing me.'

'Not before time,' Sarah added, 'you're confounded churlish this morning.'

'I'm confounded concerned about that devil!' Kite admitted, aware that he had been over-short with his wife and that Harper disapproved. 'Very well. It's your watch, Zachariah, and this could be a long job. We'll clear away the guns, and shot and charge them behind closed ports. I don't want to reveal our weak state. Then do you prepare the small arms – load every musket and pistol. I'll stand my watch down to break their fast and urge them to try and rest but don't you or your men take your eyes off the wind and the sails. We *must* try and extend the chase as long as humanly possible. It is the only chance we have.'

Kite lingered on deck as Harper busied himself and his men who, once the orders were given, were forced by habit to act again in concert. If the Old Man thought there was a chance of escape, then they would all do their best and he was at least not going to submit. Only a few Jeremiahs grumbled that Kite's action could only postpone the inevitable; the majority hoped something would turn up.

The forenoon drew on and the chasing frigate grew larger with an inexorable progress that appeared to the labouring watch to occur in fits and starts. Like a clock, the hands seemed immobile when being watched but, take your eyes off the thing for an instant and attend some other matter, and when you looked again the change was startling.

About twenty minutes before noon a tall column of white water suddenly rose in their wake, followed by the dull boom of the gun's report as it caught up with them. A small cloud blew ahead of the frigate, dissipating as it went.

No one on deck said a word. There was nothing to say. Turned heads stared forward again, searching the *Spitfire*'s sails and rigging for any adjustable advantage that would gain them even a fraction of a knot. The noise of the frigate's bow-chaser brought Kite on deck. He was followed by Sarah and, in a flutter of scarlet silk, Nisha.

Standing by the stern, Kite did not need a glass to take in the details of the enemy ship. She was a fine French frigate and the dark cluster of men about her knightheads told of the care with which her bow chase guns were being pointed. They would fire bar shot, he guessed, hoping to cripple the schooner by reducing her rig, and sooner rather than later they would find the range. The strong wind gave the heavier ship the advantage of speed and Kite had not another shred of canvas to set. He ruminated unhappily upon his fate. He seemed doomed to be frustrated at every endeavour, yet there was one trick he could try. He had done it before and, by God, he could do it again! It required split-second timing and it ran a tremendous risk, but it was the only chance he had.

'Zachariah!'

Harper was beside him in an instant. 'Sir?'

'Get Jack to pass word to the watch below that they are to muster at the bottom of the ladders but not to come on deck until summoned. Get your watch to stand by the halliards and flake them. Every halliard, d'you understand? When I give the word I want them all cast off their pins and let to run. I want every sail down, including all the square sails. Get extra men out of my watch, but let me know when you've a man at each station.'

'You don't want a commotion with all hands on deck, I guess?' Harper queried, divining Kite's intention by adding, 'You're going to dodge round into her wake and make off to windward?'

'*It's all we can do!*' hissed Kite.

'*Yessir!*'

Harper went forward and Kite envied him the catharsis of movement, then, recollecting that he could do nothing by staring at the frigate, he too turned forward, just as another column of water rose in the wake, twenty yards astern of them.

'Don't look aft!' he snapped at the apprehensive helmsman. Kite took station beside the man and called Sarah's name. 'Go quietly forward and report to Mr Harper,' he said, relieving the seaman, and then to his wife, 'Give me a hand on the tiller here. Nisha, do you go below, if you please. I would not have you exposed to any shot. The next quarter of an hour will decide our fate so perhaps you can invoke one of your gods.' He smiled as kindly as he could.

'That is the first time you have been sociable this morning,' admonished Sarah beside him.

'Frankly, my dear, I don't much care for sociability at the moment . . .' He looked forward, seeing Harper moving round the deck. The men were lifting the heavy coils of rope off the belaying pins and flaking them out on the deck so that they would run free when the turns were thrown off the pins.

'What are you going to do?' Sarah asked, leaning against the tiller beside him.

'Attempt, Sarah, it's Providence that will decide whether I achieve it . . .' and Kite explained.

'He could wreck us in passing,' Sarah observed with a toss of her head at the looming presence that seemed almost palpable behind them.

'I'm hoping that we have convinced him by now that we are simply going to run. I am fairly certain that, though he has his guns run out, he is concentrating all his efforts in shooting at our rigging.'

But he got no further as with a deep noise, a shot plunged into the sea alongside them. 'He's got our range!' Kite breathed, giving himself a quick look astern. 'And by God he'll have our wind in a few more moments!'

The French commander knew his business, or had a sailing master, an *officier bleu*, who did. Using the advantage of superior speed the frigate had edged up to windward and the *Spitfire* would soon fall in the wind shadow of the French vessel. When that happened her speed would fall off and all would be over.

And when that happened so competent an officer would have all his larboard broadside guns manned, Kite realized suddenly with a sinking of the heart. Would Harper never be ready? Why had he not set things in motion five minutes earlier? Yet he *must* hold both his hand and his tongue. It would do no good hurrying Harper, for if the halliards failed to run, it would all be wasted!

'Ready, Cap'n!'

When it did come, Harper's report took him off-balance. The mate stood himself at the main throat halliard, staring expectantly aft, and Kite could see his eyes were staring past him, fixed on the tall white pyramid of sails that drew above the starboard quarter of the schooner.

'Very well,' Kite said, his voice cracking. He ran his tongue over his dry lips and swallowed hard. His mouth was quite dry. Beside him he could hear Sarah's laboured breathing. He coughed to clear his throat. 'Stand by!' he called, then, giving one glance astern, he shouted: '*Let fall all!*'

Kite waited, poised. He must not throw the helm over until the wind was out of the heavy gaff sails, for a gybe would be fatal and he had no room to turn to starboard. Suddenly the tautly curved sails began to lose their beautiful, aerofoil shape. Instead they bellied and flapped. Aloft the gaffs of the fore and mainsails came down with a run. At the same instant the booms dropped to the extent of the topping lifts with a jar that shook the vessel. The main topsail sheet had been let to fly and the end flogged madly and unrove from the block on the extremity of the main gaff, but the sail it had been controlling flogged impotently, depriving the schooner of its power. On the foremast the upper yards ran down the topmast and landed on the cap with dull thuds and although there was a cry of warning from forward, where clearly something had snagged, *Spitfire* seemed to decelerate with such speed that Kite felt himself almost pitched forward. It was an illusion born of the tensing of his body against the tiller as he awaited the precise instant when he and Sarah must act decisively.

'*Now! Hard over!*' he grunted through gritted teeth, heaving at the tiller and dragging it to starboard. He felt Sarah throw her own weight against the heavy timber and the deck tilted as the schooner spun on her heel, carrying her way into the violent turn.

Holding the tiller over, Kite roared for all hands on deck

to make sail on the larboard tack and only then did he look at the frigate. The French man-of-war raced past, her canvas towering against the blue sky, her gingerbread work and gilding gleaming in the brilliant sunshine as the long dark streak of her gunwale, sandwiched between the golden strakes of her topsides, flew past. Kite afterwards nursed two distinct images amid that blur of impressions as the big cruiser tore past them. One was the crowd of men forward which seemed to dissolve as they streamed aft as if to keep pace with the *Spitfire*. These men and their mates already stationed round the guns loosed off a rolling but desultory broadside at the schooner, but it was clear that they had had no intimation of Kite's stratagem and although men had been stationed at the frigate's guns, they had been relaxed and unexpectant. Kite was never clear how many guns fired at them, nor was he aware of the shot passing clear over their heads. Others afterwards told of eight, twelve or twenty discharges, though how a man could have counted up to twenty in those fleeting seconds was inexplicable. Much later they found a graze in the maintopmast that so weakened the spar that it had to be sent down, but in those moments Kite was only impressed by the second impression, the sight of the French commander, standing up on a gun, one hand holding onto a backstay. Splendid in a gold-laced blue coat with red facings, Kite's opponent waved a plumed tricorne hat. Kite remembered raising his own hand and the feeling of trembling excitement that crept like a galvanic shock up and down his spine at this futile but courteous gallantry so that inexplicable tears started in his eyes.

And then he was hauling the tiller amidships and screaming out for the fore and aft sails to be hoisted again and the topsail yards to be braced sharp up. 'Larboard tack,' he roared again, 'larboard tack!'

The schooner trembled as she bucked round into the sea and the sails flogged wildly, transmitting their frustrated energy into the hull as the watch below tumbled up and lent their weight to the men struggling to rehoist the sails they had just doused.

Within a few moments the *Spitfire*'s unruly canvas had been reharnessed as the sheets were trimmed. She stood away to the north-north-west, dipping into a head sea and lifting the spray over her weather bow. Even the square topsails were redrawing, their weather leeches trembling as the yard lifts were trimmed. Only the main gaff topsail still flogged as Harper sent a man aloft to catch the sheet, and walk out to the gaff end and reeve it again. Whatever had gone wrong forward among the jib sheets had been quickly put right. All about the decks, as men recoiled the ropes, there were grins and laughter. Men hit each other with good-natured punches and Harper amidships raised his voice: 'Three cheers for Cap'n Kite and the *Spitfire*!'

When the cheers subsided, Kite bellowed his response: 'Thank you, my lads. That was better than any man-o'-war's company!'

'It was better than that one, to be sure!' said McClusky, who must have been somewhere forward, though Kite had no recollection of where Harper had placed the fellow. Here too was Muckbul Ali Rahman, whose presence on board Kite had entirely forgotten in the last few hours. Now Nisha and Maggie emerged to join the rejoicing company while Harper was coming aft to suggest they spliced the mainbrace.

'She'll be some time coming round,' Harper said, nodding astern as the frigate began to turn in their wake, 'and she'll not point as sharply as us.'

Kite stared at the enemy cruiser. In his mind's eye he conjured the image of that elegant figure acknowledging the success of Kite's *ruse de guerre*. He nodded. 'Very well, Mr Harper. Very well.'

'For Heaven's sake give the poor man a smile, William,' Sarah whispered at him.

'I don't think I can,' he replied, and indeed, he could hardly swallow, for his mouth was dry and the only moisture he felt were the ridiculous trickle of tears on his cheeks.

Chapter Fourteen

Plots and Promotions

The chase was not over, but its outcome was less uncertain and, as they all knew, darkness was only five hours away. Moreover, there was a new moon and it would be a dark night. By a fluke, Harper, looking up at the right moment to observe the great white ensign with its Bourbon lilies in gold, had also spotted the French ship's name across her stern. The *Alcmene* stood after them until they lost sight of her in the dark. Unable to chase in the schooner's direct wake by being unable to point quite so close to a wind which went down with the sun, it was clear by twilight that advantage now lay with the *Spitfire*. Although the watchers aboard the little British schooner could see the *Alcmene* in the starlight for some time after nightfall, they had lost sight of her by midnight.

At daylight Harper, then officer of the watch, clambered aloft with his glass. He could see the tiny irregularity on the horizon that marked the position of the *Alcmene*, but by noon this had disappeared and Kite tacked *Spitfire* to the southwards. In the cabin, with one of Rahman's charts spread out before him, he consulted the sea-cunny.

'Now, Mr Rahman, it was our decision not to attempt the passage of the Malacca Strait, but to stand south-east and enter the China Sea by way of the Sunda Strait. It is unfortunate that by so doing we placed ourselves in the path of that Frenchman.'

Rahman rolled his head in agreement. 'It is indeed unfortunate, Kite Sahib, but as I explained the winds in the Selat

Malacca are light and, for a fast passage, it is better to remain on the weather side of Sumatra. I am also thinking that if many French ships are at sea the Selat Malacca will be more full of them, since there is much Country trade with Pegu to the north, and Achin and along the Malay coast to the southwards.'

'Mmmm,' Kite ruminated. His thoughts were focused on their late interceptor. 'It is my belief that the *Alcmene* has but recently arrived in the Indian Seas like ourselves and that she was on her way to take up a station in the Sunda Strait. Now,' he went on, 'we should reconsider our passage because I also believe that she is likely to reach her station *here*.' Kite tapped the chart with the dividers where the great islands of Sumatra and Java were separated by the narrow outlet of the Sunda Strait. 'In which case we have not seen the last of her and, moreover, she may also be supported by Dutch cruisers, for we will not be many leagues from Batavia . . .' Kite paused and looked up. Across the small cabin Sarah and Nisha laboured with needles, thread and several yards of coloured bunting. 'It is a depressing prospect and although we might persuade a Dutchman that we are a rebel Yankee schooner by hoisting that device,' and Kite nodded at the dismembered red ensign then undergoing conversion into what was thought to be a representation of Continental American colours, 'I am by no means sanguine as to its outcome if we meet the *Alcmene* again.'

'Sanguine?' Rahman frowned.

'Oh, er, hopeful . . . Hopeful about the outcome.'

'Ah, I see . . .' Rahman nodded his comprehension. 'But, Kite Sahib, there are inside passages here, and here.' The Indian leaned forward and pointed to an extensive archipelago of small islands that littered the strait. 'We can proceed within the confines of these waters in perfect safety.'

'I never quite trust assertions of perfect safety at sea, Mr Rahman.'

'Is the Sahib not trusting me?' Rahman straightened up, one hand on his breast, his tone so hurt and outraged that both Sarah and Nisha looked up at the two men.

Kite shook his head and smiled at the affronted Indian. 'Mr Rahman, I would trust you with my life, my wife, my schooner and indeed my entire fortune, such as it is! Believe me, I can do you no greater honour, but I cannot trust you to blunt the sword of ill-fortune if it is pointing at my heart. Sometimes of late I have thought such a thing possible. If Vishnu, or whatever his name is, wishes Kite Sahib to perish in these Indian Seas, not even the considerable skills of that famous sea-cunny and inestimable topass, Muckbul Ali Rahman, can prevent the thing coming to pass.'

Nisha and Sarah exchanged glances and then stared again at the men, almost open-mouthed at this verbal outpouring from Kite. Rahman appeared to consider the matter for some time, his head wagging from side to side and his face a picture of serious contemplation. Then he looked up smiling. 'You will be a great man, Kite Sahib, of that I can make absolute prediction.'

Kite laughed. 'There is not much time for your precious prediction to come to pass, Mr Rahman. Kite Sahib is no longer young. But show me, if and when we clear this Selat Sunda of yours, do we pass to the eastwards or the west of Pulo Billiton?'

As the two men bent again to the chart, Nisha caught Sarah's eye and they both smiled.

In the event, they encountered neither French nor Dutch cruisers in the Sunda Strait, but only the native prahus in a variety of sizes, employed as both fishing and trading craft. Some boasted the rattan and matting sails of the Chinese junk and some Rahman referred to as lorchas, but Kite and Harper were relieved that none were larger than themselves and none boasted the crossed yards and artillery of a European man-of-war. Of the *Alcmene* there was no sign; she had vanished into the vastness of the ocean as mysteriously as she had emerged.

Once past the Strait they traversed the Java Sea in lighter winds and for day after day ran to the north, the heavy booms guyed out to starboard and every stitch of sail set as they reeled off the knots. Kite relinquished his watch to Rahman and the sea-cunny shared the roster with Harper and McClusky. The latter had proved able enough to be trusted with the deck in the prevailing stable weather and while he lacked the deep knowledge of a man bred to the sea, his natural intelligence rapidly acquainted him with the basic knowledge necessary for a grasp of navigation. He could work such a traverse as a fair wind enabled, and the need to maintain a sharp lookout had by now impressed itself upon the quondam clerk. Under Harper's tutelage and encouragement, McClusky began to develop ambitions in a new direction, having heard just sufficient in Bombay to whet his appetite and to persuade his lively imagination that, in due course, he too could become a nabob with a sweetly compliant Indian mistress and a fortune to be taken home and boasted of.

Even Jack Bow, whose courting of Maggie had long ago been curtailed by the harsh regime aboard ship, occupied a place of rising social importance, having become something of a steward-cum-servant to the schooner's officers. Bow attached great importance to the service of Captain Kite, whom he regarded with some awe, particularly after their encounters with enemy vessels of war. As for Kite himself, he began to relax, enjoying the privileges of master and owner, taking his fixes and plotting their position on Dalrymple's charts, but largely lounging under a spread awning in the languorous company of Sarah and Nisha. Once a day he revived his own charlatanic skills as a surgeon and dosed the clapped and poxed sailors, some of whom could hardly micturate for the burning inflammation they suffered.

Three deaths marred this idyll, two of the seamen succumbing to some infection of the bowels picked up from the stews of Bombay, and one of those with a raging venereal infection dropped quietly overboard one night.

'Don't reckon he could stand the pain in 'is piss-pipe,' the boatswain reported to Harper one morning.

Kite wrote the word 'Dead' and the date beside their names

in the muster book, reckoned their wages and noted their next of kin, if any existed, to pay what remuneration was owed when they returned home. It was an act of extreme optimism, Kite thought as he set his pen down. God alone knew whether any of them would see again the house-flags fluttering above Bidston lighthouse on the River Mersey's west bank, and see their own arrival announced to the watchers across the river in Liverpool itself.

Four days after clearing the Sunda Strait they were abeam of the Great Natuna Island and running into the deeper waters of the South China Sea. Rahman impressed upon Kite the necessity of taking their departure from the high point with great care, for from now on they would run on dead reckoning, keeping well to the east of the coast of Cochin China and maintaining a sharp lookout for the treacherous reefs which lay, like man-traps in game-rich woodland, athwart their route to the Pearl River.

'We must sound for the bank here, where there are no depths less than ten fathoms,' Rahman placed his dark index finger on a roughly delineated but unnamed group of soundings* that seemed to Kite to rise inexplicably in the middle of the sea, 'in order to avoid the reefs here.' Rahman moved his finger to the west where Kite read the legend *Paracel Islands*, a wide-spaced litter of reefs and low islands centred upon a small circular archipelago. By positively locating the lesser of the two dangers, they could avoid the greater, and thereafter set a final course for the coast of China and the Portuguese enclave of Macao at the mouth of the Pearl River, two days' sailing further north.

'Have you had much experience in these seas, Mr Rahman?' Kite asked civilly, interested in Rahman's past history as much as to confirm the value of the man's advice.

The Indian nodded and smiled. 'Oh, yes, Kite Sahib. I came here first as a boy in the *Sullamany*, owned by an Arab, and afterwards I served for four years as kelassee aboard the *Fez*

---

* Now called the Macclesfield Bank.

195

Cawdray and remained for many years in the service of the Banajees, rising to serang and tindal in several of their ships. That is where I learned English, under Captain Buchanan when he was at sea and before he went into partnership as an owner with Pestonjee Banajee. Afterwards, Captain Glasscock, the master of the *Hormuzeer*, a fine Country ship, encouraged me to take an interest in navigation. I already worked the traverse as tindal and sea-cunny, and of course I knew all the points of the compass and the principal sailings. I became an officer with Captain Glasscock, and by an' by he gave me his octant when he went home to England. He was a very fine gentleman and would have stayed in Bombay, but his wife, a very beautiful Parsee lady, she died and he had no children that survived her. Then Banajee made me naconda of the *Malabar Grab*.'

'Naconda? What is that?'

'Like you, Kite Sahib, the commander.'

Kite looked at Rahman with renewed interest. 'That impresses me, Mr Rahman.'

Rahman smiled. His face wore an expression of both pride and modesty and there were tears in his eyes.

'I am sorry that I had not rated you an officer sooner,' Kite apologized, 'I had thought you an excellent interpreter but had no idea that you were hiding other talents.'

'You were not to know, Kite Sahib.'

'You are too modest; you should have told me.'

'You would not have believed me.'

Kite looked at the Indian with a shrewd eye. 'Why, because I am an Englishman?'

'Perhaps, but mainly because you are new to the coast and have your own past and experience. Besides Hooker Sahib would not have encouraged you to favour me.'

'Because *you* are an Indian?'

'I do not quite understand what you English gentlemen mean when you say "Indian", but yes, because I am a native.'

'Ahh, I understand *that*.'

Rahman appeared to want to say more. He opened his mouth

to speak and then he seemed to think better of it, closing his mouth and shaking his head.

'What is it?' Kite asked.

'It is nothing, Kite Sahib.'

'But I see something troubles you. Tell me what it is.'

'It is only curiosity, Sahib, and curiosity is impolite.'

'And what are you curious about? Me?'

Rahman nodded and met Kite's gaze. 'A little, yes . . .'

'Go on.'

'Well, I have heard stories about you. Is it true you had a native wife?'

Kite nodded. 'Yes, it is true. She was a negro whom I bought out of slavery when I was surgeon of my first ship, a Liverpool Guineaman. We were married. She died in England many years ago. We had two children, but neither survived.'

'That is sad. Were they sons or daughters?'

'Both sons.'

'And you have had no children with Memsahib?'

'A daughter; she too died.'

'You are like Captain Glasscock.'

'But you,' Kite said, eager to divert the conversation from its lugubrious channel, 'you have many children and are a happy man who does not have to go to sea again . . .'

'Except to escape my children and my wife's mother,' Rahman said with a chuckle.

'Ah yes, I had forgot.'

The two men laughed companionably and Kite returned his attention to the chart. 'Well, now do you explain once more the procedures for bribing the local, what do you call them? Man . . . ?'

'Mandarins. Those who act as the imperial shaw-bunders, the customs-officers of the emperor who may be bought for payments of *cum-shaw*. And Kite Sahib, please trust Muckbul Ali Rahman to negotiate for you. You are inexperienced and these men will keep you dangling like a fish on a line so that, knowing the English *fan-kwei* are impatient if they do not get their own way, force up the price of the *cum-shaw* until you will pay much more than you need in order to sell your cargo. As you know, the import of opium is prohibited, so we can deposit our cargo on account in the Company's hulks moored for the purpose of acting as floating warehouses. In due season, when your cargo is sold, you will be paid and it is customary to deposit the sum in the Company's treasury in Canton in exchange for bills to be drawn on London. In this way the Company raises capital to fund its own homeward cargoes, for the Chinese want little from England and in truth buy only cotton and opium, both of which are coming from India.

'For most English and Scotch merchants, and the masters and officers trading on their own account in the ships of the Company or the Bombay or Calcutta Country vessels, the bills of exchange provide a safe way of remitting their profits to London, thus avoiding any trouble with the monopoly of the Company.'

'But you have just said the Company needs the capital in Canton,' Kite said, confused.

Rahman grinned. 'It is what I think I have heard English officers call "a matter of expedience".'

'I see,' Kite acknowledged, smiling back. 'Well, well.'

As the *Spitfire* sailed north Kite had good reason to be pleased with his circumstances. The discovery of Rahman as a man of many facets was as gratifying as the fact that Kite liked the Indian; they worked well together and Kite had asked him aft, to dine at the cabin table, along with Harper. The invitation had made it socially necessary to include McClusky too, and although one of the officers was always absent on deck, the company grew convivial, with Sarah and Nisha holding a dignifying sway over their proceedings. Oddly, although the *Spitfire* proceeded as a barely legitimate Country trader, largely protected by Kite's letter of marque and reprisal from prosecution as an interloper by assuming the alternative role of privateer, it was only now, long after Hooker's death, that their mood seemed to reflect the *Spitfire*'s original purpose on leaving Liverpool, that of a yacht.

Of course, they were all warmed by the prospect of a successful voyage, a prospect which seemed assured by the quantity of opium in their small hold, but there were other influences too. Nisha, who had been rescued from the self-immolation of suttee on the death of her first husband by the man who subsequently became her second, was now rescued from grief by a man who had become her third in all but law.

Harper's huge frame was matched by a sexual appetite, and while he could not indulge this in full during their passage, there were moments when passion overcame both propriety and prudence. Although Kite had had the temporary bulkhead that had been installed to provide private accommodation for Hooker and his wife removed, Nisha had a corner of the cabin which could be curtained off. Moreover Sarah and she had become intimate friends, sharing more than Maggie as a maid, so that Sarah was disposed to absent herself upon occasions when Kite was occupied on deck, allowing the two lovers intense, if brief, moments alone.

Only McClusky seemed left out of things. He had avoided indulgence in Bombay, Kite having drawn upon the former clerk's familiarity with a ship's business to assign the more tedious formalities of the *Spitfire* to him. It had therefore been McClusky who attended the shaw-bunder at the Custom House, and McClusky who had kept the books in the transaction that, through the mediation of Muckbul Ali Rahman, had secured them the cargo of opium. Although this had in reality amounted to very little in the way of labour, it had taken a deal of time, time which McClusky had spent in reflection. He possessed the appetites usual to a vigorous young man and had long ago conceived a desire for the older but elegant Mrs Kite. On a long voyage, plain women become beautiful and beautiful women younger. During his sojourn in Bombay McClusky had the leisure to begin to cast her husband in a new light, not that of benefactor, but of obstacle. Captain Kite seemed to be manipulating McClusky, taking advantage of the clerk's skills. McClusky, inexperienced in the sea life, had subconsciously succumbed to a shifting of his personal perceptions occasioned by these changed circumstances.

Since leaving Bombay, however, he had had yet again to reinterpret his situation. In the first place it was clear that Captain Kite desired him to take a greater part in the running of the ship and that, instead of occupying a rather undistinguished role as captain's clerk and occasional under-officer trusted with such sedentary duties as anchor watches, McClusky found himself honoured with a deck watch at sea. His lack of charity soon ascribed this to Kite's wanton desire to spend more time with his wife, reprehensible to McClusky who, in the frustration of his own desire, cast Kite in the role of sybarite, seeing him in his mind's eye lolling on the breasts of two women in that after cabin, though Zach Harper was too besotted a fool to notice!

But McClusky's logic was confused by two other influences. In the first place it was clear that he could indeed rise socially on the shoulders of Kite's bounty. This conflicted with his strong want of Sarah, but the repression to which men of McClusky's middling class were subjected, though painfully miserable, was supportable. Nor was he the only person to perceive an opportunity for social advancement. The lady's maid Maggie had in turn her own designs on McClusky. In the first weeks of the voyage, when she had been laid low by sea-sickness, Maggie had almost forgotten her flirtation with Jack Bow. Since sailing he had been sent forward to learn the business of a seaman and, odd to say on such a small vessel, she had scarcely seen him to speak to for weeks. When they had met he had seemed like a stranger, no longer the cheeky lad but a laughing young man whom Maggie now saw as dangerous, particularly after she had again escaped pregnancy by him, following a moment of weakness.

Once or twice since, Bow had been sent aft on an errand and had cornered her in the pantry. Fondling her breasts he had tried to lift her skirt and petticoat but she no longer felt the same about him. Suddenly there loomed the great fear of another pregnancy born of the uncertainty of being tossed about on the vast ocean. What happened to a girl out here if she fell for a baby? After her narrow escape and the horrors of her miscarriage, the thought terrified Maggie with a disproportionate and phobic persistence. Rejected, Bow cast her aside. His new friends told him there were women aplenty in the world and his natural optimistic adaptability made light of his rejection. Jack had found the prediction of his shipmates all too true in Bombay and, as the *Spitfire* headed north for the coast of China, undeterred by the venereal miseries of some of his former advisers, he contemplated with relish the differences he had heard claimed for the ladies of the far distant Orient.

Maggie, in the meantime, had adopted a more serious cast of mind. For her, the experience of miscarrying, the death of Hooker and the conversations of the two ladies upon whom she waited had awakened desires of another sort. The purposes of matrimony, it now occurred to her, were greater than she had at first thought. As an intelligent person, Maggie realized that the hermetic world of the schooner offered her a unique opportunity. It was true her choice was limited. Harper, who at first had fascinated her by his physique and energy, had taken rather more than a mere fancy to the widow Hooker. Maggie's reaction to this liaison was ambivalent, for while she recognized the Indian lady's claim to indisputable gentility, she was discomfited by the thought of Harper's splendid body in close proximity to the darker skin of Nisha. It was at this point that she overheard Captain Kite discussing McClusky's potential as an officer, albeit under the watchful eye of the boatswain who could make up in forehandedness what McClusky lacked in experience. McClusky's star, it appeared, was rising and she had always had a distant liking for the young clerk's appearance. Socially, of course, he was already above her, but Maggie was not slow to see that his choice of women was far more strictly limited than her own of men. Herein she scented the advantage of a proximity which might lead to concupiscent propinquity.

To these Machiavellian thoughts must be added the workings of nature. Close association with Sarah and Nisha had induced in Maggie a graceful mimicry that was devoid of pretension. In assuming some of the mannerisms of her twin mistresses along with some of their cast-off clothes, Maggie's own appearance had been transformed. While Jack dismissed her as 'stuck-up' there were men in their hammocks forward who thought of Maggie in disreputable poses as they drifted between waking and sleep. Undivided by any differences in rank, McClusky increasingly noticed the younger woman. Contemplating her attending Sarah and Nisha one morning, the wisdom of the old proverb struck him with amusing aptitude: a bird in the hand was unquestionably better than two in the bush!

Thus it was that, as the schooner raced north through the South China Sea, starting the flying fishes and the dolphins from the blue waters, the days seemed for many to be idyllic.

Chapter Fifteen

The Paracels

'In three days at the most, my darling, we shall be in sight of the coast of China.'

Kite looked up from the table upon which he had unrolled the chart as Sarah, pushing her hair back over her head, rose from the bedroll on the deck which, in the warmer latitudes, they found more comfortable than their cot. She only wore one of her men's shirts and Kite held out his arms and embraced her. They kissed and then Sarah turned to look down at the chart. She saw the group of soundings about which she had heard her husband and Rahman speak, and to the west the shoal-strewn archipelago of the Paracels.

'Three days,' she mused, still clouded by sleep.

'Four at the most. We shall be sounding for the bank this very forenoon.'

'Ahh . . .' They were kissing again, Kite feeling a thrusting tumescence as Sarah pressed herself against his lean body, when the rasp of curtain rings ended their intimacy.

'Oh, I am sorry . . .'

'It is all right, Nisha,' Sarah said quickly, throwing a quick smile at her friend. 'William has to take soundings this morning.' And then, knowing Nisha did not understand the nautical allusion, she stared into her husband's eyes and in a low voice jerked herself against him and murmured, 'But he is not dropping his lead into this sea.'

She hissed the word as a single, suggestive consonant and Kite grinned at the pun. 'Witch!' he countered as she pulled herself away and, shirt-tails flapping, danced away across the cabin. Kite caught Nisha's look as he turned to adjust himself. Beyond the stern windows the wake drew out astern and he was aware of a low swell rolling in from the east. He had not noticed it an hour earlier, when he had been on deck at dawn. Since removing himself from the watch-keeping roster, it had become his invariable habit to be on deck at dusk and dawn, to observe any changed circumstances which might threaten the *Spitfire* during the coming hours. There lurked in his mind a fear that daylight would, one day, reveal the presence of the *Alcmene*. Bold and successful though his escape from the French frigate had been, Kite was too experienced a seaman not to know that his stratagem had been blessed by Providence. A man did not enjoy such luck twice in a month.

He turned back to the cabin. The light reflected from the sea astern danced upon the deckhead and, behind her own half-drawn curtain, the top of Sarah's head was obscured by her hands as they drew off the shirt. He made to roll up the chart when Nisha caught his eye. She had not retired behind her own curtain and lay back on her pillow, watching Sarah. It occurred to Kite that, from where she lay, Nisha could see Sarah's entire body and the expression she wore was one of intense, almost ecstatic concentration.

For a moment Kite felt a shock, not of surprise, but of acknowledgement of his own stupidity, as though the obvious had only just been made clear to him. Sarah had pulled the curtain sufficiently to maintain a degree of propriety in respect of her husband, but surely she was not insensible of the fact that she was visible to Nisha?

He must have started, for he lifted one of the weights holding the chart and it rolled up. Startled from her reverie by the sudden movement, Nisha lost her rapt concentration on Sarah, and became aware of Kite's gaze upon her. In a gesture of extreme longing, Nisha stretched out a bangled arm and said in a low and intense whisper, 'She is *so lovely*, William.'

Kite felt as if the breath was being held in his throat by some extraordinary force. A strong compulsion filled his

204

body so that it seemed to expand, as though the trapped air was raised to some high and motivating temperature. Kite felt himself trembling, his lust suddenly re-aroused. He was rigid with desire. Sarah must have caught something of this atmospheric tension, for she pulled aside the remains of the curtain and stared from one to another of them. Slowly her face broke into a wide smile and she exposed herself shamelessly before them both. Kite felt the blood flush his face but Nisha was the first to move. She drew her legs from her sheets and, slipping out of the light sarong she wore about herself at night until she too was naked, she crawled across the cabin deck towards Sarah.

Kite began to move round the table as Sarah knelt to receive the approaching Nisha. He was suffused with the thunder of his racing blood and tearing at his breeches, he released himself. For a moment he thought of Harper and the mate's prior claim on the brown and trembling rump before him, but then Sarah, making a small whimpering sound, beckoned him. Her smile had gone and she wore an expression that Kite had never before seen on a woman's face.

Enticed beyond reason, Kite moved forward.

But he stumbled as the *Spitfire* rolled and he tottered ridiculously, one hand fumbling at his member. Then there was a thunderous knock at the cabin door and a voice called, 'Kite Sahib, Kite Sahib, come on deck! Please come on deck!'

There was a moment's hiatus, a dawning and rapid descent on Kite's part to the thrusting intrusion of a terrible reality. Hurriedly readjusting his breeches and sparing only a glance at the two startled women as they knelt in each other's arms, surprised and now embarrassed, he made for the door. Instinctively he reached for his telescope on the rack beside it. Appalled, almost frightened by what had happened, he felt an overwhelming relief that Rahman had not thrown the door open as Harper or McClusky would undoubtedly have done on raising such an alarm.

Outside the adjacent pantry he knocked Maggie aside as *Spitfire* gave another heavy roll. Her tray with its coffee pot and cups hit the deck with a clatter and the crash of breaking china. Briefly the thought crossed his mind that she too, in going about her morning routine, had been about to interrupt the weird tryst in the cabin. They must have been mad!

Grasping the rails at the foot of the companionway he felt the deck heel again, and then stay at a sharper inclination to larboard. Pounding up the companionway he emerged into the sunshine on deck. *Spitfire* was driving along at a spanking pace, water spurted in below the lower rims of the gun ports and washed about the lee waterways. Bracing himself, Kite stared about him.

'Where away?' he called, bringing up his glass and staring round the horizon.

'What, Sahib?'

'Where's the enemy sail?' Kite roared, spinning on his heel and seeking Rahman.

'There is no sail, Kite Sahib . . .' Rahman looked surprised as he stood on the weather rail abreast the mainmast, holding a shroud as Kite sought to master himself. Confused and guilty, Kite's brain was in a whirl. He stood almost stupidly casting ineffectually about himself, his shirt tails untucked, a man clearly called from the privy for all the world to see the haste and discomfiture of his summons.

'Then why did you call me . . . ?' he began, but Rahman realized the cause of Kite's confusion.

'It is that, Kite Sahib, see there –' Rahman gestured at the horizon and added, 'and this swell, it is getting bigger and bigger all the time. And the wind, it is freshening.'

It was then that it dawned upon Kite that it was something more than the sudden change in the wind that had alarmed Rahman. Boiling along the rim of the world to the east was a huge mass of cloud that seemed to rise with a menacing foreboding, an inexorable approach that caused poor Kite's heart to thunder again. But now there was no sensuous overwhelming of the rational, no ineluctable submission to deep and primitive pleasures. Instead he felt another primeval impulse, the only instinct stronger than the ravening desire to copulate: fear.

There was a charge in the very air they breathed and, in an instant of self-exculpation, Kite attributed their strange behaviour in the cabin below to this atmospheric electricity. The next moment he fought aside this fancy and forced his brain into a logical channel. The strange, numbing energy came with a thin veil of cloud, through which the sun shone encircled by a halo. This was but a precursor of the massive disturbance boiling up over the horizon to the east.

'Hurricane!' he called, giving voice to his comprehension. At the same minute Rahman spoke of the phenomenon called by the Chinese *taifun*: the great wind. Kite had endured a hurricane before, in the very same schooner, and the poor *Spitfire* had been severely battered. It was not an experience that he wished to repeat, but there was no time to repine. Instead he looked quickly about the deck and then shouted out, 'All hands on deck! Mr Rahman, we must secure the ship. Have your watch lay aloft and get the square topsails off her and then we will bring her up into the wind and heave to.'

'At once, Kite Sahib.'

Kite spared a fleeting thought for the two women down below. Was this a judgement for their dissolute intention? And how long had Sarah and Nisha been intimate? God, what a time to discover such a tumult of passion and lust! What did Harper know of this? And had *he* been embroiled in any similar such wild behaviour while he, Kite, had been on deck attending to the safety of the schooner? Then, as if summoned by the diabolical thought, Harper was beside him, tucking his own shirt tails into his breeches and looking to windward with concern written plain on his ugly features.

'*Hurricano!*' he said quaintly and, without awaiting any response from Kite, set about checking the lashings on the boats on their chocks amidships. In a few minutes the deck of the schooner seethed with activity. With the helm down and the staysail backed, the *Spitfire* curtseyed to the sea, swooping over the underlying swells that had grown appreciably in height and period in the last few moments. The halliards were cast off their pins and the gaffs lowered. The flogging canvas was bundled away and lashed secure; out on the bowsprit men tamed the fluttering jibs and then, with much shouting, Harper was rousing out a scrap of trysail made of heavy-duty canvas and running it up the mainmast while up forward the boatswain was preparing to hoist a storm staysail. Among this movement, Kite was pleased to see McClusky checking for loose gear and doubling the lashings on the guns. It reminded Kite of something else.

'Mr McClusky!'

'Sir?' McClusky turned, expectantly.

'When you have attended to the guns, do you and the Boatswain go below and check the cargo is secure. Set up additional toms, if you think it necessary, and then have the well pumped dry.'

'Aye, aye, sir!'

Kite turned and looked to windward again. The warmth had gone out of the sun. Now the sky immediately above the horizon was so dark that it might almost be described as black. By contrast the line of the sea was etched in a lighter tone and Kite could already see the effect of the stronger wind as the hitherto unbroken line now rucked up into the jagged saw-teeth of distant wave crests. It would be upon them within an hour, he guessed, two at the very most, and perhaps sooner. His thoughts ran hither and yon, like a weaver's shuttle. He felt the mental cramp of indecision, staring round the deck as if goaded by some instinct that urged him to do more. Then Sarah was on deck beside him. She was dressed in shirt and breeches and there was no hint of the violent passions that had so lately stirred the trio in the cabin.

'It is a hurricane,' Kite said, his voice flat, noncommittal. 'You must prepare Nisha for the worst.'

'Yes,' she said, but she did not draw away. After a moment's pause, while Kite's thoughts tossed between an urgent need to attend to his ship and the pricking diversion of unbidden lust, she said, 'William, I would not have you think . . .'

'Not now, Sarah,' he breathed distractedly, looking away, 'for God's sake, not now . . .'

'Grant me one moment's attention.' He swung back to her. 'Remember always, William, that it is you I love.'

They held each other's gaze for several long seconds and then he said, 'And I you,' whereupon she smiled and looked away, bright-eyed, turning to go below as the *Spitfire* leaned to a heavy swell and Harper came aft to demand his attention.

'She's as snug as we can make her, sir. It wants only McClusky to report the hold secure.'

Kite nodded. Suddenly he recalled what had been sub-consciously troubling him and, at almost the same moment, Rahman caught his eye and Kite beckoned him over. 'Gentle-men, we all know what we are about to endure. We are, however, in a quandary for we have not located the unnamed bank and with so powerful a wind to the eastward are in danger of being driven ashore on the Paracels to loo'ard. We cannot therefore run off before the wind unless its first onslaught is favourable. At the moment we continue to make northing, but God alone knows whether it will veer . . .'

'It *will* veer, Kite Sahib,' Rahman announced emphatically, 'in fact it has already begun to shift . . .'

The three men looked aloft at the pendant at the main truck.

'Very well,' Kite replied, 'we shall head north and somewhat to the east while we may, but the instant this becomes impos-sible and we are cast towards the west, we must heave to.'

'If we can lay to the north-east, that will do, will it not?' Harper asked.

Both Kite and Rahman nodded vigorously. 'Whether or not we find the bank, we have to hope that the reports that there is no less than ten fathoms over it are accurate. We shall have to risk passing over the top of it in order to guarantee avoiding the Paracels.'

Spitfire heeled to a violent gust and, with the precipitate change that Kite had found preposterous in one of Herr Haydn's operas, the sky grew dark and the surface of the sea skittish. Within a quarter of an hour it was blowing a full gale and Kite had sent below as many of the hands as he could. Warned by Harper, the cook had doused the galley fire after brewing up two large kettles of salt pork and biscuit and the men now fed on the hot mess in anticipation of many hours without cooked food.

Kite had no appetite, but urged by Harper he took a bowl of the stuff on deck. He was reluctant to go below and confront the two women, fearing the tumult of his emotions if he did so, for an odd temptation to abandon the schooner to her fate and to drown himself in sensuality before Providence drowned him in a watery grave seemed set fair to overwhelm him. He fought off this seductive distraction, mystified by the event of that early morning. He was no longer a young man and had passed the best of his middle years. Many men considered themselves old at his age, content to sit in the sun and watch their grandchildren play. Was that the strange imperative? That he had no children, let alone children's children, of his own? Perhaps; and did such a powerful impulse prompt him to mate with the receptive Nisha?

Good God, what *would* Harper think?

And then Harper loomed alongside him like a spectral conscience made manifest, his ugly face poked close to Kite as he shouted above the now howling gale, 'Your tarpaulin, Cap'n.'

Kite took the stiffened oiled canvas cover-all and drew it about him.

'I've seen the women are all right in the cabin, Cap'n.'

Kite stared at him, seeking some sign in his expression that told Kite he knew of the improprieties his mistress had been guilty of, but there was nothing other than Zachariah's plain, honest ugliness confronting him.

'Nisha may well be fearful in the coming hours, Zachariah.'

'Sarah will look after her, Cap'n, don't you fear.'

No, Kite thought, he need not fear that. Sarah who swore she loved him, could yet enjoy a secret intimacy with the voluptuous Indian. Sarah, Sarah . . .

All he could do was nod acknowledgement of Harper's well-meant reassurance and brace himself as a sea slapped at

Spitfire's quarter with a thud that made the entire hull tremble and sent a column of water high into the air where it was blown apart by the wind and swept the deck like buckshot.

Kite and Harper cannoned into one another and Harper shouted, 'For what we are about to receive . . . I'd better get another pair of hands on the helm to man the relieving tackles.'

Kite braced himself and *Spitfire* began to roll and scend under the onslaught of the wind and sea. Even though only two scraps of canvas were exposed to the brunt of the gale, the schooner was driving through the sea, her bow wave roiling up under her figurehead as she thrust the mass of water aside in her headlong flight.

The power in such a wind was impressive, as was the strength of the little vessel whose fabric bore this impetus and converted it through the cunning of her builders and riggers, and the skill of her crew, from the movement of a mass of air in one direction, to the passage of a ship and her cargo in another.

Kite stretched out a hand to grasp a backstay for support. He felt the thrum of it as it transmitted some of this energy downwards into the timbers of the hull. He was stung by spray driving incessantly through the air as the noise of the wind rose to a shriek. If he was foolish enough to expose the flesh of his face to it, it not only tore at his skin, but seemed to distort his very own features.

And yet he knew that the shriek was but an overture to the *taifun* itself. The great wind of the Chinese and the cyclone of the Bay of Bengal were like the hurricano of the West Indies. The mature wind blew with the booming thunder of great guns and the sea, whipped by its master, lay down in obedience, excoriated into wet air which filled every crevice of the world with the sting of salt. Moreover Kite had guessed, after his previous experience in the Atlantic, that the *taifun* blew in a vast, circular motion, and that a ship, caught and almost immobile within the system of the great storm, would, no matter how fast she drove through the water, be subject to a change in the wind's direction. What might now be a fair wind might soon be foul and at some unknown distance under their lee lay spread the reefs, islets and islands of the Paracels.

The thought was sufficient to cause a cold sweat to break out along his spine, to join the runnels of water which had defied the tarpaulin and trickled uncomfortably down his back. He tried to master the dynamics of the revolving system but could do no more than acknowledge that the slow veer of the wind would entrap them in its central eye where, he knew, the seas would rear in cataclysmic and random violence, reminiscent of the beginning and the end of all things.

All day they endured this onslaught. As the darkness of the night closed about them they were deluged with rain after which came a horrifying torrent of small birds which fluttered about their feet in such numbers that they crushed them underfoot, smearing their blood and feathers across the planking. On into the next dawning day nature raged with all its malevolent force, and clinging on to his labouring schooner Kite felt along with fear for the coming hours a sublime feeling that if death claimed him at that moment it would be supremely apt. Alongside this wild and transcendingly wondrous joy came another thought, that the violent stirrings of his own blood had possessed some of this overwhelming character, that his individuality had been subsumed by a more compelling tribal compulsion, driven by powers utterly beyond any rational comprehension.

As the typhoon boomed its way towards the first of its mighty climaxes, Kite knew with a conviction that was as powerful as any instinctive urge that he had been as simultaneously empowered and diminished by the experience of that sensual link between the three of them as he was by the experience of enduring the typhoon. The great wind that raked the surface of the South China Sea was a mighty physical reflection of the sensual turmoil that had ripped through the presumptions and pride of William Kite, merchant and mariner. Moreover, Kite thought sublimely as the wind bellowed in its fulsome triumph and he clung to the straining backstay, there was little to choose in their natural power.

Then, as if to lend majestic mystery to this gross perception, the stay upon which he relied suddenly parted, its lower end striking him across the face and shoulder like a whip in the hand of God. In the same instant the whole structure of the hull shuddered as, in a succession of fractures, it was followed by the weather rigging of the maintopmast which collapsed to leeward and thrashed about aloft, wounding the crosstrees and making a ravel of ropes and lines thirty feet above the deck.

In the two days that followed they suffered no more damage to their rigging. After a struggle aloft they managed to pass lines round the flailing maintopmast, restraining it sufficiently to prevent further mishap. Instead the level of water rose in the well so that the hands were obliged to pump for prolonged periods at frequent intervals. It was clear that *Spitfire*'s hull had suffered some damage, but Kite's anxiety for the state of the schooner was far exceeded by worry about her position. Locating the ten-fathom bank was important in that it provided the only reliable guide as to their relative location to the far greater danger of the Paracels, but it proved impossible for even a single reliable cast of the lead to be taken and the only slight indication that they might have closed the shoals was an increased breaking of the waves which Kite, Rahman and Harper thought *might* have betrayed the proximity of the reef. But having, in the absence of evidence to the contrary, convinced themselves that this was indeed the case, one of the men swore he had seen a small island to the southward. The temptation to dismiss this as a mere self-deception was too easy, and Kite had to take the report seriously, though no studying of the chart could square the two events, given the wind conditions and their likely drift under the tiny scraps of canvas they now bore. Did Kite lay the greater credence upon the sighting of supposed breakers by the officers, or the more terrifying but unverifiable appearance of the island spotted by a mere seaman? He pondered this for some time, aware that if the latter was the case then it was inconceivable that they had not ripped the bottom out of the vessel long since.

Of course, Kite could not entirely dismiss this hypothesis as fantasy. There was the evidence of the increased intake of water and, on the balance of probabilities, he thought that they had made more leeway to the east than otherwise, in which case not only could the island have indeed been there, but the breakers might not have been the ten-fathom bank, but something shallower, a part of the complex submarine obstruction making up the Paracels. As his tired mind fumbled towards this inhospitable conclusion he knew that he must assume the latter.

And yet what could he do about it? To let the schooner run off before the wind might place them in a worse condition, while remaining hove to at least retained a measure of control and left them nearer their last observed position, for all the good that that meant. As everyone else aboard the storm-tossed *Spitfire*, when not required to do their stint at the pumps, tend a fraying rope or stand a trick at the helm, grabbed what rest they could, Kite remained on deck. It was impossible for him to sleep and he kept his lonely post except when doubt nagged him and sent him below to stare at the sodden chart. Not that he gained any comfort from its blank and unsounded places, for there was no science in his contemplation. Instead he seemed like a water-diviner lacking any forked hazel twig. It was as though he held out his experience above the inscribed paper, hoping that it would give off some palpable exhalation from which he might in some way detect a fact.

But the chart was no dynamic underground spring; it was only a poor imperfect work of man and much in want of improvement. Instead, Kite's numbed brain succumbed to the vague but terrifying suggestion of providential displeasure. He had behaved grossly and the wind was the agent of God. Standing braced in the creaking cabin he felt like an allegorical figure, flanked by the soporific and prone bodies of Sarah and Nisha rolled in their blankets, pallid and half-conscious, devoid of any passionate pretensions. To add to the retributive air, empty bottles, those symbols of ultimate dissolution, rolled to and fro across the sodden deck in allegorical reproach.

As the lurid sunsets faded into the gloom of night, Kite wearily returned to the deck and lashed himself to the rail, conscious of the muttered curses of the toiling helmsmen, of the occasional comment of the officers as the watches rotated, and the dim glimmer of the binnacle light which mocked their inability to do more than keep the schooner close to the wind. But, with biblical conformity, on the third day the sun rose to a moderated wind, appearing briefly through the scud. The great boom of the typhoon had gone and even the shriek of its passage through their straining rigging sounded exhausted rather than malevolent.

As the wind finally dropped during the succeeding hours that day, Kite, his quadrant tucked into the crook of his arm, waited for the sun to show its pale face through the persisting veil of cloud. In the end it was Harper who caught a meridian altitude, snatching the instrument from Kite as he slumped in utter exhaustion under the weather rail, a loop of line about his waist, indifferent to the mate's cry that the sun seemed likely to emerge sufficiently to be navigationally useful.

Perversely Harper's triumph was as ephemeral as the solar data he applied to his observation. The parallel of latitude ran east to west, sixteen degrees and fifty-six minutes north of the equator, a line which on their chart sliced through the northern sector of the Paracels. They might lie anywhere along that imaginary line and the knowledge that they had not been driven clear of the danger only increased Kite's concern when he was finally informed. But the wind came now from the southern quarter and at least progress could be made to the northwards, enabling them to break out of the encirclement of the reefs.

Later that day they took soundings and found no bottom with the twenty-fathom lead-line. Nor was there any sign of land nor breakers to be had from the masthead. Kite turned in properly that evening in the knowledge that they were clear of the Paracels. Only the dull clunk, clunk of the pumps reminded him that they were not yet safe.

Chapter Sixteen

Of Wood and Water

A t the cry of land Kite stirred to full consciousness. He had been lying half-awake for some time, unwilling to surface and admit the truth of his real existence, preferring to remain in the penumbral world of the somnambulist rather than take up the burden of responsibility. But even this personal retreat could not resist the temptation of such a cry, and even if he *had* resisted here was Sarah rushing into the cabin to rouse him.

On deck almost the entire ship's company was assembled, so much desired was some resolution to all their uncertainties. Land, but what land? Kite could not see it at first; he was still fuddled by sleep. Experience made him raise his eyes from their scouring of the line of the horizon and there it was, a few degrees up in the sky, the rounded summit of high land faintly distinguishable from the slightly lighter tone of the surrounding sky.

'It must be Hainan,' Harper said, ranging up and doing Kite's thinking for him. 'If we can find a quiet bay, we can sort that maintopmast out and stop that damned leak.'

Kite grunted assent. 'If . . .'

Two mornings later they had found what they were looking for and stood inshore where, at the head of a small bay, a crescent of sand appeared, upon which pounded the remnant swells of the recent typhoon. The bay was surrounded by low undulating hills, covered by green vegetation and seemingly devoid of human habitation. Through his glass Kite spied the silvery flash of a stream descending from the rising ground: fresh water, and that forest would yield enough firewood to stock them for months. Within an hour of them bringing up to their anchor the boats were pulling for the shore laden with empty casks and under McClusky's command. Kite's orders were specific. There was to be no wandering off. The wooding party was to be properly supervised and the watering party was to concentrate on filling every cask as rapidly as possible, for Rahman had advised them that although there was no evidence of a village, usually betrayed by the level patches of small terraced fields on the hillside, it was almost certain that their arrival would in due course be brought to the ears of the local mandarin, who would see their presence as both illegal and as a potential for 'squeeze'.

Kite understood. Here he would find no privilege of refuge for the distressed mariner; here was only corruption, made manifest by 'squeeze' and the opportunity offered to him to sell his illegal opium at a premium. Beggars, he reminded Sarah as he explained the need for a speedy refit of *Spitfire*, could not be choosers. Quizzing Rahman, Kite was disappointed when the Indian dissuaded him from any attempt to sell the opium here, on the coast of Hainan.

'But if we are apprehended by the local mandarin, would not the offer of the sale of opium encourage a spirit conducive to our aid?'

Rahman shook his head violently. 'Oh no, Kite Sahib, it would only attract the attentions of the war junks of pirates and in all possibility those pirates would be what you are calling "hand in glove" with the mandarin.'

Kite smiled at the metaphor. 'You do not know this coast, though, do you?'

Rahman looked pained, as though an accusation lay in Kite's question. 'No, Kite Sahib, I do not, but I do know that if you try and trade outside the areas where some convention has been established, you are the more likely to be cheated than find any profit.' And when Kite appeared reluctant to accept this,

Rahman added, 'Hooker Sahib would not have traded here; he would only have traded in Macao, or near the Pearl River. Here it is too dangerous. We must leave from here as soon as possible.'

'You must listen to him, William,' Nisha broke in. Kite looked at her. The two women were engaged on some embroidery, hitherto silent as Kite conferred with Rahman and conducted the business of the ship until Nisha was moved to interrupt. It was the first time Kite had spared the widow more than a passing glance since he had watched her alluring rump crawl lasciviously across the cabin. The memory irked him and edged his response.

'Must I?'

'William,' Sarah's tone was reproachful, 'Nisha is aware of the value of Mr Rahman's advice and you would do well to heed both of them.'

Kite opened his mouth to respond sharply, but Sarah caught his eye and there was something in her expression that disturbed him far more than the memory of Nisha's wobbling buttocks. Instead he nodded. 'Very well,' he said curtly, turning to Rahman. 'Thank you.'

The incident disturbed Kite. The reawakening of the thoughts that had occupied the trio in the cabin as the typhoon boiled over the horizon threatened to compete for his attention. He felt the matter could not be left there, that sooner or later some reference to it must arise between Nisha, Sarah and himself. Moreover, he was discomfited by the thought that the intimacy between the two women guaranteed their own discussion of the affair. Was Nisha's uncharacteristic intervention evidence of an emerging attempt at domination? Had she in some way acquired the upper hand over Sarah? It seemed impossible, but so did the thought of Sarah in the arms of Nisha, and he stumbled out of the cabin in Rahman's wake, eager to divert his mind from contemplating so awkward, embarrassing but subtly fascinating, prurient and lubricious a subject.

He would make time for it later.

*   *   *

While the boats were away Harper and the remaining members of the crew, which included both the boatswain and the carpenter, shifted bales of opium, stores and gear in the hold to locate the origin of the leak. It had been expected to ease somewhat after they had fetched their anchor, but this had not happened and in fact the ingress of water had worsened significantly. It was now sufficiently serious to cause grave concern. Kite feared that to stop it altogether they would need to beach *Spitfire* and careen her. If his worst fears were realized and they had not only torn off some of the precious copper sheathing but damaged the planking of the hull by unknowingly scraping over a reef, it was almost certain that they would be compelled to take drastic measures. By the end of the day a dirty and disgruntled Harper reported to Kite, waiting in the 'tween deck, that he feared the worst.

''Tis amidships, Cap'n, 'bout the worst God-damned place it could be . . .'

'You are sure?' Kite queried, hoping against hope.

'Aye,' Harper nodded. 'It worries me that it has worsened after we anchored.'

'As if something has been disturbed and – what, fallen away?'

Harper nodded. 'Exactly, Cap'n, and I'm thinking at first that it might be some copper that has worked off, copper sheathing that was covering a split plank.'

'Or copper that came off a long time ago, admitted the shipworm and only now, after the hurricane, has become serious enough to trouble us,' Kite theorized.

'Aye, that's equally so.'

'Have you found the actual source of the leak?' Kite asked.

Harper shook his head. 'No, we got the bilge as dry as possible, which was not very,' he added, indicating the stinking wet state of his clothing, 'and I could see the water running forrard from abaft the midship's well. I gained a second access to the lower ceiling abaft the mainmast and found it trickling aft. We'll need to keep pumping through the night.'

Kite grunted agreement. 'So we've to lift the ground tier of casks amidships to get at the leak.'

'Aye, but not to fix it. 'Tis my guess we will have to beach her . . .' Harper said gloomily.

'I hope to God we don't. If Rahman's warnings are to be heeded we are exposed to the attacks of pirates who would be delighted to know we've a cargo of opium on board.'

Harper pulled a face. 'Well, Cap'n, we'd better keep the watches going, then, and not just for the God-damned pumping.'

'Quite so, but, Zachariah, get yourself cleaned up and join us for dinner. Nisha could do with some attention.'

Harper's ugly face cracked into a grin. 'I ain't sure I couldn't do with some myself, if I can summon up the energy.'

As he turned away Kite wondered why he felt less pleased for his old friend and shipmate. Was he himself jealous of having an opportunity for gratification satisfied by another or, with McClusky turned in and Rahman on deck, was he just nervous of taking dinner with the women alone? He did not seek the answer to so compromising a question but clambered up on deck to hear news of the wooding and watering parties.

By the time they sat down to dinner in the cabin they were all too tired for conversation. The ordeal of the typhoon was too recent and most of them felt their bodies swaying, a residual nervous reaction to the late violent motion of the *Spitfire*, though the schooner presently lay quietly nodding to the low swell. Nor was the food stimulating, for the fresh stores had been consumed long ago and only the duff and some bottles of Madeira enlivened the repast. The men were too much preoccupied with the leak and long silences ensued.

'Is the leak very bad?' Sarah asked, desperate to terminate one of these lacunae. Kite nodded as he chewed a particularly difficult chunk of salt pork. 'And you don't really know its cause,' she went on.

'No,' Harper broke in, laying his knife down and toying

with the stem of his wine glass. He stared unseeing at revolving Madeira.

Sarah noticed this abstraction and divined Harper's preoccupation. 'But you think you know its cause, Zachariah, do you not?'

Harper looked up sharply, like a boy caught scrumping apples. 'Well, I have a theory, 'tis true.'

'And what is that?' Kite asked, finally forcing the masticated pork down his throat.

'Well, Cap'n, d'you not think it might be a keel bolt?'

Kite, looked up sharply. 'How so? We had them drawn . . . when? Two years ago when she was docked?'

Harper's ugly face crumpled with doubt. 'I know, but somewhere I think I have heard some assertion that iron bolts and copper sheathing, when contiguous, are in some strange way inimical . . .'

Kite considered this odd proposition. Something tugged at his own memory, something overheard and not comprehended at the time. 'Inimical . . .' he said, 'but how so?'

Harper shrugged. 'I sure don't understand, Cap'n, but I'm darned certain I've heard some odd notion that 'tis so.'

'And what do you mean by *inimical*, Zachariah?' Sarah asked.

Harper shrugged again. 'It ain't no good you quizzing me, ma'am, I just don't know, but I'm damn sure that I've heard it said.'

'But what happens when these two contiguous metals are inimical? Was this rumour you heard attached to a story about a leak?' Sarah persisted, aware that it was probable that Harper's recollection had more substance than these bare bones of half-comprehended fact.

It was Harper's turn to frown now and he moved his right hand from twirling his wine glass to scratching his forehead. 'I cannot recollect, but I think it was more than that . . .'

Kite suddenly snapped his fingers and the staccato noise attracted the attention of them all. 'I recall it!' he said, his eyes gleaming. 'And I'm damned if I know why I didn't sooner!

There was a Liverpool Guineaman owned by Wyncolls and Morgan, I forget her name, but she was coppered like *Spitfire* and a few other fast slavers in emulation of some frigates which had been sheathed by the Navy Board. She went missing on the Middle Passage and there was a rumour that her hands had complained to the companies of other ships awaiting slaves in the Bonny River that she leaked like a sieve!' He frowned. 'Little notice was taken of the loss, but I do remember some discussion when it became known that the iron fastenings of the frigates had been found much wasted underneath the copper sheets.' Kite frowned.

'There were questions as to whether she should not have been fastened throughout with copper. It was all rather inconclusive—'

'Aye,' broke in Harper, 'I recall it being talked of. She was the *Ynys Mon*, Cap'n!'

'Then all our iron keel bolts are likely to be in a similar condition,' Sarah said, consternation clear on her face, 'and we are two thousand miles from a graving dock!'

'Aye, the closest is at Bombay,' Harper said, the triumph of resolving the conundrum short-lived.

'They may not all be in the same condition,' Kite temporized soberly. 'The poor *Spitfire* has just suffered a terrible wracking. Tell me, Zachariah, are you confident that only a single bolt is responsible for so large an ingress of water?'

'Well, I can say as much as it was only obvious that such was the case.'

'Very well. Then it seems to me that, although we have no grounds for complacence, we may yet return to Bombay. We must do our best to avoid heavy weather. I apprehend that this inimical quality must owe something to the immersion of these two metals in seawater, for no such circumstance happens in air. Now, each keel bolt is driven into the hull slushed with a copious amount of white lead and all were tarred, so these substances must first be eroded. It is reasonable to assume this erosion is unequal and that our recent experience has identified the greatest weakness.'

'Then we are not going to sink?' Nisha asked, leaning forward and speaking for the first time.

Kite smiled reassuringly. 'No, my dear, we are not going to sink.'

There was a long silence, then Harper said as he dabbed his grubby napkin round his mouth and thrust his chair backwards, 'Cap'n, I'd like to get to the bottom of this before the night is out.'

Kite nodded and stood up, smiling at the two women and resisting the appeal of Harper's unwitting punning. 'I agree and I'm afraid we shall have to leave you, ladies.'

They enlisted the labour of half the watch on deck and within an hour had started the bungs from the ground tier of water casks to lighten them. They could be refilled on the morrow, and while Harper waited for the water to be pumped out of the bilge they trimmed their lanterns.

They located the source of the leak almost immediately and although the head of the offending iron keel bolt seemed tight enough, the water welling past it was incontrovertible evidence that insufficient of its substance existed in the hole drilled down through keelson and keel to prevent the entry of water.

'We could not have rectified that even had we emptied the ship and beached her,' Kite said, 'and I have no idea whether there is sufficient tidal range hereabouts for even that purpose.'

Harper grunted as he bent over the gleaming black head of the bolt, his great paw twisting at it.

'I should leave well alone, Zachariah,' Kite said, 'if you disturb it we may have a veritable fountain rising in here.' Harper withdrew his hand as though it had been burnt. 'Now, let us place a heavy pad over that bolt head and see if we cannot at least reduce the inflow.'

Harper grasped the notion instantly and looked up, his weatherbeaten face a mass of highlights and dark seams in the lantern-light. 'I'll see to it.'

'Very well. I'll be on deck,' Kite replied with a tired smile.

223

The night air was cool and calm. Above them the great arch of the sky was spangled with stars. The *Spitfire*'s deck was in darkness, but for the faint starlight, for an anchor light would betray their presence to any unscrupulous predator. The schooner's waist was cluttered with the full water casks hoisted out of the boats and waiting to be struck down into the hold and Kite made his way to the taffrail, acknowledging the presence of Rahman, pale in his robe as he paced the tiny quarterdeck. Reaching the after rail Kite stretched and drew the pure air into his lungs, driving out the residue of the hold's mephitic stench. The dark presence of the land loomed high above to the west, cutting out the stars and, as his eyes grew accustomed to the darkness, showing a sharp edge against the sky. It was a tremulous moment of numinous beauty, to which a quality of eternity was added by his exhaustion. He felt unwilling to end the strange feeling of peace that pervaded his person and was filled with a longing for it to go on for ever as he seemed to float above the problems and perplexities of the world.

He had no idea how long he had been standing there when Harper joined him. He might have been dozing, though standing upright, for the discreet cough of the approaching mate made him start.

''Tis all done, Cap'n,' Harper whispered, as though aware of the sanctity of the moment. 'There is hardly a trickle now.'

Kite turned. 'Well done, Zachariah.'

'We should get some sleep, sir,' Harper said and Kite felt the American's fingers lightly touch his sleeve in a gesture of genuine concern. He was intensely moved by the gesture.

'You go below, I shall follow in a moment.'

Harper hesitated. 'Cap'n Kite?' he murmured with a slow deliberation that Kite knew presaged some important matter. Intuitively Kite knew it had nothing to do with a leaky schooner.

'What is it, Zachariah?'

'Do you think Nisha would accept a proposal of marriage from me?'

Kite was surprised and turned to stare at the pallid oval of

Harper's face. He felt a twist of pain in his own gut, aware that it was both unworthy and unkind. 'Why, my dear fellow, I really have no idea, but I see no reason why not. But think, what would you . . . I mean how would you subsist, for I do not know what is to become of any of us even if this enterprise succeeds? We are a deuced long way from Liverpool.'

'It occurred to me that I might establish myself in one of these Country ships. I have no home in America and neither Liverpool nor England hold any hopes for my prosperity or advancement. India, on the other hand . . .' Harper was buoyed up by the prospect of love and full of optimism. 'I am no longer young, Cap'n Kite,' he concluded.

'And you find the lady reciprocates your, er, affections?' Kite asked with an awkwardly strained prurience.

He could almost hear Harper's grin as the mate responded. 'Well, sure, Cap'n!'

Kite nodded. 'Well, Zachariah, I wish you success. Certainly I should be obliged if the lady was detached from my household, but that is a heartless consideration,' he added hurriedly. 'Come, we are both tired and it is long past the time for sleep.'

And taking Harper's elbow, the two men walked forward towards the companionway.

Chapter Seventeen

The Anchor

B y the following evening all the water casks, including those discharged into the bilge for ease of removal to inspect the leak, were full. Those not yet on deck lay bobbing alongside, lashed by lines in a loose raft. The garnered firewood had been cut and bundled into manageable faggots and this either filled the boats which lay astern on their painters or lay on deck ready to be stowed below. As for the wounded maintopmast, this had been finally sent down to the deck. The work had proceeded uninterrupted, though the sharp-peaked sails of two three-masted junks had been seen offshore and officers and ratings frequently cast their eyes anxiously seawards.

Having attended to the leak as best they could, Kite's next priority was to load the wood and water. This was a slow task, for access to the lower hold was impeded by the stow of opium and a lack of access in so small a vessel. The full casks were heavy and it was necessary to stow them with care, bung upwards and their round bilges free, their weight being taken on their shoulders by adjacent casks. The cut bundles of wood were easier to stow, though the hands dealing with them collected many scratches for their pains. It was a day later before Kite turned the hands' attention to the maintopmast. The parting of the rigging had over-loaded the spar, which had been bruised by shot from the *Alcmene*. Moreover, in falling, it had badly distorted the iron-work of the upper ring by which it was united to the mainmast proper. With no spare spars it was considered necessary to send a party ashore and fell a suitable tree. A careful scanning of the upper slopes of the hills had suggested that tall pines grew there. Marking a course upwards through the dense lower vegetation, Harper led his small group of men with their axes and coiled drag ropes. Kite meanwhile supervised the lowering of the damaged spar and the stripping of the blocks and rigging. He also contemplated the twisted mast-iron, aware that the small hand forge on board was quite inadequate to the task of restoring the heavy iron ring to its former accommodating shape.

'That too will have to be done ashore,' he remarked to Rahman, wiping his hands on a rag and strolling aft to where Sarah and Nisha sat at their embroidery under the awning. This was half-furled to allow the hands room to work round the base of the mainmast and Kite stood looking down at the yards of silk that lay like a bond between the two women. He had paid scant attention to the thing, but now he became aware that the length of material, which Nisha had produced after they had left Bombay, was now worked with a myriad creatures set amid the leaves of a fantastical jungle. Elephants of several sizes, some trumpeting with elevated trunks, some linked trunk to tail in a frieze, others rolling logs, formed a repetitive motif along the borders, interspersed with tigers whose predatory nature was indicated in a dozen styles of curved-backed, stalking postures that reminded Kite of the cats he had known about his boyhood village in Cumbria. Monkeys and gibbons sported among the trees, while snakes writhed through both the foliage of the trees and the long grasses that rose from the ground. The fine stitchwork was admirable and it struck Kite that he had no appreciation of the amount of skill and labour that Sarah and Nisha had put into their work.

'What is this animal?' he asked, lifting a fold of the material and pointing to a long-bodied, short-legged animal. 'I did not know there were stoats in India.'

'Nisha will tell you,' Sarah said with a smile.

'That is a mongoose,' Nisha explained, 'they sometimes kill

snakes like this cobra.' She pointed to an upright snake whose head rose from a hood.

'Good Lord,' Kite said. 'And what is it for, this magnificent tapestry?'

Nisha shrugged and cast down her eyes. 'It is to keep us amused, William,' Sarah said, 'to while away the tedious hours of this voyage and sustain our expectations.'

'I see,' he responded flatly, sensing in Sarah's tone an oblique admonishment for the boredom the women had had to endure. It was an ironic contrast with his own anxiety as he fretted about their vulnerability exposed in this bay. Like most commanders, Kite was impatient of delays, and delays born out of the inadequacy of his vessel were the most frustrating of all. While these relied upon the best efforts of the crew, over which as commander he had control, Kite instinctively wanted those efforts to be tireless and unremitting. As the hours lengthened into days, he resented the hours spent in sleep and eating; he knew it was unreasonable and fought his desire to place impossible demands upon his men, but the temptation remained and now Sarah seemed to want to complain about her plight.

The expression of discontent, mild though it was, profoundly irritated Kite. He intensely disliked any feelings that disturbed the inner equanimity of his soul and the savage sexual turmoil occasioned shortly before the onslaught of the typhoon had, he had hoped, been expiated by the long ordeal of endurance. Indeed he had felt that the numinous moment he had enjoyed after locating the leak was a sort of providential absolution, and this impression seemed heightened by the news that Harper's intentions towards Nisha would remove any source of future temptation.

Now Sarah's sharpness conveyed the impression of a discontent uncharacteristic of her as a wife. Was it only a reproach to him, or a further symptom of her attraction to Nisha? In his present frame of mind he could not see that it might also be a cry from the heart. Kite, almost overwhelmed with the cares of command, was naturally unsympathetic to the cares of the victims of boredom. Nor could he see that for the active and intelligent Sarah boredom was far greater a burden than for the Indian woman whose cultural acquiescence had once led her to accompany her first husband to his funeral pyre. Such abstractions were utterly beyond the imagination of him at the best of times, let alone now as his vessel lay at anchor disabled on the hostile coast of China, where his presence was illegal and might soon attract the attentions of pirates or imperial war junks.

In due course, however, the figures of Harper and his party, dragging a length of tree trunk, appeared on the beach. Kite buried his impatience in activity and set off in a boat to inspect the spar, taking ashore the makings of a fire, some tongs, hand-spikes, mauls and the twisted mast hoop, along with three adzes and a saw. As Harper roughly fashioned the timber to the basic size of the maintopmast, Kite located a corner of the beach where the jungle swept down over some rocks and a fire could be kindled to make a primitive forge and an adjacent boulder turned into an anvil.

Two hours later, as Harper's party began to float the rough-trimmed spar out to the *Spitfire*, Kite's improvised blacksmiths began to hammer and jemmy the twisted iron back into its old shape, annealing it in the sea that surged along the sandy shore. By that evening the restored mast-iron had been refitted to the cap of the main lower mast and awaited the completion of the topmast. This took a further day but by that afternoon, after sundry trips aloft waving rule and callipers, Harper pronounced himself satisfied. The boatswain called for turpentine, linseed oil and tallow, and the remaining iron work was fitted to the mast as it was slushed down. In due course, as the sun set, the work of rigging the spar was well advanced. As the sun dipped below the summit of the high ground and the shadow leapt out into the bay, Kite ordered work to finish for the day.

'It can be completed in the morning,' he said to the hands as they milled in the waist, tired and hungry. 'You can see to it, Mr Harper,' he said formally, 'you, Mr McClusky, may accompany me and we will go in search of some game. There are numerous ducks about and it would be a pity not to dine on roast duck before we leave this quiet spot.'

Remarking on this intention in the cabin, Sarah volunteered her own services. 'I can handle a gun as well as a foil,' she said.

Kite contemplated the proposal. It would be good to get ashore in her company, McClusky's presence notwithstanding. A shooting expedition would be harmless enough and even if they attracted the attention of the natives the junks seen off the coast had not reappeared and no Chinese had been seen throughout their sojourn in the deserted bay. Looking at the expectant Sarah he found it easy to dismiss his earlier suspicions of her motives. Instead he was reminded of a day in the country of Rhode Island, when they had first found themselves lovers. It was a long time ago, he thought sadly, and still they lived like adventurers. He smiled at his wife. 'Of course, my dear, you are a better shot than I, but we lack a gun dog and duck are difficult to recover.'

'Take Jack and give him a penny for every duck he recovers from the water,' Sarah said laughing, and the notion found favour with the others in the cabin. It was a measure of the easing of tension after the refitting of the schooner.

And so, next morning Sarah, Kite, McClusky and Jack Bow were pulled ashore and left on the beach while Harper and the hands completed the rigging of the maintopmast. For two hours the sound of musket shots rolled around the bay and those toiling on the deck of the *Spitfire* looked up to see the little puffs of powder smoke and the splashes of Jack Bow as he plunged and waded out to recover the ducks armed with a long boat-hook, for he could not swim. By noon they had a good bag and the ducks had been frightened off, so the shooting party, which had wandered along the beach for some considerable distance, began its laden march back to the landing place.

Preoccupied by their burden they took little notice of the anchored schooner and it was only when the first four-pounder gun was fired as an alarm by Harper that they realized that three junks were standing into the bay.

Kite was in the water up to his knees before he was aware of what he was doing. Fortunately Harper had despatched a boat as soon as he had become aware of the approaching junks and before discharging the gun, and this now came into view round *Spitfire*'s stern and headed for the beach, the bright sunlight flashing off its oar-blades. Kite, Sarah, McClusky and a sodden Jack stood under the hot sun and waited impatiently as the boat surged towards them. Mercifully the wind was light, scarcely ruffling the blue waters of the bay, and although it was clear that the junks were able to harness what little breeze there was, it was equally obvious that the party would reach *Spitfire* before the junks drew too close. The boat approached with the boatswain at the helm and Kite waded out with the first load of ducks, quickly forming a chain with McClusky, Jack and Sarah as they handed them out, brace by brace, as fast as they were able.

Handing Sarah aboard, Kite insisted Jack followed before he and McClusky shoved the bow of the boat off and scrambled in after them over the duck carcasses piled in the bow sheets. There they squatted uncomfortably as the boat was swung and headed out for the schooner; a few minutes later Kite was scrambling up the *Spitfire*'s side followed by the others. Harper handed him a glass with the curt remark: 'They're both armed with cannon.'

Kite levelled the telescope at the exotic craft. The three junks all had the high sterns and flat bows that made them appear ungainly to Western eyes, but they stood inshore steadily, their battened sails drawing well and their decks dark-clustered with men.

'I didn't trouble to hoist an ensign,' Harper said. It might buy them a little time, or at least cause the Chinese commander a moment's doubt as to opening fire on an unknown foreign vessel, though from what Rahman had told him Kite did not think it likely.

'Get the boats streamed astern,' Kite said without lowering

the glass, 'and then stand by to weigh. I won't lose an anchor just yet.'

'Aye, aye. I've the guns loaded and ready manned.'

'Very well. McClusky?' Kite called, raising his voice.

'Sir?'

'Leave the men at the guns, arm six men with muskets and take command of them yourself. Under no circumstances open fire until I tell you. Do you understand? Under no circumstances. I'll have no provocation here.'

'Not to open fire, aye, aye, sir.'

'Mr Rahman, get enough men to hoist the fore and main, the foretopmast staysail and the two jibs.'

'Yes, Kite Sahib.'

'And Sarah, do you hoist those Yankee colours that you and Nisha made.'

The courses of the three junks diverged. It was clear that if they intended to attack, they intended to do so on both sides and with one athwart the schooner. Kite could see a tall man in a long crimson robe with what looked like a feathered hat on. He was clearly directing operations as a number of gongs began to sound, accompanied by drums and the chattering explosions of fulminate fire-crackers. Kite kept the glass trained on the junks, switching from one to another as the sweat poured down his back. There was no doubt they were hostile, the only question was when they would open fire. He heard the rasp of sail hank on stay as the foretopmast staysail crawled aloft, then the deck was darkened by the shadow of the rising mainsail. From forward came also the rumble of the windlass.

'I can slip this anchor to a buoy!' Harper called out, even more anxious than his commander to get the ship under weigh. And then to add impetus to his suggestion, he added, 'We've still got sixty fathoms to heave in . . .'

'Very well. Slip!'

The nearest junk was within cannon shot, Kite judged, but still she stood on. Could the Chinese guns be shorter range than their own? Then he watched as she came round into the wind, parallel with *Spitfire* and, with a wild crescendo

232

of gong beating, a ragged broadside rippled along her curved side.

'Stand by at the guns!' he called out. 'And take cover!'

Unflinching, Kite counted the flashes; there were six of them and, as the shot whistled past and tore great rents in the slatting sails, it also threw splinters up from the rails and sent two men backwards with high-pitched screams. One lay dead, the other tore at his face, his feet kicking in his agony, calling upon the name of God for relief. It was clear the Chinese were firing some awful form of langridge. Kite turned and bellowed, 'Fire!'

The two four-pounders rolled back on their carriages and the breechings snapped taut as their crews bent to the task of reloading them. The shot seemed to have caused no damage to the enemy junk and then Kite heard the deep rumble of the escaping cable, felt the thrum of it through the soles of his wet shoes and acknowledged Harper's shout that the end had run clear.

'Back the headsails to larboard!' he ordered and, as *Spitfire* began to turn, he was swept by the wind of more shots that were quickly followed by the bee-like noises of small arms. 'Fire as you will! McClusky, you too!'

Kite heard McClusky's acknowledgement and, for the next few minutes the air was full of the buzzing of musket balls and the scream and whine as the Chinese shot flew about them. Showers of splinters burst upwards from the rails, holes were torn repeatedly in the sails and the scream of the wounded filled the air. Kite felt the sharp pain of a severe graze strike his upper arm like a knife cut and felt only a sudden anxiety for Sarah. Casting about he saw no sign of her. Instead, as the schooner swung, he was only aware of the three sails of one of the war junks as the relative motion of the two vessels made her slide across their bow with surprising rapidity. Their own guns were firing back, four-pounder balls that, he could see now, were thudding into the heavy timber flanks of the gaily painted craft. He looked for the tall man in the crimson robe and could see no sign of him and, as the third junk failed to get into action, *Spitfire*'s sails filled and she began to make headway with increasing speed.

Kite was wondering how long it would take to work a gun aft as a stern chaser, for he was apprehensive about their chances of escape when pursued by imperial junks, when it occurred to him that none of the three junks was following them. They seemed satisfied to be left in possession of the bay and as he ordered the guns secured, Rahman approached.

'You have left them sufficient of a trophy to take back, Kite Sahib,' he said with a wide grin.

'What the devil . . . ? Oh, you mean the anchor?'

'Of course. It is evidence of your defeat and they will gain much face.'

'I see,' Kite said, though in truth he had in fact little grasp of the subtle advantage he had conferred upon the Chinese commander.

They stood offshore slowly in the light onshore breeze. The wounded were taken below to where Kite, assisted by Sarah and Nisha, did his best for the wretched wounded. They had suffered five men killed and twelve wounded, three very severely. Kite had no hope for these and four other men gave cause for concern, but the remaining five would survive. And there was himself; grazed by some fragment, the ugly laceration would knit so he submitted to being bound up by Sarah who seemed shaken by the action, though he learned she had remained on deck and discharged her fowling piece at the enemy. Nisha had stayed below with Maggie and both now assisted in making the wounded comfortable in the tween deck.

After an hour of this work Kite went on deck where Harper was in charge. Order had been restored and both men ruefully contemplated their damaged sails. Picking up his glass, Kite levelled it astern. The three junks lay close together in the bay. He stared at them for several minutes, then he said, 'I'm going back after dark. They are not having our anchor, it is not to be lost to us so easily.'

'But—' Harper bit his protest off short.

'I'll go myself, Zachariah,' Kite said, lowering the telescope and facing the mate. 'I'll take a boat and . . .'

'How the devil will you bring an anchor off with a boat?' Harper asked, his tone exasperated.

Kite said nothing. Instead he peered astern again through the glass. Then, lowering it he said, 'Heed me a moment and I'll tell you.'

Kite hung for a moment half over the rail. His left hand rested upon a splintered section and he moved it before seeking out Harper's face in the darkness.

'You know what to do,' he said curtly.

'I still think it's madness,' Harper hissed.

Kite grunted, turned his head and looked down into the waiting boat as it towed alongside the schooner. McClusky, five oarsmen and three spare hands were already ensconced. He made to lower himself when he felt a hand touch his. He looked up. Sarah bent to him and whispered, 'Take care, my darling.'

He could see the dark pools of her eyes and thought them filled with tears.

Without a word he descended into the boat, and taking his seat and the tiller, ordered the painter slipped. As the bowman waved the painter clear, Kite put the helm over as the boat sheered out from the side of the *Spitfire*, gradually losing way as the schooner drew ahead. As soon as they were clear Kite whispered the order: 'Oars.'

With infinite care the men got out the five oars and lodged their muffled looms in the thole pins, holding them horizontal. When all were ready Kite whispered, 'Give way together.' The stroke oar set the pace, a slow, gentle rhythm that cost the men little effort and which they could make quietly. Every man, Kite and McClusky included, had his face blackened with soot from the galley chimney, and each bore a knife. Kite and McClusky had pistols, and in the bottom boards of the stern sheets nestled a boat compass and a masked lantern.

Sitting beside his commander McClusky felt a strange stomach-churning sensation, a mixture of fear and excitement that made him shake uncontrollably. This embarrassed him but no one mentioned it and Captain Kite had been particular as to the absolute necessity for total silence. To combat this unmanly loss of control, McClusky tried to think of himself as the hero he had long ago dreamed of becoming. Now, he told himself ruefully, his opportunity had come and all he wanted to do was to stop shaking. The more he tried to master the nervous shudder, the worse it became and he almost jumped when Kite touched him on the knee and moved his begrimed face towards him. McClusky bent his ear and caught Kite's words: 'Keep a sharp lookout.'

Had Kite, detecting his nervousness, given him a task to take his mind off his fear? McClusky feared so, but it would do no good to admit the matter and in any case the task was a necessary one. Turning his head he strained his eyes into the impenetrable darkness. After a moment or two it was not so impenetrable. He saw the loom of the hills against the dark grey of the cloudy sky, and caught the faint, intermittent gleam of the surf along the pallid crescent of the shoreline.

Still, it was difficult to orientate himself within the great curve of the bay and he wondered how Kite steered with such confidence, for he never looked once at the boat compass. McClusky tried to recall the last seen disposition of the junks. They had all been lying at anchor, their sails lowered, in full possession of the bay. But how could they locate them now when the schooner's boat seemed adrift and purposeless upon the vast ocean? The land breeze was getting up all the time, slapping small waves against the bow of the boat and making her rock and dip. Occasionally an injudicious oarsman, in leaning forwards and propelling his oar-blade forward, would slap one of these little wave-caps, making a noise that, McClusky thought, would betray them all. As he stared ahead McClusky perceived the matter of heroism as more complex than he had first imagined.

Then, quite close, McClusky saw the long pendant trailing

from a junk's main mast truck elevate itself above the rim of the hills. Silently he seized Kite's arm and pointed.

Kite had taken his bearings carefully that afternoon as soon as the resolution not to abandon his anchor had formed. It was not a matter of 'face' for him, it was a matter of dire necessity. The *Spitfire* carried only three anchors, her two bowers and a light kedge, so the loss of one of the bowers in so remote a location was serious. In extreme conditions one never knew when an anchor might not be the difference between life and death. Kite had noticed the tidal drift along the Hainan shore as they had stood to seaward. He had also lain anchored for long enough to have determined the times of high and low water and, although the offshore stream did not necessarily conform to the local culmination of the tidal range, he was confident that, even after dropping the junks over the horizon and waiting for the end of twilight, he could return *Spitfire* sufficiently close to the anchorage to launch the boat with a fair prospect of relocating the junks. He was less confident about what he would find the commander of the junks had done, but he guessed that the Chinese officer would have established possession of the bay beyond doubt and that his chief concern would be to ensure the foreign devils had been driven out to sea. This would mean that he would not hurry away, even though he had a trophy to prove his diligence in the imperial cause. The certainty with which Rahman had advised Kite of the importance of the anchor to the Chinese had impressed Kite and it was Rahman's hunch that he was now banking on. Kite knew that the recovery of the anchor would take some time, for the Chinese, though Rahman had told him they possessed a sophisticated windlass, would not find it easy to adapt this to accommodate the heavy cable that *Spitfire* had slipped. It was therefore Kite's assumption that the Chinese commander would delay its recovery until he was confident that the foreign devils were not going to return. Only then could he assign one of his three vessels to the task of weighing the anchor and he could not do this until daylight the following morning. From what he had observed, Kite was almost sure that one of the junks had however picked up the end of the cable and, instead of using her own anchor, now lay to that of the *Spitfire*.

With this as the basis of his plan, Kite had ordered the boat away, instructing Harper to follow them in after an hour, and now McClusky clasped his arm at the very same moment that Kite himself saw the junk's masthead. He leaned against the tiller and swung the boat's head away from the junk. First he must determine which of the three Chinese vessels actually lay to the *Spitfire*'s anchor. The bulk of the junk's hull loomed alongside as the men pulled with admirable doggedness, and Kite tried to see under her bow, but this proved impossible as they pulled past. No sound came from the junk's darkened deck and Kite took the boat ahead and then whispered the command, 'Oars!' The men ceased rowing, the oars came up horizontally; the boat lost way and the wind swung her broadside. Kite judged their leeway as it accelerated and, leaning forward, tapped the stroke oarsman's hands. 'Two strokes,' he whispered and the single oar dipped twice, adjusting the drift a little. Kite peered to larboard. In the darkness he could just make out the line of the junk's cable. He thought it had a slender, spiky appearance and instantly ordered the oarsmen to give way. The junk's cable was twisted of bamboo strands, not made of Riga hemp like *Spitfire*'s. As the oarsmen bent to their task and Kite swung the boat away in search of the second junk he was assailed by three fears. The first, that they were too close and would fall athwart the junk's bow, was soon proved groundless as the men tugged the boat clear; the second, that their proximity to the craft and their almost desperate attempts to pull away would alert any watch left on deck, took a little longer to dwindle. But the third, that they would be unable to find the other junks, or that having done so none would be secured to *Spitfire*'s anchor and cable, lasted a good deal longer.

For almost a quarter of an hour the boat pulled round in a widening circle as Kite strove to keep the first junk as a reference point. In fact several times he lost her and then found her again before finally realizing that she had vanished in the gloom to seaward. But at almost the same instant that Kite began to consider giving up his quest, McClusky grabbed his arm again and hissed a warning.

They had worked their way inshore and were almost under the bow of a second junk before Kite reacted. The next moment there was a tumbling noise forward, a suppressed curse and the boat heeled dangerously as the men, all muttering nervously, strove to keep her from oversetting. They had run foul of the very cable they were seeking and as the oar-blades were swept aft and the looms ran forward one man was hit in the face.

As the boat steadied and the men began to sort out the muddle, Kite waited for the intervention from the deck above and he hissed for silence. His anxiety communicated itself to the rest of the boat's crew and they all sat there like statues, their hearts beating with fear. But nothing happened; it appeared that the crew of the junk were all fast asleep. Realization permeated the boat slowly. Kite was unwilling to accept it as fact until he was certain; the men, persuaded sooner, grew restless at their commander's inactivity and he was compelled to hiss a second time for silence. But at last he gave the order in a whisper. 'Pass the stopper.'

A three-inch rope was clapped about the heavy cable with a rolling hitch and led forward to the bow thwart where it was made fast. As soon as this had been accomplished Kite ordered the cable itself cut. Reaching up as high under the bow of the junk as possible, the carpenter began a cautious sawing of the hemp hawser. It took some minutes but at last the final strands parted of their own accord under the weight of the junk. The end of the cable dropped into the water with a heavy splash, there was a moment's hiatus while the three-inch rope, acting as intermediary between the weight of the sinking cable and the boat, was slackened away, lowering the heavy cable to the seabed. When the bowman felt it go slack, he caught a turn; with a jerk the rope tugged the boat's bow head to wind. Kite peered astern. The high square bow of the junk was drifting away and he could see her larboard side as she swung broadside to the wind. Someone on board might notice the change of motion but with luck she would drift out to sea before anyone was alerted to the fact that they were cast loose.

Carefully Kite stood up and, his back to the junk in an attempt to obscure her from the light, he raised the lantern and uncovered it.

'I hope to God Harper sees this,' he muttered to no one in particular, voicing his thoughts without knowing it. Silent amens were added to this plea by those who heard it. When he had stood for a moment or two, Kite resumed his seat.

'Well, we must wait for Mr Harper now,' he said in a low voice.

Chapter Eighteen

The Pearl River

K ite felt an unwonted lightness in his mood as he contemplated the scene before him. The estuary of the Pearl River was hemmed to the north by the uneven outline of the coast of Kwangtung, which rippled along the horizon from west to east like a recumbent grey-green dragon. The prospect gripped his imagination for a moment in so fanciful a fashion as make him chuckle to himself. Then, mindful of his dignity, he raised his glass again. The sea, rippled by the light breeze, was filled with craft. These varied from tiny fishing sampans to large coasting junks, the latter not unlike though less gaudy than those which had sought to attack them on the coast of Hainan. Two large ship-rigged vessels were also standing north under easy sail, either East Indiamen or Country ships from Bengal or Bombay – they were too far distant for him to make out their colours with confidence. The former would, he knew, wear the gridiron ensign of John Company, whereas the latter would wear the plain and undistinguished red ensign of Great Britain. Perhaps, however, they might bear the flags of Austria or Denmark, their owners entrepreneurs, their status that of interlopers, as he was himself.

Harper had the deck and was coaxing every quarter-knot he could out of the *Spitfire* as she lifted gently to the low swell, the last remnant of the typhoon. It had taken them four days of frustratingly light breezes that had beset them since they left the bay on the coast of Hainan. Kite watched as three men forward prepared the starboard bower anchor for dropping, the same anchor that had so lately been a trophy of the Chinese.

They had had to wait for three-quarters of an hour for *Spitfire* to reach them after cutting the Chinese war junk adrift, by which time moonrise was a bare half an hour away and every moment they expected to hear shouts of alarm as the crew of the drifting junk woke to their predicament. But she had been wafted out to sea and by dawn her crew would have found themselves alone on the ocean, the coast under which they had been anchored the previous evening a blue bruise on the horizon. As for *Spitfire*, as soon as Harper had located them and taken the end of the messenger attached to the cable to the windlass, Kite and his boat's crew had clambered aboard, the boat had been streamed astern and they had bent all their efforts to heaving in the cable and its anchor. The moon had been rising as they finally broke the anchor out of the sandy bottom of the bay and, filling their sails, stood out to sea.

The two other junks had been illuminated in the moonlight but no sound or movement had come from them as they were finally swallowed up in the general obscurity of the coast astern. Daylight had found the *Spitfire* alone at sea once more. To the west the hills under which they had found shelter had given way to a low coast extending northwards as far as Hai Nan Point and the strait between Hainan Island and the mainland peninsula of Lui Chow. That forenoon they had had time to heave to and hoist in the towed boat. Moreover the following days of light breezes and calms, frustrating though they were to their progress north-east, had nevertheless allowed them the opportunity to lower the sails and repair them properly after the brief action with the war junks.

Rahman was certain the three junks had been imperial craft and not pirates. He cited the yellow colouring of their upperworks and the dragons wrought about them as indicating official status, but confessed that many such devices were 'borrowed' by less legitimate operators along the coasts of Hainan, Kwangsi and Kwangtung. It was the horse-tail streamers flying from the mastheads of the junks that clinched it, he asserted.

'They were probably on a tax-gathering voyage, and came upon us by chance, or as a result of some fishing boat's report. Although we saw no people, many will have moved inland while the typhoon raged along the coast and it is certain we were seen.'

Kite was glad to have this information after leaving the bay, but he still nursed a slight anxiety over their escape. Sooner or later the commander of those junks would report to his superiors and they in their turn might come looking for a strange schooner. He voiced this concern to Rahman.

'It is possible, Kite Sahib, but you can be certain of one thing, that the matter will be reported in a manner favourable to the Chinese mandarin in command. He will not want to lose face and he will remain attached to his story that he drove you out of the bay. After all, Kite Sahib,' Rahman said with a wide smile, 'he does not *know* it was you who cut him adrift. Indeed he will have told his officers that the cable parted, and that this proves the inferiority of your ground-tackle.' Rahman seemed delighted with this explanation, but Kite, having no such knowledge of the Oriental turn of mind, remained sceptical. He had much to concern him, for the matter of the keel bolt still undermined his confidence in *Spitfire* and they had yet to deliver themselves of the cargo of opium.

It was odd, therefore, that he felt so cheerful as they approached their destination. But the sun was warm on his back, the sky was blue and the sea a limpid green. Sarah and Nisha were on deck in their finery and he was faced with the prospect of profit after so long and arduous a voyage. Kite could not quite admit to himself that his mood of elation was the brittle unreasonable excitement of the gambler seduced by the prospect of his stake yielding him a prize. Why should he? He had been too much beset by worry not to enjoy the freedom of unconcern, no matter how transitory.

As they crept closer to the land Rahman pointed out the distant landmarks: the hill tops above Macao and the vaguely delineated cleft in the summits which marked the entrance to the Pearl River, a narrowing of the river's mouth defended by

Chinese forts and known to the British traders as the Bocca Tigris. As interlopers, Rahman had advised, they should keep to the westwards, stand north past Macao Road and anchor off Keow Island. The Indiamen worked up to Whampoa, ten miles downstream from Canton, but their own discharge of so small a quantity of illegal opium would be better effected by a local arrangement.

'You want cash, Kite Sahib, silver cash which you do not want to deposit with the Company for remittance to England.'

But now Kite vacillated. He was not certain. Might not all *Spitfire*'s keel bolts be weakened and, if they were, might not a disaster ensue?

He had kept these worries to himself, not troubling Sarah with his preoccupations. Nor did he express them to Harper, his closest professional confidant. In the end he agreed with Rahman's presumption; he had little choice, for if *Spitfire* fell apart they would probably all drown and he shied away from making himself beholden to the East India Company. He agreed with Rahman.

'And how will you negotiate a price, Mr Rahman?'

'When we have anchored, we will be approached by a shaw-bunder from the Chinese Custom House. We will open negotiations with him.'

'It is that easy?'

'The shaw-bunder wishes to live, like all men, Kite Sahib, and the emperor is distant. We must pay squeeze, but a small consignment is attractive and will make him a fortune. We are not acting on behalf of the Company, the dues and duties will be kept to a minimum because we will appeal to his greed. He will keep the matter secret because it is in his interest to do so and he will seal the lips of his boat's crew. The important thing will be to prevent pirates taking the vessel, for they will know that we are an interloper and have a private cargo, so we will insist upon a hostage.'

'And how will that prevent the intervention of pirates?' Kite asked.

'Our shaw-bunder will buy them off.'

'So a large number of people will benefit from this trans-action,' Kite remarked wryly. 'By Heaven, Mr Rahman, such a trade is not without its ironies.'

And so, as the day drew on, they stood in amongst the craft thronging Macao Road, heading north for the narrow passage of Cum-Sing-Mun, and passing south of Keow Island in a series of short boards 'rounded-to on its western side, dropping anchor in company with a quartet of small junks. The sun had already fallen below the land to the west and twilight was upon them. A village stood at the head of the bay from which, as it grew dark, several sampans shoved off, hoisting lanterns and fishing with cormorants. The birds were prevented from swallowing the larger fish after which they dived as the creatures rose to feed by having a ring round their throats.

Kite ordered the watches maintained, the guns loaded with langridge and run out. Loaded small arms were stacked about the deck and these preparations were conducted with a con-spicuous activity to dissuade any would-be thieves of the folly of any predatory enterprise.

Next morning they were surrounded by sampans selling chick-ens and fresh vegetables. Under broad straw hats and clad in loose ragged trousers, some with babies bound to their backs as they sent up their produce in woven baskets on lines, the smiling women of the islands trafficked with the *Spitfire*'s crew in wooden curios, exchanging them for coins and tobacco. The lively scene amused Sarah and Nisha, who were anxious to purchase the ivory figurines of which they had heard, but the itinerant traders were too poor to deal in such items and the two ladies were disappointed. Sarah pleaded with her husband to proceed upstream in one of the boats but Kite was adamant no one was to leave the schooner.

'I am sorry, my dear,' he said, 'but there are too many risks. You may well be taken as a hostage and God knows what might happen to you. Perhaps, in due course, we can persuade a trader down from Canton to offer you what you want . . .'

'I should like to buy some silk.'

'And so should I,' Nisha added and Kite was obliged, despite the severity of his tone, to smile at the two women, for both were charmingly eager and they had been cooped up on board, unoccupied for a very long time.

Announced by gongs at noon, a diversion offered itself as a large sampan approached. Sending for Rahman, Kite awaited its approach. Painted in bright yellow and red, a golden dragon formed its rail and two eyes marked the bow. A distant clang of gongs announced its approach and, without further ado, the sampans cast themselves off and paddled away, resting in a wide, irregular circle about the schooner and making way for the shaw-bunder.

They watched the customs officer climb delicately over the rail. He was a tall man and, Kite thought, handsome in an ascetic way. He wore a plain grey robe and on his head a small round cap which had a red button and sported a long peacock feather. As soon as he had been handed over the rail, he shoved his hands into his sleeves and stood with a quiet dignity that compelled respect. He appeared the very antithesis of the corruptible port official. Kite for his part met him with some ceremony, according gravitas to the official which, whether merited or not, could not fail to appeal to his vanity.

Wearing blue broadcloth, white breeches and a sword, Kite swept off his tricorne in a bow that would have graced the Court of the Directors of the Honourable East India Company. Also dressed formally, Harper followed his commander and then Kite presented Sarah and Nisha who dropped elegant curtsies before turning aside and indicating a table and chairs under the awning over the stern. The shaw-bunder bowed stiffly and took his seat.

Here Rahman waited, himself wearing his finest turban, trousers and white robe, offering the shaw-bunder a glass of Madeira. The Chinese official drew his hands from his robe and revealed the long, guarded fingernails of a man who did no manual labour. He was followed along the deck by four servants, one who stood behind him with a sword, another who bore a folded umbrella and the remaining two who squatted at his feet, laid ink and pens at their bare feet and drew scrolls from pouches about their waists.

As the party sat and sipped their wine, Rahman opened negotiations. He introduced the Chinese official as Lee Chew Chua, speaking to Lee in pidgin, a mixture mainly of English, Cantonese and Portuguese which was as incomprehensible as any foreign language to Kite. It reminded him of the Creole patois of the West Indies insofar as the occasional recognizable word surfaced periodically to seize the listeners' attention.

Notwithstanding this, Kite, Harper, Sarah and Nisha kept up the expressions of interest that Rahman had begged them to fake. From time to time Rahman would turn to Kite and address a few words to him, feigning deep conference and asking him the *Spitfire*'s tonnage, the number of her crew and the identity of the two women.

'They ask for Hooker Memsahib's name, Kite Sahib,' Rahman said anxiously. 'It could be a problem, they are aware that she is, as I am, Indian. I cannot say that she is my wife—'

'But I can say that she is mine, can I not?' Harper broke in.

Rahman threw him a glance of irritation at the interruption and went on addressing Kite. 'It is a matter of face, Kite Sahib, quickly we must have a name, initials will do, it is sufficiently like their own script.'

Kite, divining the urgency of the impasse, picked up the quill lying before him and on a piece of paper wrote *N.H.* then told Rahman, 'Say she is the wife of Mr Harper.'

He avoided looking at Nisha but felt both she and Sarah move awkwardly in their chairs and was aware that Nisha had drawn her veil over the lower part of her face. Lee pronounced himself satisfied and then Rahman made a long speech which, Kite divined, formed the substance of their mutual business proposition. Lee listened impassively. At one point he held up his hand and Rahman paused while Lee addressed a few words to his chief scribe. The man responded and took from his pouch a small abacus. They all watched fascinated while the fingers of the scribe flickered back and forth, sending the beads this way and that, multiplying and dividing and totting up his totals: initial cost, deduction for Lee's *cumshaw*, deduction for his own cut and the silence money to his fellow scribe, the sword-and-umbrella bearer; deduction for the pirates and the several other douceurs, sweeteners and unofficial taxes that the imperial system allowed under the notion of perquisites. Of course there was a levy that went directly into the imperial treasury, a cut in the transaction which explained why it was tolerated and why the distant emperor hypocritically permitted the pollution of his people by the Indian drug in contradiction to his own official proscription of the trade. Each sum was written down and verified by the second scribe while Lee sat, apparently aloof from these sordidly worldly computations.

Then the senior scribe made several staccato announcements and Lee nodded gravely. Turning to Rahman he made his offer. Rahman paused for several moments, then he counter-commented. They all knew from the drama of the moment, without knowing from a shred of comprehended fact, that this was the crux of their entire enterprise. After another ritual pause Lee consulted his scribe who bent again to the abacus, wrote some more columns of squiggly script in a vertical column and held up the paper for Lee to read. The hint of a tired and slightly exasperated emotion passed across Lee's face, as if he signalled an accommodation which, to the foreign devils was important, but to him meant only an augmentation of his pride.

'What does he offer?' Kite asked quietly, unable to hold his tongue any longer. Rahman turned to him with slow and contrived gravity. In a tone of voice so uncharacteristic that they all knew the Indian intermediary was putting on a skilful theatrical act for the benefit of the shaw-bunder, Rahman said, 'It is absolutely necessary that you should trust me, Kite Sahib, and not interfere, I beg you. There is much face at stake, yours included.'

Kite inclined his head as he had seen Lee do and Sarah stifled a giggle. Harper, bored with the long-winded affair, had been regarding Nisha's breasts, which rose and fell under his gaze with a wondrously distracting undulation.

Rahman spoke a few words and suddenly, in a flurry of movement, the scribe flourished his paper and placed it in front of Lee. Then the second scribe rose to his feet holding a small wooden box from which an ivory stamp was taken, inked up in red and held over the paper. Slowly Lee extended his long-nailed right hand and, placing it over the waiting hand of his scribe, pressed his *chop* down onto the paper. As the stamp was removed, the complex red monogram lay over the black script.

Rahman sighed with satisfaction and leaning forward, poured more wine. After a few moments of pleasantries Lee rose. Turning to Kite he bowed and addressed a few words. Rahman translated. 'He is appointing Chang, his senior secretary, to act on his behalf. Chang will oversee the exchange of opium for cash and we shall not see Lee again. Chang will return as our hostage.'

Kite bowed his understanding. It had clouded over now and began to rain. As Lee rose to take his departure, his umbrella-bearer extended his apparatus above his master. Kite walked forward with the Chinese official to see him and his party over the side. Clear of the encircling shelter of the umbrella Kite felt the weight of the rain which had become suddenly heavy, hissing into the sea surrounding them. He watched, fascinated despite the downpour, as Lee, mindful of his delicate fingernails, gingerly hoisted himself over the rail.

Aboard the waiting sampan the crew had donned straw hats and strange capes of reeds, which, like thatch, shot the rain off in tiny silver runnels. Unhurried and sheltered by his bearer, Lee moved aft with his sodden entourage in train. While his menials squatted down about him, he sat under an awning as the sampan cast off, the sword-bearer took up his station behind his master's chair, gongs rang and the oarsmen bent to their task.

Kite, his shoulders wet through under the heavy broadcloth, walked back to the party under the awning and watched Lee's sampan pull away. 'Well, Mr Rahman,' he asked, refilling his glass, 'for how much have you sold my soul?'

The others sat expectantly, staring at Rahman.

'For a clear profit to yourself of five hundred per centum.'

'A *clear* profit?' Kite queried incredulously. He had never felt so vulnerable, placing his entire fortune in the hands of a man of short acquaintance.

Rahman explained the ramifications of squeeze and *cumshaw*, alluding to the various recipients and beneficiaries of the transaction, including the emperor on his golden throne in distant Peking.

'Governments approve all they can tax,' he commented, sagely adding, 'as men will do anything they can obtain payment for.'

'So there is no morality at all,' Sarah said drily.

Rahman smiled and shook his head. 'No, memsahib; men must eat and feed their families. There can only be a few holy men to admire. What would the world be if any damn fool was held up as a virtuous example?'

'What indeed,' interjected Kite, 'but we shall hold you up as a virtuous man, if not a holy one, Mr Rahman, if we see such a quantity of silver come aboard.'

'It will come, Kite Sahib, and fall upon your head like this rain . . .' and Rahman, smiling broadly, gestured out over the grey waters of the bay into which the heavy rain drops fell like millions and millions of tiny silver coins.

'And it will fall upon your head too,' Kite grinned back.

'That is thanks to you, Kite Sahib.'

Kite shook his head. 'I could not have accomplished anything without your help.' Rahman rocked his head in self-deprecation and Kite, sensing his embarrassment, turned to Harper. 'Nor yours, Zachariah . . .' he began, but stopped when he beheld the two lovers. His gaze was followed by that of Sarah and Rahman and, feeling themselves the cynosure, both Nisha and Zachariah looked up.

'Ah . . . er, Cap'n Kite, Mrs Kite . . . Rahman . . . I, er, have just been accepted by Mistress Hooker.'

'Nisha!' Sarah's voice rang out and Kite swung quickly to catch his wife's expression. He found he could not read it, for it bore both delight and sadness, a sudden thickening in her voice and watering of the eyes which were swiftly translated into a movement as Sarah rose from her chair and embraced Nisha. Kite stood and held out his hand to his old and loyal friend.

'I am delighted, Zachariah,' he said gripping Harper's massive paw. Then bending over Nisha's hand he kissed it.

'I am very pleased for you, my dear,' he said, looking up into her dark and inscrutable eyes. Nisha's hand touched his face in a strange gesture that might have been mere friendship yet which, when Kite thought about it later in the waking hours of the night, seemed tinged with some regret.

Sarah was congratulating Harper when a confused Rahman asked, 'She is to become your wife?'

They all turned and looked at him. All afternoon Rahman had master-minded the commercial theatricals played out on the *Spitfire*'s narrow quarterdeck and now, at a stroke, he was lost in the delicate conventions of an unfamiliar culture. Only Nisha felt the suppressed outrage in his tone, for Rahman knew the Brahmin woman to be an outcast whom he had himself tolerated only because of the advantages associated with his attachment to Kite Sahib. His moralization to Sarah regarding the weakness of men for money had not entirely been aimed at Kite; Rahman was aware of the ironies of his own situation.

'Ah yes, Mr Rahman,' said Harper happily. 'We are to become man and wife when we return to India.'

'I am already a Christian, Topass,' Nisha said coldly and Rahman inclined his head with further embarrassment.

Kite divined this and as Sarah turned again to her friend, he took Rahman's elbow and led him forward beyond the extent of the awning. The rain had eased and Kite bent to the Indian's ear as they walked along the deck towards the watch sheltering in the narrow rain-shadow of the foremast.

'I am well pleased, Mr Rahman. If we are successful in bringing this schooner safely to Bombay, I will increase your cut by two per centum of the whole.'

Rahman stiffened and stopped to face Kite. 'Oh, Kite Sahib, that is most kind of you.'

'No, it is mere prudence. We have a long way to go and much work to do. I would have you a friend.'

'There is no need for you to buy my friendship.'

'But there may be need for me to show it.'

Rahman met his eyes and inclined his head. 'You are a good man, Kite Sahib.'

'There are too few of us,' Kite said with a wry grin. Rahman took a moment to understand the pun and then he smiled himself. 'You are off watch and must eat with us tonight,' Kite added, patting Rahman on his shoulder and turning in search of McClusky. The rain had made it prematurely dark and already the lights of the fishing sampans were bobbing out from the shoreline where the first oil lamps of the village were already alight.

As he walked aft Kite drank in the scent of the land and it was sweet. He had been right to feel happy that morning. It had been a good day.

Chapter Nineteen

The Horns of a Dilemma

R ahman warned them that there would be an inevitable delay, that the Celestials, as he disparagingly called the Chinese, did nothing at the speed wished for by Englishmen.

'Or Scotchmen, who are worse,' he added didactically, 'in their desire for the conclusion of business. We will have a few days of uncertainty before Chang joins us. This is so that Lee has our trust and gains face in Canton. More practically, he is concluding all the necessary arrangements for the transaction here. After we have our hostage, matters will move, as you will see.'

As Rahman had predicted, three days later Chang arrived, in a smaller sampan than his master, but with his own entourage of tally men that precisely established his own status in the hierarchical order. Chang spoke a smattering of English and laced his pidgin, when he wished to, with colloquial phrases conducive to trade. Kite suspected him of professional eavesdropping on the part of his master. No wonder Rahman had been embarrassed by Kite's intervention during the negotiations! He himself must have lost face before the inscrutable Celestials, but if he had, Chang gave no sign of it and was more than helpful in arranging for a sampan to come down from Canton with silks, ivories, fans and lacquer-work for the ladies to admire and purchase.

'You see, Kite Sahib,' Rahman explained happily, 'Chang will now himself gain a cut in the earnings of the ivory carvers, the fan-makers, the lacquer workers and the sampan owner, so everybody is able to live.'

'Big fleas have little fleas on their backs to bite 'em,' intoned Harper, who had overheard the comment as he watched Nisha and Sarah fingering rich and brocaded silks spread out on grass matting amidships. 'Little fleas have smaller fleas, and so *ad infinitum!*'

'You have completed the cargo tally?' Kite asked of the mate.

'Aye, and signed the manifest with that Mr Chang,' said Harper. 'It will be counted again on discharge, but Chang is satisfied that what we are trading is what we declared, first-rate Malwa opium.'

Chang was not the only visitor. On the third day a smart gig was seen pulling towards them and two blue-coated men with black tricornes clambered aboard. Called from the cabin by McClusky, Kite went on deck to find them already peering curiously about them.

'Trouble,' muttered McClusky presciently as Kite passed him.

'Gentlemen . . . ?' Kite began, approaching the two strangers, but was cut short by one of these Europeans whose sunburnt faces lent credibility to the Chinese nickname for the foreigners who had settled in their midst: 'red devils'.

'You are the master of this schooner?' one of them asked sharply.

'I am William Kite and both master and owner. Whom do I have the pleasure of addressing?'

'We are Selectmen from Canton, Captain Kite, and you, it appears, are in breach of the Honourable Company's monopoly.'

'If you would like to descend to the cabin, gentlemen, I am sure we can straighten this matter out.' Without waiting for a response, Kite turned and led the way aft. 'My departure was bruited about Bombay and I dined with President Cranbrooke . . .'

Kite clattered down the companionway and roused Sarah

and Nisha who had been sitting quietly, Nisha at her stitch-work while Sarah toyed with a watercolour of the prospect beyond the stern windows.

'Ladies, we have visitors.' Having given this announcement Kite pulled the corners of his mouth down, indicating his displeasure, then stood back and ushered the two men into the cabin. 'May I present my wife . . . and Mistress Hooker . . .'

There was a stiffly formal exchange of bows and curtsies. The Selectmen were clearly astonished to find two women aboard an interloper and there was a muttered exchange between them. One of them, apparently susceptible to Sarah's beauty as he lingered over her hand, introduced himself as Commissioner Blackstone and his companion as Commissioner Harrison.

Sarah rang for Maggie, who was set to serving wine. During this hiatus Kite requested Nisha to ask Zachariah to join them and a moment later the large, ugly American entered the cabin. Without waiting for an introduction to the newcomer and irritated by his senior colleague's obvious attraction for Mistress Kite, Harrison said, 'We understand that you are trading illegally, Captain Kite.'

'I have a letter of marque and reprisal,' Kite responded, turning to his desk to present them with the document.

'Come, sir, you have women on board. You cannot pretend that you are a privateer.'

'Oh, but we are, Commissioner, I do assure you. We have already fought an engagement with a French frigate . . .'

'A French frigate, d'you say?' Blackstone slurped his wine unalluringly in astonishment.

'What was her name?' Harrison interjected.

'*Alcmene*, I believe. And we were fortunate enough to escape her . . . Ah, here, my letter of marque.'

Kite handed the document over and Harrison and Blackstone bent their heads over the papers, muttering secretively to themselves. Kite caught Harper's eye over them and again pulled the corners of his mouth down in apprehension of the outcome. Harper responded with a confident grin. This silent exchange was terminated by Blackstone.

'But these are made out in part to –' the Commissioner looked up at Nisha – 'to *your* husband?'

'My partner in the venture,' Kite began, but Blackstone ignored him and both Selectmen now stared at Nisha, who appeared to shrink back, her bosom rising and falling under the ferocity of their scrutiny.

'And where is *your* husband, Mistress Hooker?' Harrison asked.

'Why, right behind you, gennelmen,' Harper announced, stepping forward and placing his hands upon Nisha's shoulders. Kite watched, touched that she responded by placing a hand over his.

It seemed too that both Selectmen started as Harper loomed over them and Kite, aware that Harper's quixotic motive had momentarily thrown the two Commissioners, quickly seized the initiative.

'As you see, gentlemen,' he said indicating the pile of silk brocades laid on a rush mat in the corner of the cabin, 'I am quite unable to prevent the ladies from purchasing such seductive material but I fail to see how you can accuse us of illegal trade. We have brought a small and speculative quantity of Malwa opium hither, and might therefore be said to be partaking in the Country trade in a trivial way, but as for taking a cargo for London, why, where would be the sense of it?'

The two Selectmen looked confused and Harrison bent to Blackstone's ear while Kite smiled benignly at Harper and Nisha.

After a moment Harrison, who though he might have been the junior was indisputably the more aggressive, handed back the *Spitfire*'s documents. 'You can affirm that you are not intending to load a cargo for London?'

'Absolutely not, Mr Harrison, nor Ostend, nor Amsterdam, if it please you.'

'Shame on you, gentlemen, to suspect us,' Sarah put in, flashing a radiant smile at Blackstone, who flushed darkly.

'I cannot see you on deck in action, Mistress Kite,' snapped Harrison, rising to his feet.

'Would you care to match me on deck with a foil, Mr Harrison?' Sarah flashed back. 'I am more than a match for my husband, am I not, William?'

'I think you would find my wife more than competent, Mr Harrison, nor is she a bad shot.'

But Harrison ignored the remarks and had swung round to confront Harper. 'So you are the notorious Hooker,' he said before clapping his hat upon his head, summoning Blackstone to follow and clumping up the companionway steps. For a moment the four of them stood stock-still, then Kite, putting his finger to his lips, followed the Selectmen on deck.

The watch stood about idly observing the strangers depart. McClusky was handing the manropes to Blackstone, Harrison having already descended into his gig when Kite caught up with them. Blackstone was about to throw his leg over the rail when he caught Kite's eye and said, 'Sorry to disturb you, Captain. We had information that you were loading for London.'

'Information? What information?' Kite made a deprecating gesture round the deck. 'We are a small schooner, what in Heaven's name could we carry in sufficient quantity to threaten the Honourable Company?'

'Silver, Captain, silver.'

Kite stood and watched the gig pull away. Something more than the mere commercial defence of a monopoly had motivated the Selectmen's visit and he lingered a moment, reviewing the events of the last hour. An uncomfortable apprehension was forming in his mind. How could he prove anything, though? He was a gambler, a man willing to risk all without the slightest ability to predict the outcome and with no appreciation of the part others had to play in his wager. It had all seemed so very straightforward in London and Bombay.

'William . . . William, please come below.' It was Sarah calling him from the companionway.

'What is it?' he asked, walking aft after exchanging a word with McClusky.

'Nisha is in a terrible state. What is all this about?'

'Why don't *you* ask her,' he said with laboured sarcasm. 'After all my dear, you are very close to her.'

Sarah blushed at Kite's implication and bit off a reply, bobbing angrily below. Kite followed. In the cabin Nisha sobbed in Harper's arms and Kite was moved to ask the mate to leave, but he had himself unwittingly embroiled himself in this bizarre affair and Kite could not afford to alienate him now. Kite closed the door to the companionway and the second door which led to the pantry in which Maggie was washing the glasses. Then he went aft to his desk and tucked the letter of marque away. 'Please let us all sit down, we have a few matters to discuss.'

They sat as bid, only Nisha's uncontrollable sobs breaking the silence until she looked up, aware that Kite's eyes were upon her.

'What is it, William?'

'I think you know, Nisha, better than any of us. What exactly was your late husband up to?'

'Hey, steady, Cap'n.'

Kite held up his hand. 'Zachariah, you may have acted in too precipitate a fashion for your own good. Those gentlemen came down from Canton. Now we have had no contact with Canton, nor with East India House at Macao. It is my guess that they were alerted to our presence by Lee. Lee had an interest in you, Nisha, and the name Hooker.' Kite looked at Sarah and Harper. 'Neither of you can pretend that that nasty little man Harrison did not have an interest in a man named Hooker . . .'

'But Hooker is dead, William,' Sarah put in.

'We know that, but they may well not know that in Canton.' Kite paused. 'Indeed it strikes me that they have never met Hooker . . . Until this afternoon, that is, when they met you, Zachariah. You cheerfully admitted you were Mr Hooker.'

'That's not true, Cap'n,' Harper protested.

'It's true enough for those two,' Kite said. 'It is what they wanted to believe and you wanted to believe it too, just as Sarah and I did, for we four here all had our private reasons for pretending that you were indeed Mr Josiah Hooker.' Kite was silent for a moment, then he added, 'Oddly, I think the two Selectmen anticipated finding Mr Hooker aboard, so that even if you had explained you were Zachariah Harper and not Josiah Hooker, they would not have believed you. Your assumed name, whatever way you cast the dice, is too similar to the other.'

'But, hell, Cap'n . . .'

'Moreover,' Kite went on remorselessly, 'I think that somehow when Nisha wrote her initials yesterday, Lee may have reported them as yours. N.H. looks a little like Z.H. when written askew and read by a Chinaman.'

'But the other, I mean Hooker's name, was Josiah, so where does . . . ?'

'William is right, Zachariah,' Nisha interrupted in a low tone. 'Josiah's second name was Zebulon and he used to use it in matters of trade.'

'A conceit, no doubt,' murmured Kite, thinking of the three pen scratches of the initial.

'Well, all right,' Harper went on, 'so all this is true. But what is all this about Josiah, or Zebulon Hooker, or whatever he called his God-damned name, eh?'

'Do you wish to confess, Nisha, or shall I reveal your husband's secret?' There was no reply from Nisha. 'Very well then. It was silver. Hooker carried silver clandestinely to London, a quantity of it if I am any judge . . .'

'But so what?' Harper asked. 'London is grown rich upon the wealth of the Orient.'

Kite held up his hand. 'I am not making moral judgements, Zachariah, I am only elucidating mysteries. You see the East India Company can *sell* very little in China. British manufactures are greeted by the Celestials with disdain. They must purchase tea, silk and porcelain with money and this drains their capital, so they welcome the Country trade from

Bombay and Calcutta in Indian cotton chiefly, but also in other commodities such as our lucrative lading, Malwa opium. This generates a money flow in the contrary direction, cash as they call it hereabouts, *out* of China.

'The so-called Country traders of Scots or English origin wish to remit their profits to London, both for investment return and for the removal of their capital to their home countries where, in due season, they can enjoy the benefits of their speculations in India and China. To do this and to circumvent the Company's monopolistic regulation, they deposit their cash with the Company's treasury in Canton, whither our late visitors have undoubtedly come.

'The depositors receive bills of exchange on the Company in London and thus their money is remitted as desired, while the outflow of silver from China is stemmed and available at interest from the Company, to the Chinese for further trade.'

'But that is monstrous—' Sarah began, but Kite cut his wife short.

'Monstrous or not, Sarah, that is what happens, I believe. Now we are suspected of being here to repeat the process, complete with our offending Mr Hooker, hence the animus against us from those two gentlemen. I received a scarcely veiled threat from Blackstone which I fear he would not have delivered had he not fallen under your spell, Sarah. Perhaps he has designs upon you after disposing of me.'

'Not that, William, though it is a cynical matter to be sure, what is monstrous is that you are suggesting that Josiah was murdered by agents of the Company . . . Do I take that to be your implication?'

'So it would seem.' Kite looked at Nisha. She seemed stunned as she sat, clasping Harper's large hand. 'Those dacoits were suborned in some way,' he explained, 'certainly there was not much regret shown at the Castle, who played upon my gullibility and inexperience of Oriental ways . . .'

What sounded like a scuffling outside the door to the companionway lobby intruded. 'Excuse me,' Kite said, strode to the door and flung it open. Outside Maggie was remonstrating with Rahman.

'I tried to tell him you was having a private meeting, Cap'n Kite, but he insists . . .'

'It is important, Kite Sahib,' Rahman pleaded and Kite realized that he had omitted his Indian mentor from the process: perhaps he had had a more sinister and complicit role to play. Kite motioned him into the cabin and Rahman immediately began to voice his suspicions.

'I was sleeping off watch, Kite Sahib, but Mr McClusky has just told me you have been visited by the Selectmen . . .'

Kite outlined what had transpired, voicing his suspicions as to Lee's hand in the affair. Rahman concurred, his face anxious. 'But I knew nothing of this transfer of silver, Kite Sahib. It was not something I would be made a party to . . .'

'That is true, William,' Nisha put in, sniffing back the last of her tears and Kite sensed rather than understood the gulf that divided the two Indians.

'This will affect the sale of our opium?' Kite asked, a cold certainty clamping itself around his heart.

Rahman nodded. 'Lee will try and drive the price down. Tomorrow Chang will say there are problems in Canton and that if we wish to sail soon we must accept a lower price . . . perhaps a *much* lower price . . .'

'So what are we to do?' Kite mused, anxiously rubbing his jaw.

'Mind if I say something, Cap'n?'

'Of course not, Zachariah. What is it?'

'If they're capable of murdering once, mayn't they not do it again? And seein' as how I'm now believed to be Mr Hooker . . . Well, I ain't much inclined to lay my bones down here in junk creek.'

'Oh . . .' Nisha began another bout of sobbing and Harper bent and kissed her on her veiled head.

'Hushabye, hushabye, I ain't planning on letting anything happen to old Zachariah yet awhiles.'

'We are on the horns of a dilemma, it seems,' Kite said,

looking from one to another of them. He was now the gambler who had staked and lost everything.

'There is no question, William,' Sarah said drawing herself up, 'we should not put Zachariah's life at risk. It would be better to sail at once and be damned to them all.'

'And what do we pay the hands off with, my dear, even supposing the keel bolts hold until we reach Bombay?'

'It ain't for me to say, Cap'n, but we could make for Calcutta instead. Maybe we will encounter a Country ship willing to trans-ship our opium, or maybe we could dispose of it elsewhere.'

'Of course!' Rahman smote his forehead, his eyes shining with triumph. 'It will fetch a good price in Malacca, we can sell it direct without trans-shipment, Kite Sahib! It is true it will not yield so high a profit, but,' Rahman shrugged philosophically, 'it is better than to wait here and be butchered.'

Kite smiled. 'I do not think they will butcher *you*, Mr Rahman,' he began but Rahman interjected.

'Oh, Kite Sahib, you do not understand. It is I who will disappear first, let me assure you of that.'

Kite pondered Rahman's proposition. It was clear that if Lee had indeed compromised them he would offer them only a derisory price and Kite did not like being outwitted.

'But we have our hostage!' Kite exclaimed, suddenly recollecting Chang, but Harper shook his head. Chang was not aboard. He had disappeared an hour or two before the arrival of the Selectmen, promising McClusky that they would be discharging on the morrow and he must arrange for the sampans to come down from Whampoa.

'Unfortunately McClusky believed him, Cap'n,' Hooker added.

Kite swore under his breath. It was his own fault, he should have kept a better eye upon Chang, or better briefed McClusky. It was too late anyway, and at least Rahman's contingency plan might work.

'No matter,' he said with sudden resolution, 'we cannot cry over spilt milk.'

They would weigh anchor immediately after dark, pass north of Keow Island and slip to seawards between it and Lintin to the east, he explained.

'I am unwilling to submit to coercion, but we will cheat Lee of his profit and see what we can achieve at Malacca.'

As they filed out of the cabin, Rahman asked the mate, 'What is the meaning of this spilt milk, Harper Sahib?'

'It's a saying, Rahman. You cannot drink what is on the deck, d'you see?'

Rahman smiled his gratitude. 'Of course, of course.'

And so it was that when Chang's sampan came in sight of the anchorage on the north coast of Keow next morning, there was no sign of the *Spitfire*, nor any report of where she had gone. With a heavy heart he returned to Canton to tell his master.

Chapter Twenty

A Bone of Consolation

The following day they stood to the southwards with a light north-east wind behind them which, Rahman assured Kite, was the first of the favourable monsoon.

'All the Indiamen and Country ships will be leaving the China coast within the next few weeks, Kite Sahib. The Indiamen bound for England will stand on through the Selat Sunda, others, with the Country ships, will follow us into the Selat Malacca for the Bay of Bengal, Calcutta, Madras and Bombay.'

Kite listened to Rahman's chatter, his eye on half a dozen native craft strewn about the sea ahead, his mind wandering. He was bitterly disappointed that his venture to China had collapsed in so complete and humiliating a manner and he wondered if the Company's smug officials at Bombay had some inkling of this likely conclusion for so ignorant an interloper as himself. If they had connived at Hooker's murder they were capable of anything. However, it was inconceivable that any other craft could have arrived on the China coast from Bombay sooner than *Spitfire*, despite her few days' delay off Hainan. On the other hand it was quite likely that Lee had been warned off dealing with the foreign devil who had been in action with imperial war junks. Kite discarded the thought; it was an irrelevance. What did he really know of the ramifications of the affair? He was simply speculating, and speculating wildly. Better still to curse himself for a foolish optimist in his dealings with Hooker. Why else had

Hooker hidden in a London tenement, absenting himself from the society he claimed that he desired to become a part of, but from fear of the Company's spies and informers? It was where he kept his treasure. Doubtless time and the return home of his principals, the men who had conspired with him to ship silver directly to London, would have purchased him immunity.

It was increasingly clear to Kite that Hooker had been playing a complex, dangerous and double game, for despite the concealment of his party, he had gone brazenly to East India House in Leadenhall Street. Were Woolnough and Drysdale part of the private conspiracy, despite their high office? And had they been frightened off that day when the board had sat, so that they repudiated Hooker at the moment he expected triumph? Dismissed or not, Hooker had been cast adrift, explaining his need to return to India much more convincingly than his muttered explanation of an enemy and a romantic past.

Then in Bombay Hooker's presence became a greater embarrassment than in London. Kite guessed several highly placed officials were implicated and the last thing they wanted was Hooker back on the Malabar coast. His odd behaviour in respect of Kite, what seemed some sort of an alliance with the reptilian Grindley, all done in haste and shrouded behind the bombast of his social round, carried out in suspicious solitude, seemed to indicate a further muddying of the waters. Had Hooker not, after all, banked his co-conspirators' money? Had he had it with him the whole time, thereby implicating Kite? And what risks consequently attached to Kite and the company of the *Spitfire*?

Kite concluded that he had been subjected to a clever, concealed interrogation by President Cranbrooke. His ignorance must have been as obvious as the nose on his face. He was a Liverpool man with a Loyalist American as his mate, a man with no experience of the Indian trade and clearly a dupe of the cunning Hooker. The President's lack of concern over Hooker's murder, his persuasive advice to treat the matter as suicide, all pointed to the fact that he at the very least knew who was behind the suborning of Hooker's dacoits. Whether Hooker's assassination was engineered under the clandestine auspices of the East India Company, or a secret cabal of its officials who were hand in glove with others in the China trade, did not matter. Hooker had either run foul of the former or betrayed the trust of the latter so that either party had had a motive for disposing of him.

Kite now recalled Nisha's muttered remark about paying 'it' back, a remark he, in his own selfish preoccupation, had attributed to Hooker's shameful ditching of himself. It seemed he could see now a hundred little hints that pointed to the gravity and extent of Hooker's foolish crime. Why, having encountered the gullible and disappointed Captain Kite in Leadenhall Street, had not Hooker even borne off his messenger, the even more hapless Jack Bow? The extent of Hooker's malfeasance was truly astonishing.

Not that it mattered now. It was too late to fret over having been made a dupe, though he would dearly like to know how much of her late husband's conspiracy was known to Nisha. Kite could swallow his own pride. There would be those in Liverpool who might have found it all most amusing, but by now his name would mean nothing, for he would have been forgotten as another failed shipowner, ruined by war with the American rebels. No, he would simply ship out as a common master again, as he had long ago intended to do. Nor need he return to Liverpool to do that. If he could get *Spitfire* back to Bombay, perhaps he could seek a berth in one of Banajee's Country ships. He was growing old now and he could establish Sarah in a suitable house in Bombay, he felt certain. As for the schooner, he would have to sell her, for he could not afford her docking, even in Bombay, and the state of the keel bolts troubled him deeply.

He paced the *Spitfire*'s deck, his deductions falling into place with a logic that was convincing. Nisha had confirmed her husband had trafficked in silver and, after a lifetime in trade, Kite could detect sharp practice. There was little doubt in his own mind that he had, at last, teased out the true resolution of Hooker's part in a complex monetary transaction. Then something irregular caught his eye and brought him to a standstill: there was something odd about that sampan to larboard, he thought casually. She had a sail hoisted, but it was not like the sails of the others, most of which were, in any case, lying to their nets and lines, busy about the day's fishing. Besides, was not that a man waving?

'Mr McClusky, the deck glass, if you please!'

Keeping his eyes on the distant craft, Kite took the proffered glass and peered through the lenses. Adjusting them he exclaimed, 'Why, 'tis a ship's boat!' Lowering the glass he handed it back and pointed the craft out to McClusky. 'There, what d'you make of her?'

McClusky, whose experience in these matters remained limited, was very much flattered to be asked for his opinion. After a moment he said, 'It does look like a ship's boat. Exactly like one from a big ship, sir.'

'I take it you mean an Indiaman or a Country vessel?'

'I think so, sir.'

'Then what the devil is she doing out here with her sails up and her hands waving as though they're in distress? Put the helm over and let's run down to her.'

And so fate threw them a bone by way of consolation.

'You are fortunate, gentlemen, to have fallen in with us.'

'Indeed, sir, we are.'

Kite looked at the two young officers who obviously thought themselves in heaven, ministered to by Nisha and Sarah as they tucked into the last of the duck pickled after the fowling party on Hainan. He had left the men to themselves, for they were clearly much in want of food and water before he could press themselves for an account of their misfortune and, in any case, they had had the boat to secure astern on a towline.

'I have no doubt that you have been informed by my wife here that this is the privateer schooner *Spitfire* of Liverpool and that my name is Kite . . .'

'We already knew your name, Captain.'

'They are from the *Carnatic*, William,' Sarah said, looking at him, 'Captain Grindley's ship.'

'God bless my soul! Then what has become of Captain Grindley and his vessel?'

'She was taken by a French frigate—'

'Named *Alcmene*,' Kite completed the sentence.

'How did you know, sir?'

'Intuition, Mr – er, I am sorry, I have not yet . . .'

'Davidson, sir, fourth officer of the *Carnatic*.' The young man rose and shook hands. 'And this is Cook, the second purser.'

'Mr Davidson, Mr Cook, you are very welcome. Tell me about your ordeal.'

'Well, sir, to be frank it is a mite embarrassing. Captain Grindley, d'you see, took this *Alcmene* for a British cruiser.'

'He was a man who ever knew his own mind, would you not say, Mr Davidson?' Kite asked wryly.

'Indeed, Captain Kite. He was not one to be contradicted on his own quarterdeck, certainly.' Davidson paused, then added, 'But ironically, sir, that offered us a glimmer of hope.'

'How so, Mr Davidson?'

'The whole affair was over in a quarter of an hour and we were the prisoners of a French prize crew. They were not very numerous, but they seemed confident of holding us all below decks. We had a large crew of lascars and kelassies and these were left to work the ship, not, I think, being considered a threat to the French boarding party. We, of course, were made prisoners and bound by a parole sworn by Captain Grindley. It was his assertion that he would give his parole for all the officers. Regrettably Cook and I did not consider another man's word was binding. When the ship was anchored we managed, without much trouble, to escape in a boat which the prize-master had injudiciously left on her painter under the quarter. I presume he thought the coast so hostile that there was nowhere where we could take refuge.'

'And you thought that if you could get away to sea, you might intercept a homeward-bound Indiaman . . .'

'Or a Country wallah. We did not expect a privateer like yourself, sir, but we are damned glad to see you.'

'Very happy to oblige, I'm sure, but where is the *Alcmene* now, have you any idea?' Kite asked.

'I have no idea beyond speculating that, like us, she is hopeful of picking up a homeward-bound and laden ship. On account of our late departure from Bombay we fell into his hands, but he would far rather intercept a laden homeward-bounder . . .' Davidson, relieved to have been picked up, was euphoric and his tongue was running away with him. Kite however, was concerned that the *Alcmene* was lurking somewhere ahead of the *Spitfire* and that she would fall into the trap. The little schooner was no spicier a prize than the *Carnatic*, though she had an unsold cargo of the best Malwa opium on board. He swore silently to himself and then an idea struck him.

'Do you know where your ship lay at anchor?'

'You mean where was she taken?'

'Exactly so, Mr Davidson.'

'Yes, I know where she is now lying, in a deep bay to the east of the Lamma Islands. If you have a chart, I can show you.'

'Very well.' Kite went to his desk and removed one of Dalrymple's charts and handed it to Davidson. 'Then tell me, Mr Davidson, why was the *Carnatic* sent in to the China coast and not despatched directly back to the Île de France? Have you any idea?'

Davidson shrugged. 'I can only conjecture, sir,' he said unrolling the chart, 'that we were an encumbrance. Frankly there were insufficient men to work the *Carnatic* back to the Île de France, even with a compliant crowd of lascars. I think we were left to one side, as it were, in anticipation of better prizes out of the Pearl River. If we were worth picking up at the end of the cruise, well so be it, if not we could be burnt.'

Kite nodded. 'That is logical, certainly . . .' He paused, considering matters as Davidson pointed to the China coast delineated on the chart.

'How big was the prize crew?' Sarah asked as Kite studied the chart.

Davidson turned to his beautiful interlocutor. 'Well, ma'am, perhaps twenty men, why do you ask?'

'Because my husband is thinking of recapturing her.'

Kite turned to Cook. 'And have you anything to add to Mr Davidson's account, Mr Cook?'

The junior purser shook his head. 'No, sir. Davidson's account is accurate and I could add nothing more.'

'Very well.' Kite let the chart roll up and smiled at his wife. 'My wife reads my mind.'

'Are there any questions?' Kite asked, looking round the company assembled in the cabin. Harper and McClusky shook their heads.

Davidson raised a hand. 'Cook and I wish to serve as volunteers, sir.'

'And your offer is gratefully received, Mr Davidson.' Kite turned to the two women and raised his eyebrows. Sarah made a negative gesture with her hand and Nisha lowered her eyes. Neither of the women wished to stick their heads in a hornet's nest, Nisha least of all, for she felt her presence increasingly on sufferance since the revelations in the Pearl River. Nor could Harper dislodge this from her mind and, feeling an estrangement from Nisha, he now sought the catharsis of action.

'Very well, then this is what we shall do,' Kite said, gathering the men about him as he bent over the chart.

The *Carnatic*'s boat left the schooner at two o'clock in the morning. It was commanded by Harper, with Davidson and Cook in support, and a crew of twelve men. Kite watched the dark, close-hauled quadrilateral of her lugsail disappear in the gloom. There was scarcely a breath of wind now to move the heavy schooner, though the boat was manageable and, if the wind failed utterly, her crew had had previous experience at pulling inshore with oars muffled.

They had raised the coast that afternoon and edged offshore

under only a single sail, so that if they were detected their rig was unidentifiable. Finally, shortly before sunset, they put about again. From *Spitfire*'s main crosstrees Kite had observed the masts, spars and furled sails of the *Carnatic* gleaming in the last rays of the setting sun over a spit of land at the head of the bay. As soon as it grew dark the *Spitfire* ghosted inshore, following after her boat as the wind dropped all along the coast.

Kite's plan relied upon the wind being strong enough to allow them to stand into the bay under sail but, as the hours passed, it was clear that it would not oblige them. By midnight, therefore, he had ordered the sweeps up out of the hold and the men toiled at dragging *Spitfire* through the water while Kite sought to harness the tidal stream. For Harper to attack unsupported by the schooner courted disaster and Kite paced the deck in increasing irritation, berating Rahman, who had assured him a breeze would spring up. But when the first flush of dawn began to lighten the horizon to the south-east, even the zephyrs had disappeared.

'It will come, Kite Sahib, it will come . . .'

'We cannot wait an instant longer and the noise of those damned sweeps would wake the dead!'

All along the deck the crew walked back and forth between the guns while aft Sarah, dressed in shirt, breeches and hessian boots, waited with McClusky.

'God damn it, the men will be tired out before we ask them to load a gun,' Kite muttered. He was in a lather of frustration, furious at being cheated of his last, miserable chance. If he could only . . .

'Kite Sahib!'

But Kite had felt it, smelling the dry scent of the land in its embrace. Overhead the mainsail slatted, then filled. He leapt to the helm and peered into the binnacle at the compass card.

'Steady her full and by!' he hissed at the helmsman and then, straightening up, called, 'Get those sweeps inboard. Get your heads down for an hour, we'll call you when we want you.'

With a series of dull thumps the long loomed sweeps were

drawn laboriously inboard and squared off along the deck to the boatswain's satisfaction. Kite watched Jack Bow pass some light lashings round them. The tired men flopped down on the deck, tucking themselves out of the way and, curling their arms, rested their heads. They were soon asleep.

'The true seaman can sleep on a razor's edge,' Kite remarked, his mood lifting by the second. *Spitfire* was racing through the water and it was almost impossible to imagine that only a few minutes earlier she had been becalmed. As the daylight grew, so did the breeze, and as the sun rose the prospect before them was glorious.

The large bay into which they swooped was surrounded by rising ground and a low range of mountains spread across its head. Several walled villages could be seen, their eastern ramparts catching the low rays of the rising sun, while nearer, just beyond the bulk of the *Carnatic*, stood the exotic pillar of a pagoda.

Kite lowered his glass and called for McClusky. 'Take Jack Bow, Mr McClusky, and see that all the guns are primed afresh.'

'Aye, aye, sir.' McClusky went forward and Kite summoned Rahman.

'Go round the deck and shake each man individually. Tell them to make ready and take their stations.' Rahman did as he was bid and Kite stared again at his quarry.

Against the backdrop of grey-green hills the *Carnatic* looked splendid. The sunlight caught every detail of her hull, while her masts rose against the unblemished blue of the sky. She wore the white flag of France at her stern and as it rippled out in the morning light he could see its reflection clear in the dark water under her double tiers of galleries. Along her painted strakes the dew sparkled on her blocks and the light caught her sails furled on their yards.

Suddenly he saw a puff of smoke and the sound of the warning gun rumbled over the water towards them. *Spitfire*'s approach against the rising sun would have rendered her a dark silhouette, her own ensign a black speck, her intention sinister but unconfirmed. As her company readied themselves, Kite wanted only the distance between the two vessels closed as rapidly as possible.

He turned and walked aft. Sarah straightened up. She stood with Maggie at the taffrail. 'Are you sure you wish to remain on deck?' he asked Maggie.

The little maid nodded. 'I'll load for the mistress, Cap'n,' she said.

'Then you're staying, I suppose?' he asked Sarah.

She too inclined her head but remained silent and, after he had taken off his coat, she handed him his sword on its belt. Then, as he buckled this on, she passed him a pair of pistols. 'Take care of yourself, William. I *never* loved any other but you.'

Without a word he took the pistols and shoved them into his belt. Then he bent and kissed her, holding her face in his right hand for a moment before turning and walking forward, to take his post beside the tiller.

'Mr Rahman!' he called, his voice rasping.

'Kite Sahib?'

'Man the guns! Maximum elevation and stand by!'

'Maximum elevation and standing by, sir!'

'Mr McClusky!'

'Sir?'

'Muster your boarders!'

'All mustered and arms checked.'

'Very well. Boatswain!'

'Sir?'

'Stand by forrard! Let fly the head sheets the minute I say!'

Kite took the helm. 'Go and stand by the main sheet,' he ordered the helmsman. 'Take the turns off and be ready to let it run.'

'Aye, aye, sir.'

The man ambled off and Kite, leaning on the helm and peering at the rapidly diminishing gap between the two vessels, drew his hanger. The deck was so quiet that the sword's blade rasped against the scabbard ring.

'Good fortune attend our endeavours!' he called out as, without faltering in her pace, *Spitfire* raced towards the large anchored ship whose sides began to rise above her deck as the schooner's own shadow ascended the *Carnatic*'s starboard side.

Another puff of smoke was followed immediately by the strange buzzing noise of a ball flying overhead to thwack through the mainsail with a rent that threw a bright patch of sunlight on the *Carnatic*'s open gun ports. At the same instant the boom of the gun thundered out almost overhead as Kite leaned his body on the helm and turned *Spitfire* a second before she drove bodily into the *Carnatic*'s hull.

'Let fly all sheets and spit fire!'

The sails began to shake, the deck levelled and the two four-pounders to larboard fired ineffectively into the *Carnatic*'s side, more for their numbing effect on the defenders than to inflict damage on the stout teak wales, but mainly to let Harper know they were alongside and about to board the *Carnatic*. Then there was a jarring crash, something parted forward and a grinding and splintering was accompanied by a roll to starboard. With a whoop McClusky led the *Spitfire*'s boarding party as it clambered upwards, over the main chains and the gun port lids, brandishing their cutlasses and boarding axes. Above them the French defenders poked muskets over the side, their long bayonets glistening in the strong sun, and fired down onto the *Spitfire*'s deck. Behind Kite came the spat of a discharged pistol and one of the French musketeers flew backwards. Then above him and to the left a movement caught his eye. An officer had poked a musket out through a quarter-gallery window and, enfilading the schooner's deck, sought a suitable target.

Kite drew a pistol but was distracted as the *Spitfire*'s bow swung in towards the *Carnatic*.

'Catch a turn there,' he bawled at the helmsman, waving at the end of the mainsheet. Perceiving the problem the seaman, an experienced hand, caught the end of the mainsheet round an iron rod staying the *Carnatic*'s starboard main chainwale.

But as the *Spitfire*'s stern swung out, Sarah was exposed to the clear view of the marksman in the quarter-gallery. Intent on covering the boarders, Sarah had not seen the marksman, but her energetic movements frustrated her would-be killer as he tried to follow her with the muzzle of his musket. Looking round, Kite caught a sight of the man and shot out the window above his head. The marksman flinched and the musket was realigned, the ball singing past Kite's ear an instant later. Kite sent a second ball into the quarter-gallery, howling a warning to Sarah, who swung round and, taking another loaded pistol from Maggie, laid it in wait for another appearance of the marksman.

'William!' The sharp female voice made Kite turn forward. In the opening of the companionway, standing at the top of the steps, swathed in green silk, stood Nisha. Reaching over the coaming she skidded first one then a second loaded pistol at him. He threw her his discharged weapons, picked up the loaded brace and gave her a quick grimace of gratitude. Then he made for the side of the *Carnatic*, intent on joining the fight on deck.

He was almost too late, for just as he clambered over the rail the last of Harper's men climbed over the larboard bow. Harper, Davidson, Cook and the dozen men of the boat's crew swept along the waist and caught the defenders in the rear. Entirely preoccupied by the schooner lying alongside their starboard side, whose approach they had been watching for some time, the French prize crew had no inkling of a second attack over the opposite side of the ship.

'À moi!' an officer was shouting in an attempt to rally his men and make a last stand about the foot of the mizzen mast. 'À moi, mes enfants!'

In the waist an outnumbered body of the prize crew had been surrounded and several had already thrown their weapons down in disgust, spitting on the planking as they did so.

'Secure those prisoners, McClusky,' Kite ordered, turning aft, his hanger as yet unblooded.

He confronted the French officer, who was flanked by three

men, one of whom, also an officer, was dressed in a nightshirt, his hair awry and half tied in a queue. He was wounded and bleeding profusely.

'Surrender, M'sieur, and I shall grant quarter!' All motion on the deck seemed to still as the skirmish reached its climax.

'What are you, Meester?' the wounded man queried, his voice proud and bitter. 'You 'ave no uniform. Are you a pirate?'

'I am a corsair, sir,' Kite responded.

'You are a pirate!' the French officer cried, putting up his guard.

'Surrender, M'sieur! At once or I shall shoot you dead!' They turned to see Sarah standing on the rail. She too was wounded, and Kite could see the red blood spreading on her right sleeve. In her left hand she held a pistol and the next second its report made them all jump. The ball threw the Frenchman's head back, snapping his neck and burying itself in his brain as the back of the skull opened out and a pale cloud of dissipating matter appeared briefly. At this the second officer and his last man leapt forward with a cry. Kite felt his blade engaged with a ferocious energy. The second man also lunged at him and he was compelled to swing aside to avoid the fellow's blade. His first assailant crashed against him, body to body.

'*Chien!*' howled the officer and Kite thrust him backwards so that both men recovered and came on guard again. To his right someone had caught the second man with a musket butt and he fell to his knees, dropping his empty pistol and his sword with a groan. A second prod and he stretched his length on the deck. Only one officer remained.

Kite watched the eyes of this stubbornly courageous Frenchman. He was a fraction of Kite's age and, from the poise of him, an expert swordsman. Kite felt the cold grip of fear seize his heart like a frozen fist. It was now that he wanted Sarah to blow brains out, now he wanted the *deus ex machina* of divine intervention, for he felt a sudden paralysis, as though his sword weighed a ton and had been enchanted.

'You are alone, M'sieur,' Kite said between clenched teeth. Kite saw the gleam of triumph in the younger man's eyes and it was all he could do to raise his sword in an attempt to parry the blow. It was a feeble failure and he heard the surrounding gasp at his failure, felt the nick of the *pointe* and tried to swing aside. He was saved by his attacker slithering in the gore of his dead comrade. The *pointe* of the weapon was diverted as the Frenchman lost his balance and achieved no more than a sharp cut across Kite's breast. As Kite saw the outstretched sword arm extend itself on the deck he instinctively stamped his booted foot on it.

All around him a cheer went up. Kite, shaking with relief, looked up to see Harper's ugly face grinning at him.

'I thought you'd bitten off more than you could chew there, Cap'n, just for an instant.'

Kite nodded. Sweat poured down his brow and his breath heaved in his chest, working the flesh wound like a pump handle. Out of the corner of his eye he saw Sarah and turning towards her he was confronted by the great white ensign standing out stiff in the breeze.

'Strike those colours,' he said, 'and hoist the ship's proper ensign!' Then he turned and regarded the *Spitfire*'s crew and their prisoners. Men were still catching their breath and all were grimy from the powder smoke, wounds, and the tar and tallow smeared about the *Carnatic*'s lower shrouds.

'My congratulations, Mr Harper, to you and your boat's crew, and to the rest of you. Mr Davidson, do you take me to Captain Grindley's quarters, and Mr Cook, please direct Mr Harper where best to confine our prisoners.'

'This way, then, sir.' Davidson led the way below. 'I think the captain is with all the officers in the wardroom. It has a locked door.'

Davidson proved correct. Though normally locked from within to prevent opportunist thieves in port, the French had simply reversed the process and Davidson turned the key and threw the door open. Grindley and his officers stood about the table, aware of the struggle on deck and apprehensively awaiting its outcome. Afterwards Grindley's officers admitted that they had not expected rescue by a British ship. They had persuaded themselves that they were about to be taken prisoner by the Chinese. Lugubriously they were circulating the story of a foreigner who had been shut in a cage and paraded from town to town as a curiosity for the Celestials' amusement.

Their collective surprise was therefore manifest when Kite stepped inside the gloomy wardroom. 'I give you good day, Captain Grindley,' he looked about him at the astonished faces. 'Gentlemen . . .' Then with a smile he offered a partial explanation. 'You may thank Providence and your friends Messrs Davidson and Cook for your liberty. Had they not risked all and had Providence not directed them in our grain, you would not now be under my protection . . .'

'I know you!' Grindley shoved his way forward, his face a mask of anger and humiliation.

'You know me too, Captain Grindley,' said Sarah appearing at her husband's shoulder with a smile. Her right sleeve was entirely sodden in gore, but she held a sword and a pistol butt peered from the wide leather belt about her elegantly slender waist. More astonishing, her hair, though tousled, still bore the attentive hallmark of female vanity, so tight had the queue drawn it.

Kite heard the shuffle of feet and one aside loud enough to confirm the suspicions of the dullest onlooker: 'I'll be damned! 'Tis a woman.'

'Mistress Kite!' Grindley's jaw dropped. Then he looked from her to Kite and his brow darkened. 'What do you mean, *under your protection?*' he asked with an abrupt lack of civility.

'You were taken by the French frigate *Alcmene*, were you not, Captain Grindley?' Grindley grunted assent. 'Well then, your vessel was a legitimate prize of war and I have retaken you from a French prize crew. I have a letter of marque and—'

'The devil you have!' Grindley said. 'Well, I'll be damned!'

'We had better get under weigh as soon as possible, before the *Alcmene* comes back in search of her prize. We must also alert shipping in the Pearl River of the presence of an enemy cruiser in order that a convoy may be organized. But first, Captain Grindley, you'd oblige me by trans-shipping a quantity of Malwa opium. I wish it to be sold in Canton for a decent profit and have already established a price. However, I require it to be entered on your manifest as the private venture of a, er – a Mr and Mrs Harper.'

'Who the devil are they?'

'They are your passengers insofar as accommodating them is concerned. More germane to the matter in hand, Mr Harper commands the prize crew.' Kite turned away but Grindley protested.

'I don't need a prize crew, Kite.'

'You do not command this ship, Captain Grindley,' Kite said, his tone reasonable. 'Not at the moment. It is an irony that I do, don't you think?'

PART FOUR

THE RECKONING

Chapter Twenty-One

The East Indiaman

T hey returned to the Pearl River in company with their prize and in conclusion of the *Carnatic*'s outward voyage. Here Kite arranged for Nisha and Sarah to transfer to the bigger ship, installing them in Grindley's spacious accommodation, to the intense annoyance of the displaced commander. Kite also went aboard, technically as prize master.

'I am sensible of the irony of fate, Captain Grindley,' he said with a charming smile as the *Carnatic*'s master was obliged to move his personal effects into a stateroom normally reserved for passengers. 'It is not so very long ago you offered me a position as first officer, undertaking not to burden me with the actual duty. Now I am able to offer you something similar. I should not wish to take away from you the duties attaching to command; but, on the other hand, I shall retain the direction of the ship. I hope that you can accept such a situation under the circumstances, eh? Unless, of course, you wish to make alternative arrangements for your passage back to Bombay in another vessel. What d'you say, sir?'

'That I am obliged to you, sir,' Grindley said through clenched teeth, though an instant later his tongue darted out to moisturize his lips. After a moment he asked, 'And do you intend that this arrangement should stand until we return to Bombay?'

Kite nodded. 'I can see no reason why it should not, can you?'

'Unfortunately not.'

'Then we shall have to try and rub along together as well as may be.'

Grindley made no reply, and in the succeeding weeks confined himself to the minimum of conversation with the man he uncharitably considered as his gaoler. Fortunately for the *Carnatic*, few of Grindley's officers saw the change in the ship's hierarchy in quite the same light. As far as they were concerned, Kite had saved them from an unknown fate and their commander's unpopularity lost nothing by his relegation. Most of them being youngish men thought the compensation of having two beautiful women on board sufficient a bonus to the voyage. The facts that both women were older than the majority of themselves, and that neither was unattached, simply meant that they were all able to flirt without rancour, a circumstance which added an unusual charm to the social life of the vessel.

For the return voyage to India Kite left Harper in command of *Spitfire*.

'I shall return Rahman to you for the passage back to Bombay, Zachariah,' he explained. 'However, I confess that I despise myself for leaving you myself, for I am anxious about the condition of the schooner and I would not have you think that I do so out of callous disregard for you—'

'Cap'n,' Harper interrupted, 'you *must* sail in the *Carnatic*, there's no doubt of that, otherwise Grindley will cheat you. Besides,' he added, 'we shall be keeping you in company and it wouldn't be fair on the women to leave them rattling around in that big Country wallah, even with Maggie and McClusky to look after them. We shall be all right, Cap'n, the keel ain't about to drop off this little ole schooner.'

'I hope you are right, Zachariah.'

'Well, even if I am wrong, it is better that Nisha comes with you.'

'You will miss her,' Kite said with a conspiratorial smile.

'I sure as hell will,' Harper agreed ruefully, 'but by Heaven I shall make up for it when I get back to Bombay!'

*   *   *

They lay at anchor at Whampoa for two months, the *Carnatic* was discharged of her cargo of cotton goods and Grindley was prevailed upon to act as a reluctant agent in the sale of Kite's opium. It amused Kite and Rahman, who along with McClusky had joined Kite aboard the *Carnatic* for the purposes of overseeing the negotiations over her cargo, to see Lee come aboard as shaw-bunder to deal with the inward freight of the Country ship. The Chinese official maintained his aplomb at the surprising and inexplicable sight of Kite and his Indian colleague, but ignored them in his subsequent pidgin dealings with Grindley. Ignorant of their former transaction and under pressure from Kite and Rahman, Grindley himself drove a hard bargain to which Lee had to accede, which he did with commendable imperturbability. At the conclusion of the negotiations Kite magnanimously conceded a half per cent of the profit to Grindley, which cut the ground from under the captain's feet.

More ironic was the encounter between Grindley and the Selectmen Harrison and Blackstone. The two Commissioners were clearly cronies of the Country commander and Kite afterwards told Harper that he thought he could hear Grindley actually grinding his teeth as he explained the extraordinary presence of Kite and Rahman aboard the *Carnatic*. Among the *Carnatic*'s freight, Grindley's private trade goods were consigned to Blackstone and thus the Commissioner was obliged to Kite for his recapture of the ship. It explained the man's anxiety when Kite had first acquainted the two commissioners of the presence of the *Alcmene* in eastern waters. In the event the affair was glossed over in an outward show of mutual esteem and in due course, with two other Country ships and a late East Indiaman, *Carnatic* weighed her anchor and headed south, her holds full of Chinese produce.

Kite learned Grindley was a shrewd master, and much of what he had loaded was not for the Indian market, but for London.

'You will trans-ship this in Bombay?' Kite queried as

Grindley reluctantly showed him the manifest with Lee's chop clearing ship and cargo outwards to Kite.

'No,' Grindley answered curtly, 'I was hoping that the *Carnatic* would sail for London after discharging such of her lading that is consigned for Bombay.'

'How so?' Kite asked sharply, fixing Grindley with an interrogative glare.

Grindley sighed. It was clear he was now beholden to Kite for far more than simply the release of the vessel and her cargo. His wet tongue ran about his lips as he mooted his reply.

'My anxiety in wishing you to invest in this voyage,' Grindley said in a tone that suggested the confession was causing him some agony, 'was because it is intended that the *Carnatic* should sail to London as what is called an "extra Indiaman", a vessel on charter to the Company for the duration of the voyage. A few Country ships have made the passage . . .'

'Yes, I recall them arousing considerable interest for their size and appointments,' said Kite, quietly rejoicing in the wisdom of allowing the *Carnatic*'s voyage to continue after her recapture. It amused him that, despite his rejection by the East India Company in London, he had become the *de facto* owner of an Indiaman! This thought was swiftly followed by another.

'And that is why Hooker was so keen to invest in your enterprise and take up Buchanan's share, is it not?'

Grindley nodded, his tongue flashing in the dappled light dancing off the water under the stern and reflected in turn from the cabin's deckhead.

'You were long a partner of Zebulon Hooker's, I understand,' Kite added with quiet off-handedness, picking up the manifest and casting his eyes over it. The hint of prior knowledge sprung the trap for Grindley and, without thinking, he admitted the fact. Kite laid the manifest down and turned to face him. 'Well, you should have a grand profit on such a lading if you reach the London River,' he said matter-of-factly, so that Grindley failed to notice the impact of his admission. 'It only remains to arrange matters with Mr Banajee,' Kite went on, diverting Grindley's attention further, 'for I see no reason why we should place this affair before the judgement of the prize court, do you?'

And for the first time since Kite had offered him a small commission on the sale of the Malwa opium, Grindley expressed a grudging gratitude.

'So, Captain Kite, you have brought my ship safely back to Bombay, eh?'

Kite inclined his head. It was unbearably hot in Bombay and, even in the cool shadows of Pestonjee Banajee's elegant dwelling, the constriction of his stock threatened to choke him. He could feel only the slightest breath of air from the fan being wafted gently above his ancient host's head by the immobile untouchable whose waking life consisted of this tedious task.

'And what do you intend to do with her?' Banajee went on. 'I understand that you have a letter of marque?'

'What would you like me to do with her?' Kite said, running his finger round his throat.

'I would be obliged if you did not submit her to the Admiralty Court for judgement as a prize of war,' Banajee said, a hint of wheedling in his tone. 'I am an old man, Captain, and the trouble . . . Oh, dear, the trouble . . .'

'Unfortunately, sir, I too am becoming an old man but I, in turn, am not anxious to submit the *Carnatic* to the judgement of any court and I have thus advised Captain Grindley.'

'But you are in expectation of some recompense for your trouble in recapturing the vessel, I understand.'

Kite nodded. 'Indeed. I lost one man in the attack and sustained some damage to the *Spitfire* – my schooner. At present your vessel *is* undoubtedly a prize of war, however I have yet to declare her so.' Kite shrugged, suggesting compromise.

'I know you have not been fortunate, Captain Kite, and I know that you were a man deceived by others who used you, but if I was to make you an offer,' Banajee said, his dark and swimming eyes gleaming, 'would you consider it?'

'It would entirely depend upon its merit, Mr Banajee,' Kite responded coolly.

The reclining figure stirred. Banajee rearranged his emaciated limbs. His manservant came forward to adjust his cushions, but Banajee waved him away.

'I have no sons, Captain, but sometimes a son fails the expectations of a father and a man conceives a liking for another. You are younger than I, young enough to be my son . . .'

'You flatter me, sir, I am no such thing.'

'You do not know that for certain, Captain Kite,' said the old man, smiling.

'That is true.'

'And, as you rightly say, you have earned some recompense. Did you know it was our intention to obtain a charter for the *Carnatic* as an extra Indiaman?'

Kite nodded. 'Yes, so Captain Grindley informed me.'

'After you had sailed for China, I bought up Buchanan's share of the *Carnatic*. I had not intended to do so, but I had no wish for others to trouble my life by their interfering . . . Besides,' Banajee said with, Kite realized afterwards, a significant pause, 'I found the means to hand. Now, I propose that you should take over that share and the consequent profits that arise from it. I will advance you a sum of money against such profits you may make from her onward voyage so that you and your wife may settle here in Bombay for a year or two and, who knows, perhaps for ever?'

Kite considered the matter for a moment, judging Sarah's response before he expressed his gratitude. He had enough to live off for some time from the profits of the opium sale and courteously refused Banajee's advance. 'I thank you for your offer, but it is not necessary. I shall be content, sir, if, in addition to my interest in the *Carnatic* you would fund the dry-docking of my schooner. Grindley tells me that you have a majority interest in the Wadia's graving dock.'

'Grindley's tongue is sometimes too loose,' Banajee said with a smile. 'He makes a capable ship-master but is too poor a dissembler to make a good bargain. You,' Banajee said, pointing a finger at Kite, 'are more a man of calculation . . . I like that.'

'Then matters may rest thus between us,' Kite said.

Banajee nodded. 'It is customary to shake hands, is it not?' said the old Parsee, leaning forward and extending his thin arm with its bony fingers. After they had sealed their bargain, Banajee subsided on his cushions and called for refreshment. 'We are partners, Captain Kite, and we may draw up papers to that effect tomorrow. Until you are able to find a house to your wife's liking, you must consider yourself my guest here. I have many empty rooms.'

The *Spitfire* did not go directly into dry-dock for the Royal Naval squadron commanded by Rear-Admiral Sir Edward Hughes arrived in Bombay after several defeats by a French fleet under Suffren and requisitioned the facilities. Instead *Spitfire* lay at anchor, her leaks steadily worsening, her remaining hands at the pumps regularly day and night.

In due course Hughes sailed, encountering Suffren again off Cuddalore in June 1783. Suffren, having maintained his fleet far from a base but failing to obtain reinforcement from the Dutch, was compelled to withdraw and the eastern war petered out.

In its more important North American theatre the British suffered defeat. The consequent independence of the United States of America deprived Zachariah Harper of his last chance of returning to his native land, but by the time the news reached Bombay, Harper had married Nisha and *Spitfire* had long since completed her docking.

Harper had been made permanent commander of the latest addition to the ship-owning house of Banajee and Kite, and subsequently took her on several voyages to Canton, running cargoes of opium to feed the Chinese addiction.

Several of the schooner's people went home in the *Carnatic*, among them McClusky and *his* bride. Quietly married to Maggie, McClusky sailed for London with Grindley. He had been appointed as Kite's agent, initially to keep a discreet eye on Grindley, but with instructions for a lease to be made out in his name for the house in Liverpool. Here in due course Maggie, with Mrs O'Riordan still muttering about the madness of Captain Topsy-Turvy, reigned as Mistress Michael McClusky, while her husband furthered the ship-owning enterprise of what, in the following century, became familiarly known as the B & K line.

When Banajee died and left his holdings to Kite, Kite found himself the owner of a dozen Country vessels. He made some shares over to Harper and Rahman, bringing the latter into the company as a director immediately, and the former after Zachariah declared his reluctance to go to sea any more, the profits from opium notwithstanding.

In due time Jack Bow rose to be the commander of a Country Wallah owned by B & K. In 1824 his ship lay discharging at Calcutta when the steamer *Enterprize* arrived in the Hooghli River from Britain. Her passage time had not been exceptional and she had failed to win the prize of a lakh of silver for a speedy voyage, but in common with his officers, Bow recognized the potential of the little vessel's propulsion.

Long afterwards, as an old man recounting his tale to young guests dining at his house in Bombay, Kite was apt to claim that his own fortunes took their remarkable turn for the better only after he had exposed the extent of Hooker's perfidy. He liked to imply that no good could arise directly out of evil. It was a solecism, of course, a half-truth glossed in the old man's memory by time and repetition, recounted with a certain bias in favour of its quality as a moral yarn. In fact Kite never *quite* knew for whom Hooker had acted, though in the years that followed he would glean a partial fact here and there. Hints would be made, as when Cranbrooke died and people muttered that it was impossible to know how much the man had been worth; that despite the plaudits of his colleagues and the eulogious plaque raised by a public subscription for display on the wall of the garrison church, there was a suspicion that he had had a hand in murder.

Curiously, in spite of being larger than life, Hooker himself was almost entirely forgotten, detached from the memory of all but those who had known him. The actions of Cranbrooke and his putative accomplices were commonly thought to have had something, though no one knew precisely what, to do with the impeachment of Warren Hastings, the governor whose actions the British Parliament investigated without result. Despite the fact that Hastings had been Governor of Bengal, the mud that had been flung at him by his enemies reached as far as Bombay and still stuck. Both Cranbrooke and Hooker had, of course, spent some time in Calcutta during Hastings' governorship, but this was scarcely proof of any complicity between any of the parties. Although not a shred of evidence could be found to condemn Hastings, those who recalled the Hooker affair would shake their heads knowingly, imputing a degree of half-comprehended skulduggery to Hastings' alleged and utterly unproven wickednesses.

'There could be,' they were wont to say, 'no smoke without fire.' Such superficial wisdom ignored the existence of malice and lies.

The ageing Kite, it should be made clear, *never* implied any such connection. If he strayed from the strict recounting of the truth, it was only insofar as life had taught him the manner in which men commonly conducted their affairs, namely, to their private advantage. Kite remained convinced the matter was a private conspiracy, that Hooker had acted in concert with a handful of men and that Cranbrooke, mindful of his duty in protecting the Company's interests, was somehow a party only to the disposal of Hooker. Kite was certain Cranbrooke had never been a party to the illegal private carriage of silver directly to London. As to the identity of Hooker's co-conspirators, Kite went to his grave believing that Grindley was one and the dead Buchanan another. Though he had no evidence against the latter, Grindley's half-confession combined with what Kite later discovered of the captain's character to convince him that Grindley had been involved.

It was beyond doubt that Hooker's dealings had been of a private nature and that he and Grindley had sought to double-cross their co-conspirators. How else could he have appeared in Leadenhall Street that fateful day when he first encountered Kite? Woolnough and Drysdale were not implicated, and Hooker's refuge in obscure lodgings was an attempt to conceal the location of his treasure from the London agents of those in India whom he and his accomplice Grindley were deceiving. Kite's guess was that Hooker wished to re-establish his good name with the East India Company, hence his visit that day, as a means of affording himself protection against the vengeance of his former conspirators.

If so, Kite had been right in attributing Hooker's bodily stench to the constant fear of discovery. Hooker had been a man trapped by his own greed and personality; the fact that he did not wash only added to the irony of his constantly bearing his own guilt so palpably about him!

As to who had ordered the assassination of Hooker by his own bodyguard, Kite could only conjecture. Cranbrooke likely had a hand in the affair, and Kite was convinced that Banajee knew more than he ever admitted. Some of the 'means' which came so timely to Banajee's hand and by which the old Parsee had bought up Buchanan's share in the *Carnatic* derived, Kite thought, from a certain chest of silver Chinese cash which had been spirited out of the partitioned cabin of the schooner *Spitfire* and had vanished into the tropic night a little before the wretched Hooker's soul slipped into perdition through the same window.

Often, sipping a late-night glass of arrack and regarding the anchor lights of the ships in the bay below the terrace of his house, Kite would chuckle to himself and drink to Hooker's memory. He wondered how so unlovely a man could have mustered the courage to rescue Nisha from her first husband's funeral pyre, and then concluded that it took a certain brand of courage to embark on so complicated a deception as Hooker had done. It came to Kite one such night that Hooker did not lack the courage to carry out a bold and rash act, but what he could not sustain was the longer term necessary to a complex conspiracy. It was Kite's theory that Grindley had persuaded Hooker to cheat their fellow plotters and that the impetuous quality of Hooker's character had at first eagerly acquiesced, only to realize too late that the stress of anxiety had a profound physical and mental effect upon him.

Going in to their bedroom, Kite sat on the edge of the bed and told Sarah of his theory. She listened intently and then smiled. 'I think you have unravelled the puzzle at last, my dear,' she said, taking his hand and drawing it to her breast.

He looked at her. 'You knew most of this, did you not?'

'I knew of Grindley's involvement and of Hooker's regret at his weakness at having been persuaded to cheat his colleagues.'

'Nisha told you?'

'Yes.'

'Then why did you not confide in me?'

'She was, and still is I think, terrified of repercussions. She swore me to secrecy . . .'

'And pretended she was the ignorant wife?'

'Just so. I think she thought that none of the victims of Hooker and Grindley's plot would believe that he had confided in her, particularly as she was an outcast native.'

'But he found himself unable to resist the need of confession, so ill could he handle the anxiety of it all,' Kite said, guessing.

'Yes,' Sarah confirmed.

Kite shook his head. 'The fellow must have been in an agony of regret . . .'

'It only added to poor Nisha's miseries.'

Kite looked at his wife. 'You were very close to her, were you not?'

'But I loved only you, William.'

Kite remained in Bombay until his death of heart-failure in

1804. He was survived by Sarah, who lived to hear the news of Waterloo and the defeat of Napoleon. It had been a tradition that when one of Banajee and Kite's vessels called at Bombay, her master paid his respects to 'the Old Man', as Kite came to be known. They were invariably invited to dine with Kite and his wife and after Kite's death the tradition continued for, even in old age, Sarah retained her striking looks and was much sought after for the liveliness of her conversation. Moreover, as time passed, she possessed a glamour attaching to another age, for there were few British women in Bombay who could claim to have boarded an enemy vessel in action.

Along with her shares, Sarah retained a lively interest in the company and no master failed to enjoy her society, nor to keep her fully informed as to what was going on in Liverpool, London, Calcutta, Canton, Penang or Rangoon.

Harper was killed in a dockyard accident when supervising the repair of the *Queen of Malacca* in 1807. Thereafter Sarah and Nisha dwelt together until Nisha's death of a cancer. By then the McCluskys' eldest son had settled in Bombay and with the ancient Rahman and *his* son had taken over the active running of the company's Indian operations, for after the abolition of the East India Company's monopoly in 1813, Liverpool had succeeded Bombay as the company's headquarters and McClusky as its chairman.

Of the original crew of the *Spitfire* who had first arrived in Bombay in 1781, Jack Bow was the last survivor commanding the company's first steam ship. He had been a regular visitor to Mistress Sarah and on his last visit to the old woman had begged a likeness of her. The portrait had been executed by an Indian artist and was one of a pair, the other being the Old Man himself. 'You shall have them both, Jack,' Sarah said, smiling at the grave-faced middle-aged man whom she had once known as an irresponsible youth, sowing his wild oats with a reckless abandon. 'But why on earth you should want them I have no idea.'

'I am greatly indebted to you both,' Captain Bow explained, 'but I wished to have the figurehead of the *Queen of Achin* carved after your likeness, ma'am,' he said colouring. 'She is the new steam ship, now under construction, is she not?' 'Aye, ma'am.' 'That is very flattering of you,' Sarah said, smiling at him. 'And what memorial had you in mind for my poor William?' she asked.

'Why, ma'am, take my arm, if you please . . .' Bow bent and offered his hand to the old lady. Sarah rose stiffly and, taking hold of Bow, allowed herself to be led out onto the terrace overlooking the harbour and docks. 'There is his memorial, ma'am. See: the *Queen of Pegu* discharging into lighters in the bay, the *Queen of Java* with the blue peter at the forem'st head, and a pilot is ordered to undock the *Queen of Malacca* tomorrow. And that takes no account of the *Queen of Achin* lying in the fitting-out berth.'

Sarah chuckled and squeezed her younger escort's arm in appreciation. 'You are a fine courtier, Captain Bow,' she said. 'You have no idea the extent of the difficulties he encountered.'

'Perhaps not, ma'am,' Bow said sentimentally, looking at the fine profile of Mistress Kite beside him. 'But he brought us all safely into port.'